The Heart Goes Last

ALSO BY MARGARET ATWOOD
FROM CLIPPER LARGE PRINT

Stone Mattress

The Heart Goes Last

Margaret Atwood

W F HOWES LTD

This large print edition published in 2015 by
W F Howes Ltd
Unit 4, Rearsby Business Park, Gaddesby Lane,
Rearsby, Leicester LE7 4YH

1 3 5 7 9 10 8 6 4 2

First published in the United Kingdom in 2015
by Bloomsbury Publishing Plc

A CIP catalogue record for this book is available
from the British Library

ISBN 978 1 51001 452 7

Typeset by Palimpsest Book Production Limited,
Falkirk, Stirlingshire

Printed and bound in Great Britain
by TJ International Ltd, Padstow, Cornwall

For Marian Engel (1933–1985),
Angela Carter (1940–1992), and
Judy Merril (1923–1997).

And for Graeme, as ever.

. . . with wonderful craftsmanship he sculpted a gleaming white ivory statue. . . . It appeared to be a real living girl, poised on the brink of motion but modestly holding back – so artfully did his artistry conceal itself. . . . He kissed her, convinced himself that she kissed him back, spoke to her, embraced her. . . .

– Ovid, 'Pygmalion and Galatea,'
Book X, *Metamorphoses*

'When it gets down to it, these things just don't feel right. They're made of a rubbery material that feels absolutely nothing like anything resembling a human body part. They try to make up for that by instructing you to soak them in warm water first and then using a shitload of lube. . . .'

– Adam Frucci, 'I Had Sex With
Furniture,' *Gizmodo*, 10/17/09

Lovers and madmen have such seething
  brains,
Such shaping fantasies, that apprehend
More than cool reason ever comprehends.

– William Shakespeare,
A Midsummer Night's Dream

CONTENTS

PART I
WHERE?

CRAMPED

Sleeping in the car is cramped. Being a third-hand Honda, it's no palace to begin with. If it was a van they'd have more room, but fat chance of affording one of those, even back when they thought they had money. Stan says they're lucky to have any kind of a car at all, which is true, but their luckiness doesn't make the car any bigger.

Charmaine feels that Stan ought to sleep in the back because he needs more space – it would only be fair, he's larger – but he has to be in the front in order to drive them away fast in an emergency. He doesn't trust Charmaine's ability to function under those circumstances: he says she'd be too busy screaming to drive. So Charmaine can have the more spacious back, though even so she has to curl up like a snail because she can't exactly stretch out.

They keep the windows mostly closed because of the mosquitoes and the gangs and the solitary vandals. The solitaries don't usually have guns or knives – if they have those kinds of weapons you have to get out of there triple fast – but they're more likely to be bat-shit crazy, and a crazy person with a piece of metal or a rock or even a high-heeled shoe can do a lot of damage. They'll think you're a demon or the undead or a vampire whore, and no kind of reasonable thing you might do to calm them down will cancel out that opinion. The best thing with crazy people, Grandma Win used to say – the only thing, really – is to be somewhere else.

With the windows shut except for a crack at the top, the air gets dead and supersaturated with their own smells. There aren't many places where they can grab a shower or wash their clothes, and that makes Stan irritable. It makes Charmaine irritable too, but she tries her best to stamp on that feeling and look on the bright side, because what's the use of complaining?

What's the use of anything? she often thinks. But what's the use of even thinking *What's the use?* So instead she says, 'Honey, let's just cheer up!'

'Why?' Stan might say. 'Give me one good fucking reason to cheer the fuck up.' Or he might say, 'Honey, just shut it!' mimicking her light, positive tone, which is mean of him. He can lean to the mean when he's irritated, but he's a good man underneath. Most people are good underneath if they have a chance to show their goodness: Charmaine is determined to keep on believing that. A shower is a help for the showing of the goodness in a person, because, as Grandma Win was in the habit of saying, *Cleanliness is next to godliness and godliness means goodliness.*

That was among the other things she might say, such as *Your mother didn't kill herself, that was just talk. Your daddy did the best he could but he had a lot to put up with and it got too much. You should try hard to forget those other things, because a man's not accountable when he's had too much to drink.* And then she would say, *Let's make popcorn!*

And they would make the popcorn, and Grandma Win would say, *Don't look out the window, sugar pie, you don't want to see what they're doing out there. It isn't nice. They yell because they want to. It's self-expression. Sit here by me. It all worked out for the best, because look, here you are and we're happy and safe now!*

That didn't last, though. The happiness. The safeness. The now.

WHERE?

S tan twists in the front seat, trying to get comfortable. Not much fucking chance of that. So what can he do? Where can they turn? There's no safe place, there are no instructions. It's like he's being blown by a vicious but mindless wind, aimlessly round and round in circles. No way out.

He feels so lonely, and sometimes having Charmaine with him makes him feel lonelier. He's let her down.

He has a brother, true, but that would be a last resort. He and Conor had followed different paths, was the polite way of saying it. A drunken midnight fight, with *dickhead*s and *douchebag*s and *shit-for-brain*s freely exchanged, would be the impolite way of saying it, and it was in fact the way Conor had chosen during their last encounter. To be accurate, Stan had chosen that way too, though he'd never had as foul a mouth as Con.

In Stan's view – his view at that time – Conor was next door to a criminal. But in Con's view Stan was a dupe of the system, an ass-kisser, a farce, and a coward. Balls of a tadpole.

Where's slippery Conor now, what's he doing? At least he won't have lost his job in the big financial-crash business-wrecking meltdown that turned this part of the country into a rust bucket: you can't lose your job if you don't have one. Unlike Stan, he hasn't been expelled, cast out, condemned to a life of frantic, grit-in-the-eyes, rancid-armpit wandering. Con always lived off what he could mooch or filch from others, ever since he was a kid. Stan hasn't forgotten his Swiss Army knife that he'd saved up for, his Transformer, his Nerf gun with the foam bullets: magical disappearances all, with Con's younger-brother head going shake shake shake from side to side, no way, who, me?

Stan wakes at night thinking for a moment that he's home in bed, or at least in a bed of some sort. He reaches for Charmaine, but she isn't there beside him and he finds himself inside the stinking car, needing a piss but afraid to unlock the door because of the voices yammering toward him and the footsteps crunching on gravel or thudding on asphalt, and maybe a fist thumping on the roof and a scarred, partly toothed face grinning in the window: *Lookit what we got! Cockfodder! Let's open 'er up! Gimme the crowbar!*

And then Charmaine's terrified little whisper: 'Stan! Stan! We need to go! We need to go right now!' As if he couldn't figure that out for himself. He keeps the key in the ignition, always. Rev of motor, screech of tires, yelling and jeering, pounding of heart, and then what? More of the same in some other parking lot or sidestreet, somewhere else. It would be nice if he had a machine gun: nothing any smaller would even come close. As it is, his only weapon is flight.

He feels pursued by bad luck, as if bad luck is a feral dog, lurking along behind him, following his scent, lying in wait around corners. Peering out from under bushes to fix him with its evil yellow eye. Maybe what he needs is a witch doctor, some serious voodoo. Plus a couple of hundred bucks so they could spend a night in a motel, with Charmaine beside him instead of out of reach in the back seat. That would be the bare minimum: to wish for any more would be pushing it.

Charmaine's commiseration makes it worse. She tries so hard. 'You are not a *failure*,' she says. 'Just because we lost the house and we're sleeping in the car, and you got . . .' She doesn't want to say *fired*. 'And you haven't given up, at least you're looking for a job. Those things like losing the house, and, and . . . those things have happened to a lot of people. To most people.'

'But not to everyone,' Stan would say. 'Not to fucking everyone.'

Not to rich people.

They'd started out so well. They both had jobs then. Charmaine was in the Ruby Slippers Retirement Homes and Clinics chain, doing

8

entertainment and events – she had a special touch with the elderly, said the supervisors – and she was working her way up. He was doing well too: junior quality control at Dimple Robotics, testing the Empathy Module in the automated Customer Fulfillment models. People didn't just want their groceries bagged, he used to explain to Charmaine: they wanted a total shopping experience, and that included a smile. Smiles were hard; they could turn into grimaces or leers, but if you got a smile right, they'd spend extra for it. Amazing to remember, now, what people would once spend extra for.

They'd had a small wedding – just friends, since there wasn't much family left on either side, their parents being dead one way or another. Charmaine said she wouldn't have invited hers anyway, though she didn't elaborate because she didn't like to talk about them, but she wished her Grandma Win could have been there. Who knew where Conor was? Stan didn't look for him, because if he turned up he would probably have tried to grope Charmaine or do some other attention-grabbing stunt.

Then they had a beach honeymoon in Georgia. That was a high point. There are the two of them in the photos, golden and smiling, sunlight all over them like mist, raising their glasses of – what had that been, some tropical cocktail heavy on the lime cordial – raising their glasses to their new life. Charmaine in a retro flower-patterned halter top with a sarong skirt and a hibiscus blossom tucked behind her ear, her blond hair shining, ruffled by the breeze, him in a green shirt with penguins on it that Charmaine had picked out for him, and a panama; well, not a real panama, but that idea. They look so young, so untouched. So eager for the future.

Stan sent one of those photos to Conor to show that there was, finally, a girl of Stan's that Con couldn't poach; also as an example of the success Con himself might expect to have if he'd settle down, go straight, stop doing minor time, quit fooling around on the fringes. It's not that Con wasn't smart: he was too smart. Always playing the angles.

Con sent a message back: *Nice T&A, big brother. Can she cook? Dumb penguins though.* Typical: Con had to sneer, he had to disparage. That was before he'd cut the lines, dumped his email, refused to share his address.

Back up north, they'd made a down payment on a house, a starter two-bedroom in need of a little love but with room for the growing family, said the agent with a wink. It seemed affordable, but in retrospect the decision to buy was a mistake – there were the renovations and repairs, and that meant extra debt on top of the mortgage. They told themselves they could handle it: they weren't big spenders, they worked hard. That's the killer: the hard work. He'd busted his ass. He might as well not have bothered, in view of the fuck-all he's been left with. It makes him cross-eyed to remember how hard he'd worked.

Then everything went to ratshit. Overnight, it felt like. Not just in his own personal life: the whole card castle, the whole system fell to pieces, trillions of dollars wiped off the balance sheets like fog off a window. There were hordes of two-bit experts on TV pretending to explain why it had happened – demographics, loss of confidence, gigantic Ponzi schemes – but that was all guesswork bullshit. Someone had lied, someone had cheated, someone had shorted the market, someone had inflated the currency. Not enough jobs, too many people. Or not enough jobs for middle-of-the-road people like Stan and Charmaine. The northeast, which was where they were, was the hardest hit.

The Ruby Slippers branch where Charmaine worked ran into trouble: it was upscale, so a lot of families could no longer afford to park their old folks in there. Rooms emptied, overheads were cut. Charmaine applied for a transfer – the chain was still doing well on the West Coast – but that didn't happen, and she was made redundant. Then Dimple Robotics packed up and moved west, and Stan was out without a parachute.

They sat in their newly bought home on their newly bought sofa with the flowered throw pillows that Charmaine had taken such trouble to match, and hugged each other, and said they loved each other, and Charmaine cried, and Stan patted her and felt useless.

Charmaine got a temporary job waiting tables; when that place went belly up, she got another one. Then another, in a bar. Not high-end places; those were drying up, because anyone who could afford to eat fancy food was gobbling it farther west, or else in exotic countries where the concept of minimum wage had never existed.

No such luck for Stan, with the odd jobs: over-qualified, was what they told him at the employment office. He said he wasn't picky – he'd clean floors, he'd mow lawns – and they smirked (what floors? what lawns?), and said they'd keep him on file. But then the employment office itself closed down, because why keep it open if there was no employment?

They held on in their little house, living on fast food and the money from selling the furniture, skimping on energy use and sitting in the dark, hoping things would take an upturn. Finally they put the house on the market, but by then there were no buyers; the houses on either side of theirs were already empty, and the looters had been through them, ripping out anything that could be sold. One day they had no mortgage money left, and their credit cards were frozen. They walked out before they were thrown out, and drove away before the creditors could grab their car.

Luckily Charmaine had saved up a little stash

of cash. That, and her tiny pay packet at the bar, plus tips – those have kept them in gas, and a post-office box so they can pretend to have an address if anything does come up for Stan, and the odd trip to the laundromat when they can't stand the griminess of their clothes.

Stan has sold his blood twice, though he didn't get much for it. 'You wouldn't believe it,' the woman said to him as she handed him a paper cup of fake juice after his second blood drain, 'but some people have asked us if we want to buy their babies' blood, can you imagine?'

'No shit,' says Stan. 'Why? Babies don't have that much blood.'

More valuable, was her answer. She said there was a news item that claimed a total blood renewal, young blood for old, staves off dementia and rolls your physical clock back twenty, thirty years. 'It's only been tried with mice,' she said. 'Mice aren't people! But some folks will clutch at anything. We've turned away at least a dozen baby-blood offers. We tell them we can't accept it.'

Someone's accepting it, Stan thought. You can bet they are. If there's money in it.

If only the two of them could find some place where the prospects are better. There's said to be a boom in Oregon – fuelled by a rare earth discovery, China's buying a lot of that – but how can they get out there? They'd no longer have Charmaine's trickle of money coming in, they'd run out of gas. They could ditch the car, try hitching, but Charmaine is terrified by the thought. Their car is the only barrier between them and gang rape, and not just for her, she says, considering what's out there roaming around in the night with no pants on. She has a point.

What should he do to pull them out of this ditch? Whatever he has to. There used to be a lot of jobs licking ass in the corporate world, but those asses are now out of reach. Banking's left the region, manufacturing too; the digital genius outfits have migrated to fatter pastures in other, more prosperous locations and nations. Service industries used to be held out as a promise of salvation, but those jobs too are scarce, at least around here. One of Stan's uncles, dead now, had been a chef, back when cheffing was a good gig because the top slice was still living onshore and high-end restaurants were glamorous. But not today, when those kinds of customers are floating around on tax-free sea platforms just outside the offshore limit. People that rich take their own chefs with them.

Another midnight, another parking lot. It's the third one tonight; they've had to flee the previous two. Now they're so on edge they can't get back to sleep.

'Maybe we should try the slots,' says Charmaine. They'd done that once, and come out ten dollars to the good. It wasn't much, but at least they hadn't lost it all.

'No way,' says Stan. 'We can't afford the risk, we need the money for gas.'

'Have some gum, honey,' says Charmaine. 'Relax a little. Go to sleep. Your brain's too active.'

'What fucking brain?' says Stan. There's a hurt silence: he shouldn't take it out on her. Dickhead, he tells himself. None of this is her fault.

Tomorrow he'll eat his pride. He'll hunt down Conor, help him out with whatever scam he's engaged in, join the criminal underclass. He has an idea about where to start looking. Or maybe he'll just hit Con up for a loan, supposing Con is flush. That shoe used to be on the other foot – it was Conor who'd done the hitting up when they were younger, and before Conor had figured out how to game the system – but he'll need to avoid reminding Conor of their former positions now.

Or maybe he should remind him. Con owes him. He could say *Payback time* or something. Not that he's got any leverage. But still, Con's his brother. And he is Con's brother. Which must be worth something.

PART II

PITCH

BREW

It wasn't a good night. Charmaine did try for a comforting note: 'Let's concentrate on the things we have,' she'd said into the moist, stinky darkness of the car. 'We have each other.' She'd started to reach her arm from the back seat into the front, in order to touch Stan, to reassure him, but then she thought better of it. Stan might take it the wrong way, he'd want to get into the back seat with her, he'd want them to make love, and that could be so uncomfortable with the two of them squashed in together because her head would get jammed up against the car door and she'd start to slide sideways off the seat, with Stan working away at her as if she was a job he had to get done really fast, and her head going bump bump bump. It was not inspirational.

Also she can never concentrate, because what if someone snuck up on them from the outside? Stan would be caught bare-assed, scrambling over into the front seat and trying to start the car while a gang of thugs bashed at the windows, trying to get at her. Though not her, first and foremost. What they'd want would be the truly valuable thing, which was the car. She'd be an afterthought, once they'd done away with Stan.

There's been a number of former car owners flung out onto the gravel, right around here; knifed, heads crushed in, bleeding to death. No one bothers with those cases any more, with finding out who did it, because that would take time, and only rich people can afford to have police. All those things we never appreciated until we didn't have them, as Grandma Win would say, Charmaine thinks regretfully.

Grandma Win refused to go to the hospital, once she got really sick. She said it would cost too much, and it would have. So she died right in the house, with Charmaine taking care of her up to the end. Sell the house, sugar pie, Grandma Win said when she was still lucid. Go to college, make the most of yourself. You can do it.

And Charmaine had made the most of herself. She'd majored in Gerontology and Play Therapy, because Grandma Win said that way she'd be covered both ends, and she had empathy and a special gift for helping people. She'd got her degree.

Not that it makes any difference now.

If anything happens we're on our own, Stan tells her too frequently. It's not a comforting thought. No wonder he's so rapid, those times he does manage to cram himself in on top of her. He needs to be on the alert all the time.

So instead of touching Stan last night, she whispered, 'Sleep tight. Love you.'

Stan said something. 'Love you too,' maybe, though it came out more like a mumble, with a kind of snort in it. Probably the poor man was almost asleep. He does love her, he said he'd love her forever. She was so grateful when she found him, or when he found her. When they found each other. He was so steady and dependable. She would like to be that way too, steady and dependable, although she has doubts that she can ever manage it because she's so easily startled. But she needs to toughen up. She needs to show some grit. She doesn't want to be a drag.

They both wake up early – it's summer now, the light comes in through the car windows, too bright. Maybe she should fix up some curtains, thinks Charmaine. Then they could get more sleep and not be so crabby.

They go for day-old doughnuts at the nearest strip mall, double chocolate glazed, and make some instant coffee in the car with their plug-in cup heater, which is a lot cheaper than buying the coffee in the doughnut place.

'This is like a picnic,' Charmaine says brightly, though it isn't much like a picnic – eating stale doughnuts inside the car with a light drizzle falling.

Stan checks the job websites on their pre-paid phone, but that's depressing for him – he keeps saying, 'Nothing, fuck, nothing, fuck, nothing' – so

Charmaine says why don't they go jogging? They used to do that when they had their house: get up early, jog before breakfast, then a shower. It made you feel so full of energy, so clean. But Stan looks at her like she's out of her mind, and she sees that yes, it would be silly, leaving the car unattended with everything in it such as their clothes, and putting themselves at risk in addition, because who knows what might be hiding in the bushes? Anyway, where would they jog? Along the streets with the boarded-up houses? Parks are too dangerous, they're full of addicts, everyone knows that.

'Jogging, fuck,' is all Stan says. He's bristly and grumpy, and he could use a haircut. Maybe she can smuggle him into the bar where she works, later, with a towel and a razor, and he can give himself a wash and a shave in the men's room. Not luxury surroundings, but at least water still comes out of the tap. It's rusty red in colour, but it comes out.

PixelDust is the bar. It opened in the decade when there was a digital mini-boom here – a bunch of interactive startups and app creators – and was meant to lure in those kinds of geeky kids, with toys and games such as foosball and pool and online car racing. There are big flatscreens where they once ran silent movies as cool wallpaper, though one of them is broken and the rest show ordinary TV shows, a different one on every screen. There are some little nooks and corners meant for brainy conversations – Think Tank, that section was called. The signage is still there, though someone's crossed out *Think* and written *Fuck*, because two of the semi-resident hookers turn tricks in there. After the mini-boom dried up, some smarty-pants broke the *Pixel* part of the LED sign, so now it only says *Dust*.

By name and by nature, thinks Charmaine: a layer of permanent grime coats everything. The air smells of rancid fat from the chicken wings place next door; customers bring them in here in paper bags, pass them around. Those wings are moderately disgusting, but Charmaine never says no to them when they're on offer.

The place wouldn't stay open, except that it's now the hub for what she supposes – knows, really – is the local clutch of drug dealers. It's where they meet their suppliers and customers; they don't need to worry about getting caught, not here, not any more. They have a few hangers-on, plus the two hookers, just high-spirited girls, no more than nineteen. They're both very pretty; one is a blonde, the other has long dark hair. Sandi and Veronica, decked out in T-shirts with sequins and really short shorts. They were in college before everyone around here lost their money, is what they say.

They won't last, is Charmaine's opinion. Either someone will beat them up and they'll quit, or they'll give up and start taking those drugs, which is another way of quitting. Or a pimp will move in on them; or one day they'll just drop through a hole in space and no one will want to mention them, because they'll be dead. It's a wonder none of those things have happened yet. Charmaine wants to tell them to get out of here, but where would they go, and anyway it's none of her business.

When they aren't busying themselves in the Fuck Tank, they sit at the counter and drink diet sodas and chat with Charmaine. Sandi told her they only do the hooking because they're waiting to get real work, and Veronica said, 'I work my ass off,' and then they both laughed. Sandi would like to be a personal trainer, Veronica would choose nursing. They talk as if these things might really happen one day. Charmaine doesn't contradict them, because Grandma Win always said miracles really can happen, such as Charmaine coming to stay with her – that was a miracle!

So who knows? Sandi and Veronica have been there a couple of the times that Stan has picked her up from work, and she couldn't help but introduce them. Out in the car he said, 'You shouldn't get so cozy with those hookers,' and Charmaine said she wasn't that cozy with them, but they were quite sweet really, and he said, *Sweet my ass*, which wasn't very kind in her opinion. But she didn't say so.

Once in a while outsiders blunder in, young guys usually, tourists from other, more prosperous countries or cities, going slumming, looking for cheap thrills; then she needs to be alert. She's come to know a lot of the regulars, so they leave her alone – they know she's not like Sandi and Veronica, she has a husband – and only someone new would think of trying to hit on her.

She has the afternoon shift, when it's pretty quiet. The evening would be better for tips, but Stan says he doesn't want her working then because there are too many drunken lechers, though he may have to give in on that if she's offered the slot, because their cash stash is getting really small. In the afternoons it's only her and Deirdre, who's left over from the cushier days of PixelDust – she was once a coder, she has a tattoo of a Moebius strip on her arm and still wears her hair in two little-girl brunette pigtails, that Harriet-the-Spy girl-geek look. And there's also Brad, who does the scowling at the rowdy customers when necessary.

She can watch TV on the flatscreens, old Elvis Presley movies from the sixties, so consoling; or daytime sitcoms, though they aren't that funny and anyway comedy is so cold and heartless, it makes fun of people's sadness. She prefers the more dramatic shows where everyone's getting kidnapped or raped or shut up in a dark hole, and you aren't supposed to laugh at it. You're supposed to be upset, the way you'd be if it was happening to you. Being upset is a warmer, close-up feeling, not a chilly distant feeling like laughing at people.

She used to watch a show that wasn't a sitcom. It was a reality show called *The Home Front, with Lucinda Quant*. Lucinda used to be a bigtime anchor but then she got older, so *The Home Front* was only on local cable. Lucinda went around and interviewed people who were being evicted from their homes, and you got to see all their stuff being piled on the lawn, such as their sofa and their bed and their TV, which was really sad but also interesting, all the things they'd bought, and Lucinda asked them what happened to their life, and they told about how hard-working they'd been, but then the plant closed, or the head office relocated, or whatever. Then viewers were supposed to send in money to help those folks out, and sometimes they did, and that showed the good in people.

Charmaine found *The Home Front* encouraging, because what happened to her and Stan could happen to anyone. But then Lucinda Quant got cancer and went bald and started streaming video of herself being sick, right from her hospital room, and Charmaine found that depressing, so she didn't watch Lucinda any more. Though she wished her well, and hoped she would get better.

Sometimes she chats with Deirdre. They tell their life stories, and Deirdre's is worse than Charmaine's, with fewer kindly adults like Grandma Win, and more molesting, and it has an abortion in it; which isn't a thing Charmaine could ever bring herself to do. She's on the pill for now, she gets them cheap from Deirdre, but she's always wanted a baby, though how she'll cope if she gets pregnant by mistake, with Stan and her living in their car, she has no idea. Other women – women in the past, tougher women – have dealt with babies in confined spaces, such as ocean ships and covered wagons. But maybe not cars. It's hard to get smells out of car upholstery, so you'd have to be extra careful about the spitting up and so forth.

Around eleven she and Stan have another dough-nut. Then they make a hopeful stop at a dumpster out behind a soup joint, but no luck, the stuff has already been picked over. Before noon Stan takes her to the laundromat in one of the malls – they've used that one before, two of the machines are still working – and he watches the car while she does a load and then pays for it on their phone. She got rid of their white things a while ago – even her cotton nighties – traded them for darker colours. It's too hard to keep white things clean, she hates that dingy look. Then they eat some cheese slices and a leftover bagel for lunch, with some more instant coffee. They'll have better food tonight, because Charmaine gets paid.

Then Stan drops her off at Dust and says he'll come back at seven to pick her up.

Brad says Deirdre is off, she's called in sick, but it's okay because there's nothing much happening. Just a few guys sitting at the bar drinking a brew or two. They've got fancy mixed drinks written up on the chalkboard, but nobody ever buys them.

She settles into the familiar boredom of the afternoon. She's only had this job for a few weeks, but it feels like longer. Waiting, waiting, waiting, for other people to decide things, for something to happen. It reminds her a lot of the Ruby Slippers Home and Clinic – their motto was 'There's no place like home,' which was kind of sick if you thought about it, since the people were in there because they couldn't manage in their real homes. Mostly you served the old folks food and drink at intervals, just like at Dust, and were nice to them, just like at Dust, and smiled a lot, just like at Dust. Once in a while she would get in some entertainment, a therapy clown or a therapy dog, or a magician, or a music group donating their time to charity. But mostly nothing much happened, as in those animal-cam websites with baby eagles, until all of a sudden there would be the flurry and crisis of a messy, squawky death. Just like at Dust. Though they don't beat up anyone inside the building if they can help it.

'Brewski,' says a man at the bar. 'Same as before.' Charmaine smiles impersonally and bends over to take the beer out of the fridge. Straightening up, she sees herself in the mirror – she's still in good shape, not too tired-looking despite the restless night – and catches the man staring at her. She turns her eyes away. Was she teasing, was she flaunting it, bending over like that? No, she was only doing her job. Let him stare.

Last week, Sandi and Veronica asked her if she'd like to turn a few. She could make more that way than she was making behind the bar; way more, if she'd go offsite. They had a couple of rooms nearby they could use, classier than the Fuck Tank, they had beds. Charmaine had a fresh look: the clients liked sweet, big-eyed, kiddie-faced blondes like her.

Oh no, Charmaine said. Oh no, I couldn't! Though she'd had a tiny flash of excitement, like peering in through a window and seeing another version of herself inside, leading a second life; a more raucous and rewarding second life. At least more rewarding financially, and she'd be doing it for Stan, wouldn't she? Which would excuse whatever happened. Those things with strange men, different things. What would it be like?

But no, she couldn't, because it was way too dangerous. You never knew what men like that would do, they could get carried away. They might get started on the self-expression. And what if Stan found out? He'd never go for it, no matter how much they needed the cash. He'd be destroyed. Besides, it was wrong.

STUMPED

S tan tries Conor's last known address, a boarded-up bungalow on a street that's only semi-inhabited. There might be faces looking out of some of the windows, there might not. Possibly they're only tricks of the light. There's what might once have been a communal garden, with what might be some withered pea vines. A few wooden stakes poking up from the spiky knee-high weeds. On the broken sidewalk leading up to the porch there's a skull painted in red, like the one he and Con had decorated their tool shack clubhouse with when he was ten. What had they intended? Pirates, no doubt. Weird how the symbols persist.

This house was where Con was squatting when Stan last saw him, two or was it three years ago. He'd had a message from Con, which had sounded urgent, but when he'd got here it was only the usual: Con needed a loan.

He'd found Con in a tank top and Speedo shorts, a line of spiders tattooed up his arm, throwing a knife at an inside wall – to be precise, throwing it at the outline of a naked woman drawn in purple marker – while a few of his witless buddies passed spliffs and cheered him on. Stan still had a job then and was feeling self-righteous, so he'd done the big brother thing and chewed Con out over his shiftless ways, and Con had told him to sodomize himself. One of the buddies had offered to rip Stan's head off, but Con had only laughed and said that if there were any heads to be ripped off he could do it himself, then adding, 'He's my bro, he always doles out this uptight shit before the high finance.' After some glaring, they'd done the double back pat and Stan had lent Con a couple of hundred, which he hasn't seen since but would sure like to have now. Then Stan had made a mistake and asked about that long-ago Swiss Army knife, and Con had laughed at him for getting so bent out of shape about a stupid knife, and they'd ended up trading angry insults just as if they were nine.

Stan knocks on the blistered green door. No answer, so he pushes at the door, which is unlocked. Some arsonist must have set fire to the place from within because it's semi-carbonized; hot sunlight glints off the shards of window scattered across the floor. He has the queasy idea that Conor might still be somewhere inside the house in blackened skeletal form, but there's nobody in any of the charred and roofless rooms. The smell of smoke oozes from the singed, mouse-riddled furniture.

When he comes back out there's a man peering into his car, with larceny in mind no doubt. The guy looks scrawny enough and doesn't appear to be holding a weapon, so Stan could tackle him if need be. Still, best to stand well back.

'Hey,' he says to the dingy grey shirt and balding skull. The guy whips round.

'Just looking,' he says. 'Nice car.' Ingratiating smile, but Stan isn't fooled: there's a cunning flicker in the sunken eyes. Maybe a knife?

'I'm Conor's brother,' he says. 'He used to live here.' Something shifts: whatever the guy was planning, he won't try it now. That means Con must still be alive, with even more of an evil reputation than he had two years ago.

'He's not here,' says the guy.

'Yeah, I can see that,' says Stan. There's a silence. Either the guy knows where Conor is, or he doesn't. He's trying to assess what it's worth to Stan. Then he will either lie and try to lead Stan astray, or not. A few years ago Stan would have found this situation more frightening than he does now.

Finally the man says, 'But I know where.'

'So, you can take me there,' says Stan.

'Three bucks,' says the guy, holding out his hand.

'Two. Once I see him,' says Stan, keeping his left hand in his pocket. He has no intention of paying for a blank space with no Conor in it. He has no intention of paying anyway, since he doesn't have two bucks on him. But Con will have two bucks. Con can pay. That, or mash the guy's teeth in, what's left of them.

'How do I know he wants to see you?' says the guy. 'Maybe you're not his brother.'

'That's the chance you take,' says Stan, smiling. 'Do we drive?' This could be hazardous – he'll need to let the guy sit in the front seat with him, and there might still be a weapon. But he has to risk it.

They get in, each of them wary. Down the street, around the corner. Along another street, this one with a few ratty kids kicking a deflated soccer ball. Finally, a trailer park, or at least some parked trailers. Couple of slitty-eyed guys at the entrance, one brown, one not, blocking their way. So, a fortress of sorts.

Stan stops the car, lowers the window. 'I'm here to see Conor,' he says. 'I'm Stan. His brother.'

'That's what he told me,' says the guy beside him, covering his ass.

One of the guards kicks the left front car tire half-heartedly. The other talks briefly on his cellphone. He peers through the window, then talks some more – a description of Stan, no doubt. Then motions him to get out of the car.

'Don't worry, we'll watch it for you,' says the phone-wielder, reading Stan's mind, which features at the moment a car with no tires left on it and not much of anything else. 'Just go through. Herb'll take you.'

'Pray he's the brother,' the second man says to Herb. 'Or you'll be digging two holes.'

★　　★　　★

33

Conor's out behind the farthest trailer, in a weedy open space that might once have been a house lot. He looks taller. He's lost weight; he had a slob period there for a while, but now he's trim. He's shooting at a beer can on a stump; no, a stack of bricks. The rifle is an old airgun Stan remembers from his boyhood. It used to be his, but Conor won it off him in an arm-wrestling tournament. Con's idea of a tournament was simple: you played until he won, then you stopped. It wasn't that he was bigger than Stan, but he was more devious. Also he was considerably more violent. His Off switch never worked too well when he was a kid.

Ping! goes the pellet against the can. Stan's guide doesn't interrupt, but he moves around to the side so Conor can't help seeing him.

A couple more pings: Con's making them wait. Finally he stops, leans the airgun against a cement block, and turns. Fuck, he's even shaved. What's got into him? 'Stan the man,' he says, grinning. 'How're you keeping?' He steps forward, arms wide, and they do an awkward version of the hug-and-back-pat thing.

'I brought him here,' says the scrawny man. 'You told me to watch the house.'

'Good job, Herb,' says Conor. 'Talk to Rikki, he'll give you something.' The guy shambles off. 'Brain-dead fuck. Let's have a beer,' Conor says, and they go into one of the trailers. An Airstream: high end.

It's surprisingly cool and clean in the main room.

Conor hasn't fouled it up: no contemptuous garbage or in-your-face crotch-grabbing rock posters, unlike Con's teenaged bedroom. Stan used to defend him, stick up for him to the parents, claim he'd straighten out. Maybe not such a bad thing that he hasn't. At least he seems to have a source of income, and a good one, judging from the results.

Pale grey decor, small aluminum cubes of hi-tech placed discreetly here and there, window curtains, good taste: does Con have a woman around, is that it? A tidy woman, not a slut. Or is he just making a bundle? 'It's nice,' Stan says ruefully, thinking of his own cramped, smelly car.

Con goes to the fridge, produces a couple of beers. 'I'm making do,' he says. 'How about you?'

'Not so good,' says Stan. They sit at the built-in table, upending the beers.

'Lost your job,' says Con after the right amount of silence. It's not a question.

'How'd you know?' says Stan.

'Otherwise why come looking for me?' says Con in a neutral voice. There's no point denying it, so Stan doesn't.

'I wondered maybe,' he says.

'Yeah, I owe you,' says Con. He stands up, turns his back, rummages in a jacket that's hanging on the door. 'Couple of hundred do you for now?' he says. Stan grates out a gruff thank-you, pockets the bills. 'Need another job?'

'Doing what?' says Stan.

'Oh, you know,' says Con. 'This and that. You

could keep track of stuff. Like, money. Take it offshore for us. Stash it here and there. Make us look respectable.'

'What're you up to?' says Stan.

'It's cool,' says Conor. 'Nothing dangerous. Custom stuff. On order.'

Stan wonders if he's stealing artwork. But where would there be any of that around here any more? 'Thanks,' he says. 'Maybe later.' He has no real wish to work for his little brother, even in a safe way. It would be like family welfare. Now that he has a bit of cash and some breathing room, he can look around. Find something decent.

'Any time,' says Con. 'You need a phone or anything? Fully loaded. Good for maybe a month, if you're careful.'

Why not have a second phone? That way, Charmaine and he can phone each other. While the top-up lasts. 'Where'd you get it?' says Stan.

'Don't worry, it's wiped,' says Con. 'Can't be traced.'

Stan slips the phone into his pocket. 'How's the wife?' says Con. 'Charmaine?'

'Good, good,' says Stan.

'I bet she's *good*,' says Con. 'I trust your taste. But how *is* she?'

'She's fine,' says Stan. It's always made him nervous when Con took an interest in a girl of his. Con thought Stan should share, willingly or unwillingly. A couple of Stan's girls had agreed with him on that. It still rankles.

He wants to ask Con for a firearm of some sort to thwart the nighttime thugs, but he's in a weak position and he can hear what Con would say: 'You were crap with the Nerf gun, you'd shoot your foot off.' Or worse: 'What'll you trade me? Time in the sack with the wife? She'd enjoy it. Hey! Joke!' Or: 'Sure, if you come work for me.' So he doesn't try.

The two guards walk Stan back to his car. They're much friendlier now, they even stick out their hands for a shake.

'Rikki.'

'Jerold.'

'Stan,' says Stan. As if they don't know.

As he's getting into his car, another car pulls up in front of the trailer-park entrance; a fancy hybrid, black and sleek, with tinted windows. Con has some upmarket playmates, it looks like.

'Here comes business,' says Jerold. Stan's curious to see who gets out, but nobody does. They're waiting for him to leave.

PITCH

Charmaine likes to be busy, but sometimes in the afternoons at Dust there's not much to be busy about. She's already wiped down the bar counter twice, she's rearranged some glasses. She could watch the nearest flatscreen, where a baseball replay is going on, but she isn't much interested in sports; she doesn't see why a bunch of men chasing each other around a field and trying to hit a ball and then hugging and patting butts and jumping up and down and yelling can get people so worked up.

The sound's turned down low, but when the ads are on it gets louder, and also they run the words across the bottom just to make sure you get the message. Usually the ads are cars and beer, on the sports shows, but all of a sudden there's something different.

It's a man in a suit, just the head and the shoulders, looking straight out of the screen, right into her eyes. There's something convincing about him even before he speaks – he's so serious, like what he's about to say is very important. And when he does speak, she could swear he's reading her mind.

'Tired of living in your car?' he says to her. Really, straight to her! It can't be, because how would he even know she exists, but it feels like that. He smiles, such an understanding smile. 'Of course you are! You didn't sign up for this. You had other dreams. You deserve better.' *Oh yes,* breathes Charmaine. *Better!* It's everything she feels.

Next there's a shot of a gateway in something that looks like a shiny black-glass wall, with people walking in – young couples, holding hands, energetic and smiling. Pastel clothing, springlike. Then a house, a neat, freshly painted house with a hedge and a lawn, no junked cars or wrecked sofas lying on it, and then the camera zooms in through the second-floor window, past the curtains – curtains! – and moves through the room. Spacious! Gracious! Those words they use in the real estate ads for places in the countryside and on beaches, far away and in other countries. Through the open bathroom door there's a charming deep-sided tub with lots of giant fluffy white towels hanging beside it. The bed is king-sized, with nice clean sheets in a cheerful floral design, blue and pink, and four pillows. Every muscle in Charmaine's body yearns for that bed, those pillows. Oh, to stretch out! To fall into a comfortable sleep, with that safe, cozy feeling she used to have at Grandma Win's.

Not that Grandma Win's house was exactly the same as this one. It was a lot smaller. But it was tidy. She more or less remembers a different house, from when she was little; it might have been like the house onscreen. No: it *could* have been like that if it hadn't been such a mess. Clothes rumpled on the floor, dirty dishes in the kitchen. Was there a cat? Perhaps, briefly. Something bad about the cat. She'd found it on the hall floor, but it was the wrong shape and ooze was coming out of it. *Clean that up! Don't talk back! S*he hadn't talked back – crying wasn't talking – but that hadn't made any difference, she was wrong all the same.

There was a hole in her bedroom wall the size of a large fist. Not surprising, because that was what made it, a fist. She used to hide things in that hole. A Beanie Baby. A cloth handkerchief with lace on the corner, whose was that? A dollar she'd found. She used to think that if she pushed her hand in deep enough, it would go right through, and there would be water, with blind fish and other things, things with dark teeth, and they might get out. So she was careful.

'Remember what your life used to be like?' says the man's voice, during the tour of the sheets and pillows. 'Before the dependable world we used to know was disrupted? At the Positron Project in the town of Consilience, it can be like that again. We offer not only full employment but also protection from the dangerous elements that afflict so many at this time. Work with like-minded others! Help solve the nation's problems of joblessness and crime while solving your own! Accentuate the positive!'

Back to the man's face. Not a handsome face as such, but a face you could trust. Sort of like a math teacher, or a minister. You can tell he's sincere, and sincere is better than handsome. Really handsome men were a bad idea, said Grandma Win, because they had too much to choose from. Too much what? Charmaine had asked her, and Grandma Win said, Never mind.

'The Positron Project is accepting new members now,' says the man. 'If you meet our needs, we'll meet yours. We offer training in many professional areas. Be the person you've always wanted to be! Sign up now!' That smile again, as if he's gazing deep inside her head. Not in a scary way though, in a kindly way. He only wants the best for her. She can be the person she's always wanted to be, after it was safe to want things for herself.

Come here. Don't think you can hide. Look at me. You're a bad girl, aren't you? No was the wrong answer to that, but so was *Yes.*

Stop that noise. Shut up, I said shut up! You don't even know what hurt is.

Forget those sad things, honey, Grandma Win would say. Let's make popcorn. Look, I picked some flowers. Grandma Win had a little patch at the front of the house. Nasturtiums, zinnias. Think about those flowers instead, and you'll be asleep in no time.

Halfway through the ad, Sandi and Veronica come in. Now they're sitting at the bar having Diet Cokes

41

and watching the ad too. 'Looks great,' Veronica says.

'No free lunch,' says Sandi. 'Too good to be true. That guy looks like a lousy tipper.'

'It wouldn't hurt to try,' Veronica says. 'Can't be worse than the Fuck Tank. I'd go for those towels!'

'I wonder what's their game?' says Sandi.

'Poker,' says Veronica, and they both laugh.

Charmaine wonders why that's funny. She isn't sure that they're the kind of people the man is looking for, but it would be way too snobby and also discouraging to say so, and they are nice girls at heart, so instead she says, 'Sandi! I bet you could be a nurse!' There's a website and a phone number scrolling across the bottom of the screen; Charmaine scribbles them down. She's so excited! When Stan picks her up, they can use their phone to view the details. She can feel the griminess of her body, she can smell the stale odour coming from her clothes, from her hair, from the rancid fat smell of the chicken-wings place next door. All of that can be shed, it can peel off her like an onion skin, and she can step out of that skin and be a different person.

Will there be a washer and dryer in that new home? Of course there will. And a dining table. Recipes: she'll be able to cook recipes again, the way she did after she and Stan got married. Lunches, intimate dinners, just the two of them. They'll sit on chairs while eating, they'll have real china instead of plastic. Maybe even candles.

42

Stan will be happy too: how could he not be happy? He'll stop being so grouchy. True, there's a grouchy part she'll have to guide him through first, the part where he'll say it's sure to be a scam like everything else, it's some kind of ripoff, and why bother applying because they won't get in. But nothing ventured, nothing gained, she'll say, and why don't they just try? She'll persuade him to do it, one way or another.

Worse comes to worst, she'll dangle the promise of sex. Sex in a luxurious king-sized bed, with clean sheets – wouldn't Stan like that? With no maniacs trying to break in through the window. If necessary, she'll even put up with that cramped back-seat car ordeal tonight, as a reward if he says yes. It won't be that much fun for her, but fun can wait until later. Until they're inside their new house.

PART III

SWITCH

GATEWAY

Getting into the Positron Project won't be a slam dunk. They aren't interested in just anyone, as Charmaine whispers to Stan on the bus that's picked them up from the parking-lot collection point. Some of the people on the bus can't possibly make it into the Project, they're too worn down and leathery, with blackened or missing teeth. Stan wonders if there's a dental plan in there. So far there's nothing wrong with his own teeth; lucky, considering all the cheap sugary crap they've been eating.

Sandi and Veronica are on the bus too, sitting at the back and nibbling on the sackful of cold chicken wings they've brought with them. Every once in a while they laugh, a little too loudly. Everyone on this bus is nervous, Charmaine especially. 'What if we get rejected?' she asks Stan. 'What if we get accepted?' She says it's like being picked for sports teams when she was at school: you're nervous either way.

The bus trip goes on for hours, in a steady drizzle; through open countryside, past strip malls with plywood over most of the windows, derelict burger joints. Only the gas stations appear functional. After a while Charmaine falls asleep with her head on Stan's shoulder. His arm is around her; he draws her closer. He too dozes off.

He's awake by the time the bus stops at a gateway in a high black-glass wall. Solar generation, thinks Stan. Smart, building it in like that. The group on the bus wakes, stretches, descends. It's late afternoon; as if on cue, mellow sunlight breaks through the clouds, lighting them in a golden glow. Many are smiling. They file in past the seeing-eye boundary, then through the entrance cubicle, where their eyes are scanned and their fingerprints taken and a plastic passcard with a number on it and a barcode is issued to each of them.

Back on the bus, they're driven through the town of Consilience, where the Project is located. Charmaine says she can hardly believe her eyes: everything is so spruced up, it's like a picture. Like a town in a movie, a movie of years ago. Like the olden days, before anyone was born. She squeezes Stan's hand in anticipation, and he squeezes back. 'This is the right thing to do,' she says.

They get off the bus in front of the Harmony Hotel, which is not only the top hotel in town, says the neatly dressed young man who's now in charge of them, it's the only hotel, because Consilience isn't exactly a tourist destination. He herds them into a preliminary drinks and snacks party in the ballroom. 'You're free to leave at any time,' he tells them, 'if you don't like the ambience.' He grins, to show this is a joke.

Because what's not to like about the ambience? Stan rolls an olive around in his mouth before chewing: it's a long time since he's had an olive. The taste is distracting. He should be more alert, because naturally they're being scrutinized, though it's hard to figure out who's doing it. Everyone is so fucking nice! The niceness is like the olive: it's a long time since Stan has encountered that muffling layer of smiling and nodding. Who knew he's such a fascinating dude? Not him, but there are three women, obvious hostesses, they even have name badges, deployed to convince him of his own magnetism. He scans the room: there's Charmaine, getting a similar treatment from two dudes and a girl. Her slutty hooker friends from PixelDust are in that group too. They've fixed themselves up, they even have dresses on. You wouldn't really spot them as pros.

Throughout the evening, the crowd gets thinner – a discreet weeding, Stan guesses. All those with bad attitudes, out the Discard door. But Stan and Charmaine must have passed scrutiny, because here they still are, at the end of the party. Everyone remaining is given a room reservation, for later. They also get a meal voucher, with a carafe of wine included, and another young man steers them toward a restaurant called Together, just down the street.

There's an old-fashioned tune playing in the background, white tablecloths, a plush carpet.

'Oh, Stan,' Charmaine breathes at him over the electric candles on their table for two. 'It's like a dream come true!' She picks up the rose from their bud vase, sniffs it.

It's not real, Stan wants to tell her. But why spoil it for her? She's so happy.

That night they stay at the Harmony Hotel. Charmaine has two baths, she gets so turned on by the towels. Less so by him, Stan guesses; but still, she comes across for him, so why complain? 'There,' she says afterwards. 'Isn't this better than the back seat of the car?' If they commit to the Positron Project, she says, they can kiss that horrible car goodbye and good riddance, and the vandals and thieves can tear it apart, because they themselves won't need it any more.

NIGHT OUT

The next day, the workshops begin. After the first one, they'll still be free to leave, they are told. In fact, they'll have to leave because Positron wants you to take a good look at the alternatives before deciding. As they have good reason to know, it's a festering scrap heap, out beyond the Consilience gates. People are starving. Scavenging, pilfering, dumpster-diving. Is that any way for a human being to live? So each one of them will spend what the Positron Project hopes – what it sincerely hopes! – will be their last night on the outside. To give them time to think it over, seriously. The Project isn't interested in freeloaders, tourists just trying it out. The Project wants serious commitment.

Because after that night you were either out or you were in. *In* was permanent. But no one would force you. If you signed up, it would be of your own free will.

The first day's workshop is mostly PowerPoints. It begins with videos of the town of Consilience, with happy people at work in it, doing ordinary jobs: butcher, baker, plumber, scooter repair, and so on. Then there are videos of the Positron Prison inside Consilience, with happy people at work in it as well, each one of them wearing an orange boiler suit. Stan only half watches: he already knows they're going to sign the commitment papers tomorrow, because Charmaine has her heart set on it. Despite the slightly uneasy feeling he's had – they've both had, because Charmaine said at breakfast, with lattes and real grapefruit, 'Honey, are you sure?' – the bath towels clinched the deal.

Their night outside the wall is spent in a nasty motel that Stan wagers has been tailored for the purpose, with the furniture trashed to order, stale cigarette smell sprayed on, cockroaches imported, and sounds of violent revelry in the room next door, most likely a recording. But it's enough like the real thing to make the world inside the Consilience wall seem more desirable than ever. Most likely it is the real thing, because why fake it when there's so much actual wreckage available?

In view of the racket and the lumpy mattress they have trouble getting to sleep, so Stan hears the tapping at the window immediately. 'Yo! Stan!'

Fuck, now what? He draws back the ragged curtain, peers cautiously out. It's Conor, with his two looming sidekicks watching his back.

'Conor!' he says. 'What the fuck?' At least it's Con and not some lunatic with a crowbar.

'Hi, bro,' says Con. 'Come out. I need to talk to you.'

'Fuck, now?' Stan says.

'Would I say *need* if I didn't need?'

'Honey, what is it?' says Charmaine, holding the sheet up to her chin.

'It's only my brother,' says Stan. He's pulling on his clothes.

'Conor? Why is *he* here?' She doesn't like Con, she never has; she thinks he's a bad influence who will lead Stan astray, as if he's that easy to lead. Con might get him into behaviour she doesn't approve of, like too much drinking, and darker stuff she'll never elaborate on, but she most likely means whores. 'Don't go out there, Stan, he might—'

'I can handle it,' says Stan. 'He's my *brother*, for fuck's sake!'

'Don't leave me alone in here!' she says fearfully. 'It's too scary! Wait, I'll come with you!' Is this an act, to keep him tethered so Con can't spirit him away to a den of vice?

'You stay in bed, honey. I'll be right out outside,' he says with what he hopes is gentle reassurance. Muffled sniffling from the bed. Trust Con to turn up and mess with everyone's head.

Stan slides himself out the door. 'What?' he says as irritably as he can manage.

'Don't sign in to that thing,' says Conor. He's close to whispering. 'Trust me on it. You don't want to.'

'How'd you know where to find me?' says Stan.

'What's a phone for? I gave it to you! So I traced it, dum-dum. I tracked you on that bus, all the way here. Lesson one, don't take phones from strangers,' says Conor, grinning.

'You're not a fucking stranger,' says Stan.

'Right. So, I'm telling you straight up. Don't trust that package, no matter what they tell you.'

'Why not?' says Stan. 'What's wrong with it?'

'What's wrong with it is, unless you're top management, you can't get out. Except in a box, feet first,' says Conor. 'I'm just looking out for you, is all.'

'What're you trying to tell me?'

'You don't know what goes on in there,' says Con.

'Meaning what? Meaning you do?'

'I've heard stuff,' says Conor. 'It's not for you. Nice guys finish last. Or else they get finished. You're too soft.'

Stan juts out his chin. That would have been the signal for a scuffle, once upon a time. 'You're fucking paranoid,' he says.

'Yeah, right. Don't say I didn't warn you,' says Con. 'Do yourself a favour, stay outside. Listen, you're family. I'll help you out, the same as you helped me. You need a job, some cash, a favour, you know where I am. You're always welcome. And the little lady, bring her along too.' Con grins. 'There's a place for her, any time.'

So that's it. Con has his poacher's eye on

Charmaine. No fucking way in hell is Stan falling for that one. 'Thanks, buddy,' he says. 'I appreciate it. I'll think about it.'

'Like shit,' says Conor, but he smiles cheerfully, and the two of them do the back pat.

'Stan?' comes the anxious voice of Charmaine from inside their room.

'Go comfort the little wifey,' says Conor, and Stan knows what he's thinking: *pussy-whipped*.

He watches Con walking away, with his two bodyguards; they get into a long black car, which slides off into the night, silent as a submarine. Most likely the same car he saw at the trailer park. Guys like Con who score some money always want cars like that.

Not that Stan would mind having such a car himself.

TWIN CITY

The next morning they take the final step. Stan barely even read the terms and conditions, because Charmaine is so eager to get in. After all, they've been chosen, she says, and so many have been rejected. She smiles mistily at Stan as he signs his name on the form. 'Oh, thank you,' she says. 'I feel so safe.'

Then the workshops begin in earnest; or, as one of the leaders quips, they've had the shop, now they're getting the work. They are about to learn so many astounding new things, and it will require their full concentration. Men's workshops over here, ladies' over there, because there will be different challenges and duties and expectations for each, and besides, they'll be separated for a month at a time when they're in the prison part of this project – a feature that will be explained more fully to them shortly – so they might as well start getting used to it, their first workshop leader says with a chuckle. Anyway, abstinence makes the heart grow fonder, as he is sure they know from experience. Another chuckle.

Be a loner, get a boner, thinks Stan. A rhyme of

56

teenaged Conor, who'd had a collection of rhymes like that. He watches as Charmaine and all of the other women in the group leave the room. Sandi and Veronica don't look back, but Charmaine does. She smiles brightly at Stan to show him she's confident about their decision, though she looks a little anxious. But then, he's a little anxious himself. What are these astounding new things they're about to learn?

The men's workshop leaders are half a dozen young, earnest, dark-suited, zit-picking graduates of some globally funded think tank's motivational-speaking program. In his past life, the part of it he'd spent at Dimple Robotics, Stan encountered the type. He disliked them before; but, as before, they can't be avoided, since the workshop classes are mandatory.

In a jam-packed day of back-to-back sessions, they're given the full song and dance. The rationale for Consilience, its history, the potential obstacles to it, the odds ranged against it, and why it is so imperative that those odds be overcome.

The Consilience/Positron twin city is an experiment. An ultra, ultra important experiment; the think-tankers use the word *ultra* at least ten times. If it succeeds – and it *has* to succeed, and it *can* succeed if they all work together – it could be the salvation, not only of the many regions that have been so hard-hit in recent times but eventually, if this model comes to be adopted at the highest levels, of the nation as a whole. Unemployment and crime solved in one fell swoop, with a new life for all those concerned – think about that!

They themselves, the incoming Positron Planners – they're heroic! They've chosen to risk themselves, to take a gamble on the brighter side of human nature, to chart unknown territories within the psyche. They're like the early pioneers, blazing a trail, clearing a way to the future: a future that will be more secure, more prosperous, and just all-round better because of them! Posterity will revere them. That's the spiel. Stan has never heard so much bullshit in his life. On the other hand, he sort of wants to believe it.

The final speaker is older than the zitty youths, though not that much older. His suit is of the same darkness, but it looks lusher. He's narrow-shouldered, long torso, short legs; short hair too, clippered around the neck, combed back. The look says: *I am buttoned-down.*

There's a woman with him, also in a dark suit, with straight black hair and bangs and a squarish jaw; no makeup, but she does have earrings. Her legs are good though muscular. She sits to the side, fooling with her cellphone. Is she an assistant? It isn't clear. Stan pegs her as butch. Technically she shouldn't have been here, in the men's sessions, and Stan wonders why she is. Still, better to look at her than at the guy.

The guy begins by saying they should call him

Ed. Ed hopes they're feeling comfortable, because they know – as he does! – that they've made the right choice.

Now he would like to give them – share with them – a deeper peek behind the scenes. It was a struggle to get the multiple permissions needed to set up the Positron enterprise. The powers that be did not decide easily; more than one policy guru's ass was on the line (he smirks a little at his own daring use of the word *ass*), as witness the howling when the scheme was first announced in the press. The spokesmen, or rather the spokes-persons – Ed glances at the woman, who smiles – have braved a lot of indignant screaming from the online radicals and malcontents who claim that Consilience/Positron is an infringement of individual liberties, an attempt at total social control, an insult to the human spirit. Nobody is more dedicated to individual liberties than Ed is, but as they all know – here Ed gives a conspirator-ial smile – you can't eat your so-called individual liberties, and the human spirit pays no bills, and something needed to be done to relieve the pres-sure inside the social pressure-cooker. Wouldn't they agree?

The woman in the suit glances up. What's she looking at? Her gaze sweeps over them, calm, cool. Then she turns back to her cellphone. Without a phone himself, Stan feels naked: they'd had to turn in their cells at the beginning of the workshop. They've been promised new ones, but those will work only inside the wall. Stan wonders when the new ones will be issued.

Ed lowers his voice: serious stuff coming up. Sure enough, on comes a PowerPoint with a slew of graphs. The financial big guns have concealed the true statistics to avoid panic, he says, but a shocking 40 percent of the population in this region is jobless, with 50 percent of those being under twenty-five. That's a recipe for systems breakdown, right there: for anarchy, for chaos, for the senseless destruction of property, for so-called revolution, which means looting and gang rule and warlords and mass rape, and the terrorization of the weak and helpless. That is the grim prospect staring everyone in this area right between the eyes. They've already noticed the symptoms for themselves, which is – he is sure – why they saw the desirability of signing in.

What can be done? Ed asks, wrinkling his brows. How to keep the lid on? Which it was in the interests of society at large to do, as they would surely agree. At the official leadership level, ideas were running out fast. There is only so much manpower and tax revenue that can be devoted to riot control, to social surveillance, to chasing fast youths down dark alleyways, to fire-hosing and pepper-spraying suspicious-looking gatherings. Too many once-bustling cities are stagnant or derelict, especially in the northeast, but other states are being hard hit, especially where long droughts have taken their toll. Too many of the disenfranchised are living in abandoned cars or subway tunnels or even in culverts. There's an epidemic of drugging and boozing: suicide-grade alcohol, skin-blistering drugs that kill you in under a year. Oblivion is increasingly attractive to the young, and even to the middle-aged, since why retain your brain when no amount of thinking can even begin to solve the problem? It isn't even a problem, it's beyond a problem. It's more like a looming collapse. Is their once-beautiful region, their once-beautiful country, doomed to be a wasteland of poverty and debris?

At first the solution was to build more prisons and cram more people into them, but that soon became prohibitively expensive. (Here Ed flicks through a few more slides.) Not only that, it resulted in platoons of prison graduates with professional-grade criminal skills they were more than willing to exercise once they were back in the outside world. Even when the prisons were privatized, even when the prisoners were rented out as unpaid labour to international business interests, the cost–benefit charts did not improve, because American slave workers couldn't outperform the slave workers in other countries. Competitiveness in the slave labour market was linked to the price of food, and Americans – who remain goodhearted despite everything, stray-puppy-rescuers every one – here Ed smiles indulgently, contemptuously – weren't ready to starve their prisoners to death while working them to the bone. No matter how much the prisoners were vilified by the politicians and the press as filthy dregs and toxic scum, still, heaps of stick-legged corpses can't be hidden from view indefinitely. The odd unexplained death, maybe – there has always been the odd unexplained death, says Ed, shrugging – but not heaps. Some snoop would make a phone video; such things can escape despite the best attempts to keep things under hatches, and who knows what sort of uproar, not to mention uprising, might result?

Stan feels a small prickle at the back of his neck. That's his brother Ed could be talking about! Or maybe not Con specifically; but he's pretty sure that if Ed got a close-up look at Con, he'd file him under toxic scum. It's fine for Stan to use names like that, it's within the family, and it's not that he approves of whatever it is Con is probably doing, but. Is this the kind of rumour Con's been hearing? That Positron is hardcore repressive on the subject of sticky fingers? One strike and you're out?

He'd like to phone Conor, talk to him some more. See what he knows about this place really. But he can't do that without a phone. Wait and see, he tells himself. Give the place a chance.

Ed opens his arms like a TV preacher; his voice gets louder. Then it occurred to the planners of Positron, he says – and this was brilliant – that if prisons were scaled out and handled rationally, they could be win-win viable economic units. So many jobs could be spawned by them: construction jobs, maintenance jobs, cleaning jobs, guard jobs. Hospital jobs, uniform-sewing jobs, shoe-making jobs, jobs in agriculture, if there was a farm attached: an ever-flowing cornucopia of jobs. Medium-size towns with large penitentiaries could maintain themselves, and the people inside such towns could live in middle-class comfort. And if every citizen were either a guard or a prisoner, the result would be full employment: half would be prisoners, the other half would be engaged in the business of tending the prisoners in some way or other. Or tending those who tended them.

And since it was unrealistic to expect certified criminality from 50 percent of the population, the fair thing would be for everyone to take turns: one month in, one month out. Think of the savings, with every dwelling serving two sets of residents! It was time-share taken to its logical conclusion.

Hence the twin town of Consilience/Positron. Of which they are now all such an important part! Ed smiles, the welcoming, open, inclusive smile of a born salesman. It all makes sense!

Stan wants to ask about the profit margin, and about whether this thing is a private venture. It has to be. Someone's got the lucrative infrastructure and supply contracts, walls don't build themselves, and the security systems are top grade, from what he's been able to observe at the gateway. But he stops himself: this doesn't feel like the right moment to ask, because now a great big CONSILIENCE has come up on the screen:

CONSILIENCE = CONS + RESILIENCE. DO TIME NOW, BUY TIME FOR OUR FUTURE!

A MEANINGFUL LIFE

S tan has to admit that the PR team and the branders have done well; Ed obviously thinks so too. Positron Project had changed the name of the pre-existing prison, he tells them, because 'The Upstate Correctional Institute' was dingy and boring. They'd come up with 'Positron,' which technically means the antimatter counterpart of the electron, but few out there would know that, would they? As a word, it just sounded very, well, positive. And positivity was what was needed to solve our current problems. Even the most cynical – says Ed – even the most jaundiced would have to admit that. Then they'd brought in some top designers to consult on an overall look and feel. The fifties was chosen for the visual and audio aspects, because that was the decade in which the most people had self-identified as being happy. Which is one of the goals here: maximum possible happiness. Who wouldn't tick *that* box?

When the new name and the new aesthetic were launched, Positron hit a popular nerve. Credible stratagem, said the online news bloggers. At last, a vision! Even the depressives among them said why not try it, since nothing else had worked. People were starved for hope, ready to swallow anything uplifting.

After they'd run the first TV ads, the number of online applications was overwhelming. And no wonder: there were so many advantages. Who wouldn't rather eat well three times a day, and have a shower with more than a cupful of water, and wear clean clothes and sleep in a comfortable bed devoid of bedbugs? Not to mention the inspiring sense of a shared purpose. Rather than festering in some deserted condo crawling with black mould or crouching in a stench-filled trailer where you'd spend the nights beating off dead-eyed teenagers armed with broken bottles and ready to murder you for a handful of cigarette butts, you'd have gainful employment, three wholesome meals a day, a lawn to tend, a hedge to trim, the assurance that you were contributing to the general good, and a toilet that flushed. In a word, or rather three words: A MEANINGFUL LIFE.

That was the last slogan on the last slide on the last PowerPoint. Something to take home with them, says Ed. Their new home, right here inside Consilience. And inside Positron, of course. Think of an egg, with a white and a yolk. (An egg came up onscreen, a knife cut it in half, lengthwise.) Consilience is the white, Positron is the yolk, and together they make the whole egg. The nest egg, says Ed, smiling. There's a final picture: a nest, with a golden egg shining within it.

Ed turns off the PowerPoint, puts on his reading glasses, consults a list. Practical matters: their new cellphones will be issued in the main hall. At the same time they'll receive their housing allocations. The details are explained more fully on the green sheets in their folders, but in brief, everyone in Consilience will live two lives: prisoners one month, guards or town functionaries the next. Everyone has been assigned an Alternate. One detached residential dwelling can therefore serve at least four people: in Month One, the houses will be occupied by the civilians, and then, in Month Two, by the prisoners of Month One, who will take on the civilian roles and move into the houses. And so it will go, month after month, turn and turn about. Think of the savings in the cost of living, Ed says with what is either a tic or a wink.

As for purchasing power, always a hot topic: each of them will be given an initial number of Posidollars, which can be exchanged for items they may wish to purchase at the Consilience shops or from the internal-network digital cata-logue. The sum will be topped up automatically every payday. Objects purchased to individualize the living spaces may either be stored during prison time or shared with Alternates; in case of breakage, the Alternates will of course replace such items, using their own Posidollars. There is a maintenance staff that will take care of such things as plumbing and electrical issues. And leaks, Ed says. The roof kind, not the information kind, he adds with a smile. This is supposed to be a joke, Stan guesses.

He takes a quick look at the green sheet. Single people will live in two-bedroom condos, which they will share with another single person and their two Alternates. Detached houses are reserved for couples and families: good, he and Charmaine will get one of those. Teens have two schools – one inside the prison, one outside it. Young children stay with the mothers in the women's wing, equipped with supervised play schools, kindergartens, and toddler dance classes. It's really an ideal situation for young children, and so far the parental satisfaction index is very high.

Each dwelling unit has four lockers, one for each adult. Civilian clothes, which may be selected from the catalogue, are stored in these lockers during the months when their owners are doing a prisoner shift. The orange prisoner garb is kept at the Positron Prison, worn while in prison, and left there for cleaning.

The prison cells themselves have been upgraded, and though care has been taken to maintain the theme, considerable amenities have been added. It's not as if they're being asked to live in an old-fashioned sort of prison! The prison food, for instance, is at least three-star quality. He himself enjoys nothing more because it's amazing what care and a top attitude can add to simple and wholesome ingredients.

Ed consults his notes. Stan shifts from cheek to cheek: how long is this windbag going to go on? He's got the picture, and so far there's nothing to freak out about. He could use a coffee. Better, a beer. He wonders what they've been telling Charmaine, over in the ladies' workshops.

Right, another thing, says Ed. From time to time a film crew may arrive to shoot some footage of the ideal life they will all be leading, to be shown outside Consilience as a boost to the helpful work they are doing here. They themselves will be able to view those results too, on the closed-circuit Consilience network. Music and movies are available on the same network, although, to avoid overexcitement, there is no pornography or undue violence, and no rock or hip-hop. However, there is no limitation on string quartets, Bing Crosby, Doris Day, the Mills Brothers, or show tunes from vintage Hollywood musicals.

Fuck, thinks Stan. Granny junk. What about sports, will they be able to watch any games? He wonders if there's any way of picking up a signal from outside. What's bad about football? But maybe not try anything like that too soon.

A couple more things, says Ed. There's a sign-up list for preferred jobs, in prison and in town: they should number their three top choices, with ten being the most preferred. Those who've never driven a scooter should sign up on the yellow sheet; the scooter classes will begin on Tuesday. Scooters are colour-matched to lockers, and all individuals must take personal responsibility for their scooter while it is in their care.

He, Ed, is sure they will all make a great success of this revolutionary new venture. Good luck! He gives a wave of the hand, like Santa Claus, then leaves the room. The woman in the dark suit walks behind him. Maybe she's a bodyguard, Stan thinks. Powerful glutes.

When he gets to the list of jobs, Stan chooses Robotics first. After that, IT; and third, scooter repair. He figures he could do any one of them. Just so long as he doesn't end up in Kitchen Cleanup, he'll be fine.

That evening, he and Charmaine do their first shopping with their Posidollars, and share their first meal in their new abode. Charmaine can't get over it; she's so happy she's warbling. She wants to open all the closet doors, turn on all the appliances. She can hardly wait to see what sorts of jobs they'll be given, and she's signed herself up for scooter lessons. It will all be so terrific!

'Let's go to bed,' says Stan. She's spinning out of control. He feels he needs a butterfly net to catch her, she's so hyper.

'I'm just too excited!' she says. As if, thinks Stan. He wishes he were the object of that excitement, and not the dishwasher, which she's now cooing over as if it's a kitten. He can't shake the feeling that this place is some sort of pyramid scheme, and that those who fail to understand that will be left empty-handed. But there's no obvious reason for this feeling of his. Maybe he's ungrateful by nature.

I'M STARVED FOR YOU

Stan's lost count of the exact time they've been inside the twin cities. You can get into a drifting mode. Has a year gone by already? More than a year. He's repaired scooters one month, dealt with egg-counting software in prison the next, then back to the scooters. Nothing he hasn't been able to handle.

He's listening to 'Paper Doll' on his phone ear buds while rinsing out his coffee cup. Those flirty guys, he hums to himself. At first he hated the music in Consilience, but he's begun to find it oddly consoling. Doris Day is even kind of a turn-on.

Today is switchover day, when he and Charmaine both go into the prison. How does she pass the time away from him, inside the women's wing? 'We knit a lot,' she's told him. 'In the off-hours. And there are the vegetable gardens, and the cooking – we take turns at those daily things. And the laundry, of course. And then at the hospital, my job as Chief Medications Administrator – it's a big responsibility! I'm never bored! The days just fly by!'

'Do you miss me?' Stan asked her a week ago. 'When you're in there?'

'Of course I miss you. Don't be silly,' she said, kissing him on the nose. But a nose kiss wasn't what he wanted. *Do you hunger for me, do you burn for me?* That's what he'd like to ask. But he doesn't dare ask that, because he's almost certain she would laugh.

It's not that they don't have sex. They certainly have more of it than they had in the car; but it's sex that Charmaine enacts, like yoga, with careful breath control. What he wants is sex that can't be helped. He wants helplessness. No no no, yes yes yes! That's what he wants. He's come to realize that, in recent months.

Down in the cellar, he opens the large green locker and stows away the clothes he's been wearing for summer: the shorts, the T-shirts, the jeans. He may not be using these for a while: by the time he gets back here next month, the hot weather may be over and he'll be into the fleece pullovers, though you never know with September. He won't have to do so much lawn maintenance then, which is a plus. Though the lawn will be a wreck. Some guys have no feeling for lawns, they take them for granted, they let them mat up and dry out and then the yellow ants get into them and it takes a lot of work to bring the grass back. If he were here all the time he could keep the lawn in peak condition.

Upstairs, clean towels are deployed in the bathroom, clean sheets are on the bed. Charmaine did that before she set off on her scooter for Positron. In the past couple of months he's been leaving the house after she does, so he does the final check: no bathtub ring, no orphaned sock, no ends of soap or wispy gatherings of shed hair on the floor. When they return on the first day of every second month, Stan and Charmaine are supposed to find the house pristine, spotless, hinting of lemon-scented cleaning products, and Charmaine likes to leave it that way. She says they should lead by example.

It certainly hasn't been spotless every time they've returned. As Charmaine has pointed out, there have been hairs, there have been toast crumbs, there have been smudges. More than that: three months ago Stan found a folded note; the corner was sticking out from under the refrigerator. It might originally have been attached with the silver fridge magnet in the shape of a duck, the same one Charmaine uses to post shopping reminders.

Despite the strict Consilience taboo against contact with Alternates, he read the note immediately. Though it was done on a printer, it was shockingly intimate:

Darling Max, I can hardly wait till next time.
I'm starved for you! I need you so much.
XXOO and you know what more – Jasmine.

There was a lipstick kiss: hot pink. No, darker: some kind of purple. Not violet, not mauve, not maroon. He riffled through his head, trying to recall the names of the colours on the paint chips and fabric swatches Charmaine spends so much time brooding over. He'd lifted the paper to his nose, breathed in: still a faint scent, like cherry bubble gum.

Charmaine has never worn a lipstick that colour. And she's never written him a note like that. He dropped it into the trash as if it was burning, but then fished it out and slid it back under the refrigerator: Jasmine shouldn't know that her note to Max had been intercepted. Also, it's possible Max looks under the fridge for such notes – it might be a kinky little game they play – and Max would be upset not to find it. 'Did you get my note?' Jasmine would say to him as they lay stuck together. 'What note?' Max would answer. 'Omigod, one of them found it!' Jasmine would exclaim. Then she would laugh. It might even turn her on, the consciousness of a third pair of eyes having seen the imprint of her avid mouth.

Not that she needs turning on. Stan can't stop thinking about that: about Jasmine, about her mouth. It's bad enough here at the house, even with Charmaine breathing beside him, lightly or heavily depending on what they're doing, or rather on what he's doing – Charmaine has never been much of a joiner, more of a sidelines woman, cheering him on from a distance. But at Positron, in his narrow bed in the men's wing, that kiss floats in the darkness before his open eyes like four plush pillows, parted invitingly as if about to sigh or speak. He knows the colour of that mouth by now, he's tracked it down.

Fuchsia. It has a moist, luscious feel to it. *Oh hurry,* that mouth says. *I need you, I need you now! I'm starved for you!* But it's speaking to Stan, not to the guy whose clothes repose in the locker beside his own. Not to Max.

Max and Jasmine, those are their names – the names of the Alternates, the two others who occupy the house, walk through its routines, cater to its demands, act out its fantasies of normal life when he and Charmaine aren't there. He isn't supposed to know those names, or anything at all about their owners: that's Consilience protocol. But because of the note, he does know the names. And by now he knows – or deduces, or, more accurately, imagines – a lot of other things as well.

Max's locker is the red one. Charmaine's locker is pink, Jasmine's is purple. In an hour or so – once Stan has left the house, once he's logged out – Max will walk in through the front door, open the red locker, take out his stored clothes, carry them upstairs, arrange them in the bedroom, on the shelves, in the closet: enough for a month's stay.

Then Jasmine will arrive. She won't bother with her locker, not at first. They'll throw themselves into each other's arms. No: Jasmine will throw herself into Max's arms, press herself against him, open her fuchsia mouth, tear off Max's clothes and her own, pull him down onto – what? The living room carpet? Or will they stumble upstairs, reeling with lust, and fall entwined onto the bed, so thoughtfully and neatly made up with newly ironed sheets by Charmaine before she left? Sheets with a border of birthday-party bluebirds tying pink ribbon bows. Nursery sheets, kiddie sheets: Charmaine's idea of cuteness. Those sheets don't seem right for Max and Jasmine, who would never choose such bland, pastel accessories for themselves. Black satin is more their style. Though, like all the basics in the place, the sheets came with the house.

Jasmine isn't a sheet ironer, nor does she make up the bed for Stan and Charmaine before she leaves: they find the mattress bare, and no towels set out in the bathroom either. But of course Jasmine is lax about such household details, thinks Stan, because all she really cares about is sex.

Stan rearranges Jasmine and Max in his head, this way and that, lace bra ripped asunder, legs in the air, hair wildly tangled, even though he has no idea what either of them looks like. Max's back is covered with scratch marks like a cat fancier's leather sofa.

What a slut, that Jasmine. Flaming hot in an instant, like an induction cooker. He can't stand it.

Maybe she's ugly. Ugly ugly ugly, he repeats

77

like a charm, trying to exorcise her – her and her maddening bubble-gum lipstick smell and her musky voice, a voice he's never heard. But it doesn't work, because she's not ugly, she's beautiful. She's so beautiful she glows in the dark.

No such pranks with Charmaine. No blistering fuchsia kisses, no rolling around on the carpet. A month from now it'll be 'Stanley! Stan! Honey! I'm here!' in a light, clear voice, a voice without undertones: Charmaine, wearing her blue-and-white-striped shirt, so crisp, with its faint underscent of bleach and its overtone of baby-powder-themed fabric softener.

He wouldn't have her any other way. That's why he married her: she was an escape from the many-layered, devious, ironic, hot-cold women he'd tangled himself up with until then; women too open to being raided by Conor, and by others as well. Transparency, certainty, fidelity: his various humiliations had taught him to value those. He liked the retro thing about Charmaine, the cookie-ad thing, her prissiness, the way she hardly ever swore. When they'd got married they'd pictured kids, once they could afford them. They still do picture them. Maybe that will happen soon, now that they're no longer living in their car.

He keys in the code on his locker, waits for it to flash CLOSED, climbs the cellar stairs, leaves the house. Once outside, he taps a second code into the signal pad beside the door, coding himself out.

Over at Positron, Jasmine and Max must already

have changed into the civvies they stored there last month. Now they must be checking out of their prison wings and ditching their orange prison uniforms at the main desk. Very soon they'll hop onto their scooters and make their way to this house. Stan has a voyeur's urge to hide behind the hedge, that cedar hedge he trimmed last week, tidying up the slapdash job done by Max during his last sojourn. He'll wait until they're both inside, then peer through the windows. He's figured out the sight lines, he's left the ground-floor blinds up a crack. If they go upstairs, though, he'll have no option but to set up the extension ladder, and he knows how screechy and metallic that would be.

And what if he falls off? Worse, if Max leans out the window, stark naked, and pushes him off? He doesn't know anything about Max, except from what's implied in that note; also, Max had first choice of lockers, and he chose the red one. He must be aggressive. Stan wouldn't wish to be pushed off an extension ladder by an angry naked man, a naked man to whose rippling epidermis he now adds copious tattoos. Most likely Max also has a shaved head, covered in scars and welts from all the times he's broken men's teeth and jaws with the sheer force of his bullet-shaped skull.

Stan's own skull still has a cushion of sandy hair, but it's thinning, even though he's only thirty-two. He's never used his skull to butt anyone in the mouth, though he's willing to bet Max has. Most likely Max once worked as a bodyguard for some black-jacketed, gold-chained, coke-pushing, girl-enslaving money lord, in his life before Positron. Someone like Conor, only a larger, tougher, meaner, more powerful Conor. On level ground, Stan might be able to hold his own against such a man, but on that ladder he'd be off balance. And he'd land in the hedge, bashing a jagged hole in it, after all his careful trimming.

That asswipe Max is even worse with the hedge than he is with the lawn. Stan found the hedge trimmer in the garage, its blade gummed up with slaughtered foliage. But there's no chance Max is able to focus on hedge trimming, since Jasmine leaps on the poor sod every time she sees him in his leather work gloves and starts pawing at his belt buckle.

All things considered, better not to peer in the window.

SWITCH

It's a beautiful cloudless day, not too hot for the first of August. Charmaine finds switchover days almost festive: when it's not raining, the streets are full of people, smiling, greeting one another, some walking, some on their colour-coded scooters, the odd one in a golf cart. Now and then one of the dark Surveillance cars glides through them: there are more of those cars on switchover days.

Everyone seems quite happy: having two lives means there's always something different to look forward to. It's like having a vacation every month. But which life is the vacation and which is the work? Charmaine hardly knows.

Making her way to the Consilience town pharmacy on her pink-and-purple electric scooter, she checks her watch: she doesn't have much time. She needs to key in at Positron by five-thirty at the latest, and it's already three. She told Stan she had to do some ordering for the prison hospital: that's why she was in a rush to leave the house. The month before last, her excuse was slipcovers – didn't he agree about the slipcovers, weren't they

81

a drab colour, shouldn't they both go and view the selection and put in a requisition for something more cheerful? You can't really tell from a digital image, you have to see them in person. Look, she has some fabric swatches! A floral, or maybe an abstract motif?

Anything along those lines and Stan zones out, and she can count on his not having heard a word she's said. He'd notice her if she were to suddenly disappear, but he doesn't register her much otherwise. Lately he's been treating her like white noise, like the rivulet sound on their sleep machine. This would once have hurt her – did hurt her – but now it suits her fine.

She parks the scooter in the lot behind the pharmacy, then walks around to the front. Already her heart is beating faster. She takes a breath, assumes her bustling, efficient pose, consults her little notebook as if there's something written in it. Then she orders a large box of gauze bandages, putting it on the hospital account. The bandages aren't needed, but they're also not remarkable: no one will be keeping track of gauze bandages, especially since keeping track of them happens to be her own job, every other month.

She smiles in her sunniest manner at Bill Nairn, who's putting in his last hour as pharmacist before shedding his white coat and taking up whatever role he plays inside the Positron Prison walls. Bill smiles back, and they exchange remarks about the lovely weather, then close with goodbyes. She smiles again. She has such guileless teeth: asexual teeth, nothing fanged about them. She used to worry about looking so symmetrical, so blond, but she's come to think of this as an asset. Her small teeth alarm no one: bland is good camouflage.

She hurries back to the lot, and sure enough there's a small envelope tucked in under the scooter seat. She palms it, fishtails out of the lot, makes it around the corner to a residential street, parks.

They don't use their Consilience-issue cell-phones to arrange these meetings: it's too risky, because you never know what the central IT people are tracking. The whole town is under a bell jar: communications can be exchanged inside it, but no words get in or out except through approved gateways. No whines, no complaints, no tattling, no whistle-blowing. The overall message must be tightly controlled: the outside world must be assured that the Consilience/Positron twin city project is working.

And it is working, because look: safe streets, no homelessness, jobs for all!

Though there were some bumps along the way, and those bumps had to be flattened out. But right now Charmaine doesn't intend to dwell on those discouraging bumps, or on the nature of the flattening.

She unfolds the paper, reads the address. She'll dispose of the note by burning it, though not out here in the open: a woman on a scooter setting fire to something might attract notice. There aren't any black cars in view, but it's rumoured that Surveillance can see around corners.

Today's address is in a housing development left over from some decade in the mid-twentieth century: one of the many relics from the town's past. As they've all been informed in the back-grounders, the town that's now become Consilience was founded in the late nineteenth century by a group of Quakers. Brotherly love was what they'd wanted; the town's name was Harmony, its crest was a beehive, meaning cooperative labour. The first industry was a beet-sugar mill; next came a furniture factory, then a corset company. Then there was an automobile plant – one of those pre-Ford cars – then a camera film corporation, and finally, a state correctional institution.

After the Second World War, the key industries faded until nothing was left of Harmony but a gutted downtown, several crumbling public build-ings with white columns, and a lot of repossessed houses not even the banks could sell. And, of course, the correctional institution, which was where the inhabitants had worked, when they'd worked at all.

But now, thinks Charmaine, it's all different. Such an improvement! Already the gym has been renovated, for instance. And a whole bunch of houses are being upgraded – a fresh batch of applicants will arrive any month now to fill them.

Or maybe to fill the houses that aren't so upgraded, such as the one she and Stan had lived in at first. There had been plumbing problems; more like plumbing *events,* since they were bigger than mere problems. There was the time when it rained so hard and the sewage came spouting up through the kitchen sink: that was bigger than just a problem.

Luckily they'd been approved for a transfer; she assumes their Alternates had moved to the new house as well, but maybe not. She hasn't thought to ask Max about that – whether he and his wife once lived in that earlier house. It isn't the kind of thing she talks about with Max.

Every month it's a new address: better that way. Luckily there are a lot of vacant houses, left over from when the industries were failing and the lenders were foreclosing, and from that later time when so many houses were standing empty because no one wanted to buy them. Max is a member of the Consilience Dwellings Reclamation Team when he's not living in his prison cell at Positron. The Reclamation Team are the ones who inspect the houses, then tag them either for the wrecking ball and levelling for parkland and community gardens, or else for renovation, so he's in a position to know which ones are suitable.

Max tries to choose the kind of interior decoration Charmaine prefers: she likes pretty wallpaper, with rosebuds or daisies. He does find the ones with wallpaper like that. But in each house they've used, the vandals were there, in the times when they roamed from town to town and from house to house, smashing windows and bottles and drinking and drugging and sleeping on the floor and using the bathtubs as outhouses, back before they had even started the Positron Project.

The gangs and crazies left their marks on the floral wallpaper: scrawled tags and other things. Vicious drawings. Short, hard words, written in spray paint, or markers, or lipstick, and, a couple of times, something brown and crusted that might have been shit.

'Read to me,' Max had whispered into her ear, in the first house, the first time.

'I can't,' she said. 'I don't want to.'

'Yes, you do,' Max said. 'You do want to.' And she must have wanted to, because those words were spilling out. He laughed, picked her up, pushed his hands up under her skirt. She never wears jeans to these meetings, and that's why. The next minute they were down on the bare floorboards.

'Wait!' she said, gasping with pleasure. 'Undo the buttons!'

'I can't wait,' he said, and it was true, he couldn't wait, and because he couldn't, neither could she. It was like the copy on the back of the most lurid novel in the limited-titles library at Positron. Swept away. Drugged with desire. Like a cyclone. Helpless moaning. All of that. She'd never known about such a force, such an energy inside herself. She'd thought it was only in books and TV, or else for other people.

She gathered the buttons up afterwards, pocketed them. Only two had come off. She sewed them on again, later, after her stint in Positron, before returning to the house where she lived with Stan.

She did love Stan, but it was different. A different kind of love. Trusting, sedate. It went with pet fish, in fishbowls – not that they had one of those – and with cats, perhaps. And with eggs for breakfast, poached, snuggled inside their individual poachers. And with babies.

Once Grandma Win had died, Charmaine had to make her own way; it had been thin ice with the cracks showing and disaster always waiting just beneath her, but the trick was to keep gliding. She loved Stan because she liked solid ground under her feet, non-reflective surfaces, movies with neat endings. Closure, they called it. She'd opted for Chief Medications Administrator at Positron Prison when it was offered to her because it involved shelves and inventories, and everything in its place.

Or that's all she thought it would be; but there are depths, as it turns out. There are other duties not mentioned to her at first, there's a certain amount of untidiness, there's navigation to be done. She's getting proficient at it. And it turns out she's not as dedicated to tidiness as she used to think.

It was sloppy to have left that note under the refrigerator. And that lipstick kiss was so tawdry. She keeps the lipstick in her locker; she's only ever used it on that one note. Stan would never put up with her wearing a garish hue like that – Purple Passion is its name, such bad taste.

Which is why she bought it: that's how she thinks of her feelings toward Max. Purple. Passionate. Garish. And, yes, bad taste. To a man like that, for whom you have feelings like that, you can say all sorts of things, *I'm starved for you* being the mildest of them. Words she would never have used, before. Vandal words. Sometimes she can't believe what comes out of her mouth; not to mention what goes into it. She does whatever Max wants.

His name isn't Max, of course, any more than Charmaine's name is Jasmine. They don't use their real names: they decided on that the first time, without even talking about it. It's as if they can read each other's minds.

No, not minds: each other's mindlessness. When she's with Max, she throws away her mind.

TIDY

That first time had been an accident. Charmaine had stayed behind at the house after Stan left, finishing the final tidy, as she used to do at first, before Max. 'You go on ahead,' she'd tell him to get him out of her hair, which was pulled back into her housekeeping ponytail. She liked her cleanup routine, she liked to put on her pinafore apron and her rubber gloves and tick the items off her mental list without being interrupted. Rugs, tubs, sinks. Towels, toilets, sheets. Anyway, Stan hated the sound of the vacuum. 'I'll just make up the bed,' she'd say. 'Off you go, hon. See you in a month. Have a good one.'

And that's what she was doing – making up the bed, humming to herself – when Max walked into the room. He startled her. Cornered her: there was only the one door. A thinnish man, wiry. Not unusually tall. A lot of black hair. Handsome too. A man who'd have choices.

'It's okay,' he said. 'Sorry. I'm early. I live here.' He took a step forward.

'So do I,' Charmaine said. They looked at each other.

'Pink locker?' Another step.

'Yes. You're the red one.' Backing away. 'I'm almost finished here, and then you can . . .'

'No hurry,' he said. He took another step. 'What do you keep inside that pink locker of yours? I've often wondered.'

Had he made a joke? Charmaine wasn't so good at telling when people were making jokes. 'Maybe you'd like some coffee,' she said. 'In the kitchen. I cleaned the machine, but I can always . . . It's not very nice coffee, though.' Charmaine, you're babbling, she told herself.

'I'm good,' he said. 'I'd rather stay here and watch you. I like the way you always make up the bed before you leave. And put out the fresh towels. Like a hotel.'

'It's okay, I kind of like doing it, I think it looks . . .' Now she was backed up against the night table. I need to get out of this room, she told herself. Maybe she could glide around him. She moved to the side and forward. 'I'm sorry, I have to leave now,' she said in what she hoped was a neutral tone. But he put his hand on her shoulder. He stepped forward again.

'I like your apron,' he said. 'Or whatever it is. Does it tie at the back?' The next minute – how did it happen? – her pinafore apron was on the floor, her hair had come loose – had he done that? – and they were kissing, and his hands were under her freshly ironed shirt. 'We've got a couple of hours,' he said, breaking away. 'But we can't stay

here. My wife . . . Look, I know this place . . .'
He scribbled an address. 'Go there now.'

'I'll just tuck in the sheet,' she said. 'It would look wrong otherwise.' He smiled at that. She did tuck in the sheet, though not as tightly as usual, because her hands were shaking. Then she did what he said.

That was their first vacant house. It was dim, there were dead flies, the lights didn't work, nor the water; the walls had been cracked and stained, but none of it mattered that first time, because she wasn't noticing those kinds of details. He'd left first, by the side door. Then, after she'd counted to five hundred as he'd suggested, she'd walked out the front door, trying to look hurried and official, and scootered straight to Positron Prison, where she'd checked in, handed over her civvies, taken the mandatory shower, and put on the clean orange prison-issue suit that was waiting for her. After dinner in the women's hall with the others – it was roast pork with Brussels sprouts – she'd joined her knitting circle as usual, and chatted about this and that, also as usual. But she was sleepwalking.

She ought to have been appalled by herself, by what she'd done. Instead she was amazed, and also jubilant. Had it really happened? Would it happen again? How could she contact him, or even believe in his existence? She couldn't. It was like standing on a cliff edge. It made her dizzy.

At ten o'clock she went into her double cell, where the woman she shared with was already asleep, and there was the reassuring clang of the door and click of the lock. It felt safe to be caged in, now that she knew she had this other person inside her who was capable of escapades and contortions she'd never known about before. It wasn't Stan's fault, it was the fault of chemistry. People said *chemistry* when they meant something else, such as personality, but she does mean chemistry. Smells, textures, flavours, secret ingredients. She sees a lot of chemistry in her work, she knows what it can do. Chemistry can be like magic. It can be merciless.

She slept that night as if drunk. The next day she went about her hospital duties as briskly as usual, hiding behind the grillwork of her smile. Ever since then she's been waiting: inside Positron while Max inspects vacant dwellings in Consilience; then in the house with Stan, working at her bakery job during the days; she does the pies and the cinnamon buns. Then there's an hour or two of being Jasmine, with Max, on switchover days, while he's going into Positron Prison and she's coming back to civilian life, or vice versa. A vacant house. The anxiety. The haste. The rampage.

Then more waiting. It's like being stretched so thin you feel you'll break the very next minute; but she hasn't broken yet. Though maybe leaving the note was breakage of a sort. Or the beginning of it. She should have had better control.

★   ★   ★

Stan must have read the note. It has to have been like that. He must have read it and then tucked it back under the fridge, because Max described where he'd found it, and it was a lot farther over to the right than where she'd stashed it. Ever since then, Stan has been so preoccupied he might as well be deaf and blind. When he makes love – that's how Charmaine thinks of it, as distinct from whatever it is that happens with Max – when Stan makes love, it isn't to her. Or not his usual idea of her. He's almost angry.

'Let go,' Stan said to her once. 'Just fucking let go!'

'What did you mean, "Let go"?' she asked him afterwards in her puzzled, clueless voice, the voice that had once been her only voice. 'Let go of what? What are you talking about?' He said, 'Never mind' and 'Sorry' and seemed ashamed of himself. She did nothing to discourage that. She wants him to feel ashamed of himself, because such feelings of his are a part of her disguise.

He called her Jasmine once, by mistake. What if she'd answered? It would have been a giveaway. But she caught herself and pretended she hadn't heard. Maybe Stan has fallen in love with her note, with its ill-advised fuchsia kiss. Is that funny, or is it dangerous?

What if Stan finds out? About her, about Max. What would he do? He has a temper; it was worse when they were in the car, but even since coming here he's thrown some glassware, he's sworn at things when they don't work the way he wants: the hedge trimmer, the lawn mower. He wouldn't enjoy the discovery that there is no Jasmine really, except inside Charmaine. She would lose him then. He wouldn't be able to stand it.

She needs to break it off with Max. She needs to keep them both safe – Stan as well as Max – and herself too. Just not yet. Surely she can permit herself a few more hours, a few more moments, of whatever it is. Not happiness; it isn't that.

It would have been better if Max's wife, Jocelyn, had found that note. What would she have thought? Nothing too unsafe. She wouldn't have known who 'Max' was because he never uses that name with his wife, according to him, and he doesn't have sex with her much, or nothing like the sex he has with Charmaine, so there's no need to be jealous. It's two different worlds, and Max and Jasmine are in one of them, and the wife is in the other.

For Jocelyn, 'Max' and 'Jasmine' would just be the Alternates, living in the house whenever she and her husband were in Positron. She would have thought that 'Max' and 'Jasmine' were Stan and Charmaine, if she paid any attention to that note at all. What else could she possibly have thought?

So, whew! Charmaine tells herself. Looks like you got away with it, up to now.

You said what? She hears Max's voice in her head, the way she often does when he isn't there. She invents him, she knows it; she makes up things for him to say. Though it doesn't feel like making up, it feels as if he's really talking to her. *Whew? Like a vintage funny-paper guy? Baby, you're so fucking retro, you're cool! Now I'm gonna make you say something better with your slutty purple mouth. Ask me for it. Bend over.*

Anything, she answers. Anything inside this non-house, inside this nothing space, a space that doesn't exist, between these two people with no real names. *Oh anything.* Already she's abject.

Here it is now, today's address. Max's scooter is already parked, discreetly, four derelict doors away. She can barely make her way up the front steps, her legs are so wobbly. If anyone were watching, they'd think she was crippled.

PART IV

THE HEART GOES LAST

HAIRCUT

S tan clocks in at Positron, takes a shower, changes into the orange boiler suit, lines up for the routine haircut. They like to preserve the appearance of an authentic prison, though the shorn look for convicts is archaic – it belongs with the head lice of olden times – and they no longer do the full buzz: just short enough so when it's time to leave again the hair's a respectable civilian length.

'Have a good month outside?' asks the barber, whose name is Clint. Clint has a big T on his front because he's playing the part of a Trusty. He's not one of the original criminals, the ones who were still in here when the Project began: you'd never let a dangerous offender anywhere near those scissors and razors. Outside, when he's a civilian, Clint does tree pruning. Before he signed on to the Project he'd been an actuary, but he'd lost that job when his company moved west.

It's a familiar story, though nobody talks much about what they were before: backward glances are not encouraged. Stan himself doesn't dwell on his Dimple Robotics interlude, back when he'd thought the future was like a sidewalk and all you had to do was make it from one block to the next; nor does he dwell on what came after, when he had no job. He hates to think of himself the way he was then: grimy, morose, with the air being sucked out of his chest by the sense of futility that was everywhere like a fog. It's good to have goals again, among them the discovering and seduction of Jasmine. He can almost feel her in his fingertips – the yielding, the rubberiness, the humid jungle heat.

Steady, he tells himself as he swings into the chair. Hands out of the pockets. Don't give yourself a hernia.

Clint must have learned the barbering here: they'd all had to apprentice, in order to gain or hone a practical skill of use inside Positron.

'Yeah, good month, can't complain,' says Stan. 'You?'

'Terrific,' says Clint. 'Did a little work on my house. Went to the committee, got permission, painted the kitchen. Primrose yellow, gave the place a lift. Northern exposure. Wife was pleased.'

'What's she do, inside?' Stan asks.

'Works in the hospital. Surgeon,' says Clint. 'Heart, mostly. Yours?'

'Hospital too, Chief Medications Administrator,' says Stan. He feels a twinge of pride in Charmaine: despite her pink locker, she's no airhead. It's a serious position, it comes with power. You need to be dependable, you need to be upbeat, she's told him. Also stable, discreet, and not given to dark thoughts.

'Must be a tough job sometimes,' says Clint. 'Dealing with sick people.'

'Was at first,' says Stan. 'Got to her a bit. But she's more used to it now.' She's never told him much about her work, but then, he's never told her much about his.

'You'd need a cool head,' says Clint. 'Not sentimental.'

This calls for no more than a yup. Clint decides on a tactful, snippety-snipping silence, which is fine with Stan. He needs to concentrate on Jasmine, Jasmine of the fuchsia kiss. She won't let him alone.

He closes his eyes, sees himself as one of those dorky video-game hero princes of his childhood, slashing his questing way through swamps full of tentacled man-eating plants, annihilating giant leeches, hacking through the poison brambles to the iron castle where Jasmine lies asleep, guarded by a dragon, the dragon of Max, and shortly to be awakened by a kiss, the kiss of Stan. Trouble is she's already awake, she's super awake, having sex with the dragon. Him and his big scaly tail.

Bad reverie. He opens his eyes.

Who is Max? He could be someone Stan sees often without knowing it. He could be a guy who's left his scooter with Stan for repair while he spent his month in the slammer, he could be playing a guard right now, locking Stan in at night and saying, *Stay in line.* He could even be Clint: is that possible? Could 'Clint' be a fake name? Surely not. Clint is an older guy, with greying hair and a paunch.

'There you go,' says Clint. He holds up a mirror so Stan can see the back of his own head. There's a bristly roll of fat taking shape at the nape of his neck, but only if he leans his head back. When he finds Jasmine he must remember to keep his head upright. Or forward a little. She might put her hand there, a hand with long, strong fingers tipped with nails the colour of arterial blood. At the mere thought, he feels himself flushing. Clint is whisking off the prickly hairs.

'Thanks,' says Stan. 'See you in two.'

Two months – one in, one out – until his next Clint haircut. Before then he'll be connected with Jasmine, whatever it takes.

He joins the lineup for lunch, which is always the first thing that happens after the haircut. Positron food is excellent, because if the cooking team orders up crap for you, you'll dish out crap to them the next month to get even. Works like a charm: it's amazing how many painstaking chefs have sprung into being. Today it's chicken dumplings, one of his favourites. It's an added satisfaction that he himself has made a contribution to the production of the chickens, in his Positron role as Poultry Supervisor.

Lunch hour used to be stressful in the months just after he'd signed in. At that time there were still some bona fide criminals in the place. Drug dealers, gang enforcers, grifters and con artists, assorted thieves. Seriously shaved heads, deeply engraved tats that hooked the wearer to their affiliates and advertised feuds. There were shovings in the cafeteria lineup, there were glarings, there were standoffs. Stan learned some ingenious combinations of words he would never have put together himself, even when fighting with Conor, and you had to admire the inventiveness, the poetry even. (*Pus, cock, liverwurst, mother, dog, strawberry jam:* how did that one go, exactly?) Scuffles broke out over muffins, plates of scrambled eggs were shoved into faces.

Things might escalate: stompings, the cracking of bones. Then the guards would be expected to muscle in, but only some of them had formerly been real guards, so these interventions lacked authority. Tramplings took place, kickings, punchings, chokings, hot coffee scaldings, followed by retribution behind the scenes: mysterious knifings in the showers, puncture wounds traced to double-pronged barbecue forks lifted from the kitchen, concussions caused by men somehow banging their heads repeatedly on rocks, out in the market-garden area, among the sheltering rows of tomato plants.

Throughout those days, Stan hunkered down and kept his mouth shut and tried to be as invisible as possible, knowing he was no Conor – he lacked the skill set for such hardcore games. But that period didn't last long, because the disturbances caused by the criminal elements were too great a threat to the Project. The initial thinking had been that the criminals would be sprinkled among the volunteers now making up the bulk of the prisoners, which was supposed to have an improving effect on the crims. Not only that, but they too would be let out every second month to take their turns as civilian inhabitants of Consilience, doing town-side tasks or acting as guards at Positron.

This would give them an experience they might never have had before – namely, a job – and would also earn them respect from others and a place in the community, leading to a newfound self-respect. Having prisoners act as guards and the reverse would be positive all round, went the mantra. The guards would be less likely to abuse their authority, as it would soon be their turn to be under lock and key. And the prisoners would have an incentive for good behaviour, since violent acting-out would attract retaliation. Also, there was no longer an upside to criminality. Gang dominance got you no material wealth, and you couldn't fence anything: who'd want to buy stuff that was replicated in all the Consilience furnished houses anyway? There were no illicit substances that could be bootlegged or pushed, no rackets that could be run. That was the official theory.

But it seemed some criminals wanted to throw their weight around just for the hell of it: top dog was top dog, even if there was no financial payoff. Gangs formed, non-criminals were intimidated by criminals or else drawn into circles of dark power they found newly appealing. There were home invasions in the town, trashing-and-smashing parties, maybe even – it was rumoured – gang rapes. At one point there was a threat of an uprising against Management, with hostages taken and ears cut off, but that plan was discovered in time, through a spy.

The outside forces could always have turned off the power supply and the water – any halfwit could figure that out, in Stan's opinion – but then the bad news would leak out and the Project would go down in flames, way too publicly. The model would be judged worthless. And a shitload of investors' money would have been wasted.

After surveillance was tightened, the worst troublemakers vanished. Consilience was a closed system – once inside, nobody went out – so where had they gone? 'Transferred to another wing' was the official version. Or else 'health problems.' Rumours as to their actual fates began to circulate, in furtive hints and nods. Behaviour improved dramatically.

DUTY

Lunch completed, Stan has a brief rest in his cell; then, when the chicken dumplings have settled, he works out in the weights room, concentrating on his core strength. Then it's time for his shift at the poultry facility.

Positron has four kinds of animals – cows, pigs, rabbits, and chickens. It also has extensive greenhouses that stand on the sites of demolished buildings, and several acres of apple trees, in addition to the outdoor market gardens. These, and the soybean and perennial-wheat fields, are supposed to produce the fresh food, both for Positron Prison and for the town of Consilience. Not only the fresh foods but the frozen ones, and not only food but drink: soon there will be a brewery. Some items are brought in from outside – quite a few items, in fact – but that state of affairs is viewed as temporary. In no time at all, the Project will be self-sustaining.

Except for paper products, and plastics, and fuel, and sugar, and bananas, and . . .

But still, think of the savings in other areas, such

as chickens. The chickens have been an unquali-
fied success. They're plump and tasty, they breed
like mice, eggs roll out of them with clockwork
regularity. They eat the leafy leftovers from the
vegetables, and the table scraps from the Positron
prison meals, and the chopped-up remnants of
slaughtered animals. The pigs eat the same things,
only more of them. The cows and the rabbits are
still vegetarian.

But apart from eating them, Stan has nothing
to do with the cows and pigs and rabbits, only
the chickens. These live in wire cages but are let
out for a run twice a day, which is supposed to
improve their morale. Their heating and light are
run by a computer inside a little shed, which
Stan checks periodically: there was a malfunction
once that almost resulted in roast chicken, but
Stan knew enough to be able to reprogram and
save the day. The eggs are collected via ingenious
chutes and funnels, with a digital program counting
them. Stan himself has made some improvements that reduced egg breakage, but the system's
running fine now. Mainly he spends his four-hour
shift supervising the afternoon chicken outing,
breaking up the pecking-order squabbles, and
monitoring the combs for poor health and
moping.

It's a make-work job, he knows that. He suspects
that each chicken has a chip implanted in it, with
the real supervision done that way, in a roomful

of automated chicken snoopers recording numbers on flow charts and graphs. But he finds the routine soothing.

In earlier days – during the semi-reign of the run-amok real criminals, and before the authorities had put in the spyware cameras overlooking the poultry facility – Stan got daily visitations during his shifts from men inside Positron, his fellow prisoners-for-a-month.

What they wanted was a short time alone with a chicken. They were willing to trade for it. In return, Stan would be offered protection from the furtive gang thuggery that was then running like an undercurrent beneath the orderly routines of Positron Prison.

'You want to what?' he asked the first time. The guy had spelled it out: he wanted to have sex with a chicken. It didn't hurt the chicken, he'd done it before, it was normal, lots of guys did it, and chickens didn't talk. A guy got very horny in here with no outlets, right? And it was no fair that Stan was keeping the chickens all to himself, and if he didn't unlock that wire cage right now, his life might not be so pleasant, supposing he was allowed to keep it, because he might end up as a chicken substitute like the fag he probably was.

Stan got the message. He allowed the chicken assignations. What did that make him? A chicken pimp. Better that than dead.

Conor would have known what to do. Conor would have cold-cocked the guy, turned him into chicken feed. Conor would have charged a higher price. Conor would have been running the thuggery himself. But then, Conor might not have survived, once Management started ironing out the Positron glitches in dead earnest.

Strolling between the rows of cages now, listening to the soothing clucks of contented hens, smelling the familiar ammonia scent of chicken shit, he wonders if he's ashamed of himself for his chicken pimping, and discovers that he isn't. Worse, he ponders giving the chicken option a try himself, which might ease his tormented desires by wiping the image of Jasmine off his brain with a living feather duster. But there were the surveillance cameras: a man could look very undignified with a chicken stuck onto him like a marshmallow on a stick. Most likely it wouldn't work as an exorcism: he'd only start having daydreams about Jasmine in feathers.

Cut it, Stan, he tells himself. Block it off. Suck it up. He's getting way too obsessive. There must be a drug he could take to get rid of this waking dream. No, this waking nightmare: endless tantalization, with no release. Maybe he'll ask Charmaine about some sort of calming, deflationary pill: she works in Medications, she could get her hands on something. But how can he explain his problem to her – *I'm lusting for a woman I've never seen* – much less his needs? She's so clean, so crisp, so blue and white, so baby-powder-scented. She wouldn't understand a compulsion as twisted as this. Not to mention so plain bone-ass dumb.

Maybe he needs to spend some time in the woodworking shop, after his poultry shift. Saw something in two. Pound a few nails.

THE HEART GOES LAST

C harmaine slips her green smock on over her orange basics. There's another Special Procedure scheduled for this afternoon. They always do them in the afternoons; they like to avoid the darkness of night. That way it's more cheerful for everyone, herself included.

She checks to make sure she has her mask, and her surgical gloves: yes, in her pocket. First she needs to get the key from the monitoring desk that sits at the conjunction of three corridors. There's no receptionist in the flesh at that desk, only a head box, but at least there's a head in the box. Or a canned image of a head. Whether it's live or not is anyone's guess: they do those things so well nowadays. Maybe soon they'll have robots carrying out the Special Procedures and she'll no longer be required for them. Would that be a good thing? No. Surely the Procedure needs the human factor. It's more respectful.

'Could I have the key, please?' she says to the head. It's best to treat the heads as if they're real, just in case they are.

'Log in, please,' says the head, smiling. She, or

111

it, is an attractive though square-jawed brunette with bangs and small hoop earrings. The heads change every few days, maybe to give the illusion that they exist in real time.

Charmaine can't stop herself from wondering if the head can see her. She enters her code, verifies it with her thumb, stares at the iris reader beside the head box until it blinks.

'Thank you,' says the head. A plastic key slides out of a slot at the bottom of the box. Charmaine pockets it. 'Here is your top-confidential Special Procedure for today.' A slip of paper emerges from a second slot: room number, Positron Prison name, age, last dosage of sedative, and when administered. The man must be pretty doped up. It's better that way.

She keys herself into the dispensary, locates the cabinet, codes its door open. There's the vial, all ready for her, and the needle. She snaps on her gloves.

In the assigned room, the man is attached to his bed at five points, as they always are now, so thrashing around, kicking, and biting are not possible. He's groggy but awake, which is good. Charmaine is in favour of awake: it would be wrong to carry out the Procedure on someone who's asleep, because they would miss out. On what exactly she's not sure, but on something that's nicer than it otherwise would be.

He looks up at her: despite the drugs, he's clearly frightened. He tries to speak: a thickened sound comes out. *Uhuhuhuh* . . . They always make that sound; she finds it a little painful.

'Hello,' she says. 'Isn't it a lovely day? Look at all that sunshine! Who could be down on a day like today? Nothing bad is going to happen to you.' This is true: from all she's observed, the experience appears to be an ecstatic one. The bad part happens to her, because she's the one who has to worry about whether what she's doing is right. It's a big responsibility, and worse because she isn't supposed to tell anyone what she's actually doing, not even Stan.

Granted, it's only the worst criminals, the incorrigibles, the ones they haven't been able to turn around, who are brought in for the Procedure. The troublemakers, the ones who'd ruin Consilience if they had the chance. It's a last resort. They'd reassured her a lot about that.

Most of the Procedures are men, but not all. Though none of the ones she's done have been women, yet. Women are not so incorrigible: that must be it.

She leans over, kisses this man on the forehead. A young man, smooth-skinned, golden under the tattoos. She leaves the mask in her pocket. She's supposed to wear it for the Procedure to protect against germs, but she never does: a mask would be scary. No doubt she's being monitored via some hidden camera, but so far no one has reprimanded her about this minor breach of protocol. It's not easy for them to find people willing to carry out the Procedure in an efficient yet caring way, they'd told her: dedicated people, sincere people. But someone has to do it, for the good of all.

The first time she attempted the forehead kiss, there was a lunge of the head, an attempt at snapping. He'd drawn blood. She requested that a neck restraint be added. And it was. They listen to feedback, here at Positron.

She strokes the man's head, smiles with her deceptive teeth. She hopes she appears to him like an angel: an angel of mercy. Because isn't she one? Such men are like Stan's brother, Conor: they don't fit anywhere. They'll never be happy where they are – in Positron, in Consilience, maybe even on the entire Planet Earth. So she's providing the alternative for him. The escape. Either this man will go to a better place, or else to nowhere. Whichever it is, he's about to have a great time getting there.

'Have a wonderful trip,' she says to him. She pats his arm, then turns her back so he can't see her sliding the needle into the vial and drawing up the contents.

'Off we go,' she says cheerfully. She finds the vein, slips in the needle.

Uhuhuh, he says. He strains upward. His eyes are horrified, but not for long. His face relaxes; he turns his gaze from her to the ceiling, the white blank ceiling, which is no longer white and blank for him. He smiles. She times the procedure: five minutes of ecstasy. It's more than a lot of people get in their whole lifetimes.

Then he's unconscious. Then he stops breathing. The heart goes last.

Textbook. If anything, better. It's good to be good at what you do.

She codes in the numbers that signal a successful termination, drops the needle into the recycling bin – not much sense in having sterile needles for the Procedure, so they get reused. Positron is big on anti-waste. She peels off the gloves, contributes them to the Save Our Plastics box, then leaves the room. Others will now arrive, do whatever is done. The death will be recorded as 'cardiac arrest,' which is true so far as it goes.

What will happen to the body? Not cremation; that's a wasteful power draw. And no inmates in any form, dead or alive, depart through the gates of Consilience. She's wondered about organ harvesting, but wouldn't they want them brain-dead and on a drip rather than plain old dead, period? Surely the fresher the better, when it comes to organs. Protein-enriched livestock feed? Charmaine can't believe they'd do that, it wouldn't be respectful. But whatever happens, it's bound to be useful, and that's all she needs to know. There are some things it's better not to think about.

Tonight she'll join the knitting circle, as usual. Some of them are doing little cotton hats for infants, some of them are working on a new thing – blue knitted teddy bears, so cute. 'Had a nice day?' the knitting circle women will say to her. 'Oh, a perfect day,' she'll reply.

SCOOTER

It's mid-September. In the evenings, when Stan goes for a stroll around the block, he wears a fleece jacket. A few leaves have fallen on the lawn already; he rakes them up in the early mornings, before breakfast. Not many people around at that hour. Just the odd black Surveillance car, gliding past silently as a shark. Is it protocol to give them a friendly wave? Stan has decided against it: better to pretend they're invisible. Anyway, who's inside? Those cars may be remote-controlled, like drones.

After breakfast – poached eggs if he's lucky, they're one of his favourites – and then a goodbye peck from Charmaine, he goes to his civilian job, working at the electric-scooter repair depot. It was a good choice: his one-time job at Dimple Robotics has been taken into consideration by those who hand out the jobs around here, and anyway he's always liked tinkering, messing around with machines and their digital programs. He once took apart the cheap musical toaster some joker from Dimple had given them for a wedding present and rebuilt it to play 'Steam Heat.' Charmaine had thought that was cute, at first. Though repetitive melodies can get on the nerves.

Each scooter has a number, but no name attached, because it wouldn't do for a driver to know the identity of the Alternate, in case they happen to run into each other on a switchover day. There would be grudges held, there would be arguments: Who made the dent? Who scratched the finish? What kind of a dickhead would let the battery run down, or leave the scooter out in the rain? It's not as if the things don't have covers! The scooters belong to the town of Consilience, not to any one person. Or any two people. But it's amazing how possessive you can get about this shit.

The scooter he's working on at the shop is the one Charmaine drives: pink with purple stripes. The scooters are all two-tone, to match the two lockers of their drivers. His own – his own and Max's – is green and red. It's infuriating to think of that bastard Max driving around on the scooter, with his ass-end clamped onto the very same scooter seat that Stan thinks of as his own. But better not to dwell on that. He needs to keep his cool.

Charmaine has been having trouble with her scooter for a couple of days now. The darn thing – that's how she puts it – has been sputtering at start-up, then conking out after a few blocks. Maybe something about the solar hookup?

'I'll take it in for you,' Stan offered. 'To the depot. Work on it there.'

'Oh thanks, hon, would you?' she said airily. Maybe not as appreciatively as once, or is he imagining that? 'You're a doll,' she added a bit absentmindedly. She was cleaning the stove at the time: such chores are appealing to her, she gets a kick out of dirt removal. Since it means he always has squeaky clean underwear, he's not complaining.

He'd identified the problem – frayed wiring – and spent a couple of evenings in their garage fixing the short-outs so the scooter was operating just right and he could drive it down to the depot to do some more work on it, or that's what he told Charmaine.

Really he wanted to have the scooter all to himself. In two more weeks – on the first day of October – it will be turned over to Jasmine, and he wants to customize it in advance of that event.

Why has it taken him so long to figure this out? This method of tracing Jasmine? When it's been right in front of him all the time! All he needs is a second Consilience smartphone; with a little hackwork and manipulation, he can then synch his own to it and embed the doctored phone in the scooter. Then he can track where Jasmine goes when he's in prison and recover that stored information via his own phone once he gets out. No one in the Project can access outside Wi-Fi, but they can communicate on the Consilience Wi-Fi network within the system, and view maps of the town on the Consilience interactive GPS, and that's all he needs.

It was easy enough to get hold of Charmaine's phone. She'd been so preoccupied lately she convinced herself she must have set it down somewhere, maybe at work, and who knows what happened to it? She reported it gone and they issued her another one. So far, so good. He'll be in the slammer all October, managing the chickens, but when he comes out on November 1 he'll be able to reconstruct the pathways Jasmine has been following in his absence.

And eventually those pathways will lead him somehow to a point of intersection – a place where he might be able to catch a glimpse of her, or even ambush her. On a switchover day, he'll bump into her in the supermarket aisle, or what passes for a supermarket in Consilience. He'll linger on a street corner. He'll crouch behind a shrub, on a vacant lot. Then, before she knows it, he'll have his mouth on those cherry-flavoured lips, and she'll crumple; she won't be able to resist, any more than paper can resist a lit match. Whoosh! Up in flames! Ring of fire! What a picture. He can barely stand it.

You're nuts, he tells himself. You're a stalker. You are a freaking maniac. You might get caught. Then what, smartass? Off to the hospital for your so-called health problems? What do they do in Positron to lunatics like you?

Nevertheless, he proceeds. The seat of the scooter is the best place to hide the extra phone. He cuts a slit in the fake leather, low down at the side, where it won't be noticed. There. Done. He uses a line of superglue to seal the cut; nobody who isn't looking would ever spot it.

'Good as new,' he tells Charmaine as he returns her scooter. She exclaims with joy, a cooing sound he used to find provocative but now finds sickly sweet, then gives him a perfunctory hug.

'I'm so grateful,' she tells him. But not grateful enough by a long shot. When he crawls on top of her that night and tries a few new gambits, hoping for more than her limited repertoire of little gasping breaths followed by a sigh, she starts to giggle and says he's tickling. Which is not very fucking encouraging. He might as well be porking a chicken.

But never mind. Now that he can follow Jasmine, divine her every move, read her mind, she's almost within reach. Meanwhile, he can practise for a couple of weeks by tracking Charmaine around on the scooter. It will be boring, because where can she go? The bakery where she works, the shops, the house, the bakery, the shops. She's so predictable. No news there. But he'll be able to tell whether his two-phone system is working or not.

PUSHOVER

It's already the first of October. Another switchover day. Where has the time gone?

Charmaine lies tangled in her shed clothes on the floor of the vacant house – quite a solid house this time, slated for reno rather than demolition. The wallpaper is subdued, an embossed ivy-leaf design in eggshell and truffle. The writing stands out on it: dark red paint, black marker. Short, forceful words, sudden and hard. She says them over to herself like a charm.

'You're such a surprise,' Max says to her. Murmurs in her ear, which he's nibbling. Will this be a two-in-a-row day? she wonders. She arrived at the vacant house early, hoping it would be. 'Cool as a cucumber,' Max continues, 'but then . . . That husband of yours is one lucky guy.'

'I'm not the same with him,' she says. She wishes he wouldn't ask her to talk about Stan. It's not fair.

'Tell me how you are, with him,' says Max. 'No. Tell me how you'd be with a perfect stranger.' He wants her to turn him on by describing mild atrocities. A few ropes, modified screaming. It's a game they sometimes play, now that it's fall and they know each other better.

Now she has to think about Stan. Stan in real life. 'Max,' she says. 'I need us to be serious.'

'I am serious,' says Max, moving his mouth down her neck.

'No, listen. I think he suspects.' Why does she even think that? Because Stan's been looking at her, or rather looking through her, as if she's made of glass. That's scarier than if he'd been crabby or angry, or outright accused her.

'How could he?' says Max. His head comes up: he's alarmed. If Stan walked in through the front door, Max would be out the window like a shot. That's what he'd do, she knows by now: he'd bolt, he'd sprint, he'd run like a rabbit, and that's the realistic truth. She shouldn't spook him too much, because she doesn't want him fleeing, not before there's a need. She wants to clutch him against her, the way kids clutch their stuffed animals: the thought of letting him go makes her sadder than anything.

'I don't think he knows,' she says. 'Not knows. As such. But he looks at me funny.'

'Is that all?' says Max. 'Hey. I look at you funny too. Who wouldn't?' He takes hold of her hair, turns her head, gives her a brief kiss. 'Are you worried?'

'I don't know. Maybe not. He has a temper,' she says. 'He might get violent.' That has an effect on Max.

'I would,' he says. 'Hey. I would love to get violent with you.' He raises his hand; she flinches away, as he wants her to. Now they're entwined again, snarled up in random cloth, falling down into namelessness.

Eyes closed, getting her breath back, she realizes how worried she is really: on a scale of one to ten, it's at least an eight. What if Stan really does know? And what if he cares? He could get ugly, but how ugly? He could turn threatening. His brother Conor is that way, from what Stan's told her: he'd think nothing of bashing a girl senseless if she cheated on him. What if Stan has a bad part like that hidden inside him?

Maybe she should protect herself now, while she can. If she saved just a little from each Procedure vial – if she pocketed one of the needles instead of depositing it for recycling – would anyone notice? She'd have to slide the needle in while Stan was asleep, so he'd be denied a beatific exit. Which would be unfair. But there's a downside to everything.

What would she do with the body? That would be a problem. Dig a hole in the lawn? Someone would see. She has a wild thought of stashing it in her pink locker, supposing she could even drag it down there: Stan is quite heavy. Also she might have to cut part of him off to make him fit in, though the lockers are big. But if she left him there it would make a horrible stench, and the next time

Max's wife, Jocelyn, came down to the cellar to open her purple locker she'd be sure to smell it.

Max has never said much about Jocelyn, despite Charmaine's gentle pestering. At the outset she'd vowed never to be jealous, because isn't she herself the one Max truly wants? And she isn't jealous: curiosity isn't the same as jealousy. But whenever she asks, Max stonewalls her. 'You don't need to know,' he says.

She pictures Jocelyn as a rangy, aristocratic woman with her hair skinned back from her head, like a ballerina or a schoolteacher in old movies. A distant, snobby, disapproving woman. Sometimes she has the feeling that Jocelyn knows about her and is contemptuous of her. Worse: that Max has told Jocelyn about her, that they both think she's a credulous pushover and a dime-a-dozen little slut, that they laugh together about her. But that's paranoid.

She doesn't think Max would be much help with Stan, supposing Stan was dead. Yes, Max is overpoweringly sexy, but he doesn't have backbone, he doesn't have grit, not the way Charmaine herself has them. He'd leave her holding the bag, the bagful of danger. The bagful of Stan, because she'd have to put Stan into a bag of some kind, she wouldn't be able to look at him in cold blood that way. Lying inert and defence-less. She'd remember too much about how it was when they were in love, and then when they first got married, and had sex in the ocean, and he

125

had that green shirt with the penguins on it . . . Just thinking about that shirt while at the same time thinking about Stan being dead makes her want to cry.

So maybe she does love him. Yes, of course she does! Think of how lucky she was to meet him, after Grandma Win died and she was all by herself, since her mother was gone and her father was gone in a different way, plus she had no wish to see that person ever again. Think of everything she and Stan have been through together, of what they had, what they lost, what they still had in spite of those losses. Think of how loyal he's been to her.

Be the person you've always wanted to be, they say at Positron. Is this the person she's always wanted to be? A person so slack, so quick to give herself over, so easily rendered helpless, so lacking in, lacking in what? But whatever she's lacking in, she would never want to harm Stan.

'Roll over, dirty girl,' says Max. 'Open your eyes.' At some moments he likes her to watch him. 'Tell me what you want.'

'Don't stop,' she says.

He pauses. 'Don't stop what?' It's such pauses that will make her say anything.

Has she been a fool? No question, yes. Has it been worth it? No. Maybe. Yes.

Or yes, right now.

PART V

AMBUSH

TOWN MEETING

On the evening before the December 1 switchover day there's another Town Meeting. Not that anyone actually meets up: they watch on closed-circuit TV, whether they're inside Positron Prison or out of it. The Town Meeting is to let everyone know how well the Consilience/Positron experiment is doing. Their collective Healthy Interaction scores, their Food Production goals, their Dwelling Maintenance rates: things like that. Pep talks, Zing ratings, helpful feedback. Admonishments kept to a minimum, a few new rules added in at the end.

These Town Meetings emphasize the positives. Incidents of violence are way down, they're told today – a graph pops onto the screen – and egg production is up. A new process will soon be introduced at Poultry: headless chickens nourished through tubes, which has been shown to decrease anxiety and increase meat growth efficiencies; in addition to which it eliminates cruelty to animals, which is the sort of multiple win that Positron has come to stand for! Shout-out to the Brussels Sprouts team, which has exceeded its quotas two months in a row! Let's raise the bar on rabbit production in the second half of November, there are some great new rabbit recipes coming soon. More attention to the sorting for the Waste Recycling program, please; it won't work unless we all pull together. And so on and so on.

Headless chickens, no fucking way I'd eat that, thinks Stan. He's downed three beers before the meeting started: the Consilience brewery is up and running, and the beer is better than nothing, though he can imagine what Conor would say about it. *You're joking. It's not beer, it's horse piss. What's it made out of, anyway?*

Yeah, what, he thinks, taking another swig. He lets his attention drift; Charmaine, sitting beside him on the sofa, chirps up with 'Oh, the eggs are doing well! That must be you, hon!' He talks to her, off and on, about his work in the chicken facility, but she hasn't been similarly forthcoming about her own work, which has made him curious about it. What exactly is it that she does, over at Medications Administration? It's more than just giving out pills, but when he asks questions, her face goes blank and she shuts the conversation down. Or she says everything is just fine, as if he might think it isn't.

There's something else about Charmaine that's been bothering him. During their town times, he's tracked the scooter off and on, just to make sure his two-phone system is working. Everything was as expected: Charmaine spent her time bustling here and there, to the bakery, to the shops, back to the house. But then, on the switchover days he's monitored, she's been making detours. Why would she have gone to the seedier part of town, where the unreclaimed houses are located? What was she doing? Checking out future real estate? That must be why she spent so much time inside the houses: she must've been measuring the rooms. Is she in nesting mode? Is she going to start pushing for them to get another transfer, move into a bigger house? Is she planning a baby? That's most likely her game plan, though she hasn't brought up the subject lately. He isn't sure how he feels about that: a baby might interfere with his Jasmine plans, not that these are crystal clear. He hasn't imagined much beyond that first sulphurous encounter.

He now knows where Jasmine goes during her time as a Consilience citizen: she gets on the very same pink-and-purple scooter and heads to the gym. She must work out a lot. How lithe and toned and strong her body must be.

That alarms him: she might put up a struggle when he surges out of the swimming pool like a powerful giant squid and wraps her in his wet, naked arms. But she won't struggle for long.

He's taken to going to the gym himself, checking around. Not that Jasmine would be there, she'd be inside Positron. But the weight machines, the treadmills: her alluring bum must have reposed on one of the former, her agile feet must have

131

walked upon one of the latter. Though he knows it's impossible, he half expects to find signs of her: a dropped handkerchief, a glass slipper, some fuchsia bikini briefs. Magical signs of her presence.

Sometimes when he's loitering he feels watched; perhaps by the shadowy face at the window one floor up, overlooking the gym's swimming pool. That's where the upper-management supervisors are said to get their exercise, so naturally they'd have a Surveillance person somewhere around. That thought makes him nervous: he doesn't want to be singled out, he doesn't want to be of special interest. Except to Jasmine.

The Town Meeting today skips the preliminary shots of happy workers and pie charts and focuses right in on Ed, who's in full pep-talk mode. How well they are all doing with their Project tasks – beyond Ed's highest expectations! They must be so proud of their efforts and achievements, history is being made, they are a model for future towns just like theirs; indeed, there are now nine other towns that are being reconstructed according to the Consilience/Positron model. If all goes well, soon that model will be deployed wherever the need is great – wherever the economy has flagged and left hard-working people stranded!

Better still, thanks to this model and its reordering of civic life, and the construction dollars that have been generated and the waste that's been saved, the economy in those areas is pulling out of the slump. So many new initiatives! So much problem-solving! People can think so creatively when given the chance!

Hold on, thinks Stan. What's underneath all the horn-tooting? Some folks must be making a shit-load of cash out of this thing. But who, but where? Since not that much of it is trickling down inside the Consilience wall. Everyone's got a place to live, true, but no one's richer than anyone else.

So are they all being lied to, played for suckers? Duped into doing the work while others roll around in the cash? Conor always said Stan was too trusting, that he could never sniff out a bent motive, that given the choice he'd pay top dollar for a baggie full of baking soda and stuff it up his nose. Fuck, said Conor, he'd probably even get high on it.

So how much of a dickwit have I been? Stan wonders. What exactly did I sign away? And is there really no way out except in a box, as Conor warned? That can't be true: those at the top must be able to come and go at will. But apart from Ed, he doesn't know who those top people are.

He really wants another beer. But he'll wait until this show is over, because what if the TV can see him?

Stan, Stan, he tells himself. Cool the paranoia. Why would they be interested in watching you watch them?

Now Ed has put on a fatherly frown. 'Some of

you,' he says, 'and you know who you are – some of you have been dabbling in digital experimentation. You all know the rules: phones are to be used for personal intercommunication with your friends and loved ones, but no more. We take boundaries very seriously here at Positron! You may believe you're engaging in private entertainment, and that your attempt to invade the private space of others is harmless. And so far no harm has been done. But our systems are very sensitive; they pick up even the faintest of unauthorized signals. Disconnect now – again, you know who you are – and we will take no action.'

The Consilience theme song comes on – it's the barn-raising music from *Seven Brides for Seven Brothers* – and the slogan zooms up: CONS + RESILIENCE = CONSILIENCE. DO TIME NOW, BUY TIME FOR OUR FUTURE.

Stan feels a chill. Sober up, he tells himself. That message from Ed seemed aimed at several people, so they might not be on to him personally. Still, he'll take that phone out of the scooter immediately. Never mind, he's got Jasmine in his crosshairs. On switchover days, it's first stop the house, next stop the gym.

AMBUSH

It won't be the gym, he decides: that would be too public. Instead it will be right here, at the house. On switchover day Charmaine will leave on her scooter and possibly inspect more real estate, after which she'll park the scooter at Positron Prison, after which Jasmine will get onto it and drive it here. Meanwhile, he himself will stash his pile of clean, folded clothes in the green locker, key himself out of the house, and then, instead of heading right to the prison, he'll wait in the garage. When Jasmine turns up he'll watch her go into the house. Then he'll follow, and the inevitable red-hot encounter will take place. They might not even make it upstairs, so overpowering will be their lust. The living room sofa; no, even that's too formal. The carpet. Not the kitchen floor, though: that would be hard on the knees.

They won't be interrupted by Max, because how can he get here without the scooter he shares with Stan – the red-and-green one? Which is supposed to be arriving at Positron about now, but which is still in the garage. He takes satisfaction in the thought of Max cooling his heels and checking his watch while his wayward, insatiable Jasmine is winding her arms and legs around Stan.

Now he's in the garage. It's warm for December 1, but he's shivering a bit: it must be the tension. The hedge trimmer is hanging on the wall, newly cleaned, battery charged, ready for action, not that scum-bucket Max will appreciate the care Stan has taken. The hedge trimmer would make a good weapon, supposing Max makes it to the house by some other means and there's a confrontation. The thing has a hair-trigger start button; once at full throttle, with its sharp saw whizzing around, it could take off a guy's head. Self-defence would be his plea.

If that doesn't happen and instead he gets involved in some heavy tangling with Jasmine, he'll be late for check-in. That's frowned on, but he'll have to risk it because he can't go on the way he's been going. It's eating him up. It's killing him.

There's a crack in the front door of the garage. Stan is peering through it, waiting for Jasmine to drive up on her pink scooter, so he doesn't hear the side door opening.

'It's Stan, isn't it?' says a voice. He jerks upright, whirls around. His first instinct is to go for the hedge trimmer. But it's a woman.

'Who the fuck are you?' he says. She's on the short side, with straight black hair down to her shoulders. Dark eyebrows. A heavy mouth, no lipstick. Black jeans and T-shirt. She looks like a dyke martial arts expert.

There's something familiar. Has he seen her at the gym? No, not there. It was the workshop, when they'd just signed on. She was with that dork of an Ed.

'I live here,' she says. She smiles. Her teeth are square: piano-key teeth.

'Jasmine?' he asks uncertainly. It can't be. This isn't what Jasmine looks like.

'There is no Jasmine,' she says. Now he's confused. If there is no Jasmine, how does she know there's supposed to be one?

'Where's your scooter?' he says. 'How did you get here?'

'I drove,' she says. 'In the car. I'm parked next door. By the way, I'm Jocelyn.' She holds out her hand, but Stan doesn't take it. Shit, he thinks. She's in Surveillance, which is the only way she could have a car. He feels cold.

'Now maybe you'd better tell me why you hid that phone in my scooter,' she says, withdrawing her hand. 'Or the scooter you thought was mine. I've been following it around, your clever tracker. It shows up well on our monitoring equipment.'

Somehow they're in the kitchen – his kitchen, her kitchen, their kitchen. He's sitting down. Everything here is familiar to him – there's the coffee machine, there are the folded tea towels Charmaine set out before she left – but it all seems foreign to him.

'Want a beer?' she says. A sound comes out of his mouth. She pours the beer and one for herself, then sits down opposite him, leans forward, and describes to him in way too much detail the movements of Charmaine on switchover days. In and out of the vacant houses, for months now, in conjunction with Jocelyn's husband, Max. *Conjunction* is the word she uses. Among other, shorter words.

Though Max isn't her husband's real name. His name is Phil, and she's had this kind of problem with him before. She always knows about it, and he knows she knows but is pretending not to know. He knows about the cameras hidden in the vacant houses, he knows she has access to the footage. That's part of the attraction for him: the certainty that he's performing for her. He'll stray off-track – it's an addiction like gambling, it's an illness, doesn't Stan agree, you have to feel sorry – and she'll let him run with it for a while. It's an outlet for him: in a gated city with one-way gates, outlets are limited for a man like him. He's tried to get help with this sex addiction of his, he's tried counselling, he's tried aversion therapy, but so far nothing has worked. It doesn't help that he's so good-looking. Women with overactive romantic imaginations more or less throw themselves at him. There's no shortage.

When she thinks whatever he's mixed himself up with has gone far enough, she confronts him. That shuts it down: he cuts it off with the woman in question, no loose ends. Then, after an interval of promising to go straight, he'll start on another one. It's been humiliating for her personally, even though he assures her that he's loyal to her in his heart, it's just that he can't control his impulses.

'But there's never been a wild card before,' she says. 'Not one of our own Alternates. Mine and Phil's.'

Stan's so fucking addled he can't think straight. Charmaine! Right under his nose, the slutty cheat – withholding sex from him, or doling it out in chilly slices between clean sheets. It must've been her who wrote that note, sealed it with a fuchsia kiss. How dare she show herself to be everything he was so annoyed with her for not being? And with some dipshit named Phil, married to a lady wrestler! On the other hand, how dare anyone else tag his wife as a mere outlet? 'Wild card,' he says weakly. 'You mean Charmaine.'

'No. I mean you,' she says. She looks at him from under her eyebrows. 'You're the wild card.' She smiles at him: not a demure smile. Despite her lack of makeup, her mouth looks dark and liquid, like oil.

'I need to be getting along,' he says. 'I need to check in before curfew, over at Positron. I need—'

'That's all taken care of,' she says. 'I control the identity codes. I've rearranged the data so Phil's going there in your place.'

'What?' says Stan. 'But what about my job? It takes training, he can't just—'

'Oh, he'll be fine,' says Jocelyn. 'He's not good with his hands, not like you, but he's all right with digital. He'll take care of your chickens for you, both ends. He won't let anyone interfere with them.'

Fuck, thinks Stan. Both ends. She knows about that thing with the chickens. How long has she been keeping an eye on him?

'Meanwhile,' she says. She puts her head on one side as if considering. 'Meanwhile, you'll be here, with me. You can tell me all about your interest in Jasmine. If you want to, we can listen in on Max and Jasmine, during their little vacant-house rendezvous. I've got the recordings, the surveillance videos. The sound quality's excellent, you'd be surprised. It's quite exciting. We can have a twosome of our own, on the sofa. I think it's time I got a turn at playing Phil's game, don't you?'

'But that's . . .' He wants to say, 'That's fucking warped,' but he stops himself. This woman is upper-level management, she's in Surveillance: she could make his life truly disagreeable. 'That's unfair,' he says. His voice is going all wussy.

She smiles again with her slippery-looking mouth. She has biceps, and shoulders, and her thighs are alarming; not to mention the fact that she's a sick voyeur. What has he done to himself, to his life? Why has he done it? Where is bland, perky Charmaine? It's her he wants, not this sinister and most likely hairy-legged ball crusher.

Surreptitiously he checks out the exits: back door, door to the front hall, door to the cellar stairs. What if he were to shove this woman into

140

his green basement locker, then make a run for it? But run to where? He's blocked his own exits. 'Seriously. This won't work, it's not . . . I'm not . . . I need to go,' he says. He can't bring himself to say please.

'Don't be worried,' she says. 'You won't be missed. You'll get an extra month here at the house. Then, next month, when Charmaine comes out of Positron, you can go in.'

'No,' he says. 'I don't want . . .'

She sighs. 'Think of it as an intervention to avoid possible violence. You'll have to admit you feel like strangling her, anyone would. You'll thank me later. Unless, that is, you want me to turn in a report on the rules you've broken. Want another beer?'

'Yeah,' he manages to say. He's falling deeper and deeper into the hole he dug for himself. 'Make it two.' He's trapped. 'What else do I have to do?' To avoid the consequences, is what he means, but he doesn't have to explain that. She's fully aware that she's twisting his arm.

She takes her time answering, drinks, licks her lips. 'We'll find out, won't we?' she says. 'We have lots of time. I'm sure you're very talented. By the way, I switched the lockers. Yours is the red one now.'

CHAT ROOM

On the January 1 switchover day, Charmaine is told by one of the behind-the-counter clerks to stay behind at the prison, because Human Resources needs to talk to her. She has a sinking feeling right away. Do they know about Max? If so, she's in trouble, because how many times were they told it was absolutely not allowed to fraternize with the Alternates who shared your house? You weren't even supposed to know what they looked like. Which was one of the things that made seeing Max so thrilling for her. So forbidden, so over the line.

Seeing Max. What an old-fashioned way of putting it! But then she's an old-fashioned girl – that's what Stan thinks. Though her times with Max haven't involved much actual seeing. They've been close-ups, in half-light. An ear, a hand, a thigh.

Oh please, let them not know, she prays silently, crossing her fingers. They never spelled out what would happen if you disobeyed, though Max had reassured her. He'd said it was nothing much: they just gave you a little slap on the hand and maybe changed your Alternate. Anyway she and Max were being so careful, and none of those houses had spyware in it; he should know, it was his job to know all about those houses. But what if Max was wrong? Worse: What if Max was lying?

She takes a breath and smiles, showing her small, candid teeth. 'What's the problem?' she asks the clerk, her voice higher and more girly than normal. Is it something about her job as Chief Medications Administrator? If so, she'll learn how to improve, because she always wants to do the very best possible and be all that she can be.

She hopes that's the issue. Maybe they've noted that she ignores the surgical-mask protocol, maybe they've decided she's being too nice to the subjects during the Special Procedures. The head strokings, the forehead kisses, those marks of kindliness and personal attention just before she slides in the hypodermic needle: they aren't forbidden, but they aren't mandated. They're flourishes, grace notes – little touches she's added because it makes the whole thing a more quality experience, not only for the subject of the Procedure but for herself as well. She does feel strongly that you should keep the human touch: she's always been prepared to say as much in front of a tribunal if it came to that. Though she's hoped it wouldn't. But maybe now is the time it will.

'Oh no, I'm sure it's nothing,' the clerk says. She adds that it's just an administrative formality. Someone must have keyed in the wrong piece of code; such things happen and it can take a while to unsnarl them. Even with modern technology there's always human error, and Charmaine will just have to be patient until they can trace what they can only assume is a bug in the works.

She nods and smiles. But they're looking at her strangely (now there are two of them, now there are three behind the checkout desk, one of them texting on a cell), and there's something odd in their voices: they aren't telling the truth. She doesn't think she's imagining that.

'If you'll wait in the Chat Room,' the one with the cellphone says, indicating a door to the side of the counter. 'Away from the checkout process. Thank you. There's a chair, you can sit down. The Human Resources Officer will be with you shortly.'

Charmaine looks over at the group of departing prisoners. Is that Sandi among them, and Veronica? She's glimpsed them briefly over the months – they're in prison when she is – but they aren't in her knitting group and they don't work in the hospital, so she's had no reason to get close. Now, however, she longs for a friendly face. But they don't see her, they've turned away. They've shed their orange prison boiler suits and are wearing their street clothing, they must be anticipating the fun times they're about to have, outside.

As she was, just moments ago. She's wearing a lacy white bra underneath her new cherry-coloured sweater. She chose these items a month ago to be special for Max today.

'What's wrong?' one of the other women calls over to her. Someone from her knitting circle. Charmaine must be signalling distress, she must be making a sad face. She forces up the corners of her mouth.

'Nothing, really. Some data entry thing. I'll be out later today,' she says as gaily as she can. But she doubts it. She can feel the sweat soaking into her sweater, underneath her arms. That bra will have to be washed, pronto. Most likely the cherry colour is leaking into it, and it's so hard to get dye stains like that out of whites.

She sits on the wooden chair in the Chat Room, trying not to count the minutes, resisting the urge to go back out to the front desk and make a scene, which will definitely not be any use. And even if she does get out later that day, what about Max? Their meet-up, planned a month ago. At this very moment he must be scootering toward this month's empty house; he told her the address last time and she memorized it, repeating it like a silent prayer as she lay in her narrow bed in her Positron Prison cell, in her poly-cotton standard-issue nightgown.

Max likes her to describe that nightgown. He likes her to tell him what torture it is for her to lie there alone, wearing that scratchy nightgown, tossing and turning and unable to sleep, thinking about him, living every word and touch over and over, tracing with her own hands the pathways across and into her flesh that his hands have taken. *And then what, and then what?* he'll whisper as they lie together on the dirty floorboards. *Tell me. Show me.*

What he likes even better – because she can hardly bring herself to do it, he has to force it out of her word by word – what he likes even better is to have her describe what she's feeling when it's Stan who's making love to her. *Then what does he do? Tell me, show me. And then what do you feel?*

I'm pretending it's you, she'll say. *I have to, I have to do that. I'd go crazy otherwise, I couldn't stand it.* Which isn't true really, but it's what Max likes to hear.

Last time he went further. *What if it were both of us at once?* he said. *Front and back. Tell me . . .*

Oh no, I couldn't! Not both at once! That's . . .

I think you could. I think you want to. Look, you're blushing. You're a dirty little slut, aren't you? You'd do the midget football team if there was room for them. You want to. Both of us at once. Say it.

At those moments she'd say anything. What he doesn't know is that in a way it's always both at once: whichever one she's with, the other one is there with her as well, invisible, partaking, though at an unconscious level. Unconscious to him but conscious to her, because she holds them both in her consciousness, so carefully, like fragile meringues, or uncooked eggs, or baby birds. But she doesn't think that's a dirty thing, cherishing both at once: each of them has a different essence, and she happens to be good at treasuring the

146

unique essence of a person. It's a gift not everyone has.

And now, today, she'll miss the meet-up with Max, and she has no way of warning him that she can't be there. What will he think? He'll arrive at the house early because, like her, he can hardly restrain himself. He lives for these encounters, he longs to crush her in his arms and ruin her clothing, ripping open zippers and buttons and even a seam or two, in the haste of his ardent, irresistible desire. He'll wait and wait in the empty house, impatiently, pacing the stained, mud-crusted floor, looking out through the flyspecked windows. But she won't appear. Will he assume she's failed him? Dumped him? Blown him off? Abandoned him in a fit of cowardice, or of loyalty toward Stan?

Then there's Stan himself. After the month he's just spent as a prisoner in Positron, he'll have turned in his boiler suit and put on his jeans and fleece jacket. He'll have left the men's wing in the Positron Prison complex; he'll have scootered back through the streets of Consilience, which will be thronged with people in a festive mood, some streaming into the jail to take their turn as prisoners, others streaming out of it, back to their civilian lives.

Stan too will be waiting for her, not in an abandoned building dank with the aroma of long-ago drug parties and biker sex but in their own house, the house she thinks of as theirs. Or half theirs, anyway. Stan will be inside that house, in their familiar domestic nest, expecting her to turn up at any minute and put on her apron and cook dinner while he fools around with his tools in the garage. He may even be intending to tell her he's missed her – he usually does that, though less recently – and give her a casual hug.

She relishes the casualness of those hugs: *casual* means he has no idea what she's just been doing. He doesn't realize she's returning from a stolen hour with Max. She loves that expression – *stolen hour*. It's so fifties. Like in the romantic movies they sometimes show on Consilience TV, where it comes out all right in the end.

Though *stolen hour* doesn't make sense, when you come to think about it. It's like stolen kisses: the stolen hour is about time, and the stolen kisses are about place, about whose lips go where. But how can those things be stolen? Who does the thieving? Is Stan the owner of that hour, and of those kisses too? Surely not. And even if he is, if he doesn't know about the missing time and the missing kisses, how is she hurting him? There have been art thieves who've made exact copies of expensive paintings and substituted them for the real ones, and the owners have gone for months and even years without noticing. It's like that.

But Stan will notice when she doesn't turn up. He'll be irritated, then dismayed. He'll ask the Consilience officials to do a street search, check up on scooter accidents. Then he'll contact

Positron. Most likely he'll be told that Charmaine is still inside, in the women's wing. Though he won't be told why.

Charmaine sits and sits on the hard little chair in the Chat Room, trying to keep her mind quiet. No wonder people used to go nuts in solitary confinement, she thinks. No one to talk to, nothing to do. But they don't have solitary at Positron any more. She and Stan were shown the cells, though, during the orientation tour, when they were making the big decision to sign up. The former solitary cells had been refitted with desks and computers – those were for the IT engineers and also for the robotics division they were going to build. *Very exciting possibilities there,* said the guide. *Now, let's go and see the communal dining room, and then the livestock and horticulture – all our chickens are raised right here – and after that we can look in at the Handcrafts studio, where you'll be issued your knitting supplies.*

Knitting. If she has to stay in Positron Prison another whole month she's going to get really fed up with that knitting. It was fun at first, sort of old-timey and chatty, but now they've been given quotas. The supervisors make you feel like a slacker if you don't knit fast enough.

Oh, Max. Where are you? I'm scared! But even if Max could hear her, would he come?

Stan would. He doesn't minimize it when she's scared. Spiders, for instance: she doesn't like those. Stan is very efficient with spiders. She appreciates that about him.

CHOKE COLLAR

It's late afternoon. The sun is low in the sky, the street is empty. Or it seems empty: no doubt there are eyes embedded everywhere – the lamppost, the fire hydrant. Because you can't see them doesn't mean they can't see you.

Stan is trimming the hedge, making an effort to appear not only useful but also cheerful. The hedge doesn't need trimming – it's the first of January, it's winter, despite the lack of snow – but he finds the activity calming for the same reasons nail biting is calming: it's repetitive, it imitates meaningful activity, and it's violent. The hedge trimmer emits a menacing whine, like a wasp's nest. The sound gives him an illusion of power that dulls his sense of panic. Panic of a rat in a cage, with ample food and drink and even sex, though with no way out and the suspicion that it's part of an experiment that is sure to be painful.

The source of his panic: Jocelyn, the walking Vise-Grip. She's got him shackled to her ankle. He's on her invisible leash; he's wearing her invisible choke collar. He can't shake free.

Deep breath, Stan, he tells himself. At least you're still fucking alive. Or alive and fucking. He laughs inwardly. Good one, Stan.

He's got buds in his ears, hooked up to his cell. The whining trimmer plays backup to the voice of Doris Day, whose greatest hits playlist serves as his daytime lullaby music. At first he'd had fantasies of booting Doris off a rooftop, but there isn't a lot of musical choice – they censor anything too arousing or disruptive – and he prefers her to the medley from *Oklahoma!* or Bing Crosby singing 'White Christmas.'

To the bouncy swing of 'Love Me or Leave Me,' he lops off a clutch of feathery cedar branches. Now that he's used to her, it's calming to think of Doris, ever virginal but with impressively firm bra-bolstered tits, smiling her long-ago sun-bleached smile, mixing milkshakes in her kitchen, as in the biopic of her so often shown on Consilience TV. She was the 'nice' girl, back when the opposite was 'naughty.' He has a childhood memory of an alcoholic uncle annoying young girls by calling them naughty for wearing short skirts. He was eleven then, beginning to notice.

Doris would never have opted for a skirt like that, unless for something sporty and asexual, such as tennis. Maybe it was a girl like Doris he'd been wishing for when he married Charmaine. Safe, simple, clean. Armoured in pure white undergarments. What a joke that's turned out to be.

Lonely, he hums in his head. But he won't be

allowed loneliness, not once Jocelyn gets back from her spooky daytime job. 'You should put your leather thingies on,' she said to him two nights ago, in the voice she intends as enticing. 'With the little screwdriver doodad. I'll pretend you're the plumber.' She meant what he's wearing now: the leather work gloves, the work apron with its pockets and widgets. Kink dress-ups for men, in her view. He hadn't put the leather thingies on, however: he does have some pride. Though, increasingly, less.

He stands on a stepladder to reach the topmost layer of hedge. If he shifts he might topple, and that could be lethal, because the hedge trimmer is ultra sharp. It could slice neatly through a neck with a lightning-swift move, as in the Japanese samurai films he and Conor used to watch when they were kids. Medieval executioners could take off a head with an axe in one clean chop, at least in history flicks. Could he ever do anything that extreme? Maybe, with the drumroll and the crowd of jeering, vegetable-hurling yokels to egg him on. He'd need leather gloves, only with gauntlets, and a leather face mask like those in horror films. Would his torso be bare? Better not: he needs to firm up, bulk out the muscles. He's swilling too much of that paunch-building beer: tastes like piss, but anything to get drunk.

Yesterday Jocelyn poked her index finger into the jelly roll over his lowest rib. 'Shed that flab!' she said. It was supposed to be teasing, but here was an unspoken *or else*. But *or else* what? Stan knows he's on probation; but if he fails the test, whatever it is, what then?

He has more than once pictured Jocelyn's head becoming detached from her body by means of edged tools.

Secret love, Doris sings. *Dum de dum, me, yearning, free.* Stan barely hears the words, he's heard them so often. Wallpaper, with rosebuds on it. Would Doris Day's life have been different if she'd called herself Doris Night? Would she have worn black lace, dyed her hair red, sung torch songs? What about Stan's own life? Would he be thinner and fitter if his name were Phil, like Jocelyn's cheating dipstick of a husband?

Or like Conor. What if he'd been named Conor?

No more, sings Doris. Next up will be the Patti Page top ten playlist. 'How Much Is That Doggie in the Window?' *Arf arf,* real dog barks. Charmaine thinks that song is cute. *Cute* is a primary category for her, like right and wrong. Crocuses: cute; thunderstorms: not cute. Eggcups in the shape of chickens: cute; Stan angry: not cute. He is not cute a lot these days.

Which would be better, the axe or the hedge trimmer? he muses. The axe, if you had the knack of the clean stroke. Otherwise, for amateurs, the trimmer. The tendons would cut like wet string; then there would be the hot blood, hitting him in the face like a water cannon. The thought of it makes him feel a little sick. This is the problem

153

with his fantasies: they become too vivid, then veer off into snafus and fuckups, and he gets tangled up in what might go wrong. So much already has.

You could do a good job on your own neck with the trimmer; though not with the axe. Once the trimmer was turned on it would just keep going whether or not you were still conscious. Conor once told him about a guy who committed suicide in his own bed with an electric carving knife. His cheating wife was lying beside him; it was the warmth of his blood seeping into the mattress that woke her up. He's fantasized about that too, because some days he feels so trapped, so hopeless, so dead-ended, so nutless that he'd do almost anything to get away.

But why is he being so negative? *Honey, why are you being so negative?* he hears in his head: Charmaine's chirpy, childishly high Barbie-doll voice. *Surely your life isn't that bad!* The implication being: with her in it. *Stuff it,* he tells the voice. The voice gives a little shocked *Oh,* then pops like a bubble.

HUMAN RESOURCES

Charmaine waits and waits. Why aren't there magazines to read, why isn't there TV? She'd even watch a baseball game. Plus, now she needs to go to the bathroom and there isn't one. That's really inconsiderate, and if she doesn't take control of herself she's going to get cranky. But crankiness leads to bad outcomes, if you don't have any power to back up your crankiness. People blow you off, or else they get even crankier than you. *Smile, and the world smiles with you,* Grandma Win used to say. *Cry, and you cry alone.* She must not cry: she must act as if this is normal, and boring. Just a bureaucracy thing.

Finally a woman with a PosiPad enters, in a guard uniform but with an identity badge pinned to her breast pocket: AURORA, HUMAN RESOURCES. Charmaine's heart sinks.

Aurora of Human Resources smiles mirthlessly, her eyes like sleet. She has a message to deliver and she delivers it smoothly: So sorry, but Charmaine must stay in Positron Prison for another month; and, in addition to that, she's been relieved of her duties with Medications Administration.

'But why?' says Charmaine, her voice faltering. 'If there's been any complaint filed . . .' Which is a dumb thing to say, because the subjects of her medication administrations all flatline five minutes after the Special Procedure, that's what people usually do when their hearts have stopped beating, so who is there still walking around on the planet who could file a complaint? Maybe some of them have returned from the afterlife and criticized the quality of her services, she jokes to herself. Suppose they did, they'd have been lying, she adds indignantly. She's justly proud of her efforts and her talent, she does have a gift, you can see it in their eyes. She executes well, she gives good death: those entrusted to her care go out in a state of bliss and with feelings of gratitude toward her, if body language is any indication. And it is: in the hands of Max, she has honed her skills in body language.

'Oh no, no complaints,' says Aurora of Human Resources, a sliver too carelessly. Her face barely moves: she's had work done and they went too far. She has pop eyes, and her skin is wrenched back as if a giant fist is squeezing all the hair on the back of her head. She most likely went to a session at the cosmetic school in the Positron retraining program. The surgeons are the students, so it's only natural that they'd slip up from time to time. Though Charmaine would jump off a bridge if her face looked as malpractised as that. At the Ruby Slippers Retirement Homes and Clinics, they did way better work. They could take someone seventy, eighty, eighty-five even, and have them come out looking no older than sixty.

They're most likely training the cosmetic surgeons because it's going to be really in demand here pretty soon. The average age in Consilience is thirty-three, so feeling beautiful isn't that much of a challenge for them yet, but what will happen in the Project as the years go by? Charmaine wonders. A top-heavy population of geriatrics in wheel-chairs? Or will those people be released, or rather expelled – tossed out onto the street, forced to take up life in a hardscrabble outside world? No, because the contract is for life. That's what they were all told before they signed.

But – this is a new thought for Charmaine, and it's not a nice one – there were no guarantees about how long that life might last. Maybe after a certain age people will be sent to Medications Administration for the Procedure. Maybe I'll end up there too, thinks Charmaine, with someone like me telling me everything will be fine, and stroking my hair and kissing my forehead and tucking me in with a needle, and I won't be able to move or say anything because I'll be strapped down and drugged to the eyebrows.

'If there aren't any complaints, then why?' Charmaine says to Aurora, trying not to let her desperation show. 'I'm needed in Medications, it's a special technique, I have the experience, I've never had a single—'

'Well, as I'm sure you'll agree is necessary,'

Aurora cuts in, 'considering the uncertainty as to your identity, your codes and cards have been deactivated. For the moment you're in limbo, you might say. The database crosschecking is very thorough, as it has to be, since I can share with you that we've had a few impostors in here. Journalists.' She frowns as well as she is able to with her stretched face. 'And other troublemakers. Trying to unearth – trying to *invent* bad stories about our wonderful model community.'

'Oh, that's terrible!' says Charmaine breathily. 'The way they make things up . . .' She wonders what the bad stories were, decides against asking.

'Yes, well,' says Aurora. 'We all have to be very careful about what we say, because you never know, do you? If the person is real or not.'

'Oh, I never thought of that,' says Charmaine truthfully.

Aurora's face relaxes a millimetre. 'You'll get new cards and codes if' – she catches herself – '*when* you're re-verified. Until then, it's a trust issue.'

'*Trust* issue!' says Charmaine indignantly. 'There has never been *any* . . .'

'This isn't about you personally,' says Aurora. 'It's your data. I'm sure you yourself are completely trustworthy in every way. More than loyal.' Is that a little smirk? Hard to tell on such a wrenched-back face. Charmaine finds herself blushing: *loyal*. Has Max leaked something, have they been seen? At least she's been loyal to her job.

'Now,' says Aurora, switching to efficiency mode,

'I'm placing you temporarily in Laundry. Towel-Folding – there's a shortage in that department. I've done towel-folding myself, it's very soothing. Sometimes it's wise to take a break from too much stress and responsibility, and the after-work pursuits we may' – she hesitates, searching for the word – 'the pursuits we may *pursue,* to deal with that stress. Towel-folding gives time for reflection. Think of it as professional development time. Like a vacation.'

Darn it to heck, thinks Charmaine. Towel-Folding. Her status in Positron has just taken a pratfall over a cliff.

Charmaine changes out of the street clothes she put on hours ago. (Oh shoot, look at that bra, she thinks: bright pink staining under the arms from the sweater, she'll never get it out.) There was something else. Aurora can't smile like a normal person, but it wasn't just the weird smile, it was the tone. Overly mollifying. How you'd talk to a child about to have a painful vaccination or a cow on the way to the abattoir. They had special ramps for those cows, to lull them into walking placidly to their doom.

In the evening, after four hours of towel-folding and the communal dinner – shepherd's pie, spinach salad, raspberry mousse – Charmaine joins the knitting circle in the main room of the women's wing. It's not her usual knitting circle, not the group that knows her: those women left today and were replaced by their Alternates. Not only are these women strangers to Charmaine, they view her as a stranger too. They're making it clear they don't know why she's been stuck in among them: they're polite to her, but only just. Her attempts to make small talk have been cold-shouldered; it's almost as if these women have been told some disreputable story about her.

The group is supposed to be knitting blue bears for preschoolers – some for the Positron and Consilience playgroups, the rest for export, to craft shops in faraway, more prosperous cities, maybe even in other countries, because Positron has to earn its keep. But Charmaine can't concentrate on her teddy bear. She's jittery, she's getting more anxious by the minute. It's the digital mix-up: how could it happen? The system is supposed to be bug-proof. There are IT personnel working on it right now, Aurora has told her, but meanwhile Charmaine should join some yoga groups in the gym, and stick with the daily routine, and it's too bad but numbers are numbers, and her numbers aren't showing her as being who she says she is. Aurora is sure it will work out soon.

But Charmaine doesn't believe this runaround for one instant. Someone must have it in for her. But who? A best friend or lover of one of her Special Procedure subjects? How would they even know, how would they have access? That information is supposed to be totally classified! They've found out about her and Max. It must be that. They're deciding what should be done with her. Done to her.

If only she could talk to Stan. Not Max: at the first hint of danger Max would vamoose. He's a travelling salesman at heart. *I will always treasure our moments together and keep you safe in my heart,* then out the bathroom window and over the back fence, leaving her to deal with the smoking gun and the body on the floor, which might prove to be hers.

Max is like quicksand. Quicksilver. Quick. She's always known that about him. Stan, though – Stan is solid. If he were here, he'd roll up his sleeves and tackle reality. He'd tell her what to do.

Heck. Now she's made a boo-boo with the neck of the blue teddy bear, she's knitted where she should have purled. Should she unravel the row, knit it over? No. The bear will just have to wear a little ridge around its neck. She might even tie a ribbon around it, with a bow. Cover up the flaw by adding an individual touch. *If all you've got is lemons,* she tells herself, *make pink lemonade.*

When she returns to her cell that night, she finds it empty. Her cellmate is gone; it's her month back in Consilience. But the other bed isn't made up, it's stripped bare. It's as if someone has died.

They aren't giving her a new cellmate, then. They're isolating her. Is this the beginning of her punishment? Why did she ever let herself get mixed

161

up with Max? She should have run out of the room the first minute she laid eyes on him. She's been such a pushover. And now she's all alone.

For the first time that day, she cries.

HOUSEBOY

'**H**oney, cheer up, surely life's not so bad,' Charmaine was in the habit of saying when they were living in their car, which used to grate on him: how could she be so fucking perky, with the shit that was bombarding them from all sides? But now he tries to recall her light tone, her consolations, her reassuring quotes from her dead Grandma Win. *It's darkest before the dawn.* He should man up, because she's right: surely his life's not so bad. A lot of men would be happy to trade.

Every weekday he goes to his so-called work at the Consilience electric-scooter repair depot, where he's had to fend off questions from the other guys – 'What're you doing back here? Thought it was your month to be in Positron.' To which he replies, 'Administration morons screwed up, they got my info mixed up with some other guy's. Case of mistaken identity, but hey, I'm not complaining.'

No need to add that the other guy is the douche who's been jumping his chirpy, treacherous wife, and that the Administration moron was a highly placed Surveillance spook who's recorded her husband's encounters with Charmaine in grainy but surprisingly erotic videos. Stan knows they're surprisingly erotic because he's watched them with Jocelyn, sitting on the exact same sofa where he used to sit with Charmaine to watch TV.

That sofa, with its royal blue ground and overall design of off-white lilies, had meant tedium and a comforting routine; the most he'd ever done on it with Charmaine had been hand-holding or an arm around the shoulders, because Charmaine claimed she didn't want to do bed things except where they belonged, in a bed. A wildly false claim, judging from those videos, in which Charmaine required nothing more than a closed door and a bare floor to release her inner sidewalk whore and urge Phil to do things she'd never allowed Stan to do and say things she'd never once said to Stan.

Jocelyn, smiling a tight but lip-licking smile, likes to watch Stan watching. Then she wants him to re-create these videos, playing Phil, with her in the role of Charmaine. The horrible thing is that sometimes he can; though it's equally horrible when he can't. If he roughs her up and fucks her, it's because she told him to; if he isn't up to it, he's a failure; so whichever it is, he loses. Jocelyn has transformed the neutral sofa with its bland lilies into a nest of torturous and humiliating vice. He can barely sit down on it any more: who knew that a harmless consumer good made of fabric and stuffing could become such a crippling head-games weapon?

He hopes Jocelyn has been recording these scenes, and will make Phil watch them in his turn. She's mean enough for it. No doubt Phil's wondering why he's still in prison, and is trying bluster – *There's been a mistake, I'm supposed to be leaving now, just let me contact my wife, she's in Surveillance, we'll get this straightened out.* Stan takes an acidic pleasure in imagining this scenario, as well as the stonewalling stares and hidden snickering among the guards, because haven't they got their orders, which come from higher up? *Just cool it, buddy, look at the printout, Positron identity numbers don't lie, the system's hackproof.* That twisted fuckwit Phil had it coming.

Holding this thought keeps Stan going during his sexual command performances with Jocelyn, which are a good deal more like tenderizing a steak than anything he finds purely pleasurable.

Oh, Stan! comes the pert, giggly pseudovoice of Charmaine. *You get a kick out of it, you must! You know you do, well, most of the time anyway, and every man has those letdown moments, but the rest of the time don't think I can't hear those groans, which have to be enjoyable for you, don't deny it!*

Ram it, he tells her. But Charmaine, with her angel face and devious heart – the real Charmaine – can't hear him. She can't know that Jocelyn's been messing with their lives, paying her back for stealing Phil; but on the first of the month she'll find out. When she walks into this house, expecting to find Stan, it will be Phil who'll be waiting for her. He won't exactly be pleased about it either, would be Stan's guess, because a quick hit of supercharged nooky snatched on the run is not at all the same as all day every day.

That's when Charmaine will discover that the fire of her loins is not who she thinks he is – not the Max of her fever dreams, whose fake name she invokes over and over in those videos – but a much less alpha male, who will look very different in plain daylight. Saggier, older, but also jaded, shifty-eyed, calculating: you can see that in his face, on the videos. She and Phil will be stuck with each other whether they like it or not. Charmaine will have to live with his dirty socks, his hairs in the sink; she'll have to listen to him snoring, she'll have to make small talk with him at breakfast; all of which will put a damper on the bodice-ripper she's been acting out.

How long will it take for the two of them to get bored, then fed up with each other? How long before Phil resorts to domestic violence, just for something to do? Not long, Stan hopes. He wouldn't mind knowing that Phil is smacking Charmaine around, and not just as a garnish to sex, the way he does onscreen, but for real: somebody needs to.

But Phil better not push it too far, or Charmaine may stick a grapefruit knife into his jugular, since behind that blond puffball act of hers there's something skewed. A chip missing, a loose connection. He hadn't recognized it when they'd been living together – he'd underestimated her shadow side, which was mistake number one, because everyone has a shadow side, even fluffpots like her.

There's another thought, not so pleasant: when Phil and Charmaine take up domestic life in this house, what will become of him, Stan? He can't stay in the house with them, that's clear. Will Jocelyn spirit him away to a secret love-nest and chain him to her bedpost? Or will she tire of treating him like an indentured studmuffin, of hotwiring his mind and watching him jerk around like a galvanized frog, and let him re-enter Positron for a much-needed rest?

Though maybe she'll alter the schedule even further: maybe she'll just keep Stan here with her, playing her warped game of house, and let the other two cool their jets inside the slammer. Switchover day will roll around and Charmaine and Phil will be all set to put on their civvies and beeline it to their seedy rendezvous, but then some gink in a uniform will tell them there's been a delay, and they won't be coming out of Positron right now. Which will mean three months straight for Charmaine. She must be going nuts.

Phil will already have guessed that Jocelyn has found him out, yet again; he'll wonder whether she's finally given up on him. He'll be in an advanced state of anxiety if he has any sense at all. He must know his wife is a vengeful harpy, deep inside her business-suit-neutral cool and her long-suffering pose of tolerance.

But Charmaine will be confused. She'll run through her gamut of girly manipulations with the Positron management: dimpled blond astonishment, lip-quivering, outrage, tearful pleading – but none of it will do her any good. Then maybe she'll have a real meltdown. She'll lose it, she'll wail, she'll crumple to the floor. The officials won't put up with that: they'll haul her upright, hose her down. Stan would like to see that; it would be some satisfaction for the contempt with which she's been treating him. Maybe Jocelyn will let him watch on the spy-cam.

Not likely. His access to spy-cam material is limited to Charmaine and Phil writhing around on the floor. Jocelyn really gets a jolt out of those. Her demand that he duplicate the action is pathetic: she must know he can't feel any real passion. At those moments he'd drink paint thinner or stuff a chili pepper up his nose – anything to dull his brain during these mutually humiliating scenes. But he needs to convince himself that he's next door to an automaton, he needs to keep the action going. His life may depend on it.

Last night Jocelyn tried something new. She has all the access codes to everything, as far as he can tell, so she opened Charmaine's pink locker and rummaged around in Charmaine's stuff and found a nightgown she could fit into. It had daisies on it, and little bows – very far from Jocelyn's functional style, which was maybe the point.

Jocelyn is in the habit of sleeping in the spare room, where she also keeps her 'work,' whatever it is; but last night, after lighting a scented candle, she'd put on that nightgown and tiptoed into his room. 'Surprise,' she'd whispered. Her mouth was dark with lipstick, and as she pressed it down on his he'd recognized the aroma of the lipstick kiss on that note he'd found. *I'm starved for you! I need you so much. XXOO and you know what more – Jasmine.* Like a moron, he'd fallen for this sultry Jasmine, with her mouth the colour of grape juice. What a mirage! Then, what a disappointment.

And now Jocelyn wanted to be who? Dragged out of sleep, he was disoriented; for a moment he didn't know where he was, or who was pressing herself against him. 'Just imagine I'm Jasmine,' she murmured. 'Just let yourself go.' But how could he, with the texture of Charmaine's familiar cotton nightgown under his fingers? The daisies. The bows. It was such a disconnect.

How much longer can he go on starring in this bedroom farce without losing it completely and doing something violent? He can keep himself steady when he's working at the scooter depot: solving mechanical problems levels him out. But as the workday nears its end he feels the dread building. Then he has to get onto his scooter and motor back to the house. His goal is to dump a few beers into himself, then pretend to concentrate on yard work before Jocelyn turns up.

It's risky to combine beer fog with power tools,

but it's a risk he's willing to take. Unless he numbs himself, he might find himself doing something stupid.

But Jocelyn is high up on the status ladder; she must have every one of her snatch hairs monitored, with a SWAT team ready to spring into lethal action at any threat. Stan would surely trigger some alarm while making even the most innocuous move against her, such as roping her up and stowing her in Charmaine's pink locker – no, not the pink one, he doesn't know the code; in his own red locker – while he makes his getaway. But getaway to where? There's no route out of Consilience, not for those who've made the dick-brained mistake of signing themselves in. Signing themselves over. DO TIME NOW, BUY TIME FOR OUR FUTURE.

You got suckered, says Conor's voice inside his head.

Here comes Jocelyn in her darkened, softly purring spook vehicle. She must have a driver, because she always exits from the back seat. They're said to be working on a bunch of new robotic tech stuff at Positron that's going to help this place pay its way, so maybe it's a bot driving the car.

He has a wild impulse to sprint over with the hedge trimmer, turn it on, threaten to shred both Jocelyn and her robot driver unless they take him to the main Consilience gateway, right now. What if she calls his bluff and refuses? Will he go for it, and be left with a dead car full of electronics and mangled body parts?

But if it works, he'll make her drive him right through the gateway, into the crumbling, semi-deserted wasteland outside the wall. He'll jump out of the car, make a break for it. He wouldn't have much of a life out there, picking through garbage dumps and fighting off scavengers, but at least he'd be in charge of himself again. He'll find Conor, or Conor will find him. If anyone knows how to play the angles out there, it will be Con. He'll have to eat his pride, though. Do some back-tracking. *I was wrong, I should have listened to you,* and fucking etcetera.

Though maybe better not to try the hedge-trimmer move on Jocelyn. She can probably activate the alarm system by flexing her toes. Not to mention her fast moves: those Surveillance types must take martial arts training. Learn to crush windpipes with their thumbs.

Now she's getting out of the car, feet first. Shoes, ankles, grey nylon. Any guy seeing those legs would have to be turned on. Wouldn't they?

Hang on to that thought, Stan, he tells himself. It's not all downside.

PART VI

VALENTINE'S DAY

LIMBO

It's the tenth day of February, and Stan is still in limbo. Charmaine didn't reappear on the switchover day, as he'd been both hoping and fearing she would. Hoping, because – he has to admit – he misses her and wants to see her, especially if she replaces Jocelyn. Fearing, because would he lose his temper? Tell her he's seen the videos of her with Max, confront her with all the lies she told him, belt her one, the way Con might? Would she be defiant, would she laugh at him? Or would she cry and say what a mistake she's made and how sorry she is, and how much she loves him? And if she does say that, how will he know she means it?

He himself would be on shaky ground. What if Jocelyn takes her side, what if she shares what she knows about Stan's pursuit of the fake Jasmine and adds in a few details about what she and Stan have been doing on the blue sofa? And elsewhere. Many elsewheres. The inside of his head turns to a snarl of string every time he tries to picture his reunion with Charmaine.

'I think you two need more time apart,' was what

Jocelyn said about it, as if he and Charmaine were squabbling children who'd been given a time-out by a loving but strict mother. No, not a mother: a decadent babysitter who'd shortly be charged with corrupting minors, because right after that prissy little sermon, Stan found himself on the blue sofa with its chaste but by now grubby lilies enacting one of Jocelyn's favourite scenes from the frequently replayed video-porn saga featuring their two energetic spouses.

'What if it were both of us at once?' he found himself growling as if from a great distance. The voice was his, the words were Max's. The script called for some handwork here. It was hard to remember all the words, synchronize them with the gestures. How did they manage it in films? But those people got multiple takes: if they did it wrong, they could do it over. 'Front and back?'

'Oh no, I couldn't!' Jocelyn replied in a voice intended to sound breathless and ashamed, like Charmaine's on the video. And it did kind of sound that way: she wasn't acting, or not entirely. 'Not both at once! That's . . .'

What came next? His mind went blank. To gain time he tore off a few buttons.

'I think you could,' Jocelyn prompted him.

'I think you could,' he said. 'I think you want to. Look, you're blushing. You're a dirty little slut, aren't you?'

When would this be over? Why couldn't he just skip all the role-playing crap, cut to the chase, get to the part where her eyes rolled back in her head and she screamed like ripped metal? But she didn't want the short-form. She wanted dialogue and ritual, she wanted courtship. She wanted what Charmaine had, right there onscreen, and not a syllable less. It was pitiful, once Stan stopped to think about it: as if she'd been left out, the one kid not invited to the birthday party, so she was going to have her own birthday party, all by herself.

And she *was* having it all by herself, more or less, because Stan wasn't present in any real sense. Why doesn't she just order herself a robot? he thought. Among the guys down at the scooter depot, talk has it that full production has begun on the new and improved sexbots that are in the trial stage somewhere in the depths of Positron. Maybe it's an urban legend or wishful thinking, but the guys swear to it: they have the inside track. It's said to be a line of Dutch-designed prostibots, some for the domestic market, but the majority for export. The bots are supposed to be really life-like, with body heat and touch-sensitive plastic fibre skin that actually quivers, and several different voice modes, and flushable interiors for sanitary purposes, because who wants to catch a dick-rotting disease?

These bots will cut down on sex trafficking, say the boosters: no more young girls smuggled over borders, beaten into submission, chained to the bed, reduced to a pulp, then thrown into sewage lagoons. No more of that: plus, they'll practically shit money.

But it won't be anything like the real thing, say the detractors: you won't be able to look into their eyes and see a real person looking out. Oh, they've got a few tricks up their sleeves, say the boosters: improved facial muscles, better software. But they can't feel pain, say the detractors. They're working on that feature, say the boosters. Anyway, they'll never say no. Or they'll say no only if you want them to.

Stan doubts all of this: the empathy modules at Dimple Robotics wouldn't have convinced a five-year-old. But maybe they've made strides.

The guys joke about applying to be prostibot testers at Positron. It's said to be a wild experience, though creepy. You get to choose the voice and phrase option, the bot whispers enticing flatteries or dirty words; when you touch her, she wriggles; you give her a jump. Then, while the rinse cycle is kicking in – that part is weird, it sounds a little too much like the drain on a dishwasher – you have to fill out a questionnaire, check the ratings boxes for likes and dislikes of this or that feature, suggest improvements. As an on-demand sexual experience, it's said to be better than the bonk-a-chicken racket that used to go on at Positron, they add. No squawking, no scratchy claws. And better than a warm watermelon too, the latter being not all that responsive.

There must be male prostibots for the Jocelyns

of this world, thinks Stan. Randy Andy the Handy Android. But such an item wouldn't suit Jocelyn, because she wants something that can feel resentment, and even rage. Feel it and have to repress it. He knows quite a lot about her tastes by now.

The night before New Year's Day, she'd made popcorn and insisted they eat it while watching the video prelims: Phil's arrival at the derelict house, his restless pacing, the breath mint he'd slipped into his mouth, his swift preening of himself in the reflection of a shard of glass left in a shattered mirror. The popcorn was greasy with melted butter, but when Stan moved to get a paper towel, Jocelyn laid a hand on his leg; lightly enough, but he knew a command signal when he felt one. 'No,' she said, smiling that smile he increasingly can't read. Pain, or intent on causing it? 'Stay here. I want your butter all over me.'

At least it was something extra, that butter. Something Phil and Charmaine hadn't done. Or not on the videos.

And so it went on. But toward the end of January, Jocelyn's ardour or whatever it was had flagged. She seemed distracted; she worked in her room at the computer she'd set up in there, and instead of wanting sex on the sofa she'd taken to reading novels on it, with her shoes off and her feet up. He knows more about her now, or more about the story of herself she's using as a front. How did she get into the Surveillance business? he'd asked her, for something to do at the breakfast table.

'I was an English major,' she said. 'It's a real help.'

'You're bullshitting me, right?'

'Not in the least,' she said. 'It's where all the plots are. That's where you learn the twists and turns. I did my senior thesis on *Paradise Lost*.'

Paradise what? The only thing that came to Stan's mind was a nightclub site in Australia he'd once seen online when looking for soft porn, but the place had shut down years before. He wanted to ask Jocelyn if that book was made into an HBO mini-series or something, in case he might have seen it, but he didn't do that because the less ignorance he displayed, the better. Already she was treating him like a brain-damaged spaniel, with a mixture of amusement and contempt. Except when he was in full-throttle pelvic action. But that was happening less and less.

Some nights he found himself drinking beer alone because Jocelyn was out of the house. He felt relief – some of the performance pressure was off – but also fear, because what if she was about to discard him? And what if the destination she had in mind for him was not Positron Prison but that unknown void into which the bona fide criminals originally warehoused at Positron had vanished?

Jocelyn could erase him. She could just wave her hand and reduce him to zero. She'd never said so, but he knew she had that power.

But the first of February had come and gone, with no switchover for him. He'd finally dared to bring the subject up: when, exactly, would he be leaving for Positron?

'Missing your chickens?' she'd said. 'Never mind, you might be joining them soon.' This made his neck hair stand up: the nature of the chicken feed at Positron was a matter for grisly rumour. 'But first I want to spend Valentine's Day with you.' The tone was almost sentimental, though there was an underlayer of flint. 'I want it to be special.' Was *special* a threat? She watched him, smiling a little. 'I don't want us to be . . . interrupted.'

'Who'd interrupt us?' he said. In old movies, the kind they showed on the Consilience channel – comic movies, tragic movies, melodramatic movies – there were frequent interruptions. Someone would burst through a door – a jealous spouse, a betrayed lover. Unless it was a spy movie, in which case it would be a double agent, or a crime movie in which a stool pigeon had betrayed the gang. Scuffles or gunshots would follow. Escapes from balconies. Bullets to the head. Speedboats zigzagging out of reach. That's what those interruptions led to, though followed by happy endings. But surely no such interrupting was possible here.

'No one, I suppose,' she said. She watched him. 'Charmaine is perfectly safe,' she added. 'She's alive and well. I'm not a monster!' Then that hand on his knee again. Spider silk, stronger than iron. 'Are you worried?'

181

Of course I'm fucking worried, he wanted to shout. *What do you think, you twisted perv? You think it's a kiddie picnic for me, being house slave to a fucking dog trainer who could have me put down at any minute?* But all he'd said was, 'No, not really.' Then, to his shame: 'I'm looking forward to it.' He's disgusted with himself. What would Conor do in his place? Conor would take charge, somehow. Conor would turn the tables. But how?

'Looking forward to what?' she said with a blank stare. She was such a gamester. 'To what, Stan?' when he stalled.

'Valentine's Day,' he muttered. What a loser. Crawl, Stan. Lick shoes. Kiss ass. Your life may be hanging by a thread.

She smiled openly this time. That mouth he would soon be obliged to mash with his own, those teeth that would soon be biting his ear. 'Good,' she said sweetly, patting his leg. 'I'm glad you're looking forward to it. I like surprises, don't you? Valentine's Day reminds me of cinnamon hearts. Those little red ones you sucked. Red Hots, they were called. Remember?' She licked her lips.

Cut the crap, he wanted to say. Drop the fucking innuendo. I know you want to suck my little red-hot heart.

'I need a beer,' he said.

'Work for it,' she said, abruptly harsh again. She moved her hand up his leg, squeezed.

TURBAN

harmaine is called in to verify her data: sit for the retina scan, repeat the finger-printing, read *Winnie the Pooh* for the voice analyzer. Will these steps re-authenticate her profile for the benefit of the database? It's hard to tell: she's still alone in her cell, still shunned by the knitting circle, still stuck in Towel-Folding.

But the next day Aurora from Human Resources turns up in the laundry room and asks Charmaine to accompany her upstairs for a chat. The other towel-folders look up: is Charmaine in trouble? They probably hope so. Charmaine feels at a disadvantage – she's covered in lint, which is diminishing – but she brushes herself off and follows Aurora to the elevator.

The chat takes place in the Chat Room beside the front checkout counter. Aurora is pleased to be able to tell Charmaine that she will have her cards and codes restored to her – or not restored; confirmed. Just as Aurora has been assuring her that the database glitch has been repaired and she is now once again who she's been claiming she is. Aurora smiles tightly. Isn't that good news?

Charmaine agrees that it is. At least she has a code identity once again, which is some comfort. 'So can I leave now?' she asks. 'Go back home? I've missed a lot of Out time.'

Unfortunately, says Aurora, Charmaine can't depart from Positron quite yet: the synchronization is off. Although in theory she might move into the guest room of her own house – Aurora makes a laughing sound – her Alternate is of course now living in the house they share, it being that person's turn. Aurora understands how upsetting all this must be for Charmaine, but the proper rotation must be preserved, with no interaction between Alternates. Familiarity would inevitably lead to territorial squabbling, especially over such comfort items as sheets and body lotion. As they have all been taught, possessiveness about our cozy corners and favourite toys isn't limited to cats and dogs. How we *wish* it were. Wouldn't life be simpler?

So Charmaine must continue to be patient, says Aurora. And in any case she's been doing such a good job with the knitting – the blue teddy bears. How many has she knitted now? It must be at least a dozen! She'll have time for a few more of them before she leaves, hopefully at the next switchover day, which is when? The first of March, isn't it? And it's almost Valentine's Day – so, not long to go!

Aurora herself has never learned to knit. She does regret that. It must be calming.

Charmaine clenches her hands. One more of

those darn teddy bears with their bright, unseeing eyes and she's going to go sideways, right off the tracks! They've filled bins of them. She has nightmares about those teddies; she dreams they're in bed with her, unmoving but alive. 'Yes, it is calming,' she says.

Aurora consults her PosiPad. She has another piece of good news for Charmaine: as of the day after tomorrow, Charmaine will be taken off towel-folding and will resume her former duties as Chief Medications Administrator. Positron does reward talent and experience, and Charmaine's talent and experience have not gone unnoticed. Aurora gives an encouraging grimace. 'Not everyone has the soft touch,' she says. 'Coupled with such dedication. There have been incidents, when other . . . other operatives have been tasked with the, with the task. With the essential duty.'

'When do I start?' asks Charmaine. 'Thank you,' she adds. She's thrilled to be getting away from the towel-folding. She looks forward to re-entering the Medications Administration wing and following that remembered route along the hallways. She visualizes approaching the desk, accessing the possibly real head on the screen, advancing through the familiar doors, snapping on the gloves, picking up the medication and the hypodermic. Then on to the room where her Procedure subject will await, immobile but fearful. She will soothe those fears. Then she will deliver bliss, and then release. It will be nice to feel respected again.

Aurora consults her PosiPad again. 'I see here that you're set to resume your duties tomorrow afternoon,' she says. 'After lunch. When we make a mistake here, we do move to rectify it. Congratulations on a good outcome! We've all been rooting for you.'

Charmaine wonders who's been doing the rooting, because she hasn't noticed anyone. But like so many things around here, maybe the rooting has taken place behind the scenes. 'Goodness, I'm late for a meeting,' says Aurora. 'We have a whole new group of prisoners coming in, and all at once! Any further questions or points of information?'

Yes, says Charmaine. While she herself has been detained in Positron, what has Stan been told about her situation? Surely he's been worried about her! Does he know why she wasn't there? At home. Was he told what happened? Or did he think she'd just been subtracted? Sent to Medications? Erased? She hasn't dared to ask about this before – it might have sounded like complaining, it might have cast suspicion, it might have interfered with her chances for exoneration – but she's been cleared now.

'Stan?' says Aurora blankly.

'Stan. My husband, Stan,' says Charmaine.

'That's not information I have access to,' says Aurora. 'But I'm sure it's been taken care of.'

'Thank you,' says Charmaine again. To demand any more answers during this delicate transition that's taking place – this rehabilitation – might be pushing her luck.

Then there's Max, kept equally in the dark. Longing for her! Lusting for her! He must be going crazy. But she couldn't ask Aurora about Max.

'Could I maybe just send him a message?' Charmaine says. 'Stan? For Valentine's Day? To let him know I'm okay, and that I . . .' A tremulous pause on the verge of tears, which she feels she might really shed. 'That I love him?'

Aurora stops smiling. 'No. No messages while in Positron. You know better than that. If prison isn't prison, the outside world has no meaning! Now, enjoy the rest of your experience here.' She nods, stands up, and bustles out of the Chat Room.

At least there won't be much more of these darn towels, Charmaine thinks as she folds and stacks, folds and stacks. Maybe you can get a lung disease from the fluff. As she's wheeling her completed set over to the Outtake window, there's a sort of murmuring behind her, coming from the other women in Towel-Folding. She turns to see: it's Ed, the CEO of the Positron Project, ushering in an older woman who isn't wearing an orange boiler suit. On her head she has something that looks like a turban, decorated with red felt flowers. They're coming toward her.

'Oh my gosh!' Charmaine says. It just sort of comes out of her. 'Lucinda Quant! I used to love your show, *The Home Front*, it was so . . . I'm so glad you got better!' She's babbling, she's making a fool of herself. 'I'm sorry, I shouldn't . . .'

'Thanks,' says Lucinda Quant gruffly. She seems pleased. She's quite leathery, or at least her skin is. She didn't used to look like that on TV, but maybe it's the illness.

'I'm sure Ms Quant appreciates your support,' says Ed in that suave voice he has. 'We're giving her a quick tour of our wonderful project. She's considering a new show called *After the Home Front*, so she can tell the world about the wonderful solution we have here, to the problems of homelessness and joblessness.' He smiles at Charmaine. He's standing close to her. 'You've been happy here, haven't you?' he says. 'Since coming to the Project?'

'Oh yes,' says Charmaine. 'It's been so, it's been so . . .' How can she describe what it's been, considering everything, such as Max and Stan? Is she going to cry?

'Excellent,' Ed says. He pats her arm and turns away, dismissing her. Lucinda Quant gives Charmaine a sharp glance from her beady, red-rimmed eyes. 'Cat got your tongue?' she says.

'Oh no,' says Charmaine. Is Ed going to make trouble for her because she didn't say the right thing? 'It's only . . . I wish I could've been on your show.' And she does wish that, because then maybe people would've sent in money, and she and Stan would never have felt the need to sign on.

SHUFFLE

S tan does the countdown: two more days before Valentine's Day. The subject hasn't come up again, but every once in a while he catches Jocelyn looking at him speculatively, as if measuring him.

Tonight they're on the sofa as usual, but this time the upholstery will remain unsullied. They're side by side, facing forward, like a married couple – which they are, though they're married to other people. But they aren't watching the digital gyrations of Charmaine and Phil tonight. They're watching actual TV – Consilience TV, but still TV. If you drank enough beer, slit your eyes, wiped the context, you could almost believe you were in the outside world. Or the outside world in the past.

They've tuned in at the end of a motivational self-help show. So far as Stan can make out, it's about channelling the positive energy rays of the universe through the invisible power points on your body. You do it through the nostrils: close the right nostril with the index finger, breathe in, open, close the left nostril, breathe out. It gives a whole new dimension to nose-picking.

The star of the show is a young light-haired woman in a skintight pink leotard. She looks familiar, but then such generic women do. Nice tits – especially when she does the right nostril – despite the air bubble chatter coming out of her mouth. So, something for everyone: self-help and nostrils for the women, tits for the men. Distractions. They don't go out of their way to make you unhappy here.

The pink leotard woman tells them to practise every day, because if you focus, focus, focus on positive thoughts, you'll attract your own luck to yourself and shut out those negative thoughts that try to get in. They can have such a toxic effect on your immune system, leading to cancer and also to outbreaks of acne, because the skin is the body's largest organ and extra sensitive to negativity. Then she tells them that next week the feature will be pelvic alignment, so they should all reserve their yoga mats at the gym. She signs off with a freeze-frame smile.

Could that be Sandi, Stan wonders, Charmaine's erstwhile low-rent friend from PixelDust? No, too pretty.

New music comes on – 'Somewhere Over the Rainbow,' sung by Judy Garland – and with it the Consilience logo: CONSILIENCE = CONS + RESILIENCE. DO TIME NOW, BUY TIME FOR OUR FUTURE.

Yes, it's another Town Meeting. Stan yawns, tries not to yawn again. He opens his eyes wider. Here come the usual head-deadeners: the graphs, the statistics, the hectoring disguised as uplift. Violent incidents are down for the third time in a row, says a small guy in a tight suit, and let's keep that arrow moving: shot of a graph. Egg production is up again. Another graph, then a shot of eggs rolling down a chute and an automatic counter registering each egg with a digitized number. Stan has a pang of nostalgia – those chickens and eggs were once *his* chickens and eggs. They were his responsibility, and, yes, his tranquility. But now all that has been taken away from him and he's been demoted to chief toe licker for Jocelyn the spook.

Suck it up, he tells himself. Close the right nostril, breathe in.

Now another face comes on. It's Ed the confidence man, onscreen to make them all feel confident, but an Ed who's more substantial and assured, weightier in manner, more full of himself. Maybe he's scored a major contract. In any case, he's puffed up with the importance of what he's about to deliver.

The Project has been going well, says Ed. Their unit, here at Consilience, was the first, the pioneering town, and others in the chain have similarly prospered. Head office is getting inquiries daily from other stricken communities, who see the Project as a way of solving their own problems, both economic and social. There are different, more old-fashioned solutions to these problems – Louisiana has kept its honey-hole model, the for-profit hosting of recalcitrants from other states, and Texas is still dealing with its criminality statistics by means of executions. But many jurisdictions are looking for a more *rewarding* . . . for a more *humane,* or at least a more . . . for something more like Consilience. There is every reason to believe that their twin city is being viewed at a high level as a possible model for the future. Full employment is hard to beat. He smiles.

But now, a frown. In fact, says Ed, the model has been shown to be so effective – so conducive to social order, and, because of that, so positive in economic terms, and indeed so positive for the invest – for the *supporters* and *visionaries* who'd had the courage and moral fibre to see a way forward in a time of multiple challenges . . . The Consilience model has been, in a word, so successful that it has created enemies. As successful enterprises always do. Where there is light, it does seem a rule that darkness will shortly appear. As it now has, he is sorry to inform them.

An even deeper frown, a thrusting of the forehead, a lowering of the chin, a raising of the shoulders: an angry-bull stance. Who are these enemies? First of all, they are reporters. Muckraking journalists trying to worm their way in, to get evidence . . . to get pictures and other material that they can distort for so-called exposés, in order to turn the outside world against everything the Positron Project stands for. These shady so-called reporters aim to undermine the foundations of returning prosperity and to chip away at trust, that trust without which no society can function in a stable manner. Several journalists have actually made it inside the wall, pretending they wanted to sign on, but luckily they were identified in time. For instance, just the other day a female TV journalist with excellent credentials had been given a mini-tour under strict conditions of confidentiality but had been discovered in the act of taking clandestine pictures intended to present a slanted view.

How to explain the wish of such people to sabotage such an excellent venture? Except by saying they are maladjusted misfits who claim to be acting as they do in the interests of so-called press freedom, and in order to restore so-called human rights, and under the pretense that transparency is a virtue and the people need to know. But isn't it a human right to have a job? Ed believes it is! And enough to eat, and a decent place to live, which Consilience provides – those are surely human rights!

These enemies, not to mince words – says Ed – have already been involved in stirring up protest gatherings, luckily quite small ones, and have been writing hostile blog posts, though happily without credibility. None of this has gone very far as yet, because what evidence do such malcontents have for their scurrilous allegations? Scurrilous allegations that he will not dignify by repeating. These people and their networks must be identified, and then they must be neutralized. For, otherwise, what will happen? The Consilience model will be threatened! It will be attacked on all sides by what may seem at first like small forces, but together in a mob those forces are not small, they are catastrophic, just as one rat is negligible but a million rats is an infestation, a plague. So the sternest of measures must be taken before things get out of control. A solution is required.

And such a solution has indeed been devised, though not without much careful thought and the rejection of less viable alternatives. It is the best solution available at this time and in this place: they can take Ed's word for that.

And this is where he needs their cooperation. For the jewel in the middle of Consilience – Positron Prison, to which they have all given so much of their time and attention – Positron Prison has been chosen for a vital role in that solution. Every resident of Consilience will have a part to play, if only by keeping out of harm's way and being alert to subervsion from within, but for the present they can best help by simply going about their daily routine as if nothing unusual is happening, despite the unavoidable disruptions that may occur in that routine from time to time. Though it is earnestly hoped that such disruptions will be kept to a minimum.

Remember, says Ed, these enemies, if they succeeded, would destroy everyone's job security and very way of life! They should all bear that in mind. He has great faith in the common sense of the citizens of Consilience, and in their ability to recognize the greater good and to choose the lesser evil.

He allows himself a tiny smile. Then he is replaced by the Consilience logo and the familiar sign-off slogan: A MEANINGFUL LIFE.

Stan has found this news of interest, if it is news. Are there really subversives? Are they really trying to undermine the Project? What would be the point? He himself has fucked his life up, but for the other people in here – anyone he knows, at least – this place beats the hell out of what they had before.

He looks sideways at Jocelyn. She's staring thoughtfully at the screen, on which a toddler in the Positron preschool is playing with a blue knitted teddy bear, a ribbon around its neck. They've taken to running kiddie pictures after the Town Meetings, as if to remind everyone not to stray off the course Consilience has set for them, because wouldn't they be endangering the security and happiness of these little ones? No one but a child abuser would do that.

Jocelyn switches the TV off, then sighs. She's looking tired. She knew what Ed was going to say, Stan thinks. She's in on his solution, whatever it is. Maybe she wrote the speech.

'Do you believe in free will?' she asks. Her voice is different; it's not her usual confident tone. Is this some kind of trap?

'How do you mean?' says Stan.

★   ★   ★

The first truck arrives the next morning. It's unloaded at the main gates: Stan sees this as he scooters to work. The people herded out are wearing the regulation orange boiler suits, but they're hooded, their hands plasticuffed behind their backs. Instead of being driven straight to Positron, they're shuffled along the street, shepherded by a batch of guards. The prisoners must have some way of seeing out the front; they don't stumble as much as you'd think. Some are women, judging from the shapes muffled beneath their baggy clothing.

No need to parade them like this unless it's a demonstration, thinks Stan. A demonstration of power. What's been going on in the turbulent world outside the closed fishbowl of Consilience? No, not a fishbowl, because no one can see in.

The other guys in the scooter repair depot glance up as the silent procession shuffles past, then return to their work.

'Sometimes you miss the newspaper,' one of them says. No one replies.

THREAT

C harmaine saw the Town Meeting on TV, along with everyone else in the women's wing. Nobody had much to say about it, because whatever was happening wouldn't affect them, especially while they were inside the prison, so why worry about it? In any case, said someone in the knitting circle, so what if a reporter got in, because what could they report? There wasn't anything bad going on inside Consilience. The bad stuff was on the outside; that's why all of them had come in, to get away from it. Nods all round.

Charmaine isn't so sure. What if some reporter happened to find out about the Procedure? Not everyone would understand about that; they wouldn't understand the reasons for it, the good reasons. You could put a really unpleasant headline on such a story. She has a flash of herself, in a front-page photo, in her green smock, smiling eerily and holding a needle: DEATH ANGEL CLAIMS SHE SENT MEN TO HEAVEN. That would be horrible. She'd be the target of a lot of hate. But Ed won't let the reporters get in here, and thank goodness for that.

The next evening, after the communal meal in the women's dining room – chicken stew, Brussels sprouts, tapioca pudding – they all file into the main space, where the knitting circle meets. The teddy bear bin is half empty; it's their task to fill it before the month is out.

Charmaine takes up her allotted bear and sets to work. But when she's done only two rows, one knit, one purl, there's a stir. Heads turn: a man has walked into the room. This is almost unheard of, here in the women's wing. It's Ed himself, looking the same as when she saw him in Towel-Folding, though less relaxed. His shoulders are back more, his chin is up. It's a marching stance.

Behind him is Aurora with her PosiPad, and another woman: black hair, squarish face, a strong body, like someone who works out a lot – boxing, not yoga. Nice legs in grey stockings. Charmaine recognizes her: she's one of the talking heads from the validation screen in Medications Administration. So those heads are real after all! She's always wondered about that.

Is it her imagination, or has this woman singled her out, given her a brief nod, a quick smile? Maybe she's a secret ally – one of the behind-the-scenes rooters, one of those who's restored Charmaine to her rightful job. Charmaine gives a little nod in her direction, just in case.

Aurora speaks first. Here is Ed, their president and CEO – they will of course recognize him from his excellent Town Meeting presentations – and he has some very simple but very crucial instructions to give them at this juncture.

Ed begins with a smile and a gaze around the room. On the TV he's always friendly, makes eye contact, he somehow includes everyone in. He's doing that now, putting them at their ease.

He begins to talk. He knows they've seen the Town Meeting, and he has something to add about the crisis they are all facing – well, it isn't a crisis yet, and it's his job, and their job too, to make sure that it never becomes one. Scrutiny from the outside world is something Ed welcomes – he's happy to go out and speak on behalf of all of them here, and to gather support – but he will not allow the inmates to be pestered and slandered, because that is the aim of those who are set against them: pestering and slandering. Why should they be subjected to such treatment? It would be most unfair, after all the hard work they've been doing.

The women are nodding. He has their sympathy. How thoughtful he is, protecting them in this way.

The situation is under control, he continues, but meanwhile he's calling upon all of them to exert themselves even more than usual, in order to repel the barbarians at the gates who have declared themselves against the new way of ordering society they have been creating right here. The new order that is a beacon of hope, a beacon that risks being deliberately sabotaged.

But necessary steps are being taken. Some of those saboteurs have been identified, and they are

199

being brought right here to Positron to be dealt with. Sticklers might not view such a move as strictly legal, but desperate situations require a certain bending of the rules, as he is sure they will agree.

He would ask them to help out in the following ways. No fraternizing with those new-style prisoners, even if an opportunity may present itself. Any unusual sounds are to be ignored. He can't say what these sounds might be, other than unusual, but they will know them when they hear them. Otherwise they are to carry on as normal, and to mind – he will put this colloquially – to mind their own business.

As if it's been orchestrated, there's a scream. It's distant – hard to say whether it's a man or a woman – but it's definitely a scream. Charmaine holds herself perfectly still; she wills herself not to turn her head. Did the scream come over the sound system? Was it from outside, in the yard? There's an imperceptible rustling among the women as they steel themselves against hearing.

Ed has paused a little, to make room for the scream. Now he continues. And finally, he says, he will now share with them, and he does apologize for this: during this crisis, and he does expect it to be cleared up soon, Positron Prison will not be the comfortable and familiar haven of friends and neighbours that they have helped to nourish. Regrettably, it will become a less trusting and open place, because that is what happens in a crisis – people must be on guard, they must be sharper, they must be harder. But after this interlude, if the forces acting for the greater good are successful, the normal pleasant and congenial atmosphere will return.

Now he hopes they will relax and keep on with what they're doing. He'll just stroll around and watch them at their work, because it is deeply encouraging to him to see them so peacefully and usefully employed.

'I guess that means keep on knitting,' Charmaine's neighbour says to her. The knitting circle is being friendlier to her now that they know she's got her old job back.

'What was he talking about?' says another. 'What sounds? I didn't hear anything.'

'We don't need to know,' says a third. 'When people talk like that, it means don't even listen, is what they mean.'

'I didn't get that about a crisis,' says a fourth. 'Did something blow up?'

Dang it to heck, thinks Charmaine. I dropped a stitch.

Then Ed is standing right beside her. He must have crept up. 'That's an attractive blue bear you're knitting,' he says to her. 'It will make someone very happy.' Charmaine looks up at him. He's against the light: she can hardly see him.

'I'm not very good at it,' she says.

'Oh, I'm sure you are,' he says as he turns away. It comes to her in a flash: *He knows about Max.*

She can feel herself blushing with shame. Now why did she have that thought? Why would he have any reason to know? He's too important to be bothered with people like her. She only had that thought because of the way she is, the way she can't shake Max out of her head. Out of her body. The way she can't get clear.

VALENTINE'S DAY

It's Valentine's Day. Stan lies in bed. He doesn't want to get up, because he doesn't want to plod through the hours ahead, expecting to be ambushed at any minute by whatever foul or embarrassing surprise Jocelyn's planning to spring on him. Will it be a red cake plus tawdry heart-sprinkled crotchless lingerie for Jocelyn – or, worse, for himself? Will there be a soppy and mortifying declaration of love from her, with the expectation of an equally soppy and mortifying one from him in return? Hard-shelled women like her can have slushy interiors.

Or will it be Option B – *We're done here, you fail.* Sandbag to the back of the skull from the lurking goon she's got hidden in the broom closet – he casts her regular chauffeur for that, supposing there is one and not merely a bot – then a needle in the arm to keep him out cold; then dragged into that creepy stealth car with the darkened windows and hauled off to Positron to be processed in whatever way they process people there. Then into the chicken-feed grinder, or wherever they dispose of the parts. The cake and the melting, tender, velvet-eyed confession, or the iron-fisted sandbagging? She's capable of either.

Having bullied himself upright, he pulls on his scooter-depot work clothes, then sneak-foots along the upstairs hall to listen at the top of the stairs. She must be in the kitchen; there are food smells and clinkings. He descends gingerly, peers around the doorframe. She's sitting at the kitchen table texting on her phone, a plate of tousled breakfast leftovers in front of her. She's wearing her I-mean-business outfit: tidy suit, gold earrings, the grey stockings. Her reading glasses are perched on her nose.

No cake. No goon. Nothing out of the ordinary.

'Sleep in?' Jocelyn says pleasantly. Should he say 'Happy Valentine's Day,' then advance and give her a kiss to forestall any nastiness? Maybe not. Maybe she's forgotten what day it is.

'Yeah,' he says.

'Bad dreams?'

'I don't dream,' he says, lying.

'Everyone dreams,' she says. 'Have an egg. Or two. I poached them for you. They might be a little hard. Coffee's in the thermos.' She turns the two eggs out onto a piece of toast: they've been done in heart-shaped poachers. Is this the Valentine surprise? Is this all? He feels massive relief. Get real, Stan, he tells himself. She's not so bad. All she wanted was a bit of fun, plus getting back at her letch of a husband.

She's looking at him to see his reaction. 'Thanks,' he says. 'That's nice. It's a nice . . . a nice gesture.' She gives one of her all-teeth smiles. She isn't deceived for an instant, she knows he hates this.

'You're welcome,' she says. 'A token of my appreciation.'

A tip for the houseboy. Demeaning. He needs to wolf down the food, then beat it out of the house. Hightail it down to the scooter depot, make small talk, rewire some circuits, hit something with a hammer. Take a breather. 'I'm a bit late for work,' he says, to prepare her for his rapid exit. He slabs one of the eggs into his mouth, squeezes it down.

'You won't be going to your job today,' she says in a neutral voice. 'You'll be coming with me, in the car.'

The room darkens. 'Why?' he says. 'What's up?'

'I suggest you eat that other egg,' she says, smiling. 'You'll need the energy. You're going to have a long day.'

'Why is that?' he says as calmly as he can. He peers down over the edge of the next half-hour. Mist, a sheer drop. He feels sick.

She's poured herself a coffee, she's leaning in across the table. 'The cameras are off, but not for long,' she says. 'So I'm going to tell you this very quickly.' Her manner has changed completely. Gone is the awkward flirtation, the dominatrix pose. She's urgent, straightforward. 'Forget every-thing you think you know about me; and by the way, you kept your cool very well during our time together. I know I'm not your favourite squeeze toy, but you would have fooled most. Which is why I'm asking you to do this: because I think you can.'

She pauses, eyeing him. Stan swallows. 'Do what?' he says. Lie, steal, inflict wounds? Conor things? Something from the shadowlands: it has that feel.

'We need to smuggle somebody to the outside – outside the Consilience wall,' she says. 'I've already switched your database entries. You've been Phil these past months, but now you're going to be Stan again, just for a few hours. Then after that we can get you out.'

Stan feels dizzy. 'Out?' he says. 'How?' Nobody gets out unless they're upper management.

'Never mind how. Think of yourself as a messenger. I need you to take some information out.'

'Just a minute,' says Stan. 'What's going on? Who's we?'

'Ed's right about some things,' says Jocelyn. 'You heard him on the Town Meeting. There really are some folks who want to expose the Project. But they aren't all out there. Some of them are in here. In fact, some of them are in this room.' She smiles: now her smile has an almost elfish quality. Dangerous though this conversation must be, she's enjoying it.

'Whoa, just a minute,' says Stan. This is too

206

much in one sound bite. 'How come? I thought you were part of the top management in this place. You're high up in Surveillance, right?'

'I am. As a matter of fact, I'm Ed's founding partner. I supported the Project in the early stages. I believed in it; I believed in Ed. I worked hard on it. I thought it was for the best,' says Jocelyn. 'I bought the good-news story. And it was true at first, considering the alternative, which was a terrible life for a lot of people. But then Ed brought in a different group of investors, and they got greedy.'

'Greedy about what?' says Stan. 'It's not like this place makes a profit! On the fucking Brussels sprouts? And the chickens? I thought it was more about saving money, or like a charity thing, right?'

Jocelyn sighs. 'You don't honestly believe this whole operation is being run simply to rejuvenate the rust belt and create jobs? That was the original idea, but once you've got a controlled population with a wall around it and no oversight, you can do anything you want. You start to see the possibilities. And some of those got very profitable, very fast.'

Stan can hardly follow. 'I guess the building contractors must be making . . .'

'Forget the contracting end,' says Jocelyn. 'It's a sideshow. The main deal is the prison. Prisons used to be about punishment, and then reform and penitence, and then keeping dangerous offenders inside. Then, for quite a few decades, they were about crowd control – penning up the young, aggressive, marginalized guys to keep them off the streets. And then, when they started to be run as private businesses, they were about the profit margins for the prepackaged jail-meal suppliers, and the hired guards and so forth.' Stan nods; he understands all of this.

'But when we signed on,' he says, 'it wasn't like that. They didn't lie about what we'd have, inside. We got the house, we got . . . Before, we were broke, we were miserable. In here we were a lot happier.'

'Of course you were,' says Jocelyn. 'At first. So was I, at the beginning. But this isn't the beginning any more.'

'What's the bad news, then?' says Stan.

'Suppose I told you about the income from body parts? Organs, bones, DNA, whatever's in demand. That's one of the big earners for this place. It was going on in other countries first, and they were making a killing; that aspect was too tempting for Ed. There's a big market for transplant material among aging millionaires, no? Ed's bought into a retirement-home chain, and he's set up the transplant clinics right inside each of the branch facilities. Ruby Slippers Retirement Homes and Clinics: it's big. The main operation is in Las Vegas, for the cutting edge. He figures there'll be less scrutiny there, because anything goes. He doesn't miss a trick.'

'Just a minute,' says Stan. 'Whose body parts? It's still the same number of guys in Positron, I know them, they're not being sliced up for organs, it's not as if anyone's vanishing. Not once we got rid of the real criminals.'

'Yes, Ed thinks it's a shame we ran out of those,' says Jocelyn. 'He's got plans to import some more, take them off the hands of the public, so to speak. But your guys are the good citizens of Consilience, they keep the place running day to day, they're the worker ants. They'll stay in place. The raw material's being shipped in from outside.'

The truck. The hooded, shuffling prisoners. Oh great, thinks Stan. We're stuck in a grainy black-and-white retro-thriller movie. 'You mean they're rounding people up, carting them here? Killing them for parts?'

'Just undesirables,' says Jocelyn, smiling with her big teeth. She's kept some of her badass sarcasm, anyway. 'But now *undesirable* is whoever Ed says. Ed says the next hot thing is going to be babies' blood, by the way. It's being talked up as very rejuvenating for the elderly, and the margin on that is going to be astronomical.'

'That's . . .' Stan wants to say 'fucking gruesome,' which doesn't begin to cover it. Or else he could say, 'You're shitting me.' But he remembers that thing he heard about the mouse experiments; also she seems deadly serious. 'Where are they planning on getting the babies?'

'There's no shortage,' she says with that other

smile of hers, the ironic one. 'People leave them lying around. So careless.'

'Has anyone heard about this?' he says. 'Out there? Have they put it together, shouldn't they . . .'

'That's what Ed's worried about,' says Jocelyn. 'That's why the ultra-tight security. A few rumours were circulating, but he's managed to shut them down. Now nobody connected with a news outlet can get within a mile of this place, and as you know, no information is allowed out. That's why we have to send a person, such as you. You'll be taking a digitized document dump and some videos, on a flash drive. We'll try to set you up with a key media target. Someone who's not pals with Ed's political friends, and who's willing to take a chance on breaking the story.'

'So I'm supposed to be what?' says Stan. 'The errand boy?' The one who gets shot, he thinks.

'More or less,' says Jocelyn.

'Why don't you take it out yourself? This document dump.'

Jocelyn looks at him pityingly. 'No way,' she says. 'It's true I have a pass, I can go out. I've been setting up the outside operations, paying off the people we hire to do the less legal things Ed's got us involved in. But I'm monitored the whole time. To make sure I stay safe, is Ed's excuse. He trusts me as far as he trusts anyone, but increasingly that's not much. He's getting jumpy.'

'Why didn't you make a break for it? Just get

out?' says Stan. It's most likely what he himself would have done.

'I helped build this,' says Jocelyn. 'I need to help fix it. Now, time's up. We have to move.'

SANDBAG

They're in the car now; he can scarcely remember walking out to it. In front of them there's a driver – a real one, not a robot. The driver sits upright, his grey shoulders straight, the back of his head noncommittal. The streets glide past.

'Where are we going?' says Stan.

'Positron,' says Jocelyn. 'Our exit strategy for you begins there. Need to get you prepped, then see you through the day. This move is not without risks. It would be very unfortunate if you got caught.'

The driver, thinks Stan. It's always the driver, in movies. Listening in. Spying on everyone. 'What about him?' he says. 'He's heard all this.'

'Oh, that's only Phil,' says Jocelyn. 'Or Max. You'll recognize him from the videos.'

Phil turns around, gives a brief smile. It's him, all right – Charmaine's Max, with his handsome, narrow, untrustworthy face, his too bright eyes.

'He's been such a help in creating motive,' says Jocelyn. 'We chose Charmaine because we thought she might be . . .'

'Susceptible,' says Phil.

'Sufficient to have stood but free to fall,' says Jocelyn.

'What?' says Stan. This is some slur on Charmaine. He clenches his fists. Steady, he tells himself.

'She was a gamble,' says Jocelyn.

'But she paid off,' says Phil.

The lying bastard, he wasn't even sincere, thinks Stan. He was shitting poor Charmaine all along. Setting her up. Leading her astray for motives different from the ones you're supposed to have when you lead someone astray. It's as if Charmaine wasn't good enough for him; not good enough for a genuine illicit passion. Which, if you think about it, is actually a criticism of Stan. His hands are burning: he'd like to strangle the guy. Or at least give him a solid punch in the teeth.

'Motive for what?' says Stan.

'Don't be sulky,' says Jocelyn. 'For why I'd want to have you eliminated. I have superiors. I'll need to account to them for my decision.'

'Eliminated? You're going to do what?' Stan almost shouts. This is getting more demented by the minute. Underneath the heroic talk, is she a psychopath after all? With designs on his liver as a bonus?

'Whatever you want to call it,' says Jocelyn. 'Among our Management group, we call it "repurposing." I have the discretionary power for that, and I've made those kinds of decisions before, when things have gone seriously . . . when I've had

213

to. For this particular scenario – the one geared toward getting you past the wall in one piece – anyone likely to be checking up on me, such as Ed, knows power corrupts, they'll have experienced that first-hand. They'll see how I'd be tempted to use my own power for personal reasons. They may not approve of that, but they'll buy it. The evidence is all there, supposing I might ever need to use it, which I hope I won't.'

'Such as?' says Stan. 'Evidence?' He's feeling cold all over and a little dizzy.

'It's on record, every minute of it – everything you'd need to establish a reason. Phil and Charmaine, their torrid affair, which I have to say Phil threw himself into; but he's good at that. Then my own degrading and jealous attempts to re-enact that affair and punish Charmaine through you. Why do you think we had to go through all that theatrical sex in front of the TV? Your reluctance was fully registered, believe me – the lighting was good, I've seen the clips.' She sighs. 'I was a little surprised you didn't take a swipe at me. A lot of men would have, and I know you almost lost it a couple of times; I worried about your blood pressure. But you've shown impressive restraint.'

'Thanks,' says Stan. He has a moment of pleasure at having been tagged 'impressive.' Cripes, he tells himself. Are you buying this? Do you believe for one nanosecond that this stone-cold bitch wasn't getting off big-time on treating you like a fucking galley slave? Do you trust the two of them?

No, he answers. But do you have any choice? Pull back, say you won't do it, and they'll likely kill you.

'It was a plus that you had to force yourself,' says Jocelyn. 'Your reluctance played well, though it was hardly flattering. Anyone watching would conclude it was sex at virtual gunpoint.'

'She's not really like that, underneath. She can be very attractive,' says Phil gallantly. Or maybe even honestly, thinks Stan. Tastes differ.

'I agree,' he says, because agreement is called for. 'It was hardly at gunpoint, it was . . .'

Jocelyn crosses her legs. She pats Stan's thigh as if steadying him. 'Anyway, those who might have to be shown those videos will see why I might want to get rid of you. And by means of Charmaine, for, after all, she filched my husband, right? Double punishment. It has to be watertight, this stunt. Something that can fool Ed, supposing he'll go looking. He'd buy that kind of malice, coming from me. He thinks I'm hardass as it is. That's why I'm his right-hand gal.'

Is this leading where Stan thinks? His hands are clammy. 'What stunt?'

'The part where Charmaine goes in to work in Medications Administration – where on a normal day she administers an exit dose to someone slated for repurposing – and then finds out that the next Special Procedure she has to perform is on you. And then she does perform it. But don't worry – unlike the others, you'll wake up afterwards. And

215

then we'll be halfway there, because you won't be in the database anymore except in the past tense.'

Stan's getting a headache. He can hardly follow this. So that's what Charmaine's been doing at her confidential job. She's been . . . He can't believe this. Fluffy, upbeat Charmaine? Fuck. She's a murderess.

'Wait. You haven't told her?' he says. 'Charmaine? She'll think she's killed me?'

'For her, it has to be real,' says Jocelyn. 'We don't want her to act, they'd see through it: they have facial-expression analyzers. But Charmaine will believe the set-up. She's really good at believing.'

'She enters readily into fantasies,' says Phil. Is that a grin?

'Charmaine won't kill me,' says Stan firmly. 'No matter . . .' *No matter how far into her you got, you lying dickshit,* he wants to say but doesn't. 'If she thinks it'll kill me, she won't go through with it.'

'We'll find that out too, won't we?' says Jocelyn, smiling.

Stan wants to say, *Charmaine loves me,* but he's not completely sure of that any more. *And what if there's a mistake? What if I really do die?* he'd like to ask. But he's too chickenshit to admit he's chickenshit, so he keeps quiet.

Phil starts the car, moves them soundlessly along the street toward Positron Prison. He turns on the dashboard radio: it's the Doris Day playlist. 'You Made Me Love You.' Stan relaxes. That crooning voice is such a safe place for him now. He closes his eyes.

'Happy Valentine's Day,' says Jocelyn softly. She pats his thigh again.

He hardly even feels the needle go in; it's just a slight jab. Then he's over the edge of the misty cliff. Then he's falling.

PART VII

WHITE CEILING

WHITE CEILING

Stan enters consciousness as if coming up from a well full of dark molasses. No, a well with nothing in it, because he didn't have any dreams. The last thing he can recall is being in the car, the black Surveillance car with darkened windows, with Jocelyn sitting beside him in the back seat and her smug, treacherous dipstick of a husband doing the driving.

He has an image of the back of Phil's head – a head he wouldn't mind perforating with a broken bottle – and then another of Jocelyn putting her sturdy but manicured hand out to pat his knee in the patronizing way she had, as if he was a pet dog. The black sleeve of her suit. That was his last snapshot.

Then the prick of the needle. He was gone before he knew it.

But look, she didn't kill him! He's still in his body, he can hear his heart beating. As for his mind, it's clear as ice water. He doesn't feel drugged; he feels refreshed and hyper-alert, as if he's just chugged a couple of double espressos.

He opens his eyes. Fuck. Nothing. Maybe he's been sent to the stratosphere after all. No, wait, it's a ceiling. A white ceiling, with light reflecting down from it.

He turns his head to see where the light's coming from. No, he doesn't turn his head, because his head won't turn that far. Something's restraining it, and his arms, and, yes, his legs too. Triple fuck. They've got him strapped down.

'Fuck!' he says out loud. But no, he doesn't say that. The only sound that comes out of his mouth is a slobbering zombie sound. But urgent, like a car in a snowbank spinning its wheels. *Unhuhuh. Unhuhuh.*

This is horrible. He can think, but he can't move and he can't speak. Shit.

Charmaine hardly slept a wink all night. Maybe it was the screams; or they might have been laughs – that would be nicer; though if they were laughs, they were loud, high, and hysterical. She'd like to ask some of the other women if they heard anything too, but that's probably not a good idea.

Or maybe her sleeplessness came from over-excitement, because really she's super excited. She's so excited she can only peck at her lunch, because this afternoon she gets to resume her real job. After putting in her morning session of towel-folding, she got to throw away the shameful Laundry Room nametag and replace it with her rightful one: Chief Medications Administrator. It feels blissful, as if that nametag has been lost and now it's been found; like when you misplace your scooter keys or your phone and then they turn up and you get a rush of luckiness, as if the stars or fate or something has singled you out for a win. That's how happy her rightful nametag makes her feel.

The other women in her section have noticed that nametag: they're treating her with new respect. They're looking at her directly instead of letting their eyes slide past her like she was furniture; they're asking her sociable questions such as how did she sleep, and isn't this an awesome lunch? They're handing her small, chatty praises, like what a good job she's doing with the blue teddy bears, even though she's such a crappy knitter. And they're smiling at her, not half-smiles either, but full-on total-face smiles that are only partly fake.

It isn't at all hard for her to smile back. Not like the past weeks, when she was exiled to Towel-Folding, when she felt so lonely and isolated and her own smile felt cracked, as if there was a broken cement sidewalk right behind her teeth, and her mouth felt shrunken and clogged, and the other women spoke to her in sentences of two words because they didn't know what kind of disgrace she was in.

Charmaine couldn't blame them, since she didn't know that herself. She tried her utmost to believe

223

it was just a trivial mistake: you always had to try your utmost to believe the positive, because what did believing the negative ever get you except depressed? Whereas with the positive you found the strength to carry on.

And she had carried on.

Though it had been hard, because she'd been so scared. What were they really planning for her? She's sure there's more than one of them. The only one they actually show much of is Ed, but there has to be a whole bunch of them behind the scenes, talking everything over and making important decisions.

Have they been sitting in their boardroom, discussing her? Do they know she's been cheating on Stan? Have they got photos of her, or voice recordings, or, even worse, videos? She'd said that to Max once – 'What if there's a video?' – but he'd only laughed and said why would there be a videocam in an abandoned house, and he only wished there was so he could relive the moment. But what if he has been reliving the moment, and those other men have been reliving it too?

It makes her blush all over to think of them watching her and Max in those vacant houses. She wasn't herself with Max, she was some other person – some slutty blonde she wouldn't speak to if they were standing in a checkout line together. If that other Charmaine tried to strike up a conversation with her she'd turn away as if she hadn't heard, because you're known by the company you keep and that other Charmaine is bad company. But that Charmaine has been banished, and she herself – the real Charmaine – has been restored to good standing, and she has to keep it that way no matter what.

She gazes down the table at the rows of women in their orange boiler suits. She doesn't know them very well because they've basically not been speaking to her, but their faces are familiar. She scans their features as they chew away at their lunches: isn't this a warm, fuzzy, grateful feeling she's getting, because each one of them is a unique and irreplaceable human being?

No, this is not a warm, fuzzy, grateful feeling. To be honest, she doesn't like these women much. Grandma Win would say she wouldn't trust any of them as far as she could throw them, which isn't very far since most of them are overweight. They should burn more energy, take the dancercise classes, or work out in the Positron gym, because sitting on their fat butts knitting those stupid blue bears plus eating the desserts is piling the pounds onto them and they're blowing up like blimps. And deep down she doesn't give a crap about each of them being a unique and irreplaceable human being, because they didn't treat her like one. They treated her like something that got stuck on their shoe.

But that's the past, and she must not look back in anger or hold on to grudges, because such behaviour is toxic, as the girl in the pink outfit says on the TV yoga show, so now she's dwelling on blessings. How blessed they all are to be tucked in here when so many other people are having a bad time outside the wall, where – according to Ed – everything's going to ratshit. Even more ratshit than it was going to when she lived out there.

The lunch is chicken salad. It's made with chickens raised right here at Positron Prison, in healthy and considerate surroundings, over at the men's wing; and the lettuce and arugula and radicchio and celery are grown here as well. Though not the celery, now that she thinks of it – that comes in from outside. But the parsley's grown here. And the spring onions. And the Tiny Tim tomatoes. Despite her lack of appetite she picks away at the salad, because she doesn't want to look ungrateful. Or, worse, unstable.

Here comes the dessert. They've set it out on the table at the far end of the room; the women get up in order, row by row, and stand in line for it. Plum crumble, the women murmur to one another, made with red plums from Positron's very own orchard. Though Charmaine has never worked in that orchard herself or even talked to anybody who's worked in it, so how would she know if it even exists? They could be bringing those plums in here in cans and nobody but whoever opens the cans would be any the wiser.

These skeptical notions about Positron are

coming to her more frequently. Don't be so stupid, Charmaine, she tells herself. Change the channel, because why would you even care about where the plums come from? And if they want to fib about plums to make us all feel better, what's the harm?

She picks up her helping of plum crumble in its sturdy pressed-glass dish. There's cream added, from Positron's own cows; not that she's ever seen those cows either. She nods and smiles at the other women as she files past them, sits back down at her place, stares at her crumble. She can't help thinking it looks like curdled blood, but she draws a marker across that thought, blacks it out. She should try to eat just a bit: it might steady her nerves.

She's been away from the Medications Administration job so long. Maybe she's lost her touch. What if she makes a shambles of the Special Procedure the next time she does it? Gets cold feet? Misses the sweet spot in the vein?

When you're actually doing the Procedure you don't have big-picture worries, you exist in the moment, you only want to get it right and do your duty. But over the past two months she's been at a distance, and from a distance what she does in Medications Administration doesn't always look the same as what she ought to do, supposing she was just a person.

Are you having qualms, Charmaine? asks the little voice in her head.

No, silly, she answers. I'm having dessert. Plum crumble.

The women at her table are making *mmm* sounds. Red crumbs cling to their lips.

HOOD

S tan tries again. He uses all his strength, pushing up with his arms and thighs against the straps – they must be straps, though he can't see them. No dice. What is this, Jocelyn's warped idea of another kinky sex game?

'Charmaine,' he tries to call. His throat slurs, his tongue is like a cold beef sandwich. Why's he calling her anyway, as if he can't find his socks, as if he needs help with his top shirt button? What kind of a help-me-mommy-wife-whine is that? Maybe part of his brain is dead. *Dumbass,* he tells himself: *Charmaine can't hear you, she isn't in the room.* Or not so far as he can see, which isn't far.

Oh, Charmaine. I love you, baby. Get me out of this!

Wait a minute: now he remembers. According to Jocelyn, Charmaine is supposed to kill him.

Two o'clock. The first Procedure of the afternoon is scheduled for three. After leaving the dining area, Charmaine heads back to her cell to spend a little quiet time alone. She needs to prepare herself, both physically and mentally; and also

229

spiritually, of course. Do some deep breathing, the way they show it on TV. Fix her makeup, which is energizing. Calmness, positive energy: that's what she needs.

But when she opens the door to her cell, there's someone already in it. It's a woman, in the standard orange boiler suit but with a hood over her head. She's sitting on the bed. Her wrists are attached together in front with plastic handcuffs.

'Excuse me?' says Charmaine. If it weren't for the hood and the cuffs, she would have pointed out that this is her cell, and as far as she knows there hasn't been a new cell assignment. And then she would have said, Please leave.

'Don't . . .,' says the woman's voice, muffled by the hood. Then there's something else that Charmaine doesn't catch. She goes over to the bed – risky, because what if this is a maniac who might snap at her or something – and lifts the hood up and back.

This is a shock. This is definitely a shock. It's Sandi. It can't be Sandi! Why would it be Sandi? She stares at Charmaine with watery, blinking eyes. 'Charmaine, Christ,' she says. 'Put the hood back on! Don't talk to me!'

Charmaine is confused. Sandi never did bad things, apart from the hooking, but that was instead of a job, so why would she need to do it in Consilience? Her hair's a wreck. Her cheek-bones are more prominent than they were: maybe she's had work done. Has she maybe been pushing? Talking to a journalist? But how?

'Sandi! What are you doing in my cell?' she says. That doesn't sound very gracious, but it's not as if she meant it meanly. Sandi's leg is chained to the bedframe, her ankles are shackled. This is serious.

'Don't talk loud,' Sandi whispers. 'They must've fucked up, stuck me in the wrong place. Pretend you don't know me! Or you might get in trouble.'

'Are you a, you know. A criminal element?' Charmaine asks – has to ask, though maybe she shouldn't. Sandi's a nice girl at heart, she can't be a criminal element, and anyway the criminal elements she's used to dealing with at Medications Administration have all been men. She can't see Sandi murdering anyone, or doing any of the other things that get you strapped down five ways on a gurney. 'What did you do? I mean, did you do anything?'

'I tried to get out,' Sandi whispers. 'I tried to get myself smuggled through the wall in a bag of trash, where they send it down that chute to the truck outside. I had sex with one of those trash guys, the ones in the green vests, you know the ones. He ratted on me but not until after the sex, the fucker.'

'But, honey, why would you want to get out?' Charmaine whispers. That's mystifying to her. 'It's so much better—'

'Yeah, it was at first, it was going great, I was

231

helping at the gym and then they picked me to make those yoga videos, I got some work done, cheekbones mostly, and they did the makeup, and all I had to do was put on that pink suit and read the script and do a few poses.'

'I thought it was you,' Charmaine says untruthfully. 'You were great, it looked like you were an expert!' She's a little jealous. What an easy job, and with star power too. Not like her own job. But hers is more important.

'So then Veronica came back one day,' Sandi whispers. 'We were sharing a condo, she was training at the prison hospital, and she was all excited, they'd offered her a promotion, to this special unit they have there.'

'What was it?' Charmaine says. Maybe something bland, like Pediatric.

'It was in Medications Administration,' says Sandi. 'She went the next day to start the training. But when she came back she was upset. Veronica never gets upset normally.' Sandi pauses. 'You mind scratching my back?'

Charmaine scratches. 'A little to the left,' says Sandi. 'Thanks. So she said, "Basically they want me to kill people. Underneath all the bullshit, that's what it is."'

'Oh gosh,' says Charmaine. 'Not really!'

'No shit,' says Sandi. 'So she told them no, she couldn't do it. And the next day she was gone. Just gone. Nobody knew where she went, or else they wouldn't say. I asked at her work, and they looked at me in this weird way and said that information was not available. It was creepy! So I wanted out.'

'You're not allowed out!' Charmaine whispers. 'Remember what we signed! Couldn't you just explain to them . . .' She knows this is futile, because rules are rules, but she wants to hold out hope.

'Forget it,' says Sandi. 'I'm fucked.' Her teeth are chattering. 'No free lunch for me, I should've known. Now you need to put the hood back on and call a guard, and say why is this person in your cell, and they'll clear me out of your way.'

'But I can't just . . .,' says Charmaine. 'What will happen to you?' She's going to cry. This is wrong, it *has* to be wrong! The chains, the handcuffs . . . Maybe they'll only put Sandi in Towel-Folding or something. But she can't get herself to believe that. There's a dark light rippling around Sandi, like dirty water. Charmaine puts her arms around her. She's so cold. 'Oh, Sandi,' she says. 'It will be okay!'

'Just do it,' says Sandi. 'You don't have the choice.'

CHERRY PIE

The white ceiling is even more boring than Consilience TV. Hardly anything's going on up there, though there has been a fly, which has helped to pass the time. Scram, fly, Stan thought at it, to see if he could control it by broadcasting his mental electrical waves. But he couldn't.

The other thing on the white ceiling is a small, round silver circle. It's either a sprinkler or a videocam. He closes his eyes, then opens them: he should stay awake if possible. He concentrates on the chain of causes and effects and lies and impostures – some of them his – that has stranded him in this tedious or possibly terrifying cul-de-sac.

Which will terminate with Charmaine in a lab coat walking in here in about five minutes, or at least he hopes it's that soon because he really needs a piss. The poor mouse will think she's about to send some serial killer or child murderer or old-person batterer to the next life. But when she approaches the gurney he's strapped onto, it won't be an unknown criminal element waiting for her: it will be him.

What will she do then? Scream and run away? Throw herself onto his body? Tell Positron there's been a terrible mistake?

Maybe she'll flick a hidden switch to turn off the videocam, then unstrap him, and they'll hug each other, and she'll whisper, 'I'm so sorry, can you ever forgive me for cheating, you're the one I really love,' and so on, though there won't be time for the drawn-out grovelling and cringing he has the right to expect. But he'll squeeze her reassuringly, and then she'll show him – what? A trapdoor? A secret tunnel? A set of clothes to wear as a disguise?

He's watched way too much TV, over the years. On TV there are last-minute escapes, and tunnels, and trapdoors. This is real life, numbnuts, he tells himself. Or it's supposed to be.

But there has to be some last-minute plot flip like that, because Charmaine would surely never stick the death drug into him, or whatever it is she does. She'd never go the whole hog. She's too tender-hearted.

Unhuhuh, he says to the ceiling. Because now he's not so sure about her tender-heartedness. He's not sure of anything. And what if something has fucked up, and the Positron spooks have caught up with double-dealing Jocelyn and arrested her, or maybe even shot her?

And what if, when the door opens, it isn't Charmaine who walks through it?

They're probably watching him right now,

through that silver circle. They've probably tortured Jocelyn, made her cough up her entire subversive plan. They probably think he's in on it.

I didn't know! It wasn't me! I've done nothing! he screams in his head.

Unhuhuhuh.

Shit. He's wet his pants. But it doesn't seep, it doesn't trickle. Have they got him in diapers? Crap. Not a good sign.

So he can't be the first person who's been here and done the pant-wetting thing. You can't say they don't cover the angles.

It takes Charmaine a while to regain her calm after the two guards have hauled Sandi away. By the armpits, because she couldn't walk very well, what with the shackles.

'No need to mention this to anyone,' the first guard had said. The second one gave a kind of barky laugh. Neither of them was anyone Charmaine had ever seen before.

She takes some yogic breaths, she clears her mind of negative vibrations. Then she washes her hands, and after that she brushes her teeth: it's like a cleansing ritual, because she likes to feel pure in heart when going into a Procedure. She checks herself in the mirror: there she is, the same sweet, roundish baby-face she's always relied on at home and school; she hasn't changed that much since being a teenager, though she's a little dark under the eyes. She pulls a few strands of her blond hair forward to frame her face. But she's thinner. She's lost weight over the past while, slightly too much weight, and she's looking pale. She's been so worried, and she's still worried, because even though her name's been cleared and she has her job again, what will the future bring? Once she's back at the house.

The very worst – well, almost the worst – would be if they told Stan about Max. Then what will happen when she sees Stan? He'll be really mad at her. Even if she cries and says she's sorry, and how can he ever forgive her, and he's the one she really loves, he still might want a divorce. The mere possibility makes her tearful. She'd feel so unsafe without Stan, and people would gossip about her, and she'd be all alone in Consilience, forever, because you can't get out. But she might not feel very safe *with* Stan, either.

As for Max, yes, she does remember hoping he might leave his wife for her so they could be together and she could be crushed in his embrace like a stepped-on blueberry muffin every minute of every day. He'd say, 'There's no one like you, bend over,' while nibbling on her ear, and she'd melt like toffee in the sun.

But on some level she's always known that would be impossible. She's been a distraction for him, but not a necessity of life. More like a super-strong mint: intense while it lasted but quickly finished. And, to be fair, he's been the same thing for her, and if he was offered to her on a serving platter in exchange for Stan, she would say no thanks, because she could never depend on Max: he's too fast with his mouth, he's like a TV ad, pushing something dark and delicious but bad for you. Instead she would say, 'I choose Stan.' She does feel quite certain that this is the choice she would make.

Though what if Stan rejects her, despite her new, virtuous intentions? What if he throws her out, tosses her clothes onto the lawn for everyone to see, and then locks the door on the inside? Maybe it will happen at night, and she'll be outside in the rain, scratching on the window like a cat, begging to be taken back. *Oh, I've ruined everything,* she'll wail. Her eyes water up just picturing it.

But she'll refuse to think about that, because you make your own reality out of your attitude, and if she thinks about it happening, then it will. Instead she'll think about Stan's arms going around her and him saying how miserable he's been without her and how happy he is that they're finally together once more. And she'll stroke him, and cuddle him, and it will be like old times.

Because the days will fly past and it will be switchover in a couple of weeks, and she can finally leave Positron for her month as a civilian again. She'll be working at her Consilience job in the bakery, and she won't have to think about screams or women with hoods chained to her bed, and she'll smell like cinnamon from the cinnamon buns, such a cheerful smell, and not like the floral scent of the fabric softener from Towel-Folding in Positron, which if you have to breathe it all day is truly chemical and sickly. She won't use that fabric softener on her own laundry any more, ever. She'll be back in her own house, with her pretty sheets and the bright kitchen where she cooks such nice breakfasts, and she'll be with Stan.

Because why would they even tell him about Max, supposing they know? Considering that the whole point of Consilience is for things to run smoothly, with happy citizens, or are they inmates? Both, to be honest. Because citizens were always a bit like inmates and inmates were always a bit like citizens, so Consilience and Positron have only made it official. Anyway, the point is the greatest happiness all around, and telling Stan would mean less happiness. In fact it would mean more misery. So they won't do it.

Already she can picture, no, feel Stan's arms around her; and then the way he nuzzles the side of her neck and says things like, *Yum. Cinnamon. How's my little bun?* Or he used to say things like that, comfort-food kinds of things, though he was slacking off lately. Almost ever since she got tangled up with Max, come to think of it. But he'll say those things again, because he'll have missed her and worried about her. *How's my cherry pie?* Not like the things Max says, which are more like, *I'm going to turn you inside out, after this you won't be able to crawl. Beg me for it.*

Stan maybe isn't the most . . . well, the most. The most of whatever you'd call Max. But Stan loves her, and she loves him.

She does really. That thing with Max was only a blip, it was an animal episode. She'll have to stay away from Max in future. Though it might be hard, because Max is so passionate about her. He'll try to get her back, no question. But she'll have to put her fingers in her ears and grit her teeth and roll up her sleeves and resist temptation.

Though why shouldn't a person have both? says the voice in her head.

I'm making an effort here, she answers. So shut up.

She looks at her watch: two-thirty. Half an hour to go. The waiting is the worst thing. She's never been so trembly before a Procedure.

She smiles her I-am-a-good-person smile, the smile of an absent-minded angel with a childish lisp. That smile has seen her through many difficult places, or at least it has since she's been grown up. It's a Get Out of Jail Free card, it's a rock concert wristband, it's a universal security password, like being in a wheelchair. Who would question it?

To give herself confidence she applies blush all over her pale face, then a thin coat of mascara on the eyelashes: nothing too overdone. Positron allows makeup in jail; in fact it encourages makeup, because looking your best is good for morale. It's her duty to look her best: she's about to become the last thing some poor young man will see on this earth. That's a big responsibility. She doesn't take it lightly.

Charmaine, Charmaine, whispers the small voice in her head. You are such a fraud.

So are you, she tells it.

HEADGAME

S tan must have drifted off, but he comes awake with a start. That fucking fly is walking all over his face, and he can't get at it.

'Fucking fly,' he tries to say. *Fuuuuuh. Fluuuh.* Nope, no speech functions so far. Drug's got his tongue. He hopes this isn't permanent: he won't be able to buy anything except with little notes. *Hi, my name is Stan and I can't talk. Gimme ten bottles of booze.* He won't care what kind, he'd drink elephant piss. After what he's been through he'll want to get falling-down blind drunk. Oblivious.

It will make a good story though. Once he gets out. Once he hooks up with Brother Conor and his band of merry men, and erases himself from the radar of everyone and everything to do with Positron, because what rule is there that says he has to be Jocelyn's flunky and mule boy once he's out? Let her handle her own weird shit. He'll have to get Charmaine out too, of course. Maybe. If possible.

Now the fly's trying to get into his eye. Blink blink, turn the head: it's not very scared of eyelashes, but it moves. Now it's going into his nose. At least he has some control over his nostrils: he blows it out. His back is terminally itchy, he has a cramp in his leg, his diaper is sodden. More than anything, he wants this to be over. This stage, this phase, this powerlessness, whatever it is. Let's get this show on the road, he'd shout, if he were capable of shouting. Which he isn't. But he hopes he will be soon. He has a lot of shouting to catch up on.

Charmaine makes her way through the familiar corridors to the Medications Administration reception area, where three corridors come together. She's wearing her green smock over her orange boiler suit; her latex gloves are in her pocket, as well as her face mask in case of germs. She'll put it on before she goes into the room – that's the rule – but then she'll take it off again, because why should anyone's last view of a human face be so impersonal? She wants whoever it is to be able to see her reassuring smile.

She's a little nervous; probably they're monitoring it, this nervousness of hers. And most likely it counts in her favour, because during the training course she took they'd put some electrodes on you and then showed you pictures of people undergoing the Special Procedure and measured how you reacted. What they were looking for was a certain amount of jitteriness, but not so much that you'd lose control. They'd weeded out the ones who stayed totally calm and cold, and also those who'd showed too much eagerness. They didn't want people who got pleasure out of doing this – they didn't want sadists or psychopaths. In fact, it was the sadists and psychopaths who needed to be – not *euthanized,* not *erased,* those words are too blunt. Relocated to a different sphere, because they were not suited to the life of Consilience.

Maybe that's what will happen to Sandi, but in a nicer way. Maybe they'll just take her someplace else, like an island, with the other people on it who are like her. People who don't fit in, but not criminal elements. Surely that's what they'll do.

Now she's reached Reception, and there's the check-in box with the flatscreen on the front. The head is already there: it must be expecting her. Today it's the woman with the dark hair and bangs. It's the same woman who was with Ed when he'd visited the knitting circle the night before, the one with the hoop earrings and the grey stockings. Someone important. Charmaine feels a slight chill. Yogic breath, she tells herself. In through the nose, out through the mouth.

The head smiles at her. Is it only a recorded image this time, or is it a real person?

'Could I have the key, please?' Charmaine asks it, as she is supposed to.

'Log in, please,' the head says to her. It's still smiling, though it seems to be looking at her more intently than usual. Charmaine presses her thumb to the pad, then gazes at the iris reader until it blinks.

'Thank you,' says the head. The plastic key slides out of the slot at the bottom of the box. Charmaine puts it into her lab coat pocket, waits for the slip of paper with the details of the Procedure printed on it: room number, name, age, last dose of sedative, and when administered. It's necessary to know how alert the subject may be.

Nothing happens. The head is staring at her with a meaningful half-smile. Now what? thinks Charmaine. Don't tell me the dratted databank has messed up my identity numbers again.

'I need the Procedure slip,' she says to the head. Even if it's only a canned image, her request will surely register.

'Charmaine,' the head says to her. 'We need to talk.'

Charmaine feels the hair stand up on the back of her neck. The head knows her name. It's talking to her directly. It's as if the sofa has spoken.

'What?' she says. 'What did I do wrong?'

'You didn't do anything wrong,' the head says, 'yet. But you're on probation. You must undergo a test.'

'What do you mean, probation?' says Charmaine. 'I've always been good at this job, I've never had any complaints, my job assessment score has been . . .' She's twisting the latex glove in her right-hand pocket; she tells herself to stop. It's bad to show agitation, as if she's in some way guilty. She's up

245

for their darn test, whatever it is: she's willing to bet her technique and fulfillment against anybody's. They can't fault her, except for not wearing her face mask, but who in their right mind would care about that?

'It's not your competence that's in question,' says the head. 'But Management has had some misgivings about your professional dedication.'

'I've always been extremely dedicated!' Charmaine says. Somebody must have been gossiping about her, telling lies. 'You have to be dedicated to do this job! Who says I haven't been dedicated?' It must be that sneaky Aurora, from Human Resources. Or someone in her knitting group, because she wasn't peppy enough about those darn blue bears. 'I love my job, I mean, I don't love having to do what I do, but I know it's my duty to do it, because it has to be done by someone, and I've always taken the best care and been very meticulous, and . . .'

'Let's call it loyalty,' says the head.

Why did the head say *loyalty*? Is *loyalty* about her and Max? 'I've always been loyal,' she says. Her voice sounds weak.

'It's a matter of degree,' says the head. 'Please pay attention. You must carry out the Procedure as usual today. It is very important that you complete the task that has been assigned to you.'

'I always complete the task!' says Charmaine indignantly.

'Today, this time, you may encounter a situation

that you find challenging. Despite this, the Procedure must be carried out. Your future here depends on it. Are you ready for that?'

'What kind of situation?' Charmaine asks.

'You have an option,' says the head. 'You can resign from Medications Administration right now and go back to Towel-Folding, or some other undemanding form of work, if you feel you are not up to the test.' It smiles, showing its strong, square teeth.

Charmaine would like to ask if she could have some time to think it over. But maybe that wouldn't be taken well: the head could see it as a flaw in her loyalty.

'You must decide now,' says the head. 'Are you ready?'

'Yes,' says Charmaine. 'I'm ready.'

'All right then,' says the head. 'You have now chosen. There are only two kinds of people admitted to the Medications Administration wing: those who do and those who are done to. You have elected the role of those who do. If you fail, the consequences to yourself will be severe. You may find yourself playing the other role. Do you understand?'

'Yes,' says Charmaine faintly. That was a threat: if she doesn't eliminate, she'll be eliminated. It's very clear. Her hands are cold.

'Very well,' says the head. 'Here are the details of your Procedure for today.' The slip of paper slides out of the slot. Charmaine picks it up. The room number and the sedative information are there, but the name is missing.

'There isn't any name,' Charmaine says. But the head has vanished.

CHOICE

Stan lets his mind float free. Time is passing; whatever will happen to him is about to happen. There's not a thing he can do about it.

Are these my last minutes? he asks himself. Surely not. Despite his earlier moment of panic, he's now oddly calm. But not resigned, not numbed. Instead he's intensely, painfully alive. He can feel his own thunderous heartbeat, he can hear the blood surging through his veins, he can sense every muscle, every tendon. His body is massive, like rock, like granite; though possibly a little soft around the middle.

I should have worked out more, he thinks. I should have done everything more. I should have cut loose from . . . from what? Looking back on his life, he sees himself spread out on the earth like a giant covered in tiny threads that have held him down. Tiny threads of petty cares and small concerns, and fears he took seriously at the time. Debts, timetables, the need for money, the longing for comfort; the earworm of sex, repeating itself over and over like a neural feedback loop.

249

He's been the puppet of his own constricted desires.

He shouldn't have let himself be caged in here, walled off from freedom. But what does freedom mean any more? And who had caged him and walled him off? He'd done it himself. So many small choices. The reduction of himself to a series of numbers, stored by others, controlled by others. He should have left the disintegrating cities, fled the pinched, cramped life on offer there. Broken out of the electronic net, thrown away all the passwords, gone forth to range over the land, a gaunt wolf howling at midnight.

But there isn't any land to range over any more. There isn't any place without fences, roadways, networks. Or is there? And who would go with him, be with him? Supposing he can't find Conor. Supposing, unthinkable, that Conor is dead. Would Charmaine be up to such a trip? Would she even want him to smuggle her out? Would she consider it rescue? She's never liked camping, she wouldn't want to do without her clean flowered sheets. Still, he has a brief flash of longing: the two of them, hand in hand, walking into the sunrise, all betrayals forgotten, ready for a new life, somewhere, somehow. With maybe some strike-anywhere matches, and . . . what else would they need?

He tries to visualize the world outside the wall of Consilience. But he has no real picture of that world any more. All he sees is fog.

*   *   *

Charmaine keys herself into the dispensary, locates the cabinet, codes open its door. She finds the vial and the needle. She pockets them, snaps on her latex gloves, then walks along the corridor to the left.

These corridors are always empty when she's on her way to a Procedure. Do they do that on purpose, so nobody will know who has terminated which person? Nobody, that is, except the head. And whoever is behind the head. And whoever may be watching her right now, from inside a light fixture or through a tiny lens the size of a rivet. She straightens her shoulders, adjusts her face into what she hopes is a positive but determined expression.

Here's the room. She opens the door, steps quietly in. Removes her face mask.

The man is lying on his back, attached to the gurney at five points, as he should be. His head is turned a little away from her. Most likely he's staring at the ceiling, whatever part of it he can see. And most likely the ceiling is staring back at him.

'Hello,' she says as she walks over to the gurney. 'Isn't it a lovely day? Look at all the lovely sunshine! I always find a sunny day is really cheering, don't you?'

The man's head turns toward her, as far as it can turn. The eyes meet hers. It's Stan.

'Oh my gosh,' says Charmaine. She almost drops the needle. She blinks, hoping the face will change into the face of someone else, a total stranger. But it doesn't change.

'Stan,' she whispers. 'What are they doing to you? Oh, honey. What did you do?' Has he committed a crime? What kind of a crime? It must have been very bad. But maybe there was no crime, or just a little one, because what sort of a crime would Stan have done? He's sometimes grumpy and he can lose his temper, but he's not mean as such. He's not the criminal type.

'Did you try to find me?' she says. 'Honey? You must have been crazy with worry. Did you . . .' Has his love for her driven him over the edge? Has he found out about Max and killed him? That would be terrible. A fatal threesome, like something she'd see on the TV news, back at Dust. The sleazier news.

'*Uhuhuhuh,*' says Stan. There's a trickle of drool coming out of the corner of his mouth. Tenderly she wipes it away. He's killed for her! He must have! His eyes are wide: he's pleading with her, silently.

This is more horrible than anything. She wants to rush out of the room, run back to her cell and shut the door and throw herself onto the bed and pull the covers over her head, and pretend that none of this has ever happened. But her feet don't move. All the blood is draining out of her brain. Think, Charmaine, she tells herself. But she can't think.

'Nothing bad is going to happen to you,' she

says as she usually does, but it's as if her mouth is moving by itself, with a dead voice coming out. Though the voice is trembling.

Stan doesn't believe her. *'Uhuhuhuh,'* he says. He's straining against the bands that hold him in place.

'You're going to have such a great time,' she says to him. 'We'll have this done in a jiffy.' There are tears running out of her eyes; she blots them away with her sleeve, because such tears won't do and she hopes no one has seen them, not even Stan. Especially not Stan. 'You'll be home really soon,' she tells him. 'And then we'll have a lovely dinner, and watch TV.' She moves behind him, out of his line of vision. 'And then we'll go to bed together, the way we used to. Won't that be nice?'

The tears are coming harder. She can't help herself, she's flashing on the two of them when they were first married, and planning – oh, so many things for their new life together. A house, and kids, and everything. They were so sweet then, so hopeful; so young, not like the way she is now. And then it hadn't worked out, because of circumstances. And it was a strain, so many tensions, what with the car and everything, but they'd stayed together because they had each other and they loved each other. And then they'd come here, and at first it was so lovely, so clean, everything in its place, with happy music and popcorn in front of the TV, but then . . .

Then there was that lipstick. The kiss she'd made with it. Starved. Her fault.

Get hold of yourself, Charmaine, she tells herself. Don't be sentimental. Remember it's a test.

They're watching her. They can't be serious about this. They can't expect her to – not kill, no, she will not use the *kill* word. They can't expect her to relocate her own husband.

She strokes Stan's head. 'Shhh,' she says to him. 'It's okay.' She always strokes their heads, but this time it's not any old head, it's Stan's head, with his bristly haircut. She knows every feature of his head so well, each eye, each ear, and the corner of the jaw, and the mouth with Stan's teeth in it, and the neck, and the body that's attached to it. It's almost glowing, that body: it's as clear to her as anything, each freckle and hair, as if she's looking at it through a magnifying glass. She wants to throw her arms around that body to hold it still, keep it in this present moment, because unless she can stop time, this body doesn't have a future.

She can't do the Procedure. She won't do it. She'll march out of here, back to Reception, and demand to talk with the woman's head in the box. 'I'm not falling for this,' she'll say. 'I'm not doing your stupid test, so just take a flying leap.'

But wait. What will happen then? Someone else will come in and relocate Stan. The bad thing will happen to him anyway, and whoever it is will not do it in a considerate and respectful way, not the way she does. And what will become of her,

Charmaine, if she fails the test? It won't just be back to Towel-Folding, it will be into the plastic cuffs and the hood and the shackles, like Sandi; then onto the gurney with the five straps. That must be why they put Sandi in her cell: as a warning. She's shivering now. She can hardly breathe.

'Oh, Stan,' she whispers into his left ear. 'I don't know how things got this way. I'm so sorry. Please forgive me.'

'*Uhuhuhuh*,' says Stan. It's like a dog whimper. But he's heard her, he understands. Is that a nod?

She kisses him on the forehead. Then, taking a big chance, she kisses him on the mouth, a heart-felt, lingering kiss. He doesn't kiss her back – his mouth must be paralyzed – but at least he doesn't try to bite her.

Then she sticks the needle into the vial. She watches her hands, in their latex gloves, moving like seaweed; her arms are heavy, as if she's swimming in liquid glue. Everything's in slow motion.

Standing behind Stan, she feels gently for the vein in his neck, finds it. His heart beats like percussion under her fingertips. She slides in the needle.

Then a jolt, then a spasm. Like electrocution.

Then she hits the floor.

Blackout.

PART VIII

ERASE ME

BINNED

When Stan wakes up, he's no longer strapped down. He's curled up on his side, lying on something soft. He's dizzy, and he's got a crashing headache, like three prime hangovers all at once.

He unglues his eyelids: several pairs of big white eyes with round black pupils are staring into his. What the shit are these? He struggles to sit up, loses his balance, flounders in a mound of small, yielding, fuzzy bodies. Enormous spiders? Caterpillars? Despite himself, he yelps.

A grip, Stan, he tells himself. Get two, they're cheap.

Ah. He's lying in a large bin filled with knitted blue teddy bears. Those are the white round-pupilled eyes watching him. 'Fuck,' he says. Then he adds, for good measure, 'Fucking hell!' At least he's got his voice back.

He's in a warehouse with metal rafters and a dim strip of fluorescent lighting overhead. Peering over the side of the bin, he scopes out the floor: cement. That must be why they put him on top of the teddy bears: there's nothing else in this place that's in any way soft. Someone's been thoughtful.

He feels around his own body: parts all accounted for. Thank crap they got rid of the diaper or whatever that was, though it's humiliating to visualize the removal process. They've even put some new clothes on him: an orange Positron boiler suit plus a fleece jacket. And thick socks, because it's cold as a witch's tit in here. Stands to reason: it's February. And why heat a warehouse with nothing in it but teddy bears?

What next? Where is everyone? Not a good idea to shout. Maybe get up, find the exit? But wait: one of his legs is tethered to the side of the metal bin with, yes, a nylon cuff. That must be to keep him from wandering around, leaving this warehouse, bumping into whoever's outside the door. Nothing to do but wait until Jocelyn comes and tells him what the fuck he's supposed to do.

He checks over the warehouse interior once again. More bins like the one he's lying in, arranged in a row. That's a freaking large number of teddy bears. Also – over toward what he's now identified as the doors, a small one for people, a big sliding one for trucks – there are some stacks of long boxes that look a lot like coffins, narrower at one end. He sure hopes he's not shut up in here with a bunch of soon-to-be-rotting corpses.

Which is what Charmaine must think he already is himself, the sad, deluded rabbit. Her distress wasn't faked: those tears were real. She was shaking when she felt his neck and then stuck the needle into it: she must've truly believed she was murdering him. She must've passed out right after that: in the split second before the drug hit him and he went out in a blissful swirl of coloured lights, he'd heard the impact as she did a vertical face-plant onto the floor.

If he'd had money on the proposition that Charmaine would never go through with it, he'd have lost the bet. She's amazing in her own way, Charmaine; under all that froth she has guts, he has to give her that. He thought she'd let love get in the way, that she'd lose her nerve and start whimpering and back off. That she'd maybe throw herself onto him, wreck the plan. So much for his ability to second-guess: Jocelyn's fix on Charmaine had been better than his.

Poor Charmaine, he thinks. She must be putting herself through hell right now. Remorse, guilt, and so forth. How does he feel about that? Part of him – the vengeful part – is saying, Serves her right. Her and her cheating heart, and he hopes she writhes in anguish and boo-hoos her angelic blue eyes out. Another part is saying, To be fair, Stan, you've cheated on her too, both in intention and in deed. True, you thought you were chasing a different purple passion than the one you caught. With whom you had sex on many occasions, and though your heart may not have been into it, your body was. Or into it enough. So let bygones be bygones and wipe the slate.

Yeah, says the vengeful part, but dumb Charmaine doesn't know about Jocelyn, so if you ever get back together with her you can hold her fling with Max/ Phil over her head forever. Tell her you've seen the videos. Repeat back to her the things she says on them. Turn her into a handful of soggy tissue. Wipe your boots on her: there would be some satisfaction in that. Not to mention the fact that she murdered you. She'll be your slave, she'll never dare say no to you, she'll wait on you hand and foot.

Either that or she'll put rodent poison in your coffee. There's a steely side to her. Don't discount it. So maybe you should strike first, given the chance. Dump her. Toss her clothes onto the lawn. Lock the door. Or hit her on the head with a brick. Is that what Conor would do?

You forget, he tells himself. I'll probably never be back inside that house again. Unless something goes wrong once I'm outside the wall, I'll never be back in Consilience. That life is gone. I'm supposed to be dead.

Should he be angry about that? Maybe not: being dead is for his own good. On the other hand, he didn't ask to be dead, he didn't wish it upon himself. He's simply been assigned, as if he's a member of an army in which he's never enlisted. He's been fucking drafted, against his will, and meanwhile he's in here chained to a binful of knitted bears, and that sadistic bitch Jocelyn seems to have forgotten all about him, and despite the headache he's starting to feel hungry. Plus he's freezing his nuts off. It's so cold that he can see his breath.

He lies down again, covers himself with blue teddy bears. They'll be some insulation. The only thing to do right now is go to sleep.

TEATIME

When Charmaine wakes up, she's alone. And she's back in her house. Their house, hers and Stan's; or rather hers and Stan's once, but now only hers, because Stan will never be in this house again. Never, never, never, never, never. She starts to cry.

She's lying on the sofa, the royal blue one with the pretty off-white lilies; though with her face up close to it like this, she can see that it needs cleaning, because someone's been spilling coffee on it, and other things. She can remember pretending to dislike this pattern, pretending to want to change it, pretending she was going to look at fabric swatches as an excuse to leave the house early on switchover days so she could be with Max. Stan could be counted on to take no interest whatsoever in slipcovers or wallpaper or any of those things. His lack of interest once annoyed her – weren't they supposed to be home-building together? – but after that she'd welcomed it, because it was a blind spot of his that gave her some time with Max. Now it makes her cry because Stan is dead.

There. She said it. *Dead.* She cries harder. She's sobbing, her breath coming in staccato gulps. Stan, what have I done to you? she thinks. Where have you gone?

Though she's crying as hard as she can, she nevertheless notices a strange thing: she's no longer wearing her orange boiler suit. Instead she has on a peach-and-grey checked outfit in a light wool weave, with a flared skirt and a fitted jacket. There's supposed to be a matching blouse, which is peach imitation silk, with peach flamenco dancer ruffles on the front, but that isn't the blouse she has on, which is a blue floral print and doesn't go with the outfit at all. She selected the peach-and-grey ensemble with care from the 'Smile in Style' section of the digital catalogue just after she and Stan signed in to Consilience. It was a choice between the peach and grey and the other combos, the navy blue and white, which was a little too Chanel for her, and the lime green and orange – no contest there because she can't wear lime green, it washes her out.

Plus she folded up this outfit and stored it in her pink locker in the cellar along with her other civilian clothes right before going in for her latest stint at Positron. So someone has the code to her locker, and someone has been rummaging through her things. The very same somebody must have taken off the boiler suit and dressed her up in the checked outfit, with the wrong blouse.

'Feeling better now?' says a voice. She looks up

265

from the sofa. Holy heck, it's Aurora from Human Resources, with the overdone face job that makes her look like a gecko: unmoving cheek muscles, pop eyes. Aurora is about the last person she wants to see, not only here and now but ever.

She's carrying a tray – Charmaine's tray, she picked it herself, from the catalogue's tray options – with a teapot on it. Charmaine's teapot, though it came with the house. Charmaine feels invaded. How dare Aurora barge into her home while she herself is passed out on the sofa and simply take over the kitchen as if she owns it?

'I've made you some nice hot tea,' says Aurora with a pitying, maddening demi-smile. 'I understand you've had a shock. You hit your head when you fainted, but they don't think you were concussed. You should have a CAT-scan though, just to be sure. I've arranged that for you, later today.'

Charmaine can't get out a word. She struggles to control her tears. She's heaving, she's gasping; snot is running out of her nose. 'Go ahead, have a good cry,' says Aurora, as if granting royal permission. 'A good cry clears the air. Not to mention the sinuses,' she adds: her version of a joke.

'Did you open my locker?' Charmaine manages to squeeze out.

'Now why would I do that?' says Aurora.

'Someone did,' says Charmaine. 'Because I'm wearing different clothes.' The thought of Aurora changing her clothes like a Barbie doll's while she was out cold gives her a shuddery feeling all over.

'I expect you did it yourself, and just don't remember it. You must have had an episode of temporary amnesia,' says Aurora in that know-it-all voice of hers. 'A shock like the one you've had can bring on a fugue state. You were on the sofa when I got here ten minutes ago.' She sets the tea tray down on the coffee table. 'The brain is very protective, it decides what we choose to remember.'

Charmaine feels anger flooding her, pushing out the grief. If she'd been down in the cellar getting stuff out of her locker she'd remember it, in addition to which she never would've picked this blouse. What kind of a fashion loser do they think she is? Who brought her back here from Medications Administration, anyway?

She pulls herself upright, swings her legs down onto the floor. She absolutely, totally does not want Aurora to see her in this state, the state of a mud puddle. She wipes her nose and eyes on her sleeve since a tissue is lacking, brushes the damp hair back off her forehead, pulls her face into a semblance of order. 'Thank you,' she says as crisply as she can. 'Actually, I'm fine.'

Does Aurora know about what Charmaine has done to Stan? Maybe she can bluff, conceal her weakness. Say she fainted because she had her period or low blood sugar or something.

'Well, that's very strong of you,' says Aurora. 'I mean, not many people would have such a firm

267

sense of duty and loyalty.' She sits down on the sofa beside Charmaine. 'I have to admire you, I really do.' She pours the tea into the cup – Charmaine's cup, with the pink rosebuds that Stan never liked. But he never liked tea anyway, he was a coffee kind of guy, with cream and two sugars. She represses a sob.

'I really should apologize, on behalf of Management,' says Aurora, setting the cup down on the coffee table in front of Charmaine. 'It was so tactless of Logistics.' She's put a cup for herself on the tray; she busies herself with filling it. Charmaine takes a gulp of tea. It does help.

'What do you mean?' she says, though she knows perfectly well what Aurora means. Aurora's enjoying this. She's relishing it.

'They should have booked you for someone else's Procedure,' says Aurora. 'They shouldn't have put you through such an ordeal.' She measures the sugar into her own cup, stirs it.

'What ordeal?' says Charmaine. 'I was just doing my job.' But it's no use: she can see that in the tidy non-smile on Aurora's over-lifted face.

'He was your husband, wasn't he?' says Aurora. 'Your most recent Procedure. According to the records. Whatever the state of your private life together, and that is none of our business and I don't want to pry, but whatever that state, carrying out the Procedure must have been . . . truly a difficult decision for you to make.' She cranks up her smile, a smile of smarmy understanding.

Charmaine feels like whacking her across the face. What do you know about it, you shrivelled-up prissy-pants? she would like to yell.

'I just do my job,' she says defensively. 'I follow the prescribed routine. In all cases.'

'I appreciate your desire to – shall we say – blur the outlines,' says Aurora. 'But we happen to have taped the entire process, as we do at random, for quality control. It was very . . . it was touching. Watching you struggle with your emotions. I was moved, I really was, we all were! We could see you faltering, it was only natural, I mean, who wouldn't? You'd have to be inhuman. But you did overcome them, those emotions! Don't think we haven't noted that. The overcoming. Of the emotions. In fact, our chief himself, Ed, would like to thank you in person, and a little bird told me, it's not official, but I think there might be a promotion in the offing, because if anyone deserves it for the heroic—'

'I think you should leave now,' says Charmaine, setting down her cup. In one more minute she is going to throw that cup and everything in it. Smack-dab in the middle of Aurora's prefab face.

'Of course,' says Aurora with a half-smile like a perfectly symmetrical slice of lemon. 'I do feel your pain. It must be so, well, so painful. The pain that you feel. We've booked a trauma counsellor for you, because of course you will be experiencing survivor's guilt. Well, more than just *survivor's*

269

guilt, because with a survivor, all they did was survive, whereas you, I mean . . .'

Charmaine stands up abruptly, knocking over her cup. 'Please get out,' she says as steadily as she can. 'Right now.'

Go on, says her little inner voice. Bash this teapot over her head. Cut her throat with the bread knife. Then drag her downstairs and hide the body in your pink locker.

But Charmaine refrains. There would be telltale bloodstains on the rug. Plus, if they'd videoed her with Stan and the needle, they might have a way of doing that inside this house as well.

'You'll feel differently tomorrow,' says Aurora, standing too, still smiling her flat, stretched smile. 'We all adjust, in time. The funeral is on Thursday, that's in two days. Electrical accident at the chicken facility, is the explanation we're giving; it will be on the news tonight. Everyone at the funeral will want to offer condolences, so you should be prepared. I'll arrange a car for six-thirty, to pick you up for your concussion CAT scan; it's after hours, but they'll be waiting for you specially. In your state, you shouldn't be driving your scooter.'

'I hate you!' Charmaine yells. 'Evil witch!' But she waits until after the door has closed.

COFFEETIME

'**S**tan,' says a voice. 'Time to move.' Stan opens his eyes: it's Jocelyn. She's shaking his arm. He stares at her groggily.

'About fucking time,' he says. 'And thanks for leaving me in cold storage. Do you mind unshackling me? I need to take a leak.' He has an image of how the next few minutes would go if this were a spy film. He'd deck Jocelyn, knock her out, find her keys, snap her onto the bin, steal her phone so she couldn't call for help when she woke up – she must have a phone – and then go out and save the world all by himself.

'Don't do anything spontaneous,' says Jocelyn. 'I'm the only thing standing between you and rigor mortis. So pay very close attention, because I can only go over this once. I'm due at a top-level meeting, so we have almost no time.' She's wearing her business get-up – the trim suit, the little hoop earrings, the grey stockings. Strange to think of her prone underneath him or naked on top of him, where she has often been – legs splayed, mouth open, hair wild, as if blown by a squall. That seems like a different planet.

271

She unlocks his tether, helps him to climb down out of the teddy bear bin. He's still wobbly. He staggers in behind the bin, takes a piss – he can't see any other place to do it – then staggers back out again.

She has a small thermos of coffee with her, thank fuck for that. He guzzles greedily, washing down the two painkiller pills that she hands him. 'For the headache,' she says. 'Sorry about it, but that drug's the only one we could use. Mimics the effects of the real thing but without the finale.'

'How close did I get?' says Stan.

'Nothing worse than a strong anesthetic,' she says. 'Think of it as a holiday for your brain.'

'So,' says Stan. 'I was wrong about Charmaine. She went for the bull's-eye.'

'She couldn't have been better,' says Jocelyn with an irritating smile. 'Acting wouldn't come close.'

You callous asshole, he thinks. 'You know you're a triple-grade shit,' he says. 'Putting her through that. You've fucked up her head for life.'

'She's a little shaken, yes,' says Jocelyn evenly. 'For the present. But we'll take care of her.' Stan doesn't find this too reassuring: *take care of her* could mean something less than kind.

'Good,' he says nonetheless.

'But I expect you're hungry,' says Jocelyn.

'Understatement,' says Stan. Now that he thinks about it, he's ravenous.

Out of her handbag Jocelyn produces a cheese sandwich that he scarfs down in one bite. He could use a couple more of those, plus some chocolate cake and a beer. 'Where exactly the fuck am I?' he says, once he's swallowed it all down.

'In a warehouse,' says Jocelyn.

'Yeah, I got that. But am I still inside Positron Prison?'

'Yes,' says Jocelyn. 'It's part of the facility.'

'So, are those coffins?' He nods toward the oblong boxes.

Jocelyn laughs. 'No. They're shipping crates.'

Stan decides not to ask what they might be shipping. 'Okay, so,' he says, 'where do I go? Unless you plan to keep me in here with these fucking bears.'

'I can understand your irritation,' says Jocelyn. 'Bear with me, pardon the pun.' She gives him a big-toothed grin. 'There are two things you have to remember, for your own safety during your time here. First, your name is now Waldo.'

'Waldo?' he says. 'Can't I be . . . Shit!' In no way does he see himself as a Waldo. Wasn't that some kind of cartoon rabbit on kids' TV? Or a fish? No, that was Nemo. A cartoon thing, anyway. *Where's Waldo?*

'It's a databank move,' says Jocelyn. 'You're replacing a previous Waldo. He had an accident. Don't look at me like that, it was a real accident, involving a soldering iron. You're inheriting his code, his identity. I've gone into the system and spliced in your biometrics.'

'Okay,' he says. 'So I'm fucking Waldo. What's the second thing?'

'You'll be on a Possibilibots team,' says Jocelyn. 'Just watch the others and follow orders.'

'Possibilibots?' says Stan. Is this something he's supposed to know? He can't place the term; he's feeling dizzy again. 'Any more coffee?'

'Possibilibots makes a Dutch-designed line of exact-replica female sex aids,' says Jocelyn. 'For home and export. I'm sure you'll find the work interesting.'

'You mean those prostibots? The sex robots? The guys at the scooter depot were talking about them.'

'That's the unofficial name for them, yes. Once they're put together and tested for performance, they're packed into these boxes' – she indicates the stacks of coffin-shaped containers – 'and shipped outside Consilience, for deployment in amusement centres and other franchise areas. The Belgians are nuts about them, certain models. And some of the other models are very big in Southeast Asia.'

He thinks for a moment. 'And who will they think this Waldo is? The one I'm supposed to be? Won't they wonder where the other Waldo has gone?'

'They never knew that Waldo. They don't even know there was a Waldo. He was deployed elsewhere. But if they check the databank, you'll be Waldo in there. Don't worry, just keep saying your name is Waldo. And remember, the job here is the key to transferring you safely to the outside world.'

'When do we do that?' says Stan. And through

274

some beam-me-up-Scotty sleight of hand? An underground tunnel? Or what?

'You'll be approached by someone here. The password is "Tiptoe Through the Tulips." I can't tell you any more, in case you're suspected and questioned. In a perfect world I'd be overseeing the questioning, but it's not a perfect world.'

'Why would I be questioned?' says Stan. He doesn't like any of this. Now that he's getting close to it, he no longer wants to be shipped to the outside world, because who knows what extreme crap is going on out there? It could be total anarchy by now. Given the choice, he'd elect to stay in Consilience, with Charmaine. If only he could rewind to day one, wipe all that Jasmine crap, treat Charmaine the way she wanted to be treated, whatever that was, so she'd never go wandering off. The mere thought of her, and of the house he once found so boring, makes him feel weepy.

But he can't rewind anything. He's stuck in the present. What are his options? He wonders what would happen if he snitched on Jocelyn. Her and her philandering scumbucket of a husband. But who would he snitch to? It would have to be someone in Surveillance, and whoever it is would surely report directly to Jocelyn herself, and then he'd be dog food.

He'll have to take his chances, go through with the Waldo charade, be Jocelyn's courier, in the name of freedom and democracy, no doubt. Not that he gives much of a flying fuck about freedom and democracy, since they haven't performed that well for him personally.

'You're unlikely to be questioned so long as you stick to the Waldo cover,' says Jocelyn. 'But there are no unsinkable boats. I'm late for that meeting. Here's your Waldo nametag. All clear?'

'Sure,' he says, though it's clear as rust paint. 'Where do I go now?'

'Through that door,' says Jocelyn. 'Good luck, Stan. You're doing fine so far. I'm counting on you.' She pecks him on the cheek.

His impulse is to wrap his arms around her, clutch on to her like a lifeline, but he resists it.

AJAR

Charmaine has a little time before the car arrives to take her for the scan; not that she thinks she needs a scan, but better to humour them. She wanders around the house – her house – putting things back in order. The tea towels, the pot holders. She hates it when the kitchen implements are left lying around, like the corkscrew. That corkscrew has definitely been put to use, by Max and his wife. They've always been slack on the tidying details.

In the living room there's a table lamp out of place. She'll fix that later: she doesn't feel like crawling around on the floor looking for the wall socket. And there's something in the DVD player of the flatscreen TV: its little light is flashing. What has Max been watching? Not that she's still obsessed with him, not after the shock she's had. Killing Stan has wiped Max from her mind.

She pushes Play.

Oh. Oh *no*.

The blood rushes to her face, the screen swims. It's shadowy, it's out of focus, but it's her. Her and Max, in one of those empty houses. Racing toward each other, colliding, toppling to the floor. And those sounds coming out of her, like an animal in a trap . . . This is awful. She pushes Eject, snatches up the silver disc. Who's been watching it? If it's only Max, reliving their moments together, then she's kind of safe.

What to do with it? Putting it in the trash would be fatal: someone might find it. And if she breaks it into pieces, all the more reason for them to reconstruct it. She takes it into the kitchen, slides it in between the refrigerator and the wall. There. Not a terrific hidey-hole, but she's improvised hidey-holes in the past, and that worked out okay, so it's better than nothing.

Act normal, Charmaine, she tells herself. Supposing you can remember what normal is.

She's unsteady on her feet, but she makes it to the powder room off the front hall, where she splashes water on her face, then wipes it off and leans in closer to the mirror. Her hair's a bird's nest, her eyes are puffy. Maybe some cold teabags? And she can spray product on her hair, which will keep it in place for the short-term.

Stan didn't like the scent of the hair product: he said it made her smell like paint remover. She's nostalgic even for his annoying put-downs.

Don't cry any more, she tells herself. Just do one thing at a time. Get from hour to hour and day to day like a frog jumping on lily pads. Not that she has ever seen a frog doing that except on TV.

Her makeup and stuff is in the bedroom. She stands at the bottom of the stairs, looking up. It seems like a long climb. Maybe down to the cellar first, check out her locker. Get out of this stupid floral print blouse, find the right one, the peach with the ruffles. It's easier to go downstairs than up. As long as you don't fall down them, Charmaine, she warns herself.

Her knees are weak. Hold on to the railing. That's the girl, as Grandma Win would say. Put one foot on the first stair, then the other one beside it, like when you were three. You need to take care of yourself, because who else will?

There. Standing on the solid cellar floor, swaying like a, like a. Swaying.

Now she's standing beside the four lockers, which are side by side. They're horizontal, with lids that lift up, like freezer chests. Her locker, pink. Stan's, green. Then the lockers of the Alternates, which are purple and red. The red one is Max's, and the purple one belongs to that wife of his, whom Charmaine hates on principle. If she could wave a magic wand and make both of those lockers disappear, she would, because then she could make that whole chunk of the past disappear as well. None of it would ever have happened, and Stan would still be alive.

She leans over to punch in the code for her locker. The lid is open a little, from whoever has been rummaging in her things. Here's the peach blouse. She takes off her suit jacket and the blue print blouse and struggles into the peach one. Struggles because one of her shoulders is sore: she must have hit it when she passed out. Doing up the buttons is hard because of her shaky fingers, but she manages it. She puts the suit jacket back on. Now she feels less discordant.

And here are all her civilian clothes, including the ones she had on the last time she checked in at Positron. The cherry-coloured pullover, the white bra. Someone must have brought them back here and put them away; they must know her code. Well, of course they know her code, because they know everyone's code.

She used to hide things in this locker. She used to think they were truly hidden. How ditzy that had been. She'd bought that cheap fuchsia lipstick that smelled like bubble gum so she could put kisses on her notes for Max. *I'm starved for you,* silly things like that. She should get rid of it. Bury it in the backyard.

She'd wrapped that lipstick in a handkerchief and tucked it into the toe of one of her shoes with the high heels, right here.

But it's gone. It isn't there.

She feels around with her hands. She needs to bring a flashlight: it's most likely rolled out somehow when whoever it was pawed through her stuff. She'll find it later, and when she does she'll throw it far, far away. It's a memento, and *memento* means something that helps you remember. She'd rather have a forgetto.

It's a joke. She has made a joke.

You are a shallow, frivolous person, says the little voice. Can't you keep it in your stupid head that Stan is . . .

Not another word, she tells it. She shuts the top of her locker, codes it CLOSED. As she turns to leave, she sees that Stan's green locker is ajar. Someone's been in there too. She knows she shouldn't look in. It will be bad for her to see Stan's familiar clothes, all neatly folded – the summer T-shirts, the fleece jacket he used to wear when he pruned the hedge. She'll start thinking about how those clothes are empty of Stan forever, and she'll start crying again, and then it will be the puffy eyes, only twice as puffy.

Better to erase it all. She'll call the Consilience removal service tomorrow and have them come in and take away Stan's clothes. She can start anew, in a whole different place; they'll put her in one of the condos for singles. Maybe there's a special building for widows. Even though she'll be a lot younger than the average widow, she can do those widow things with the other widows. Play cards. Look out the window. Watch the leaves change colour. It will be peaceful at any rate, being a widow.

So she should not upset herself by messing around with Stan's coffin. With Stan's locker. But she walks over anyway and lifts the lid.

The locker's empty.

ERASE ME

She's sitting on the cellar floor. How long has she been doing that? And why was it such a shock, finding Stan's locker empty? She should have expected it. Naturally they would come and clear away his things. To save her the distress. They're very thoughtful, the Consilience team.

Maybe it was that gloating meanie, Aurora, she thinks. Can't keep her nosy nose out of it. Rolling around in my sadness like a dog in poo.

The doorbell rings.

She could just sit here until they go away. She's not up to getting her head CAT-scanned, not right now.

But the bell rings again, and then she can hear the door opening. They have the door code, of course they do. She pulls herself upright, makes it to the cellar stairs, and climbs.

There's a woman in the living room. She's bending over, doing something to the TV, even though it's off. Dark hair, a suit.

'Hello,' says Charmaine. 'Sorry I was late answering the door. I was just down in the cellar, I was . . .'

The woman straightens up, turns. She smiles. 'I'm here to take you to your CAT scan appointment,' she says.

The small hoop earrings, the bangs, the square teeth. It's the head from the Reception box at Medications Administration.

Charmaine gasps. 'Oh my gosh,' she says. She sits down on the sofa like a stone falling. 'You're the head!'

'Excuse me?' says the woman.

'You're the talking head! At Reception. In the box. You told me to kill Stan,' says Charmaine. 'And now he's dead!' She should not be saying these words, but she can't help it.

'You've had a shock,' says the woman in a compassionate voice that does not fool Charmaine for one second. They pretend to be sympathetic, they pretend they're helping. But they have other ideas in mind.

'You said it was a test,' says Charmaine. 'You said I had to follow the Procedure, to show I was loyal. So I darn well followed it, because I am darn loyal, and now Stan's dead! Because of you!' She can't stop the tears. Here they come again, out of her puffy eyes, but she doesn't care.

'You're confused,' says the woman calmly. 'It's normal to blame others. The mind in shock reverts to the habits of childhood, and provides agency; we find it hard to grasp the randomness of the universe.'

'That is total garbage and you know it,' says Charmaine. 'It was you. You were in that Reception box. What I want to know is why? Why did you want to kill my Stan? He was a good man! What did he ever do to you?'

'It's important for you to see a doctor,' says the woman. 'They'll check for concussion, then give you a sedative to help you sleep. I'm so sorry about your husband, and the terrible accident at the Positron Prison chicken facility. The fire was caused by faulty wiring. But because of your husband's swift action, most of the chickens were saved, as well as a number of his co-workers. He was heroic. You should be proud of him.'

I have never heard such a bag of pure twaddle in my entire life, thinks Charmaine. But what should I do? Play along, pretend to believe her? If I don't, if I keep on telling the truth and pushing her to tell it as well, she'll say I'm unstable. Disruptive, hallucinating, off the charts. Call in the Surveillance heavies, haul me off to a cell, shackle me to a bed like Sandi, then stick a drug into me; and then, if I don't so-called improve, it might get terminal.

She takes a breath. Breathe out, breathe in.

What they want is compliance. The opposite of disruptive. 'Oh, I *am* proud of Stan,' she says. Gosh, does her voice ever sound so phony. 'I am so proud of him, I really am. I'm not surprised he sacrificed himself to save other people, and the chickens too. He was always such an unselfish man. And an animal lover,' she adds for good measure.

The woman smiles her deceptive smile. Underneath

that business suit she's muscular, thinks Charmaine. She could tackle me, have me down in an instant. I wouldn't win a scuffle with her. And she's not wearing a nametag. How do I know she is who she says she is?

'I'm glad you agree,' says the woman. 'Keep that story firmly in mind. Consilience Management will do whatever is required to help you with the grieving process. Is there anything you feel you need right now? We could send someone over to stay with you tonight, for instance. Provide some company, make you a cup of tea. Aurora from Human Resources has kindly offered.'

'Thank you,' says Charmaine demurely. 'That's very kind of her, but I feel sure I can manage.'

'We'll see,' says the woman. 'Now it's time for us to get you to that CAT scan appointment. They're waiting for you. The car's outside. Do you have a coat?'

'I think it's in my locker,' says Charmaine, but when the woman opens the hall closet, there it is, her coat: hanging on a hanger, ready for her. It's like a stage prop.

A pale pink smear lingers in the west, from where the sun has set; there's a light dusting of snow. The woman takes Charmaine's arm as they go down the walk. There's a dark silhouette in the front of the car: the driver. 'We'll sit in the back,' says the woman. She opens the door, stands aside for Charmaine. They certainly do treat you like

285

royalty when they decide to take care of you, thinks Charmaine.

Now the inside car light is on. As she gets into the car, Charmaine sees the driver's profile. She gives a small scream. 'Max!' she says. Her heart opens like a hot rose. *Oh save me!*

The driver turns his head, looks at her. It's Max all right. How could she ever forget him? His eyes, his dark hair. That mouth. Soft but hard, urgent, demanding . . .

'Pardon me?' says the man. His face is immobile.

'Max, I know it's you!' she says. How dare he pretend not to recognize her!

'You're mistaken,' says the driver. 'I'm Phil. I drive for Surveillance.'

'Max, what in heck is going on? Why are you lying?' Charmaine almost shouts.

The man has unpinned his nametag. 'Look,' he says, handing it to her, 'Phil. That's what it says here. My nametag. That's me.'

'Is there a problem?' says the woman, who's now sliding into the back seat beside Charmaine.

'She says my name is Max,' says the driver. He sounds truly puzzled.

'But it is!' says Charmaine. 'Max! It's me! You lived for our next meet-up! You said that a hundred times!' She reaches for him over the car seat; he pulls back.

'I'm sorry,' he says. 'You've confused me with someone else.'

'You think you can hide behind that stupid nametag?' Charmaine says. Her voice is rising.

'I'm sure we can set this straight,' says the woman, but Charmaine ignores her.

'You're trying to erase me!' she cries. 'But you can't change one single minute of everything we did! You loved it, you lived for it, that's what you said!' She needs to stop, she needs to stop talking. She's not going to win this one, because what proof does she have? Except the video: she's got the video. But it's back in her kitchen.

'I've never seen her before in my life,' says the man. He sounds aggrieved, as if Charmaine has wounded his feelings.

This is hurtful. Why is he doing it? Unless – Charmaine, don't be so dumb! – unless this woman is his wife or something. Now that would make sense. If only she could be alone with him!

'I apologize,' the woman says to him. 'I should have warned you. She's had a shock, she's a little delusional.' She lowers her voice. 'That was her husband today, at the chicken facility fire. It's a shame, he was so brave. We'll go to the hospital now, please.'

'No problem,' says the man. He puts the car in gear. Charmaine hears the locks clicking shut. Holy shoot, she thinks. I am darn well not delusional. You can't be mistaken about a man who's done those kinds of things to you. With you. But what if that woman knows about us? What if the two of them have planned this thing together? Is this about Max wanting to get rid of me? Blow me off, like a failed blind date? What a coward.

Don't cry, she tells herself. Now is not the time. There's nobody on your side.

She'll need to keep her wits about her if she wants to lead any kind of a half-decent life in Consilience from now on. The life of a respected widow, keeping her mouth zipped, her smile at the ready. Rather than ending up in a padded cell; or worse, as a blank line in the databank.

She'll have to bury the truth about Stan, and the truth about Max too, as far down inside her own head as she can. Make sure she doesn't blurt things out, ask the wrong questions the way Sandi did. Or give the wrong answers, like Veronica. Even if she could tell someone, and even if they believed her, they'd pretend not to, because they'd see the truth as botulism. They'd fear contamination.

She's on her own.

PART IX

POSSIBILIBOTS

LUNCH

Stan's in the Possibilibots cafeteria with the guys from his team – his new team, the team he's just been inserted into. He's having a beer, that weak, urine-coloured beer they're brewing now; plus a side of onion rings and some fries to share, and a platter of Buffalo wings. Sucking the fat off a wing, he reflects that he himself might have tended the owner of this wing when it had been covered with feathers and attached to a chicken.

The guys on his team look normal enough, just ordinary guys sitting around in the cafeteria having lunch, like him. Not young, not old; fit enough, though a couple of them are getting plump around the middle. They've all got nametags. His says WALDO, and he really needs to remember that his name is Waldo now, not Stan. All he has to do is to stay Waldo until someone hands him the flash-drive with the hot-potato crap he's supposed to be smuggling out and reveals what he's supposed to do to get himself past the wall. Or else until he figures out how to make a break for it on his own.

Tiptoe Through the Tulips is supposed to be the

signal, the secret handshake. Will his unknown contact speak it or sing it? He hopes there won't be singing. Who chose that annoying tune? Jocelyn, naturally: along with her other complex personality traits, she has a warped sense of humour. She'd relish the idea of compelling some poor sod to croak out that brain-damaged ditty. Not one of the guys at lunch looks like the Tiptoe Through the Tulips kind; nor do any of them look like a possible undercover contact. But then, they wouldn't.

Waldo, Waldo, he tells himself. *You are Waldo now.* It's a feeble name, like something in a kids' kitten book. The other names around the table are more solid: Derek, Kevin, Gary, Tyler, Budge. He's only just met them, he knows nothing about them, so he has to keep his mouth shut and his ears open. And they know nothing about him except that he's been sent to fill a vacancy on their team.

There've been a lot of yuks at the lunch table, a lot of in-jokes that Stan didn't catch. He's trying to read the facial expressions: behind the genial grins there's a barrier, behind which a language foreign to him is being spoken, a language of obscure references. Around the room, at other cafeteria tables, there are other knots of men. Other Possibilibots teams would be his guess. He's doing a lot of guessing.

The cafeteria is a long room with light green walls. Frosted-glass windows down one side: you can't see out. On the side without the windows there are a couple of retro-looking posters. One of them shows a little girl of six or seven in a ruffled white nightie, rubbing one eye sleepily, a blue teddy bear cradled in the crook of her other arm. There's a steaming cup of something in the foreground. SLEEP TIGHT, says the slogan. It's like a hundred-year-old poster for a malted bedtime drink.

The other poster shows a pretty blond girl in a red and white polka-dot bikini and a pin-up pose, hands clasped around one drawn-up knee, the foot in a slingback red high heel; the other leg extended, the shoe dangling from her toe. Pouty red lips, a wink. Some writing in, it must be, Dutch.

'Looks like a real girl, yeah?' says Derek, nodding at the pin-up girl. 'But it's not.'

'Fooled me too,' says Tyler. 'They did that poster in a fifties style. Those Dutch are so far ahead of us!'

'Yeah, they've passed the legislation and everything,' says Gary. 'They anticipated the future.'

'What's it say?' Stan asks. He knows what they're making at Possibilibots. Replica women; slut machines, some call them. There was earnest talk about them among the fellow scooter repair guys: the real-life pain they might prevent, the money they might make. Maybe all women should be robots, he thinks with a tinge of acid: the flesh-and-blood ones are out of control.

'It's Dutch, so who knows what it says exactly,' says Kevin. 'But something like *Better than real.*'

'And is it?' says Stan. 'Better than real?' He's feeling more relaxed now – nobody suspects him of not being Waldo – so he can risk a few offhand questions.

'Not exactly. But the voice options are great,' says Derek. 'You can have silent, or, like, moans and screams, even a few words: *more, harder,* like that.'

'In my books they're not the same,' says Gary, head on one side as if tasting a new menu choice. 'I didn't go for it that much, myself. It was too, you know, mechanical. But some guys prefer it. No limp-dick worries if you fuck up.'

'So to speak,' says Tyler, and they all laugh.

'You need to fiddle with the settings,' says Kevin, reaching over for the last onion ring. 'It's like a bicycle seat, you need to make the adjustments. You guys want another round of beers? I'll get them.'

'I vote yes,' says Tyler. 'And throw in some more of those hot wings.'

'Maybe you just picked the wrong model,' says Budge to Gary.

'I don't think they'll ever replace the living and breathing,' says Gary.

'They said that about e-books,' says Kevin. 'You can't stop progress.'

'With the Platinum grade, they do breathe,' says Derek. 'In, out. I prefer that. With the ones that don't breathe, you sense there's something missing.'

'Some have got heartbeats too,' says Kevin. 'If you want to get fancy. That's the Platinum Plus.'

'They should stick some knee pads into the kit, anyway,' says Gary. 'Mine got stuck in high gear, I skinned my knees, damn near crippled myself, and I couldn't turn the damn thing off.'

'You might like that feature in a real one,' says Kevin, who's back with the beers and wings. 'No Turn-off button.'

'Trouble is, with some of the real ones, there's no Turn-on button,' says Tyler, and this time it's laughs all round. Stan joins in: he can relate to that.

'But you need to remind yourself they're not alive; they're that good, the top grade anyway,' Derek says to Stan. Of all of them, he seems the biggest booster.

'We should let old Waldo try it out,' says Tyler. 'We all did, first chance we had! Let him have a test run. What about it, Waldo?'

'It's not officially allowed,' says Gary. 'Unless you've been assigned for it.'

'But they turn a blind eye,' says Tyler.

Stan gives what he hopes is a lascivious grin. 'I'm game,' he says.

'Bad boy,' says Tyler lightly.

'So you don't mind bending the rules,' says Budge. 'Pushing the boundaries.' He gives Stan a genial smile, the smile of an indulgent uncle.

'Depends, I guess,' Stan says. Has he made a mistake, put himself at risk? 'There's boundaries, and then there's boundaries.' That should hold it steady for a while.

'Okay then,' says Budge. 'First the tour, then the test run. Step this way.'

EGG CUP

Charmaine slept poorly last night, even though she was in her own bed. Of course this bed isn't really hers, it belongs to Consilience, but still, it's a bed she's used to. Or she *was* used to it when Stan was in there with her. But now it feels alien to her, like one of those scary movies where you wake up and find you're on a spaceship, and you've been abducted, and people you thought were your friends have had their brains taken over, and they want to do kinky probes; because Stan isn't in this bed with her any more and he will never be in it again. Face it, she tells herself: you kissed him goodbye and then you stuck the needle into him, and he died. That's reality, and it doesn't matter how much you cry about it now because he's still dead and you can't bring him back.

Think about flowers, she tells herself. That's what Grandma Win would tell her. But she can't think about them. Flowers are for funerals, that's all she can see. White flowers; like the white room, the white ceiling.

She hadn't meant to kill him. She hadn't meant

to kill *him*. But how else could she have acted? They wanted her to use her head and discard her heart; but it wasn't so easy, because the heart goes last and hers was still clinging on inside her all the time she was readying the needle, which is why she was crying the whole time. Then the next thing she knew, she was lying on her own sofa with a headache.

At least she didn't have a concussion. That's what they told her at the Consilience clinic after the CAT scan. They'd sent her home with three kinds of pills – a pink one, a green one, and a yellow one – to help her relax, they said. She hadn't taken those pills, however: she didn't know what was in them. Slipping a person some kind of knockout thing was what those aliens did before they got you onto their spaceship, and then you woke up with tubes going into you, right in the middle of a probe. There aren't any aliens really; but still, she didn't trust what might happen to her while she was sleeping like a baby.

'You'll sleep like a baby' was what Aurora had said about those pills. She'd been at the clinic, waiting for Charmaine. They were all in on it, whatever it was: Aurora, and Max, and that woman who'd driven her to the clinic, the woman with dark hair and hoop earrings.

Thinking about what happened, Charmaine feels maybe she shouldn't have blurted out, 'You're the head in the box!' Telling a person they were a head in a box was too blunt.

She'd messed up on the subject of Max too. She shouldn't have let on she knew him at all, much less make those pathetic demands. But it was too stupid, him claiming his name was Phil. Phil! She could never have flung herself into the arms of a man called Phil. Phils were pharmacists, they were never in the daytime-TV shows, they had no inner shadows and banked-up flames of desire. And Max did, even in that ugly driver's uniform he was wearing. She knew he longed for her; she's sensitive, she has an instinct for knowing that.

Then she got it: she should act dumb, because they were messing with her head. She'd seen movies like that: people disguising themselves as other people and pretending not to know you; then, when you accused them of doing it, they'd say you were crazy. So it's safer to go along with whatever made-up version of themselves they want to put out there.

Though if she could corner Max alone, and make him kiss her, and get a firm grip on his belt buckle – a familiar buckle, one she could undo in her sleep – then his cover story would smoke and burn and turn to ash, like the flammable thing it is.

After they'd driven her back from the clinic and she'd crawled into bed, Charmaine kept as quiet as a mouse. She couldn't even pace the floor or wail because Aurora had insisted on sleeping in the guest bedroom. Someone needed to stay with Charmaine, said Aurora. Considering the shock of the chicken facility tragedy, Charmaine might do some rash thing that Aurora was obviously dying to spell out.

'We wouldn't want to lose you too,' she said in her falsely considerate voice, the one she used to demote people. The dark-haired woman, who'd said she was from Surveillance, had backed Aurora up. *Strongly advisable* was the phrase she used about Aurora staying over. Though, she added, Charmaine was free to make her own decisions.

Like heck I am, Charmaine thought. 'Leave me the heck alone!' she'd wanted to scream. But you didn't argue with Surveillance. Pick your battles, her Grandma Win used to say, and there was no point in getting into a tug-of-war over whether or not pushy Aurora with her pulled-back fail of a face was going to muss up Charmaine's neatly ironed floral sheets.

And muss up the clean towels. And waste a rose-scented miniature guest soap; though she and Stan never had any guests, because no one you'd known before could get into Consilience for a visit, you couldn't even phone them or email them. But just thinking you might some day have a real guest, like an old high school friend, people you hoped wouldn't stay long and they most likely hoped it too, but still, it was nice to catch up – just thinking about it was a comfort. She tried to see Aurora as that sort of a guest, instead of a watchdog; and that was when she finally went to sleep.

★   ★   ★

'Rise and shine,' says Aurora's voice. Darn it if she isn't barging in the door, carrying Charmaine's tray with Charmaine's teacup on it. 'I've made you a wake-up tea. My goodness, you really did need that beauty sleep!'

'Why, what time is it?' Charmaine asks groggily. She acts groggier than she is so Aurora will think she's taken those pills. She'd flushed a couple of them down the toilet, because she wouldn't put it past Aurora to count.

'It's noon,' says Aurora, setting the teacup down on the nightstand. There's nothing on that stand, none of the usual clutter – the nail file, the hand lotion, the lavender aromatherapy sachet pincushion – only the alarm clock and the tissue box. And Stan's nightstand has been cleared off as well. Where have they put it all? Maybe better not to make a fuss about that. 'Now, you take your time, no hurry. I've fixed us brunch.' She smiles her tight, wrinkle-free smile.

What if it's not her real face? thinks Charmaine. What if it's only stuck on and there's a giant cockroach or something behind it? What if I grabbed her by both of the ears and pulled, would the face pop off?

'Oh, thank you so much,' she says.

The brunch is laid out on the sunny-nook kitchen table: the eggs in the little hen egg cups Charmaine ordered from the catalogue as a tribute to Stan's chicken work, the coffee in the mugs with gnomes

301

on them, a grumpy one for Stan and a happy one for Charmaine, though sometimes she'd switch them around for fun. Stan needed more fun in his life, she'd tell him. Though what she'd meant was that she needed more fun in her own life. Well, she'd got some. She'd got Max. Fun plus, for a while.

'Toast? Another egg?' says Aurora, who has taken full possession of the stovetop, the pots, the toaster. How has she known where to find everything in Charmaine's kitchen? A horde of folks has been trooping in and out of her house, it seems. The place might as well be made of cellophane.

'More coffee?' says Aurora. Charmaine looks down at the mug: Aurora has given her the happy gnome. She feels tears trickling down her cheeks. Oh no, not more crying; she doesn't have the strength for it. Why had they wanted to kill Stan? He wasn't a subversive element; unless he'd been hiding something from her. But he couldn't have been, he was so easy to read. Though that's what he'd thought about her, and look how much she'd hidden from him.

Maybe he'd found out something about Positron, something really bad. Dangerous chemicals in the chickens, and everyone was eating them? Surely not, those chickens were organic. But maybe the chickens are part of some terrible experiment, and Stan discovered it and was going to warn everyone. Could that be the reason they wanted him dead? If so, he really was a hero, and she was proud of him.

And what happened to the bodies, really? After the Procedures. She'd never asked; she must have known that it would be crossing a line. Is there even a cemetery in Consilience? Or Positron Prison? She's never seen one.

She wipes her nose on the serviette, a cloth one with a robin embroidered on it in tiny stitches. Aurora reaches across the sunny-nook table, pats her hand. 'Never mind,' she says. 'It will be all right. Trust me. Now, finish your breakfast, and we'll go shopping.'

'Shopping?' Charmaine almost shouts. 'What in the heck for?'

'The funeral,' says Aurora in the mollifying voice of an adult to a balky child. 'It's tomorrow. You don't have a single stitch of black in your entire wardrobe.' She opens the closet door: there are all Charmaine's suits and dresses, hung up tidily on quilted hangers. Who took them out of her locker?

'You've been going through my closet!' Charmaine says accusingly. 'That's not your right, that closet is my private—'

'It's my job,' says Aurora more strictly. 'To help you get through this. You'll be the star feature, everyone will be looking at you. It would be disrespectful for you to wear . . . well, pastel flowers.'

She has a point, thinks Charmaine. 'Okay,' she says. 'I'm sorry. I'm on edge.'

'It's understandable,' says Aurora. 'Anyone would be, in your place.'

There has never been anyone in my place,

Charmaine thinks. My place is just too weird. And as for you, lady, don't say *understandable* to me, because what you understand is nothing. But she keeps that observation to herself.

TOUR

After lunch is over, Stan gets the tour. Or Waldo gets the tour. Waldo, Waldo, drill it into your head, he tells himself. He hopes to fuck there's no other Stan in this unit, because then he might make a slip. Someone would call his real name and his head would snap up, he wouldn't be able to stop himself.

Budge leads Stan and the rest of the team along a long hallway, blandly painted, blandly tiled. On the walls there are glossy photographs of fruit: a lemon, a pear, an apple. Round white-glass light fixtures. They turn a corner, turn another corner. No one teleported in here would have a clue where he was – what city, what country even. He'd just know he was somewhere in the twenty-first century. All generic materials.

'So, there's basically six divisions,' Budge is saying, 'for the standard economy-class models: Receiving, Assembly, Customization, Quality Control, Wardrobe and Accessories, and Shipping. Past that door you have Receiving, but we won't bother going through, there's nothing to see, it's just guys unloading boxes from the transport trucks.'

'How do the trucks get in?' asks Stan, keeping his voice neutral. 'I never saw any big trucks driving through the streets of Consilience.' It's a scooter town; even cars are a rarity, reserved for Surveillance and the top brass.

'They don't come through the town,' says Budge casually. 'This place is an extension, built onto the back of Positron Prison. The back portway of Receiving opens onto the outside. 'Course, we don't let any of those truckers come in here. No information exchange, that's the policy – no gawkers, no leakers. As far as they know they're delivering plumbing fixtures.'

Now that's interesting, Stan thinks. An outside portal. How can he wangle a job in Receiving without appearing overly eager about it?

'Plumbing fixtures,' he says with a chortle. 'That's good.' Budge grins happily.

'The boxes have only the parts,' says Kevin. 'Made in China like everything else, but it doesn't pay to assemble them over there and ship the bots here. Not enough quality control.'

'Plus there would be breakage,' says Gary. 'Too much breakage.'

'So they come in units,' says Budge. 'Arms, legs, torsos, basically the exoskeleton. Standard heads, though we do the customizing and skinning here. There's a lot of special orders. Some of the end users are very specific in their requirements.'

'Fetishists,' says Kevin.

'Stalkers,' says Tyler. 'They'll get one made with

the face of someone they're hot for but can't have, such as rock stars, or cheerleaders, or maybe their high school English teacher.'

'It can get sleazy,' says Budge. 'We get some demand for female relatives. We even had a great-aunt once.'

'That was a gross-out,' says Kevin.

'Hey. Everyone's different,' says Derek.

'But some are more different than others,' says Budge, and they all laugh.

'The info storage chips are already installed, and the voice elements, but we have to 3-D-print some of the neural connections,' says Gary. 'On the custom jobs.'

'We put the skin on last,' says Tyler. 'That's a skilled operation. The skin's got sensors, it can actually *feel* you. With the more expensive line, it can get goose bumps. When you're in contact, up close and personal, it's really hard to tell the difference.'

'But after you've seen one of them being assembled, you can't shake the knowledge,' says Budge. 'You know it's just an *it.*'

'They've done double-blind tests though,' says Gary. 'Real ones and these. These had a 77 percent success rate.'

'They're aiming for 100 percent,' says Kevin, 'but no way they'll ever get there.'

'No way,' Budge echoes. 'You can't program the little things. The unexpecteds.'

'Though there's these settings on them,' says Kevin. 'You can push Random and get a surprise.'

'Yeah,' says Tyler. 'She says, "Not tonight, I've got a headache."'

'That's no surprise,' says Kevin, and they laugh some more.

I need to come up with some jokes, Stan thinks. But not yet: they haven't accepted me completely. They're still reserving judgment.

'Up ahead we're coming to Assembly,' says Budge. 'Have a look, but we don't need to go in. Remember car factories?'

'Who remembers those?' says Tyler.

'Okay, movies of them. This guy does nothing but this, that guy does nothing but that. Specialized. Boring as hell. No latitude for error.'

'Get it wrong and they can have a spasm,' says Kevin. 'Flail around. That's not pretty.'

'Bits can come off,' says Gary. 'I mean bits of you.'

'One guy got clamped. He was stuck like a trapped rat for fifteen minutes, only it was more like a gyroscope. It took an electrician and three digital techs to unplug him, and after that his dick was shaped like a corkscrew for the rest of his life,' says Derek.

They laugh again, looking at Stan to see if he believes this. 'You're a sicko,' Tyler says to Derek affectionately.

'Think of the upside,' says Kevin. 'No condoms. No pregnancy woes.'

'No animal was harmed in the testing of this product,' says Derek.

'Except Gary,' says Kevin. More chuckles.

★　　★　　★

'This is it, in here,' says Budge. 'Assembly.' He uses his card key to open a double door, with a notice on it warning against dust and digital devices, these last to be turned firmly off, because, as the sign says, delicate electronic circuits are being activated.

Assembly lines are what Stan would expect to see, and that's what he does see. Most of the work is being done by robotics – attaching one thing to another, robots making other robots, just like the assembly at Dimple Robotics – though there's a scattering of human overseers. There are moving belts conveying thighs, hip joints, torsos; there are trays of hands, left and right. These body parts are man-made, they're not corpse portions, but nonetheless the effect is ghoulish. Squint and you're in a morgue, he thinks; or else a slaughterhouse. Except there's no blood.

'How flammable are they?' he asks Budge. 'The bodies.' It's Budge who seems to have the authority. And the card key for the doors: Stan must take note of which pocket he keeps it in. He wonders what other doors that key can open.

'Flammable?' says Budge.

'Supposing a guy is smoking,' says Stan. 'Like, a customer.'

'Oh, I don't think they'll be smoking,' says Tyler dismissively.

'Can't walk and chew gum at the same time,' says Derek.

'Some guys like a smoke, though,' says Stan. 'Afterwards. And maybe some talking, just a few words, like "That was awesome."'

'At the Platinum level it's an option,' says Tyler. 'The lower-tech models can't make small talk.'

'Fancy language costs extra,' says Gary.

'There's a plus though, they can't pester you, like, did you lock the door, did you take the garbage out, all of that,' says Budge.

A married man then, Stan thinks. He's overcome with a wave of nostalgia: it smells like orange juice, like fireplaces, like leather slippers. Charmaine once said things like that to him, in bed. *Did you lock the door, honey?* He warms toward Budge: he, too, must once have led a normal life.

BLACK SUIT

Black flatters me, thinks Charmaine, checking herself in the powder room mirror. Aurora had known where to take her shopping, and though black has never been her colour, Charmaine's not negative about the results. The black suit, the black hat, the blond hair – it's like a white chocolate truffle with dark chocolate truffles all around it; or like, who was that? Marilyn Monroe in *Niagara,* in the scene right before she gets strangled, with the white scarf she should never have worn, because women in danger of being strangled should avoid any fashion accessories that tie around the neck. They've shown that movie a bunch of times on Positron TV and Charmaine watched it every time. Sex in the movies used to be so much more sexy than it became after you could actually have sex in the movies. It was languorous and melting, with sighing and surrender and half-closed eyes. Not just a lot of bouncy athletics.

Of course, she thinks, Marilyn's mouth was fuller than her own, and you could use very thick red lipstick then. Does she herself have that innocence, that surprised look? *Oh! Goodness me!* Big doll eyes. Not that Marilyn's innocence was much in evidence in *Niagara*. But it was, later.

She widens her eyes in the mirror, makes an *O* with her mouth. Her own eyes are still a little puffy despite the cold teabags, with faint dark semicircles under them. Alluring, or not? That would depend on a man's taste: whether he's aroused by fragility with a hint of smouldering underneath, or perhaps by a hint of a punch in the eye. Stan wouldn't have liked the puffy-eyed look. Stan would have said, What's wrong with you? Fall out of bed? Or else, Aw, honey, what you need is a big hug. Depending on which phase of Stan she's remembering. *Oh, Stan . . .*

Stop that, she tells herself. Stan's gone.

Am I shallow? she asks the mirror. Yes, I am shallow. The sun shines on the ripples where it's shallow. Deep is too dark.

She considers the black hat, a small round hat with a little brim – sort of like a schoolgirl hat – that Aurora said was just right for a funeral. But does she have to wear a hat? Everyone did, once; then hats disappeared. But now, inside Consilience, they're appearing again. Everything in this town is retro, which accounts for the large supply of black vintage items in Accessories. The past is so much safer, because whatever's in it has already happened. It can't be changed; so, in a way, there's nothing to dread.

She once felt so secure inside this house. Her

and Stan's house, their warm cocoon, their shelter from the dangerous outside world, nestled inside a larger cocoon. First the town wall, like an outside shell; then, Consilience, like the soft white part of an egg. And inside Consilience, Positron Prison: the core, the heart, the meaning of it all.

And somewhere inside Positron, right now, is Stan. Or what used to be Stan. If only she hadn't . . . what if, instead . . . Maybe she herself is a kind of fatal woman, like Marilyn in *Niagara,* with invisible spider webs coming out of her, entangling men because they can't help it, and the spider can't help it either because it's her nature. Maybe she's doomed to be sticky, like chewing gum, or hair gel, or . . .

Because look what she's done without meaning to. She's caused Stan's funeral, and now she has to go to it. But she can't reveal her guilt at the funeral, she can't cry and say, *It's all my fault.* She'll have to behave with dignity, because this funeral will be very solemn and pious and reverential, it will be the funeral of a hero. What the whole town believes, because it was on the TV, is that there was an electrical fire in the chicken facility, and Stan died to save his fellow workers.

And to save the chickens, of course. And he did save them: no chicken had perished. That fact has been emphasized in the news story as making Stan even more truly heroic than if he'd saved just people. Or maybe not more heroic, only more touching. Sort of like saving babies: chickens were little and helpless too, though not so cute. Nothing with a beak can be truly cute, in Charmaine's opinion. But why is she even thinking about Stan saving chickens? That fire was made up, it had not in any way happened.

Stop dithering, Charmaine, she tells herself. Get back to reality, whatever that turns out to be.

The doorbell's chiming. She teeters down the hall on her black high heels: it's Aurora, who slipped out earlier to change into her funeral outfit. Behind her, waiting by the curb, is a long dark car.

Aurora's wearing a Chanel-style suit, black with white piping: way too boxy for her figure, which is boxy anyway. Dump the shoulder pads, Charmaine finds herself thinking. The hat is a sort of modified shovel design that does nothing for her, but no hat could. It's like her face is stretched like a rubber bathing cap over a large bald head. Her eyes are way too far to the sides.

When Charmaine was little and *recession* was a dirty word and not a fact of life, Grandma Win told her that no one should be called ugly. Instead, such people should be called unfortunate. It was just good manners. But years later, when Charmaine was older, Grandma Win told her that good manners were for those who could afford them, and if an elbow in the ribs for the person trying to barge in front of you was what it took, then an elbow in the ribs was the tool you should use.

Aurora smiles her unsettling smile. 'How are you

feeling now?' she says. She doesn't wait for an answer. 'Bearing up, I hope! The suit looks perfect.' Again she doesn't wait for an answer. She steps forward, and Charmaine steps back. Why does Aurora want to come in? Aren't they going to the funeral?

'Aren't we going to the funeral?' says Charmaine in a voice that sounds – to herself – plaintive and disappointed, like a child who's been told it won't be taken to the circus after all.

'Of course we're going,' says Aurora. 'But we need to wait for a very special guest. He wanted to be here in person, to support you in your loss.' She's holding her cellphone, Charmaine sees now; she must have just made a call. 'Oh, look, here he is now! Johnny on the spot!'

A second black car oozes down the street and draws up behind the first. So Aurora arranged to come early, to make sure that Charmaine is still holding it together and not staggering around and raving; then she sent an all-clear signal on her phone, and here comes the mystery man.

It's Max. She knows it is. He's slipped away from that cold and controlling woman, the head in the box. He's snuck off, the way he used to, and very soon she'll be wrapped in his familiar arms. Nothing stands between them except Aurora – how to get rid of her? – and also the funeral, the one she has to go to. Already she can hear the ripping of black cloth as Max tears off her layers, destroys her lace, flings her down

315

on . . . But what is she thinking? She needs to attend.

Though wait: Aurora can go to the funeral in her own car, and Charmaine and Max can take the second one, and sink back into the luxurious upholstery, and then, one hand on her mouth, a cascade of buttons, teeth on her throat . . . Because the funeral isn't real, Stan isn't actually in a coffin there, but he's dead, so it won't count as cheating.

No, Charmaine, she tells herself. Max can't be trusted, he's already shown that. You can't let yourself be swept away on a tidal wave of treacherous hormones. *Oh please! Let yourself!* says her other voice.

But the man getting out of the second car isn't Max. It takes Charmaine a moment to identify him: it's Ed. Ed himself, alone, come just to see her. Now that's a surprise! Aurora is beaming at her as if Charmaine has won the lottery.

'He wanted to make the effort,' she says. 'It's a tribute to you. And to your husband, of course.'

Does Charmaine feel flattered? Yes, she does. This feeling is not a good thing morally, she knows that. She should be too distraught by the death of Stan to feel flattered about anything. But still.

She smiles uncertainly. It can be very appealing, uncertainty – a sort of bashful, hesitant, but guilty look, especially if not fake. And hers is not fake, because right now she's thinking, even as she smiles: *What does he want?*

TIPTOE THROUGH THE TULIPS

Receiving and Assembly were straightforward enough: nothing they couldn't do at Dimple Robotics. 'Here's where the Blue Fairy works the magic,' says Budge. 'And Pinocchio comes to life.'

They're in Customization. None of the workers here are robots: too much individualized detailing, says Tyler, especially when finishing the heads. Stan wants to see them work the facial features, especially the smiles. He has a professional interest, from his job at Dimple. The Empathy Model he'd worked on could smile, but it was the same smile every time. Though what else did you need for checking out groceries? Put two eyes on anything and basically it looks like a face.

'They do the hairstyling over there,' says Tyler. 'Everything with the hair, like the beards and moustaches. Lumbersexual is a trend.'

'The what?' says Stan in a slightly too loud voice. 'There are guy prostibots? Since when?'

Kevin shoots him a look. 'Possibilibots is for everyone,' he says.

Of course, thinks Stan. It's the age of tolerance.

Stupid fucking me. Anything goes, out there in the so-called real world; though not inside Consilience, where the surface ambience is wholesomely, relentlessly hetero. Have they been eliminating gays all this time, or just not letting them in?

'Granted, most of the orders are for females,' says Tyler. 'Though that could change. But as yet there's not much capability, except at the Platinum level.'

'Because these economy bots can't walk around or anything,' says Kevin. 'Limited mobility. No locomotion. So mostly it's just the missionary position. They do what's required and that's about it, whereas with guy on guy—'

'Got it,' says Stan. He doesn't need the details.

'Anyway, some of the male items are for the older women customers,' says Derek. 'They say they feel more comfortable with a bot. They don't have to turn out the lights.' There's a shared chuckle.

'You can get all different age groups, different body types,' says Budge. 'Fat, thin, whatever. Grey hair, there's some requests for that.'

'Over here is the Expression Department,' says Gary. 'There's a menu of basics. Then on top of those, the folks here can make a few tweaks. Only thing is, once you've set the expression it can't be changed. The functioning human face has thirty-three sets of muscles, but the full deck would be way too expensive to build, maybe impossible.'

Stan watches with interest as a tech runs one of the faces through its repertoire of smiles. 'That's really advanced!' he says. 'Really. It's kind of amazing.'

'This is only the lower end,' says Budge modestly. 'But most users are in transient-client situations. The gated amusement parks, the casinos, the big-show venues, the destination malls; or the designated cheap-bot quarters in places like Holland, and increasingly right here at home. A few rust-belt towns have already been rejuvenated by setting up a cheap-bot shop, or that's what we hear.'

'The pro girls are pissed about it,' says Derek. 'It's undercutting their prices. They've held demonstrations, tried to smash displays, torn the heads off some of the bots, got arrested for destroying private property. It's not a small investment, setting up a facility.'

'But those joints make a bazillion,' says Gary. 'Vegas is totalling more out of these than the slots, or so they say. But it stands to reason, it's almost all margin once you've put in the front money. No food to buy, no death as such, and it's multiple use squared. There's the lube, you do have to front a lot of that. But those girls are sturdy! A real one could only do, say, fifty gigs a day, tops, without breaking down, whereas with these it's endless.'

'Unless the flushing and sanitation mechanisms malfunction,' says Derek.

Stan picks up an order form off one of the

worktables. There's a coded checklist, with letters and boxes. 'That's for the standard expressions,' says Budge.

'What's W?' Stan says.

'That's for Welcoming,' says Budge. 'But sort of neutral, like a flight attendant. T+H is Timid and Hesitant, L+S is for Lustful and Shameless. A+B is for Angry and Belligerent; not too much demand for that, you might think, but you'd be wrong. The V is for Virgin, which is T+H plus a few other adjustments.'

'Now, over here is Customization Plus,' says Tyler. 'This is where the customer sends in a photo and the body type is chosen to go with it, and the face is sculpted to look like the photo. Or as much as possible. Those are all private orders. Of course we do the dead celebrities for the more entertainment-oriented venues. A lot of those in Vegas.'

'It's like being able to go wild in Madame Tussaud's,' says Kevin. 'There's a big demand.'

Stan looks with curiosity at the special custom work that's underway. Brunettes at one table, redheads at another. Over here are the blondes.

And here is Charmaine, gazing up at him out of her blue eyes from a disembodied head. A photo of her is clipped to a stand on the table. He recognizes it: it's one with both of them in it, taken on their honeymoon at the beach, way back before any of this happened. He kept it in his locker.

But he himself has been cut out of the photo.

There's just a blank where he once grinned and posed, chest out, biceps flexed.

A shiver runs up his spine. Who's been going through his stuff? Could it be that Charmaine has ordered up a replica of her own head and scissored him out of her life?

Who to ask? He glances around. The operative assigned to Charmaine's head is on a coffee break. Anyway, what would the worker know? They just follow instructions. The order form is taped in place on the worktable; the expression checked in the box is T+H, with an added V. But the customer's name is inked out.

Steady, he tells himself. 'Who ordered this head?' he asks too casually.

Budge gives him a straight look. Is it a warning? 'Command performance,' he says. 'Ultra-special order. We've been told to be very meticulous with it.'

'It's going right to the top,' says Kevin. 'Not my type, personally – too vanilla – but someone up there must like that style.'

'The instructions are *extra lifelike*,' says Gary.

'We can't afford to screw it up,' says Tyler.

'Yeah, we really have to tiptoe through the tulips on this one,' says Budge.

Tulips. Tiptoeing. Kindly Budge with the pot belly is supposed to be his subversive contact? Budge, who looks like Charmaine's happy-gnome coffee cup? Surely not!

'Tiptoe through the what?' he says.

'Tulips,' says Budge. 'It's an old song. Before your time.'

Fucking crap. Spymaster Budge, confirmed. I really need a drink, thinks Stan. Right fucking now!

PART X

GRIEF THERAPY

HANDCREEP

Charmaine sits in the back seat of the long, smooth, silent car. Beside her is Ed, who has just helped her into it, one hand on her black-suited elbow.

'It's so good of you to come and collect me,' she says to him tremulously. 'In person.' Her lower lip really is quivering, a tear really is trickling out of her eye. She blots it with the tip of her black cotton glove. That glove tip feels like a soft, dry rabbit foot, stroking her gently.

She and Stan once had a rabbit foot. It was in the car when they'd bought it, along with a bunch of other junk. Stan wanted to toss it, but Charmaine said they should keep it because some rabbit had sacrificed its life so they could have good luck. So sad. The mascara, she thinks: is it running? But it would be crass at this moment to take the compact out of her black clutch bag to see.

'It's the very least I could do,' says Ed. He sounds almost shy. He pats her arm, a tentative pat that stops short of being too familiar. His voice is flatter and tinnier than it is when it's coming out of the TV, and he himself is shorter. She'd been sitting down the time he came to Positron and made that scary speech, and then complimented her on the blue teddy bear she'd been knitting; he'd seemed taller then, but she'd been looking up. She guesses he stands on a box when he's doing the important TV broadcasts about the tremendous progress and how they must all overcome the subversive elements. But right now, if you happened to glance in through the window, not that you could glance in because the glass is tinted, you would never guess that Ed is the big cheese of Consilience. The biggest cheese of all.

Why are important men called big cheeses? Charmaine wonders; she needs to distract herself, she does not want to deal with the fact that Ed has patted her arm again, and this time his hand has hovered, then descended and remained, just below her elbow. You would never say big cheese about a woman, even an important one. And Ed looks sort of like a cheese, because of his slickness; the round kind of cheese with wax all over the outside that kids used to love. They used to trade for that cheese in order to get the wax. It was red, and you could peel it off the cheese and mould it into little figures, like dogs or ducks. That's what had been valued, the wax; the cheese was only an add-on. It wasn't flavourful, but at least it wasn't awful.

Maybe that's what Ed would be like in bed, she thinks. Not flavourful but not awful. Something you didn't want that had to be accepted because of something you did want. He would have to be encouraged, he would have to be cheered on. Rapid breathing, false crescendos. Then there would be his gratitude, she'd have to cope with that. She would rather be the one feeling gratitude. Just thinking about all of it makes her tired.

How far could she force herself to go, supposing it comes to that? Because it will, if she allows it. She can tell, because of the look Ed is giving her now, a kind of damp, sickly, pious look. Reverence crossed with hidden lust, but behind that a determination to get what he wants. It's a dangerous look disguised as niceness. First they wheedle, but if you won't do that thing they want, they get hurtful.

Never mind, she tells herself. Think about flowers, because now you're safe. Except she isn't safe. Maybe no one can ever be safe. You run into your room and you slam the door, but there isn't any lock.

'It is absolutely the least we could do,' says Ed. 'We want to be here for you, in your great loss.'

'Thank you,' Charmaine murmurs. What to do about the hand? She can't push it away; that would be rude, and she would lose the edge it gives her. Not that she has the edge exactly, but it's an edge of sorts, as long as she neither offends him nor encourages him. What if she grasped the hand in both of hers and started to cry? No, that might turn him on even more. He might lunge, clumsily. She can't have him lunging just before the funeral.

'You've been brave,' Ed continues. 'You've been
. . . loyal. You must feel very alone now, as if there's
no one you can confide in.'

'Oh, I do,' says Charmaine. 'I do feel alone.' No
lie there. 'Stan was so—'

But Ed doesn't want to hear about Stan right
now. 'We want to assure you that you can rely on
us, on all of us in Management here at Consilience.
If you have any concerns, any problems, any fears
or worries you want to share . . .'

'Oh, yes. Thank you. That makes me feel so . . .
protected,' she says with a little intake of breath.
Fat chance she'd ever share her fears, especially
the ones she's having right now. This is thin ice.
Powerful men don't take well to rejection. Rage
could result.

There's a pause. 'You can rely on . . . me,' says
Ed. The hand squeezes.

What a nerve, thinks Charmaine with indigna-
tion. Making advances to a widow – to a woman
whose husband has just died heroically in a tragic
chicken accident. Even if he hasn't, and even if
Ed knows he hasn't. He knows, and he'll use that
knowledge as a weapon. He'll whisper her husband-
killing guilt into her ear, then he'll seize her in his
cheesy arms and stick his cheesy mouth on hers
because she has committed a terrible crime and
this is how she'll be expected to pay.

If he tries that I'll scream, thinks Charmaine.
No, she won't, because no one would hear her
except the driver, who has surely been trained to

ignore any noises from the back seat. And a scream would blow her edge right out of the water.

What to do, how to act? She can't let herself be taken for granted. If Ed must be endured, she'll need to make him beg a little. If only for form's sake. It will have to be a negotiation, like asking for a pay raise, not that she ever did that when she had a real job, at Ruby Slippers. But suppose he's open to a negotiation, what could she get from him in return?

Luckily the car is drawing up to the curb, because they're at the funeral chapel. Ed has removed his hand, and the door on his side is being opened from the outside, not by the driver but by a man in a black suit. Then her own door is opened and Ed helps her out. There's a crowd gathered, with that muted look – like stuffed cloth – that people waiting for funerals used to have back when funerals were still done properly around here. When people still had the money to put into them. Before dead people were simply cast adrift.

Ed offers his arm and leads Charmaine on her shaky black high heels and her slender black suit through the clustered people. They draw back to let her pass because she is sanctified by mourning. She keeps her eyes lowered and does not look around or smile, as if she's in deep grief.

She *is* in deep grief. She is.

QUALITY CONTROL

'Down the hall,' says Budge. 'Next stop, Quality Control. Hang in there, we're almost done.' He pats Stan's shoulder.

This has to be a signal. Stan clamps down on his urge to laugh. This whole thing is crazed. Charmaine's head? Budge the spook? You couldn't make it up. He's finding it hard to take it seriously. But it is serious.

Quality Control, says Kevin, is where they put the bodies through their paces before they attach the heads. It's to test the mechanical and the digital, says Gary, especially the writhing and the smoothness of the pelvic action. The space is filled with the motion of thighs and abdomens, like some grotesque art installation; there's a soft pulsing sound and a smell of plastic.

'Waldo, you want a ride round the block on one of these?' says Derek. Stan reflects that, come right down to it, nothing turns him on less than the sight of a dozen headless, naked plastic bodies miming the act of copulation. There's something insect-like about it.

'I'll take a rain check,' he says. They all laugh.

'Yeah, right, we didn't want to either,' says Tyler.

'They fix that smell later on,' says Gary. 'They add synthetic pheromones, and then there's a choice of orange blossom, rose, ylang-ylang, chocolate pudding, or Old Spice.'

'I'd say you need the head, at the very minimum,' says Budge. 'They stick them on after the bodies have checked out Affirmative. It's tricky, a lot of neural connections; all that work would be wasted if the body's defective.'

Stan looks down the line, to the far side of the room: it's like an operating theatre over there. Bright overhead lights, air purifiers. They're even wearing full caps and surgeon's masks.

'You don't want any hairs or dust getting into those heads,' says Derek. 'It can screw up the reaction time.'

They proceed to Wardrobe and Accessories. Racks of clothes stand ready – ordinary street clothing, business suits, leather outfits, feathers and sequins and gaudy costumes; also rolling shelves, with many different wigs. Movie sets must have looked like this, back in the days of Technicolor musicals.

'Here are the Rihannas and the Oprahs,' says Kevin. 'And the Princess Dianas. Those are the James Deans and the Marlon Brandos and the Denzel Washingtons and the Bill Clintons, and that's the Elvis aisle. It's mostly the white jumpsuit model they go for, with the studs and spangles, but there's other choices. The black with gold embroidery, that's popular. Not with the old ladies though, they want the white.'

'And this is the Marilyn section,' says Budge. 'You can have five different hairstyles, and in the outfits you get a choice too, depending on what movie. That's from *Gentlemen Prefer Blondes,* the pink dress; there's the black suit from *Niagara,* and over there is the all-girl jazz band one from *Some Like It Hot . . .*'

'Where are these headed for?' says Stan. 'The Oprahs. Are they that into Oprah, in Holland?'

'You name it, someone's gonna be fetishistic about it,' says Derek.

'Our biggest customers are the casino operations,' says Gary. 'The ones in Oklahoma, but they can be puritanical there. Even though these aren't real women and so forth. Whereas, Vegas. It's whatever, whenever, and the place is knee-high in cash. The rust-belt stuff never hit there.'

'Not the upmarket venues, anyway,' says Budge. 'Shedloads of foreign tourists, big spenders. Your Russians, your Indian millionaires, your Chinese, your Brazilians.'

'No regulations,' says Tyler. 'Sky's the limit.'

'Whatever you can think of, it's either up and running already or it will be,' says Derek.

'There's a lot of Elvises and Marilyns there anyway,' says Kevin. 'Alive ones. So the replicas blend right in.'

'What's that over there?' says Stan. He's spotted a bin full of knitted blue teddy bears.

'They're for the kiddybots,' says Kevin. 'They get dressed in the white nighties or the flannel pjs. They're boxed in flannelette sheets, and each one has a bear tucked into the package for extra-realistic effect.'

'That is fucking sick,' says Stan.

'I hear you,' says Derek. 'Yeah, it's sick. We agree, we felt the same when we found out about this product line. But they aren't real.'

'Who knows? Maybe these bots are sparing real kids a whole lot of pain and suffering,' says Kevin. 'Keeps the pervs off the streets.'

'I don't fucking buy that!' says Stan. 'They'll use these for dry runs, they'll practise up, then they'll . . .' Zip it, he tells himself. Don't get involved.

'But a lot of customers do buy it, if you see what I mean,' says Gary. 'They buy it like hotcakes. This vertical is a big earner for Possibilibots. Hard to argue with the bottom line.'

'Jobs are at stake, Waldo,' says Derek. 'Mega-jobs. Folks out there have bills to pay.'

'That's not a good reason,' says Stan. They're all watching him now, but he pushes on. 'How can you go along with this? It's not right!'

'It's time for your trial run,' says Budge. He gives Stan's shoulder a little nudge, turning him toward the exit. ' 'Scuse us, guys. I've got it set up in one of the private test rooms. There's some things a man needs to do alone.'

Laughter. 'Have a good trip,' says Derek. Gary adds, 'Heavy on the lube.'

'Down here,' says Budge. 'Nothing much left on the tour proper, except Shipping,' he says. 'It's mainly carting the boxes around; they're all packed and locked by the time they get to Shipping. That's my department, Shipping. Want to grab a beer?'

'Sure,' says Stan. He almost blew it back there, over the kiddybots. And those fucking blue teddy bears. What pervert dreamed that one up? 'How about the trial run?' he says.

'Forget it. We've got other business,' says Budge. 'Tulip business.'

'Right,' says Stan. Is he supposed to know what that means?

'In here – it's my office.' They go in; standard cubicle, desk, couple of chairs. Minibar: Budge gets two beers, pops the tops.

'Take a seat.' He leans forward across the desk. 'My job is to ship you. You and whatever you're taking with you. I don't know why and I don't know what, so no point asking.'

'Thanks,' says Stan, 'but . . .' He wants to ask about Charmaine, about her head. Is she in danger from some twisted stalker? If so, he can't leave Positron. He can't just desert her.

'No need for thanks,' says Budge. 'I'm just a

hired gun, I do what I'm told. It's one of our specialities, people-moving.' He doesn't look like a friendly uncle any more: he looks efficient. 'Me, for instance. To get me inside, they tucked me into a box of torsos, along with the ID I'd need. It worked fine. But you're our first try at shipping someone out.'

'Who's this we?' says Stan. 'You mean Jocelyn.'

'First off, your brother, Conor,' says Budge. 'We go way back. We did some time together when we were kids.'

'Conor!' says Stan. 'How did he get into this?' Trust fucking Conor. Not that he does. He remembers the sleek dark car in front of the trailer park, that time he went to see Con. Who's the pay pal?

'Same way he gets into everything,' says Budge. 'We got a call, we made a deal. We have a reputation for keeping our word. Doing what we've been paid for.'

'Mind my asking who paid you?' Stan asks.

'Classified,' says Budge, smiling. 'So, here's the plan. We'll put you into an Elvis outfit, then into a bot shipping crate. An Elvis would be the closest to your size.'

'Wait a minute!' says Stan. 'You want me to be a sexbot? You're pimping me out? No fucking way, that won't—'

'It's only for the shipping part,' says Budge. 'There's not a lot of options. You can't just walk out of here. And they check every Management vehicle and match up the biometrics. Remember,

335

even though they think you're dead, your data will still be on file. But inside the shipping box, and to the casual glance . . .'

'I don't look like Elvis,' says Stan.

'You will when we add the outfit and the finishing touches,' says Budge. 'And it's not the real Elvis you need to resemble, it's the imitation Elvises. Not hard to look like one of them.'

'What do I do when I get there?' says Stan.

'We're sending a guide out with you,' says Budge. 'She'll help you.'

'She?' says Stan. 'The only women I've seen in here have been plastic.'

'The prostibots are just one of the solutions that Possibilibots is marketing,' says Budge. 'There's something even more advanced.' He checks his watch. 'Showtime.'

They go out into the hallway, turn a corner, then another corner. More framed pictures of fruits: a mango, a kumquat. The fruit, he notes, is getting more exotic.

'Bots can't hold a real conversation,' says Budge. 'Even the best of them. Today's tech isn't there. But higher up the income scale, the customers want something they can show off to their friends; something less like, less like—'

'Less like a brain-dead trashbunny,' says Stan. What's Budge leading up to?

'Let me put it to you,' says Budge. 'Suppose you could customize a human being through a brain procedure.'

'How do you mean?' says Stan.

'They use lasers,' says Budge. 'They can wipe your attachment to anyone previous. When the subject wakes up she imprints on whoever's there. It's like ducklings.'

'Holy crap,' says Stan.

'So, shorthand: choose a babe, give her the operation, stick yourself in front of her when she's waking up, and she's yours forever, always compliant, always ready, no matter what you do. That way nobody feels exploited.'

'Wait a minute,' says Stan. 'Nobody's exploited?'

'I said nobody *feels* exploited,' says Budge. 'Different thing.'

'Women sign up for this?' says Stan. 'For the brain op?'

'Not sign up, exactly,' says Budge. 'Wake up is more like it. That way there's more freedom of selection. The clients wouldn't likely want anyone desperate enough to sign up of their own accord.'

'So, they fucking kidnap people?' says Stan.

'Not to say I'm endorsing it,' says Budge.

'That's . . .' Stan doesn't know whether to say *evil* or *brilliant*. 'Don't they – don't these women care about their earlier lives? Don't they resent—'

'Not if the laser job is done professionally,' says Budge. 'But it's still experimental. It hasn't been entirely perfected. Some clients have been willing to take the chance anyway, but mistakes have occurred.'

'Like what?' says Stan.

'You'll see when you meet your guide,' says Budge. 'She didn't turn out the way she was supposed to. That was one very pissed-off client! But he'd signed the terms and conditions, he knew the risks.'

'What went wrong?' Stan asks. He's already imagining. She wants to hump dead people, or dogs, or what?

'Timing,' says Budge. 'But it makes her an ideal operative, because she can never be distracted by a man.'

'What *can* she be distracted by?' Stan asks.

Budge stops in front of a door, knocks on it, opens it with his card. 'After you,' he says.

SACRIFICE

The funeral chapel is one size fits all. No crosses or whatnot, but there's a giant pair of praying hands and a picture of a sunrise. The colour scheme is powder blue and white, like the Wedgwood-style teacups Grandma Win used to have. There are huge banks of white flowers: they've really gone all out.

The chapel is filled to overflowing. The women from the bakery where Charmaine works when she's not in prison are here, and so are the knitting groups – her original group and that other group she hardly knows at all. They must have let these women out of Positron on passes for the funeral. Quite a few are wearing black hats – berets, pancake shapes, modified cloches – so she's made the right choice hatwise.

There are a number of Stan's fellow workers from the scooter shop. They nod at her deferentially because she's the widow, but there's an extra layer of deference as well. It must be the presence of Ed, who has tucked her arm within his and who is leading her up the aisle carefully, respectfully. He places her in the front pew, then sits down beside her, his thigh not touching hers, thank goodness, but still too close.

Aurora is on the other side of her, and on the other side of Ed is the woman from Surveillance, wearing a pillbox hat. She looks a bit like Jackie Kennedy.

And on the other side of that woman is Max. Charmaine can feel a thin filament of superheated air stretching between them, like the inside of an old light bulb: incandescent. He feels it too. He must feel it.

Ignore this, she tells herself. It's an illusion. You are in mourning.

The chapel has fold-down pews in case any dead person has a kneeling family. Charmaine wasn't brought up as a kneeler, but she'd like to be able to kneel right now – put her hands on the back of the pew in front, then place her forehead on those hands as if in despair. That way she could just zone out, which would help her get through this bogus funeral. Or she could spend the time thinking about what in heck she's going to do if Ed makes a move on her, such as putting his hand on her thigh. But she can't do any kneeling, because she's in the front row. She has to sit up straight and act noble. She squares her shoulders.

Now they're playing organ music, some kind of hymn. If they play 'You'll Never Walk Alone,' like in some of the Consilience TV funerals, she doesn't know if she can stand it. She is walking alone, she always will be. Here comes a tear.

340

Toughen up. Just pretend you're at the hairdresser's, says the little voice.

The coffin is closed, due to the hideous burns that Stan is supposed to have suffered as he threw himself upon the defective main switch, then frizzled as the current shot through him. That's what it said on the TV news, but really the coffin is closed because Stan isn't in it. She wonders what they've done with him and what they've put into the coffin instead. Most likely some old cabbages or bags of lawn clippings: something of the right weight and sogginess. But why have anything in there at all? No one's going to look inside.

What if she called their bluff? Said, *I want to see my darling Stan one more time.* Made a scene, threw herself on the coffin, demanded they wrench off the lid. Then, when they refuse, she could turn to the congregation and tell them what's really going on: *Innocent people are being killed! Like Sandi! Like Stan! And there must be dozens of others . . .* But they'd surround her in a minute and haul her away to calm her down, because after all she's out of her mind with grief. Then she'd be erased, just like Stan. *Oh, Stan . . .*

Dang it, more tears. Aurora squeezes her hand to show support. Ed is going pat pat, and in one more minute he's going to snake his arm around her. There's black on her white hanky: the mascara. 'I'm all right,' she manages to gasp in a half-whisper.

Now there's a soloist, a woman from Charmaine's

knitting group, the second one. She's got that solemn soprano expression on her face, she's inflating her lungs and sticking out her black frilly boobs and opening her mouth, and this will be awful, because Charmaine recognizes the organ-music tune: 'Cry Me a River.' The woman's way off-key. Charmaine covers her face with her gloved hands, because she might laugh. No losing it, she tells herself firmly.

The soprano's done, thank heavens. After the rustling and coughs die down, one of Stan's scooter co-workers delivers a message from what he calls Stan's Team. Bowed head, foot shuffling. *Great guy, Stan; stepped up to the mark, proud of him, made the sacrifice for all of us, miss him.* Charmaine feels sorry for the speaker, because he's been deceived. Like everyone else.

Then Ed unglues himself from her arm, straightens his tie, and walks to the podium. He clears his throat and out pours his TV voice, warm and reassuring, strong and believable. It comes to her as bursts of sound, like a scratched CD. *Brought together malfunction regrettable sacred deplorable admirable brave enduring heroic forever.* Then, *Join loss spouse help hope community.*

If she didn't know the truth, Charmaine would be convinced. More than convinced, won over. Get through it, you windbag, she thinks at Ed.

Now six of Stan's Team are moving forward. Now they're rolling the coffin down the aisle. Now the music starts up: 'Side by Side.'

I can't take this, thinks Charmaine. That should have been us, me and Stan, travelling along as we used to, through all kinds of weather, even inside that smelly old car, just as long as we're together. Here come the tears again.

'Stand up,' Aurora is telling her. 'You need to follow the coffin.'

'I can't, I can't see,' Charmaine gasps.

'I'll help you. Up you come! People will want to pay their respects at the reception.'

Reception. Egg salad sandwiches with the crusts cut off. Asparagus pinwheels. Lemon squares. 'To me? Respects?' Charmaine stifles a sob. That's all she needs, a hysterical outburst. 'I couldn't, I couldn't eat anything!' Why does death make people so hungry?

'Take a deep breath,' says Aurora. 'That's better. You'll shake their hands and smile, it's all they expect. Then I'll drive with you back to the house, and we can discuss your grief therapy. Consilience always provides that.'

'I don't need any grief therapy!' Charmaine almost screams.

'Oh, you do,' says Aurora with her sham compassion. 'Oh, I think you really do.'

We'll see about that, Charmaine thinks. She starts to pace down the aisle, Aurora's steadying hand on her elbow. Ed has materialized again and flanks her on the other side, his arm stuck onto her back like a squid.

PERFECT

Budge eases the door open, stands aside to
let Stan go first. The room they enter is
the closest thing to a genuine old-fashioned
room that Stan has seen in some time. The Dimple
Robotics golf course had a bar like that. There's
wood panelling, there are floor-length curtains,
there are oriental carpets. There's a fire burning
in the fireplace, or a quasi-fire: gas, maybe. There's
a leather-look sofa in front of it.

Sitting on the sofa with her long legs stretched
out is one of the most gorgeous women Stan has
ever seen. Lustrous dark hair, shoulder-length;
perfect tits, the tops of them just barely displayed.
She's wearing a simple black sheath, a single strand
of pearls. What a classy piece of ass, thinks Stan.

She smiles at him, the neutral smile she might
give a puppy, or an elderly aunt. There's no charge
coming from her, no chemistry.

'Stan, I'd like you to meet Veronica,' says Budge.
'Veronica, this is Stan.'

'Veronica,' says Stan. Is this the same Veronica?
That hooker from PixelDust who Charmaine used
to tell him wasn't really her friend? If so, she's had

quite a makeover. She'd been pretty before, but now she's drop-dead stunning. 'Do I know you?' he asks, then feels dumb because every man she meets must ask her that.

'Possibly,' says Veronica, 'but the past no longer applies.' She extends a hand. Manicured nails, burgundy. Expensive watch, Rolex. Cool palm. She gives him an LED smile: light, but no heat. 'I understand I'm taking you to the other side.'

Stan shakes the hand. Take me fucking anywhere, he thinks. This is what he once thought Jasmine would look like – Jasmine, the fatal fantasy. He needs to watch it here, not let himself be hauled around by the gonads. Listen up, he tells his dick silently. Keep it zipped.

'Sit down, have a drink,' says Veronica.

'Do you live here?' says Stan.

'Live?' says Veronica. She arches a perfect eyebrow.

'This is the honeymoon suite,' says Budge. 'Or one of them. Where the customized individuals first meet their . . . their . . .'

'Their owners,' says Veronica with a precious-metal laugh. 'It's supposed to be lust at first sight on behalf of the, of the people like me, but they missed the target in my case. The man walked in to collect on his investment and there was nothing.'

'Nothing?' says Stan. Why isn't she angry? But Budge said they weren't, or not so you'd notice. They don't seem to miss what they've lost.

'No spark between us. Not a twinge. He was

furious about it, but there was nothing I could do. Consilience gave him the choice of a refund or a second pick. He's still thinking about it.'

'They couldn't do Veronica over again,' says Budge. 'Too risky. She might come out drooling.'

'He wanted just me,' says Veronica, shrugging. 'But I can't. It wasn't my fault.'

'It was some stupid, well-meaning nurse,' says Budge. 'The guy's photo was there, as agreed, in case he got held up in a meeting. But the nurse gave her a comfort toy. Like she was a kid.'

'My head was turned that way, so he was the first thing I saw,' says Veronica. 'His two gorgeous eyes, gazing into mine.' The mishap doesn't seem to have bothered her. 'Luckily I can take my loved one with me everywhere I go. I keep him in this carry bag, right here. I'd show him to you, but I might lose control. Even talking about him is the most incredible turn-on for me.'

'But,' says Stan. 'But you're so beautiful!' Is this a joke, are the two of them messing with him? If not, what a fucking waste. 'Have you tried—'

'Any other man? I'm afraid it's no use,' says Veronica. 'I'm just plain frigid when it comes to real live men. The mere thought of them in that way makes me feel a little sick. That was programmed in when they did the operation.'

'But she's smart,' says Budge. 'Good in an emergency, and she has a swift kick. And she follows orders, so long as it isn't about sex. So you'll be in safe hands.'

346

'And I won't rape you,' says Veronica with a sweet smile.

If only, thinks Stan. 'Mind if I look?' he asks politely, indicating the black carry bag. He has an urge to see what he's already thinking of as his rival.

'It's okay,' says Veronica. 'Go ahead. You'll laugh. I know you don't believe me about this whole thing, but it's true. So I'm just telling you: don't have any hopes about me. I'd hate to wreck your nuts.'

Not such a total makeover, thinks Stan. She's still got her street mouth.

The bag has a zipper. Stan undoes it. Inside, staring up at him with its round blank eyes, is a blue knitted teddy bear.

GRIEF THERAPY

Charmaine makes it through the reception somehow. She manages the receiving line and the hand-clasping and the meaningful glances, and the arm strokings, and even the hugs from both of her teddy bear knitting groups. That second group hardly talked to her at all, as if she'd done something wrong; but now that she *has* done something wrong they're all mushy and huggy, with their breaths of egg salad sandwiches. Which just goes to show, as Grandma Win would have said. But what does it go to show? That people are delusional?

We're so sorry for your loss. Buzz off! Charmaine wants to yell. But she smiles feebly and says to each one of them, *Oh, thank you. Thank you for all your support.* Including when I really needed it and you treated me like puppy throw-up.

Now they're in Aurora's car, and Aurora's in the front seat, and Charmaine is eating the asparagus pinwheel she wrapped in a paper napkin and tucked into her clutch bag when no one was looking, because despite everything she has to keep

348

up her strength. And now they're at Charmaine's house, and Aurora is removing her unflattering black hat in front of the hall mirror. And now she's saying, 'Let's just kick off our shoes and get comfortable. I'll make some tea, and then we can start your grief therapy.' She smiles with her stretched face. For a fleeting instant, she looks afraid; but what has she got to be afraid of? Nothing. Unlike Charmaine.

'I don't need any grief therapy,' Charmaine mutters sulkily. She feels bodiless and also unbalanced, as if the floor is tilting. She teeters over to the sofa on her high heels and plunks herself down. She'll be darned if she lets these mean, slippery people give her grief therapy. What would they want to therapize about? The way Stan is supposed to have died or the way he really did die? Whichever, it will be a major brainwreck.

'Trust me, it will do you good,' says Aurora as she disappears into the kitchen. She'll put a pill in the tea, thinks Charmaine. She'll blot out my memory, that's likely their idea of grief therapy. In the kitchen the radio turns on: 'Happy Days Are Here Again.' Charmaine's neck prickles: are they playing that on purpose? Do they know about her habit of humming her favourite upbeat tunes while she readies herself to do the Procedures?

Aurora enters in her stocking feet, carrying a tray with a plate of oatmeal cookies and three cups. Not two, three. Charmaine feels cold all over: who's in the kitchen?

'There,' says Aurora. 'Girls' tea party!'

The woman from Surveillance saunters out of the kitchen. She's holding a blue knitted teddy bear. Her expression is – what? Sarcastic, Charmaine would once have said. More like inquisitive. But concealing it.

'What're you doing in my kitchen?' Charmaine says. Her voice is squeaky with outrage. Really it's too much! Privacy invasion! Ease up, she tells herself: this woman could obliterate you with one word.

'In point of fact, every other month it's *my* kitchen,' says the woman. 'My name is Jocelyn. I happen to live here when I'm not working from Positron.'

'Jocelyn? You're my *Alternate*?' says Charmaine. 'So you're . . .' Oh no. 'Max's wife! Or Phil, or whatever he . . .'

'Maybe we should have our tea first,' Aurora offers, 'before we get into the—'

'Never mind which wife is whose,' says Jocelyn. 'We can't waste time on the sexual spaghetti. I need you to listen very carefully to what I'm about to say. Many lives will depend on it.' She gives Charmaine a severe stare, like a gym teacher's.

Goodness, thinks Charmaine. Now what have I done?

'First of all,' says Jocelyn, 'Stan isn't dead.'

'Yes, he is!' says Charmaine. 'That's a lie! I know he is! He *has* to be dead!'

'You think you killed him,' says Jocelyn.

'You told me to!' says Charmaine.

'I told you to carry out the Special Procedure,' says Jocelyn, 'and you did. Thank you for that, and for your overreaction; it was a great help. But the formula you administered merely induced temporary unconsciousness. Stan is now safely inside a facility adjacent to Positron Prison, awaiting further instructions.'

'You're lying again!' says Charmaine. 'If he's alive, why did you make me go through that whole funeral thing?'

'Your grief had to be genuine,' says Jocelyn. 'Facial expression recognition tech is very precise these days. We needed everyone watching you to endorse a reality in which Stan is dead. Dead is the only way he can be effective.'

Effective at what? Charmaine wonders. 'I just don't believe you!' she says. Is that a butterfly of hope somewhere inside her?

'Listen for a minute. He sent you a message,' says Jocelyn. She fiddles with the blue teddy bear, and out of it comes Stan's voice: *Hi, honey, this is Stan. It's okay, I'm alive. They'll get you out, we can be together again, but you have to have faith in them, you have to do what they say. I love you.* The voice is tinny and sounds far away. Then there's a click.

Charmaine is stunned. This has to be fake! But if it really is Stan, how can she trust that he's being allowed to speak for himself? She has an image of him with a gun to his head, being forced to record the message. 'Play it again,' she says.

351

'It self-erased,' says Jocelyn. She's taken a little square thing out of the bear; she crushes it under her heel. 'Security reasons. You wouldn't want to be caught with a hot teddy bear. So, will you help Stan?'

'Help Stan do what?' says Charmaine.

'You don't need to know that yet,' says Jocelyn. 'Stan will tell you, once we get you out. Or far enough out, at any rate.'

'But he knows I killed him,' says Charmaine, starting to sniffle again. Even if the two of them do get back together outside Positron, how can he ever forgive her?

'I'll tell him you knew it wasn't real,' says Jocelyn. 'The death drug. But then I can always un-tell him, after which he'll hate you, and you can stay locked in here forever. Big Ed has a hard-on for you, and he won't take giggle for an answer. He's having a sexbot made in your image.'

'He's making a what?' says Charmaine.

'A sexbot. A sex robot. They've already sculpted your face; next they'll add the body.'

'They can't do that!' says Charmaine. 'Without even asking me!'

'Actually, they can,' says Jocelyn. 'But once he's practised on that he'll want the real thing. Eventually he'll tire of you, if history's top bananas are any guide – think Henry the Eighth – and then where will you end up? On the wrong end of the Procedure, is my guess.'

'That's so mean,' wails Charmaine. 'Where am I supposed to go?'

'You can stay here at the mercy of Ed, or you can take a chance with us, and then with Stan. One or the other.' Jocelyn takes a bite of her cookie, watching Charmaine's face.

This is awful, thinks Charmaine. A sexbot of herself, that is so creepy-crawly. Ed must be crazy; and despite the message he sent, Stan must be totally mad at her. Why does she have to choose between two scary things? 'What do you want me to do?' she asks.

What they want her to do is easily spelled out. They want her to snuggle up to Ed, get close to him but not too close – remember, she's a grieving widow – then report back with anything he says and anything she might come across, for instance in his bureau drawers or his briefcase, or maybe on his cellphone, if he gets careless; but that part – the carelessness part – will be up to her. Encourage him to think with his dick, an appendage not noticeably overloaded with brains. That's in the short run, and the short run is all they're asking for right now. Or so Jocelyn says.

'Do I have to, you know,' says Charmaine. 'Go all the way?' The idea of having Ed slither around on her naked body gives her the queasies.

'Absolutely not. In fact, that's crucial. You need to delay,' says Jocelyn. 'If he starts coming on strong, tell him you're not ready yet. You can plead sorrow for a while. He's part of the reality in which Stan is dead, so he'll understand that. He'll even welcome it. He's never seen those videos of you and Phil – I've made sure of that – so he thinks you're modest. That's part of his obsession with you: so hard to find a modest girl these days.' Is that a twitch, an almost-smile? 'If you don't want to help us, we could show him the videos. His reaction would be adverse. At the very least, he'd feel betrayed.'

Charmaine blushes. She *is* modest, it's just that . . . The thing with Max wasn't her true self, it couldn't have been. Maybe he was using some kind of hypnotism on her. The things he made her say . . . All of which have been recorded. This is blackmail! 'All right,' she says reluctantly. 'I'll try.'

'An appropriate decision,' says Aurora. 'I'm sure you'll come to realize that, in time. You'll be helping me – you'll be helping us – more than you know. Here, have a cookie.'

DRESSUPS

In the room at Possibilibots where Budge has stashed him, Stan dozes fitfully. He's dreaming of blue bears: they're outside the window, peering in at him. They clamber up onto the sill, they wiggle suggestively, they stare at him with their round, inexpressive eyes. Now they're laughing at him, displaying rows of pointed shark teeth. And now they're squeezing into his room through the half-open window, dropping onto his bed . . .

He wakes with a start and a muffled bark but it's only Veronica, shaking his arm. 'Hurry,' she tells him. There's bad news: over at Ed's office, IT has discovered that some crucial files have been copied. That would be the files on the flashdrive Stan will be taking out. There's bound to be a thorough search in the morning. Luckily, a rush order has come in at Possibilibots: five Elvises are leaving for Vegas at three a.m., and one of them will be him. She and Budge have everything ready and waiting in Shipping, but he needs to come right now.

He pulls on his clothes and follows her. She's wearing jeans and a T, ordinary-enough clothes, though with her inside them they look like silk. Life is unfair, he thinks, as he watches her undulate through the hallways.

She has all the right passcards as she leads him through a series of doorways to Shipping. 'You'll find everything you need in the men's,' she says. 'I'll be in the ladies', getting my own outfit on.'

'You're coming to Vegas too?' he says stupidly.

'Of course I am,' she says. 'I'm your minder. Remember?'

There's not much time to spare. The Elvis costume is hanging in one of the stalls. Stan shoehorns himself into it: it's half a size too small. Could he have gained that much weight on Positron beer, or was whoever picked this fucking outfit for him a bondage fetishist? The white bell-bottoms on the jumpsuit are too tight, the platform shoes pinch his toes, the belt with the big silver and turquoise buckle just barely makes it around his waist. Did Elvis wear a girdle, or what? He must've suffered from a permanent case of crotch cramp. The jacket is encrusted with studs and spangles, with a little cape attached; the collar sticks up like a Dracula cloak, the shoulder pads are grotesque.

The black wig is slippery – some sort of synthetic – but he manages to pull it on over his own hair. His head is going to cook in this thing! The eyebrows adhere on quite easily, the sideburns less so; he has to try twice. He applies bronzing powder with the brush supplied: instant tan. This is like

Halloween, when he was a kid. It's probably a crappy job, but who's going to see him? No one, if he's lucky.

All that remains are the chunky rings – he'll leave them till last – and the fake lips, top and bottom, which come supplied with their own Insta-glue. Not a total success; the lips feel precarious, but at least they stick on.

He poses in front of the mirror, does a lopsided grin; though he barely needs to grin because the lips are doing the grinning for him. Underneath them, his own lips are semi-paralyzed. He wiggles his new black eyebrows, flings back his head, smooths his hair. 'You handsome devil,' he says. 'Back from the dead.' The faux lips are hard to manoeuvre, but he'll get the hang of it. Oddly, he does look something like Elvis. Is that all we are? he thinks. Unmistakable clothing, a hairstyle, a few exaggerated features, a gesture?

There's a discreet knock: it's Veronica in her Marilyn getup, her hair hidden under a short blond wig. She's chosen the black suit from *Niagara,* with the skintight skirt and the white scarf. Her mouth glistens like slick red plastic. He has to admit she looks terrific; she even looks like the real Marilyn. She's got a large black carry bag, which doubtless contains her knitted blue fetish.

'Ready to go?' she says. 'I'll tuck you into your case, then Budge will do the same for me. Your cargo is in the belt buckle, don't lose it! We have

357

to hurry. Wait, let me even out your skin tone a bit.' She locates the brush, powders his face some more. She's standing way too close; this is torture, but she seems unaware of that. He longs to crush her against him, bury his nose in her Marilyn hair, smash his rubbery mouth onto her bright red lips, futile though that would be. 'There,' she says. 'Now you're perfect. You look just like an Elvis bot. Let's pop you in.'

The transport case is marked ELVIS/UR-ELF in stencilled block letters; it's one of the set of five stacked on the loading dock, ready for shipment. Beside it are five smaller cases labelled MARILYN/UR-MLF, one of which is standing open. It's lined with pink satin, with Styrofoam packing moulds to prevent breakage. His own packing case is lined with blue. 'Is this safe?' he says as he clambers in. 'How will I breathe?'

'There's air holes,' she says. 'They aren't very noticeable because no real bot would need them. I'm positioning this hot water bottle, it's empty. See, it's right beside your elbow. You should be able to move your arms enough to pee into it, if you have to. Here's a few pills in case you get panicky, they'll put you right under, don't take more than two at a time. Oh, and here's your bottled waters, I'm giving you three, we wouldn't want you to shrivel up, and a couple of tear-and-shake Little Hotties hand warmers, in case it gets cold on the plane. And an energy bar if you feel hungry. I'll make sure they let you out once we arrive!'

What if they don't? Stan wants to yell. 'Okay,' he says, trying to sound nonchalant.

'If there's a booboo and the wrong person finds you, just say you were drugged, and you have no idea how you got into the packing case,' says Veronica. 'In Vegas, they'll find that believable. Now, have a good sleep! Here comes Budge, it's my turn.'

She lowers the top, and Stan hears the catches being snapped shut. Now he's in the dark. Shit, he thinks. This better work. Best case, he makes it to Vegas, then gives Veronica the slip, ditches this outfit, and travels – how? – to rejoin Conor, because a life of outlawry is a lot more appealing to him than anything else that's going on right now. Though that wouldn't work, because Conor, via Budge, has a contract to deliver him to whoever, so that's what he'll do.

Worst case . . . He has an image of himself inside the packing case, abandoned in a nighttime airport in, say, the wilds of Kansas, yelping to emptiness: *Help! Let me out!*

Or, worse yet, identified as a terrorist threat by some addled sniffer dog and detonated by Homeland Security. Sideburns and silver all over the place. *What the hey! I think Elvis has left the building!*

He squirms around inside the slippery satin cocoon, trying to get comfortable. He doesn't want to take a pill, he's had enough of drugs lately. It's completely dark; a few hours in here and he'll start seeing things. The air is already stuffy; it reeks of glue, from the lips. Maybe it will make him high, and therefore less anxious. When did he set out along the path that's led to this dark cul-de-sac, how has he managed to agree to this crazed escapade, what's become his so-called life? Will he ever manage to see Charmaine again? If only he'd stolen her sculpted head: at least then he'd have something tangible.

The image of her lovely, pale, tear-streaked face floats before him. She's had few real choices; she's as unprepared for all this crap as he is. Lying in the satin-lined void with the Elvis collar itching his neck and the Elvis wig steam-cooking his scalp, he forgives her everything: her rancid interlude with Phil/Max, the moment when she thought she was killing him, even her obsession with slipcovers and those gnome coffee mugs. He should have cherished her more, he should have taken better care of her.

Right beside his ear he hears Veronica's voice. She's whispering. *Hi, Stan. There's a mic in your shoulder pad and one in my bear. It's our own walkie-talkie, ultra secure, just you and me. Letting you know it's okay, I'm in my own box, we're moving out. Signing off now. Just relax.*

As if, Stan thinks, as he feels his feet end lifting into the air. Fucking hell.

PART XI

RUBY SLIPPERS

FLIRT

Charmaine and Ed are having dinner at Together, which is the very same restaurant where Charmaine had dinner with Stan the first night they were at Consilience, before they'd actually signed in. It had been so magical then. The white tablecloths, the candles, the flowers. Like a dream. And now here she is again, and she must try not to remember that first time, back when everything was still simple with Stan, back when she herself was still simple. When she'd been able to say what she really felt.

Now nothing is simple. Now she's a widow. Now she's a spy.

She's finding this date with Ed a little difficult. More than a little: she doesn't know how to play this, because it's unclear what he wants, or not what: when. Why can't he just blurt it out?

'Are you feeling all right?' Ed says with concern, and she says, 'I'll be fine, it's just . . .' Then she excuses herself and goes to the ladies' room. Grief must be expected to overcome her from time to time, which it does, truly, only just not right now. But the ladies' is a reliable place, a place a girl

363

can retreat to at moments like this. The dinner hasn't even started, and already she needs a time-out.

It's soothing in here; luxurious, like a spa. The countertops are marble, the sinks are long and made of stainless steel, with a line of tiny faucets endlessly shooting thin streams of silvery water. The towels aren't paper, they're soft white cotton pile, and happily there's no air dryer that blows your skin into flesh ripples up as far as your wrists; she hates those, they make you realize that your skin could be peeled off like an orange rind. When there are no towels, she'd rather take her chance with the microbes and wipe her hands on her skirt.

There's lotion that claims to be made from real almonds: Charmaine rubs it on her inner arms, breathes it in. If only she could just stay in here, for ever and ever. A woman place. Sort of like a nunnery. No, a girl place, pristine, like the white cotton nighties she had at Grandma Win's, when she could be clean, and not hurt and afraid. A place where she feels safe.

The toilets play a tune when you wave your hand in front of the toilet paper dispenser. The tune is the theme song of Together; it's from some old song about not having a barrel of money and wearing white-trash clothes, and having to travel along, side by side, all of which was more or less the way it had been when she and Stan were living in their car; but in the song, none of that matters because the two of them are together, singing a song. A song about being together, for the restaurant called Together.

It's lying, that song. Not having any money does matter, and having to wear those worn-out clothes. It's because all those things matter that they signed in to the Project.

She checks herself in the mirror, refreshes her lips. Why is it she's finding Ed so hard to be with? It's because he's like that weirdo psycho nerd who admired her so much in high school, what was his name . . .

Get real, Charmaine, her reflection says to her. He didn't just admire you. He had a nauseating sexual crush on you, he used to slip anonymous notes into your locker, to which he seemed to have the combination even though you changed the lock twice. Those notes – typed, but not emailed, not texted, he was smarter than that – those notes listed your body parts and which ones he most wanted to slide his hands over or into. Then came the day of the damp tissue left inside her jacket pocket, reeking of jerkoff; that was truly icky. Why had he thought she'd find it in any way attractive?

Though perhaps the goal was not to attract her. Perhaps the goal was to repel her, then overwhelm her despite her aversion. The wet dream of a boy who hoped he was a lion king but who was really just a slimy loser.

She returns to the dining room. Ed stands up, holds her chair for her. The avocado with shrimp appetizer is in place, and a bottle of white wine in a silver bucket. He raises his glass and says, 'To a brighter future,' which really means 'To us,' and what can she do but raise her glass in return? She does it modestly, though. Tremulously. Then she sighs. She doesn't have to fake the sighing. *Sigh* is what she feels.

She blots the corner of her eye, folding the trace of black mascara up in the serviette. Men don't like to think about makeup, they like to think everything about you is genuine. Unless of course they want to think you're a slut and everything about you is fake.

'I know you must find it hard to believe in a brighter future, so soon after . . .,' he says.

'Oh yes,' she says. 'It is hard. It's so hard. I miss Stan so much!' Which is true, but at the same time she's pondering the word *slut*. Just one letter over from *slit*. It was Max who'd pointed that out, pinning her to the floor, *Say it, say it* . . . She presses her legs together. What if she could still . . .? But no, Jocelyn stands between them, with her sarcastic look and those black-mailing videos. She'll never let Charmaine be together with Max, ever again.

That's over, Charmaine, she tells herself. That's gone.

'He died a hero,' Ed says piously. 'As we all know.'

Charmaine looks down at her half-eaten avocado. 'Yes,' she says. 'It's such a comfort.'

'Though in fairness,' he says, 'I have to tell you that there are some doubts.'

'Oh,' she says. 'Really? What kind of doubts?' A wave of cold sweeps up from her stomach. She flutters her eyelashes. Is she blushing?

'Nothing you need to be troubled with right now,' he says. 'An irresponsible rumour. That Stan didn't die in that fire but in a different way. People will make up some very malicious things! Anyway, accidents do happen and data gets mixed up. But I can take care of that rumour for you. Nip it in the bud.'

You jerk, she thinks. You're bribing me! You know I killed Stan, you know I have to pretend he died saving chickens, and now you're twisting my arm. But guess what, I know something you don't know. Stan isn't dead, and pretty soon I'll be together with him again.

Unless Jocelyn is lying.

'You still working on that?' says the server, a brownish young man in a white dinner jacket. At Together they want everything to look like an old movie. But no one in an old movie would ever have said, *You still working on that?* as if eating is some kind of a job. He forgot to say *ma'am.*

'No thank you,' she says with a quavery little smile. Too sad, too refined, too battered by fate, to do anything so hearty, so greedy, so gross, as chewing: that's her story. She can pig out when she gets back home. There's a packet of potato chips in the cupboard, unless Jocelyn and Aurora

367

have helped themselves the way they've helped themselves to everything else in her life.

The server whisks the plate away. Ed leans forward. Charmaine leans back but not too far back. Maybe she shouldn't have worn the black V-neck. It wouldn't have been her choice, but Jocelyn had selected it for her. That, and the push-up bra underneath. 'You have to suggest that he might be able to look all the way down,' she'd said. 'But don't let him actually do it. Remember, you're in mourning. Vulnerable, but inaccessible. That's your game.'

Working in secret with Jocelyn like this – it was exciting in a way. She has to admit that. She'd made her face up carefully, with a little extra powder for the pallor.

'I respect your sentiments,' says Ed. 'But you're young, you have a whole life ahead of you. You should live it to the fullest.' Here comes his hand, planing slowly across the white tablecloth like a manta ray in one of those deep-sea documentaries. It's descending onto her own hand, which she shouldn't have left so carelessly lying around on the table.

'It doesn't feel like I could do that,' says Charmaine. 'As if I could live it to the fullest. It feels like my life is over.' It would be shockingly rude to remove her hand. It would be like a slap. His hand covers hers: it's damp. Pat, pat, pat, squeeze. Then, thankfully, withdrawal.

'We've got to get the roses back in your cheeks,'

says Ed. Now he's being fatherly. 'That's why I ordered steak. Bump up your iron.'

And here's the steak in front of her, seared and brown, branded with a crisscross of black, running with hot blood. On the side, three mini-broccolis and two new potatoes. It smells delicious. She's ravenous, but it would be folly to show it. Tiny, ladylike bites, if any. Maybe she should let him cut it up for her. 'Oh, it's too much,' she breathes. 'I couldn't possibly . . .'

'You need to make an effort,' says Ed. Will he go so far as to pop a morsel into her mouth? Will he say, 'Open up?' To head him off, Charmaine nibbles a sprig of broccoli.

'You've been so kind,' she says. 'So supportive.' Ed smiles, his lips now glossy with fat.

'I'd like to help you,' he says. 'You shouldn't go back to your old work in the hospital, it would be too much pressure. Too many memories. I believe I have a job you might like. Nothing too demanding. You can ease yourself into it.'

'Oh,' says Charmaine. She must not sound eager. 'What sort of job?'

'Working with me,' says Ed. 'As my personal assistant. That way, I can keep an eye on you. Make sure you're not overstrained.'

You don't fool me, thinks Charmaine. 'Oh, well, I'm not sure . . . That sounds . . .,' she says as if wavering.

'No need to discuss it now,' he says. 'We have lots of time to do that later. Now eat up, like a good girl.'

That's the role he's chosen for her: good girl. She feels a sudden wave of longing for Max. Bad girl was what she was for him. Bad, and deserving of punishment. She leans forward to cut up a potato, and Ed leans forward too. She knows exactly what the view is from his vantage point: she's rehearsed the angles in the mirror. A curve of breast, with an edging of black lace.

Is he sweating? Yes, make that a definite. Is that his knee, giving her own knee the gentlest of nudges under the table? Yes, it is: she knows a knee under the table when she feels one. She moves her own knee away.

'There,' she says. 'I'm eating. I'm being good.' She looks at him over the rim of her wineglass: her blue-eyed look, her child's look. Then she takes a sip of wine, pursing her lips into a pout. Maybe she'll leave a lipstick kiss on the glass for him, as if by accident. A pale kiss, a shadow of a kiss, like a whisper. Nothing too blatant.

SHIPPED

S tan wakes and sleeps, wakes and sleeps, wakes. He's taken one of the pills Veronica gave him, which conked him out though not for long enough, and now he's hyper-alert. He doesn't want to take any more pills, because what if the plane lands soon? He can't be asleep for that: he may need to spring into full-throttle action, though he's got no image of what kind of action. Saving the world in a blue cape and an Elvis ducktail wig doesn't convince him, even as a fantasy. But it would have an element of surprise if the enemy thinks he's a robot.

What enemy? Back at Positron the enemy is Ed – control-freak body-parts salesman, potential baby-blood vampire – but who will the enemy be once he gets to Las Vegas? In the pitch-blackness a parade of potential enemies scrolls across his eyeballs. Corrupters of Charmaine, kidnappers of Veronica, platoons of slavering men much more lecherous than he is, with scaly skins and clawlike fingernails and slitty-pupilled lizard eyes. In addition to which they have superhuman strength and can walk up the sides of skyscrapers as if they were human silverfish.

There goes one of them now, leaping from rooftop to rooftop, Charmaine under one arm, Veronica under the other. But it's Stan to the rescue. Luckily his blue Elvis cape and his silver belt buckle have magic powers. 'Drop those women or I'll sing "Heartbreak Hotel." It won't be pretty.' The monster shudders and clutches a hand to either pointed ear; while he's distracted, Stan presses his silver buckle and a lethal ray shoots out of it. The monster screams and disintegrates. Both scantily clad beauties tumble, their diaphanous garments fluttering. Stan vaults forward, flies through the air, and catches the wilted lovelies in his outstretched arms. They're too heavy, he's losing altitude, he's about to crash! Which wilted lovely should he save? And which will therefore go splat? He can't save both of them. Considering that Veronica will never hump anyone but a stuffed animal, maybe he should stick with Charmaine.

So much for that daydream, which lands him right back in the breakfast nook with him and Charmaine fighting over which one of them has cheated the most, and then whether Charmaine really wanted to kill Stan, and then tears. 'How could you believe that about me! Don't we love each other?' Yes or no? Maybe isn't allowed. No matter how he plays it, he'll come out an asshole. Or else a wimp. Are those his only choices?

★   ★   ★

He eats the energy bar, which tastes like coconut-flavoured sawdust. It's freezing cold in here. How long is this fucking flight going to go on? Why doesn't he have a light-up watch? It's totally dark, not to mention noisy. He knows – he knows with the rational part of his mind – that he's inside a satin-lined shipping crate, which in turn is strapped into place, along with four other Elvises, inside an aluminum Unit Load Device, which in turn is in the cargo hold of a transcontinental plane; but with the other part of his mind – by far the larger part at the moment – he thinks he's been buried alive. *Get me out! Get me out!* he screams silently. As if in answer, there's the muffled barking of a dog. Some gloomy pet, the slave and toy of a bejewelled concubine, herself no doubt the gloomy pet of a suavely sadistic plutocrat. He sympathizes.

Like a fool, he's drunk two of the bottles of water packed for him by Veronica, and now, of course, of course! he needs a piss. Veronica's instructions were that he was to pee into the empty hot-water bottle, but where the fuck is it? He gropes around, locates it snarled up in his cape, unscrews the top. Why didn't they give him a flashlight? Because he might forget to turn it off, and then the light beams coming through the air holes would give him away, and they'd unsnap his cover, guns at the ready. *Yo! Bro! This Elvis is not a robot, this Elvis is alive! Undead Elvis! Get the garlic and the spike!*

Calm down, Stan, he orders himself. Next contest challenge: unzipping Elvis's fly. He fumbles

373

around. The zipper sticks. Of course! Of course! 'Fuck, shit,' he says out loud.

'Stan, is that you?' comes the whisper in his ear. Veronica, over their Virtual Private Network; her voice, even her whispering voice, sends a jolt of sexual electricity through his spine. 'Keep your voice down, there may be monitor bugs in the cargo hold. Is everything okay?'

'Yeah, it's fine,' he whispers back. He's not about to tell her he couldn't get his dick out of his white flares, result being he's just wet himself.

'Why are you awake? Are you worrying?'

'Not really, but . . .'

'It's all arranged. They won't ask you anything. Just follow the plan.'

What fucking plan? Stan wants to ask but doesn't. 'Okay, cool,' he says.

'Did you take a pill?'

'Yeah, I did, earlier. But I don't want to take another, I need to stay alert.'

'It's okay, take one if you want to. Take two, it'll be fine. Are your hands cold? Remember you've got those Little Hotties. You just tear the package open and give it a shake, and it heats up.'

'Thanks,' he whispers. Even now, with things really not going so good, really going quite terrible in here, since he's squelching around on warm, damp, aromatic satin that will soon be cold, damp, smelly satin, he can't help picturing Veronica as she lies inside the ULD beside his. Sculpted perfection, so smooth, so curved, so inviting. Little

Hottie. How he'd like to tear her package open and give her a shake, feel her heat up.

Stan, Stan, he tells himself. This is a mission you're on. Can you stop thinking like a pre-human sex-crazed baboon for maybe just one minute? It's his hormones, it must be his hormones. Is he responsible for his hormones?

'How much longer?' he whispers.

'Oh, maybe an hour. Go back to sleep, okay?'

'Okay,' he whispers back. He drifts into a semi-doze, but then, right in his ear, he hears her whispering voice again.

'Oh, baby. Oh, yes. You're so soft! You're so strong!'

For one instant, he thinks she's talking to him. No such luck: she's making out with the blue knitted bear. She must have forgotten to turn off the mic at her end, or else she's torturing him for some obscure reason. Because it is torture! Is it worse to listen in, or not to listen? Wait, wait, he wants to shout. I can do that better!

'Yes, yes . . . oh, harder . . .'

This is obscene! In desperation he swallows three of the handy pills and plummets into oblivion.

FETISH

The morning after Charmaine's dinner with Ed, Jocelyn arrives at the house in her sleek black car. No chauffeur this time, no Max/Phil: she must have driven herself. Aurora's with her.

Charmaine watches the two of them from the front window as they come up the walk, each in a tidy businesslike suit. She's at a disadvantage: in her housecoat, no makeup, her hair every which way. She feels like she has a hangover, even though she drank almost nothing: it's the toxic effect of Ed.

Jocelyn does Charmaine the courtesy of ringing the doorbell even though she has a key, and Charmaine says, 'Come in' even though they'll come in anyway.

'I'll make some coffee,' Aurora says, using her most efficient voice.

'Thanks, you know where everything is,' says Charmaine. This is supposed to be a rebuke to Aurora for the way she's snooped all over Charmaine's life, but either Aurora doesn't pick up on that or she pays no attention. Jocelyn follows Charmaine into the living room.

'Well?' she says. 'Get the hook in? Not that he wasn't up to the gills already.'

Charmaine describes her evening, including the food, and everything Ed said, and everything she said in return. She includes the job offer, but Jocelyn already knew about that, because Ed asked her advice about it. She's more interested in the body language. Did Ed take her arm as they left the restaurant? Yes, he did. Did he put his arm around her waist, at any time? No, he did not. Did he try to kiss her goodnight?

'There was a moment,' says Charmaine. 'He kind of loomed forward in that way they have. But I stepped back and said thank you for the lovely evening and for being so understanding, and then I slipped inside the door.'

'Excellent,' says Jocelyn. ' "Understanding," good choice. Right up there with "I think of you as a friend." You need to keep him at arm's length without actually pushing him away. Can you do that?'

'I'll try,' says Charmaine. Then she just has to ask, because why else is she doing all this: 'Where's Stan? When can I see him?'

'Not yet,' says Jocelyn. 'You've got a few cards to play for us first. But he's safe enough, don't worry.'

Aurora comes in with the tray and three mugs of coffee. 'Now, about your new job,' she says. 'Here's what we want you to wear.' They've been through her clothes again, they've added a couple more outfits; they've got it all planned out.

Aurora makes her nervous. Why is she in cahoots with Jocelyn? Why would she risk her job? Has she done some criminal thing Jocelyn knows about? Charmaine can't imagine what.

For her first day as Ed's personal assistant, Charmaine has on a black suit with white trim and a high collar. There's a white blouse underneath; it has a frilly white bow at the neck, a cross between angel feathers and underpants. She sits at a desk outside Ed's office and does nothing much. She has a computer on which she's supposed to keep track of Ed's appointments, but his onscreen calendar seems to run itself and he posts dates on it without consulting her. Still, she has a good idea of his whereabouts most of the time, for whatever that's worth. He asks her to email a few people and tell them he can't see them because he has prior commitments; he asks her to look in his address files for some contact numbers in Las Vegas. One of them is at a casino, one seems to be a doctor's office, but one is at the new Ruby Slippers headquarters they've opened after taking over the chain, which makes her go all nostalgic. If only she still had her old job, in the Ruby Slippers local branch where she'd once been so content.

Or she'd been content enough. Being nice to the residents and planning special entertainment events for them wasn't what most people would call stimulating, but it was rewarding to be able to shine a ray of happiness into people's lives, and she was good at that, and she'd felt appreciated.

Ed walks past her desk, says, 'How's it going,' goes into his office, shuts the door. A trained dog could do this job, she thinks. It isn't really a job, it's an excuse. He wants me where he can get his hands on me.

But he doesn't get his hands on her. He doesn't take her to lunch, or make any moves on her at all, apart from some benign smiling and an assurance that she'll soon get used to things. He doesn't even ask her to go into his office except to bring him coffee. She's had a little daydream – a little nightmare – of Ed cornering her in there, and then locking the door and advancing on her with a leer. But that doesn't happen.

What's in the drawers of her own desk? Only some pens and paper clips, that kind of thing. Nothing to report there.

There's one other thing, she tells Jocelyn, who's come over in the evening to debrief her. There's a map on the wall behind Ed's desk, with pins in it. Orange pins are the Positron Prisons that are going up. Ed has told her it's now a franchise: there's a basic plan, there are instructions; it's like hamburger chains, only with prisons. Red pins are for the Ruby Slippers branches. There are more of those, but that company has been going longer.

Ed seems very proud of the map. He made sure she was watching him the day he stuck a new pin into it, near Orlando.

On the fifth day of her job, three state governors called and Ed got quite excited. 'They want one in their state,' Charmaine heard him saying on his phone. 'The model's proving itself! We're cooking with gas!'

At the end of the week he went to Washington for a meeting with some senators – Charmaine arranged the tickets and booked the hotel – but although he seemed pleased when he came back, he didn't tell her what happened.

'Did you go into his office while he was away?' asks Aurora.

'It's bugged,' says Charmaine. 'He told me that.'

'I'm in charge of the bugging, remember?' says Jocelyn. 'That's how I know your house is clean. Next time go in. Have a look around. Not on his computer, though. He'd know about that.'

In the middle of the second week, Charmaine says, 'I don't get it. According to both of you, he's mad for me . . .'

'Oh, he is,' says Aurora. 'He's at the moping stage.'

'But he hardly looks at me, and he hasn't asked me out again. And the job's a nothing. Why does he want me there?'

'So nobody else can get you,' says Jocelyn. 'He's

asked me to shadow you to and from work, and to report anyone – any man – who visits you at home. Needless to say I don't report myself. Aurora, yes, I report her. She's supposed to be doing grief therapy with you.'

'But what . . . I don't see where this is going,' says Charmaine.

'I don't exactly myself,' says Jocelyn. 'But he's got his double of you almost finished. Have a look.'

She brings up a window on her PosiPad: grainy footage of a corridor, Ed walking along it. He goes in through a door. 'Surveillance footage,' she says. 'Sorry about the quality. This is over at Possibilibots, where they're making the sex robots.' Charmaine remembers Stan saying something about that, but she hadn't paid much attention, she'd been too preoccupied with Max. Real sex with him was so, was so . . . *Divine* isn't the word. But if you could have that, why bother with a robot?

Inside the room, bright light. A couple of men are there, one with glasses, one without. They have green smocks on. There are a lot of wires and gizmos.

'How's she coming?' Ed asks the two men.

'Almost ready for a trial run,' the glasses one says. 'Just the standard prostibody for now, with the regular action. We can't make the custom body without the measurements, and some photos for detail.'

'That'll come later,' says Ed. 'Let's have a look.'

Segue across to a table, or is it a bed? A flower-patterned sheet over a body shape. Daisies and carnations. Ed turns down the corner of the sheet.

There's Charmaine's head, her very own head, with her very own hair on it, slightly dishevelled. She's sleeping. She looks so lifelike, so alive: Charmaine would swear she can see the rise and fall of the upper torso.

'Oh my gosh!' she says. 'It's me! That is so . . .' She feels a chill of terror. On the other hand, it's thrilling in a strange way. Another one of her! What will happen to her?

Ed leans over, strokes the cheek gently. The eyes open, widen in alarm.

'Perfect,' says Ed. 'Did you program the voice yet?'

'Just put your hands around her neck,' says one of the men, the one with the glasses. 'Give a tender squeeze.'

Ed does so. 'No! Don't touch me!' says Charmaine's head. The eyes close, the head is thrown back in an attitude of surrender.

'Now kiss her neck,' says the man without glasses. 'A small bite is okay, but don't bite too hard.'

'You wouldn't want to break the skin,' says the other. 'You could get a short.'

'Those can be ugly,' says the one without glasses.

'Okay, here goes,' says Ed as if he's about to jump into a swimming pool. His head goes down. The camera sees two white arms come up, encircle him. There's a moan from underneath Ed.

'You hit it out of the park,' says the one with glasses.

'The moan means you're on target,' says the other. 'Wait till you try the main action.'

'Genius,' says Ed. 'Exactly to spec. You guys deserve a medal. When can I take delivery?'

'Tomorrow,' says the one with glasses. 'If you're willing to go with this iteration. There's only a couple more adjustments.'

'You don't want to wait for the custom body?' says the other.

'This one will do for now,' says Ed. 'When I've got the stats and the pics I'll send it back to you for the replacement.' He bends over the head, which is sleeping again. 'Goodnight, sweetheart,' he murmurs. 'I'll see you very soon.'

The film ends. Charmaine feels dizzy. 'He's going to have sex with her?' She feels strangely protective of her fabricated self.

'That's the idea,' says Jocelyn.

'Why doesn't he just . . . I mean, he could ask me instead. He could practically force me to do it.'

'He's afraid of rejection,' says Aurora. 'A lot of people are. This way, he'll never be rejected by you.'

'By the way, heads-up,' says Jocelyn. 'He's asked me to plant some cameras in your bathroom, to take the pictures for the custom body.'

'But you won't do it,' says Charmaine. 'Will you?' Displaying herself for an unseen camera, pretending she doesn't know it's there . . . that's the kind of thing Max might have asked her to do. Did ask. *Turn this way. Raise your arms. Bend over.* The joke was that there really were cameras.

'It's my job,' says Jocelyn. 'If I don't do it he'll know something's wrong.'

'Fine. I just won't have any baths,' says Charmaine. 'Or showers,' she adds.

'I wouldn't take that attitude if I were you,' says Aurora. 'It's not helpful. Think of it like acting. We want him to go through with his plan.'

'It's partly business,' says Jocelyn. 'You're like a demonstration model. Can you imagine what a market demand there would be for customized robots like this, once they've got all the kinks worked out of the process?'

'In addition to those, we think he's working on a sort of blend. Not that we know for sure,' says Jocelyn.

'A blend of what?' says Charmaine.

'Heavens, look at the time!' says Aurora. 'I need my beauty sleep!'

'I think I'll pay a visit to Possibilibots,' says Jocelyn. 'Just to make sure the security is tight around Ed's special project. We wouldn't want any sabotage the first time he takes it out for a drive around the block.'

'A what?' says Charmaine. 'Why are you talking about a car?'

Jocelyn actually laughs. She doesn't laugh much

as a rule. 'You're terrific,' she says to Charmaine. 'It's not a car.'

'Oh,' Charmaine says after a minute. 'Now I get it.'

MALFUNCTION

The next day Ed isn't at the office. There's nothing on his schedule to suggest where he might be. Charmaine takes the liberty – or else the chance – of knocking on his door. When there's no answer she goes in. No sign of him. Desk neat as a pin. She peeks quickly into a couple of his desk drawers: there are a few folders, but all they have in them is expansion plans for Ruby Slippers. No receipts for plane tickets, nothing. Where could he have gone?

She isn't supposed to contact Jocelyn during the day, not by text, not by phone or email: no snail trails, is Jocelyn's motto. With no orders to follow, she occupies her mind by painting her nails, which is a very soothing thing to do when you're anxious and keyed up. Some people like to throw objects, such as glasses of water or rocks, but nail painting is more positive. If more world leaders would take it up there would be less overall suffering, in her opinion.

After so-called work, she goes straight home. Jocelyn's waiting for her in the living room, sitting on the sofa with her shoes off and her feet up.

Charmaine is pained by the sight of those feet. As long as Jocelyn keeps all her clothes on it seems improbable that Max/Phil could ever have made love to her, but with the shoes off, displaying feet with real toes . . . And she has terrific legs, Charmaine has to give her that. Legs that Max/Phil's hands must have stroked, in an upward direction, many times.

Charmaine can't imagine Jocelyn in the grip of passion, she can't imagine her saying the kinds of words Max likes to hear. She's always so in control of herself. Nothing short of a thumbscrew could make her lose it.

'I'm having a scotch,' Jocelyn says. 'Want one?'

'Why, what's happened?' says Charmaine. Is there a shock coming? 'What's happened to Stan?'

'Stan's fine,' says Jocelyn. 'He's relaxing.'

'All right then,' says Charmaine. She flops down into the easy chair; she's so relieved her knees feel weak. Jocelyn swings her feet over and onto the floor, pads across the room to pour Charmaine's drink. 'Water, I think,' she says, 'but no ice.'

It's not even a question. Darn it, Charmaine thinks, when will she stop bossing me around? 'Thank you,' she says. She kicks her own shoes off. 'There was a funny thing today,' she says. 'Ed wasn't there. At his office. And there's nothing on his calendar, no appointment. He's just vanished.'

'I know,' says Jocelyn. 'But he hasn't vanished. He's in the Positron hospital infirmary. He's had an accident.'

'What sort of an accident?' says Charmaine. 'Is it serious?' Maybe it's a car crash. Maybe he will die, and then she won't have to worry about whatever was supposed to come next. But if Ed dies, she'll lose whatever power she's got. She won't have any function for Jocelyn. She'll be disposable.

She has a quick thought: Why not do what Ed wants? Become his whatever. Mistress. Then she'd be safe. Wouldn't she?

'Painful accident, I expect,' says Jocelyn. 'Judging from the video surveillance records. But temporary. He'll be back to normal soon enough.'

'Oh no,' Charmaine says, 'did he break something?'

'Not break. But he got a little bent out of shape.' Jocelyn smiles, and this time it's actually a friendly smile. 'He got tangled up with you, as a matter of fact.'

'Me?' says Charmaine. 'That's not possible. I never . . .'

'Okay, your evil twin,' says Jocelyn. 'The prostibot with your head. He got carried away. He squeezed your neck too hard, and then he bit you.'

'Not me,' says Charmaine. Jocelyn's teasing. 'It's not *me!*'

'Ed thought it was,' says Jocelyn. 'Those things can be convincing when combined with a personal fantasy, which is always the magic ingredient, don't you agree?'

Charmaine blushes, she can't help herself. So

Jocelyn hasn't forgiven her: she's still holding it against her, that time with Max. With Phil. 'What did I . . . what did it do?' she asks. 'To Ed?'

'Some kind of electrical short,' says Jocelyn. 'Those circuits are so sensitive; the smallest thing can throw them off, such as a foreign object – such as, oh, a pin. Maybe it was inserted deliberately. Some resentful functionary. Who knows how it could've happened?'

'That's awful,' says Charmaine.

'Yes, it's terrible,' says Jocelyn. Would you call that a grin? It's not exactly a sweet smile. But Jocelyn's not in the habit of those. 'Anyway, the thing went into spasm, trapping Ed inside it, and then it started thrashing around.'

'Oh my goodness,' says Charmaine. 'He could've died!'

'Which would have been a business disaster for Possibilibots if the news leaked out,' says Jocelyn. 'Luckily, I was keeping tabs on him, so I sent the paramedics in before too much damage was done. They've got some ice packs on him, and they're using anti-inflammatories. There shouldn't be too much bruising. But don't be surprised if you see him walking like a duck.'

'Oh my goodness,' says Charmaine again. She's got her hands over her mouth. Whatever she thinks of Ed, it wouldn't be nice to laugh. A person is a person, however much of a weirdo they may be. And pain is pain. Just thinking about that pain makes a tingly wire shoot up her back.

'He was fairly mad at you, though,' Jocelyn continues in her detached voice. 'He sent you back to the shop. He ordered you to be destroyed.'

'Not me!' Charmaine says. 'Not actually me!'

'No, of course not. You know what I mean. The boys at the shop said they were sorry, and they'd tested it beforehand, but as he'd been informed, it was a beta and these things happen. They said they could debug it, but he told them not to bother because he's through with substitutes.'

'Oh,' says Charmaine. She has a sinking feeling. 'Does that mean what I think? You told me not to let him . . .'

'That still goes,' says Jocelyn. 'He'll be back on his feet again soon, and then you'll have to keep yourself in view but out of reach. It's crucial; I must emphasize how important that is, and how important you are. We're absolutely depending on you. Play the piece of cheese to Ed's rat. You're clever, you can do it.'

It's not very nice being told you're a piece of cheese, but Charmaine is pleased that Jocelyn has called her important. Also clever. Up till now, she's had the impression that Jocelyn thinks she's an idiot.

UNPACKED

Stan jolts awake. It's still dark, but he's moving rapidly through the air, feet first. Then there's a bump. Muffled voices. Snap, snap, snap, snap: the fasteners on his casket. The lid lifts, light streams in. He blinks in the dazzle. White-clad arms reach for him, hoist him into a sitting position.

'Upsy-daisy!'

'Wow, what stinks?'

'Get him some other pants. Make that a whole other outfit.'

'Don't be harsh, he didn't do it on purpose.'

'All together now! Heave-ho!'

Stan is lifted out of the satin coffin, stood on his feet. How long has he been asleep? It feels like days. He shakes his head, tries to unslit his eyes. The room is lit with a bank of overhead LEDs – hyper-bright, but that's because he's been in the dark so long. He seems to be in an office; there are filing cabinets, a couple of desks. A computer terminal.

Two Elvises, in white and silver with blue capes, are holding him by the arms; three more are surveying him. Each has the hairdo, the belt buckle, the epaulettes, the lips. The fake tan. Propped against the walls there are seven or eight more, but those don't seem to be real.

'Don't let go of him, he'll fall over!'

'Oh dear, his mouth fell off!'

'He looks like the walking dead.'

'Make yourself useful for once, get him some coffee.'

'I'd say a sports drink.'

'Why not both?'

Another Elvis bustles in, carrying yet another Elvis outfit. Stan blinks. Cripes, how many Elvises are there?

'Here we go,' says the tallest one; he seems to be the leader. 'Let's get you into something more comfortable. Don't be embarrassed, everyone here's wet themselves at least once in their life.'

'And most of them weren't locked in a packing crate,' says another. 'There's a washroom over there.'

'We won't peek!'

'Or maybe we will!' Laughter.

Fuck. They're all gay, Stan thinks. A roomful of gay Elvises. Is this a mistake, is he in the wrong place? He hopes they're not expecting . . . How can he tell them he's as straight as a Kansas highway without sounding rude?

'Thanks,' he mumbles. His lips are numb. He starts toward the washroom. His legs wobble; he pauses, leaning against a desk. 'Where's Veron

. . . where's the Marilyn I came with?' Better not to mention Veronica's name until he can figure out what's going on. How do these gay Elvises fit into Jocelyn's plan? Or are they just a way station? Maybe Veronica was supposed to collect him but didn't make it, so he got delivered here by mistake.

What if Jocelyn doesn't know where he is? He could lie low for a while with the Elvises, then head for the coast, blend in with the local population. Say he's doing a tech startup. Get a job as a waiter. After that, figure out how to reconnect with Charmaine, supposing that's possible. But how? For starters, he doesn't have any money.

'*That* Marilyn? She's with the Marilyns,' says the chief Elvis. 'They don't live here.'

'It's quite a different clientele. It's all men, with the Marilyns. Help yourself to the bronzer in there, touch yourself up. Stick your mouth back on. Oh, and there's a box of sideburns.'

Stan wants to ask about the clientele for the Elvises, but that can wait. He totters into the washroom, shuts the door. He peels himself out of his damp, whiffy white pants, dumps them into what he assumes is a laundry hamper, dampens a towel, sponges himself off. He changes his jacket and cape as well, but he keeps the belt he came with, along with its buckle. He runs his fingers over it, back and front – if it has a document dump flashdrive inside, there must be some way of opening it – but he can't find any button or catch.

He does the belt up – after his time in transit, at least he's thinner – then checks his face in the mirror. What a wreck. Dangling sideburn, smeared tan, wandering eyebrows. He repairs his mouth as best he can – there's some glue in with the spare 'burns – and adds bronzer. He lifts his top lip, tries for a signature sneer. Grotesque.

Outside the door they're discussing him. 'What do you think? Is he UR-ELF material?'

'Can he sing?'

'Let's find out. He'd have to do the full bump and grind, it doesn't work without that.'

'You're telling *me*!'

'Oh stop it for once, try to be helpful.'

Stan makes his exit from the washroom. The Elvises are encouraging.

'*Much* better!'

'A new man!'

'I love a new man!'

'Here, have a coffee. Sugar?'

The Elvises sit Stan in a desk chair, watch him while he takes a few sips of coffee. He dribbles: the fake lips are hard to manipulate. 'You have to go like *this*,' says one of the Elvises, pushing his mouth out into a kind of snout. 'You'll get used to it after a while.'

'Thanks,' says Stan.

'Try that in a lower register. *Thu-hanks*. Project

from the solar plexus. More like a growl . . . Elvis had an *amazing* range.'

'Now,' says the chief Elvis, 'what position do you see for yourself? Here at UR-ELF we have a wide choice. We've got Singing Elvis – dances, parties, anything that needs a little showtime; we charge the highest fees for them. Wedding Elvis, you'd need to get certified so it's legal, but that's not hard around here. Escort Elvis – that's for going to events, taking them out to dinner and maybe a show.'

'And Chauffeur Elvis, if that's what they want,' says one of the others. 'Sightseeing around town and like that; they might want you to take them shopping. I like that the best. And Bodyguard Elvis, for the heavy gamblers, so no one tries to snatch their purse. Oh, and Retirement Home Elvis; we do the hospitals too, palliative care. It can get depressing though, I warn you.'

'Singing Elvis is the most fun,' says a third Elvis. 'You can really express yourself!'

'I can't sing,' says Stan. 'So that's out.' Expressing himself is the last thing he wants right now. He'd only howl. 'Which is the least demanding? To begin with?'

'I think maybe the retirement homes,' says the chief Elvis. 'In there, they won't know the difference.'

'Darling, you'll knock 'em dead.'

Do they think I'm gay too? Stan wonders. Shit. Where the fuck is Veronica, and why didn't

Budge prepare him for this part? Nobody ever said he would have to perform in this Elvis racket. Are they laughing at him? They don't seem at all curious about why he was in a packing case, so that's one good thing.

RUBY SLIPPERS

The Elvises have prepared a space for him in the Elvisorium, which is what they call the fifties split-level bungalow shared by several of them. He sleeps on a fold-out cot in the laundry room, a tacit admission that he won't be staying forever. 'Just until your Catcher in the Rye shows up,' says the chief Elvis. 'That Marilyn of yours should be along soon.'

'Meanwhile we get to take care of you,' a second one chimes in. 'Lucky us!'

'We're doing it for Budge,' says the chief Elvis. 'Not that he doesn't pay well. Full room and board.'

Stan asks how long he's supposed to wait, but the Elvises don't seem to know. 'We're just your cover, Waldo,' says the chief Elvis. 'Keep you fed, get you some bookings, make you look real. We get to play the Seven Dwarves to your Snow White!' They think this is funny.

They give him a few days of leisure while they decide how to fit him in. They tell him he should explore the street life, see the Strip, so worth it! Though they insist he has to wear the full costume

every time he goes outside. He'll be less conspic-
uous that way: Elvises are a dime a dozen in this
town. If anyone comes up to him and wants their
picture taken with him, all he has to do is pose
and smile, and accept the crumpled bill they might
offer. He must resist all invitations to sing. He
should nod at any other Elvis he might meet – a
courtesy – but avoid conversation: not all the
Elvises are from their agency, UR-ElvisLiveForever,
and it wouldn't be good if those other, inferior
Elvises started asking him questions.

These Elvises – his own Elvises – know he's
hiding from something, or that someone might be
looking for him; shady business, anyway. But
they're discreet and don't ask him for any details.
Not even where he came from. Not even his last
name.

He wanders the streets an hour at a time, taking
in the sights, posing for the odd photo. He can't
stay out any longer: everything's too hot, too
bright, too gaudy, too supersaturated. Many jovial
tourists stroll here and there, making the most of
their absences from reality, shopping and bar-
hopping and taking selfies with the impersonators.
On the main drag there's at least one of those per
corner: white-gloved mice, Mickey or Minnie;
Donald Ducks; Godzillas; pirates; Darth Vaders;
Greek warriors. There's a fake Roman Forum, a
miniature Eiffel Tower, a Venetian canal complete
with gondolas. There are other replicas, though
Stan can't make out what they're imitating. The

place swarms with vendors: balloon animals, street food, carnival masks, souvenirs of every kind. Several old women dressed as gypsies shove post-cards at him, showing barely dressed young girls, with phone numbers.

Back at the Elvisorium, he takes frequent showers and dozes a lot. At first he has trouble sleeping in the daytime because the singing Elvises like to practise their acts, accompanied by backup tracks turned up way too high. But he's soon acclimatized.

Nobody comes to collect his belt buckle, with its precious, scandalous data. He sleeps with it under his pillow.

He's chewing on a hot dog at a street café, sheltering from the sun as best he can, when a Marilyn slides onto the seat beside him. 'It's Veronica,' she whispers. 'Everything okay? Guys treating you right? Still got that buckle?'

'Yeah, but I need to know—'

'Holy shit, look, both of them together! That is so fabulous! Can we get a picture?' Red-faced dude in an *I ♥ Vegas* T, his grinning wife, two bored-looking teens.

'Okay, just one,' says Veronica. She throws back her head, does the Marilyn smile, links her arm with Stan's; they pose. But several other camera-wielding couples are closing in on them. This could be a mob scene.

'Catch you later,' she smiles. 'Gotta dash!' She

kisses Stan on the forehead, leaving – he supposes – a big red mouth. She doesn't forget the almost-limping Marilyn ass wiggle as she moves away. She's got a new red carry bag; he can only suppose that her gigolo of a teddy bear is inside it.

His first official postings are to the palliative care wing of Ruby Slippers; it's the same chain that Charmaine used to work for before they both lost their jobs, so the decor has a familiar feel to it. He doesn't allow himself to think too much about what went wrong between the two of them, or where Charmaine is now. He can't afford to brood. Day by day is how he needs to play it.

The job isn't hard. Once he's been ordered up by a friend or a relative, all he has to do is get himself into costume and into the role. Then he delivers bouquets of flowers to elderly patients – elderly female patients, since the Marilyns do the men. The palliative care nurses welcome him: he's a spot of brightness, they claim: he keeps the patients interested in life. 'We don't think of the clients here as dying,' one of them said to him on his first visit. 'After all, everyone's dying, just some of us more slowly.' Some days he believes this; other days he feels like the Grim Reaper. The Angel of Death as Elvis. It kind of fits.

For each delivery he shows his identity card with the UR-ELF logo at Reception, passes through Security, and is escorted as far as the patient's room door. There he makes a dramatic entrance, though not too dramatic: a noisy surprise might be fatal. Then he presents the flowers with a bow and a swirl of his cape, and just a suggestion of pelvic action.

After that he sits beside the hospital beds and holds the frail, trembling hands, and tells the patients that he loves them. They like to have this message delivered in the form of Elvis's hit song titles – 'I Want You, I Need You, I Love You,' or 'I'm All Shook Up,' or 'Let Me Be Your Teddy Bear' – but he doesn't have to sing these songs, just whisper the titles. Some of the patients hardly know he's there, but others, less feeble, get a kick out of him and think he's a fine joke.

Yet others believe he's real. 'Oh, Elvis, you're here at last! I knew you would come,' one old woman exclaims, throwing her matchstick arms around his neck. 'I love you! I always loved you! Kiss me!'

'I love you too, honey,' he growls in return, placing his rubbery lips on her wrinkled cheek. 'I love you tender.'

'Oh, Elvis!'

When he first began he felt like a shit-for-brains fool, capering around like this in a phony get-up, pretending to be someone he isn't; but the more he does it, the easier it becomes. After the fifth or sixth time he really does love these old biddies, at least for a moment. He brings such joy. When was the last time anyone was so truly happy to see him?

PART XII

ESCORT

ELVISORIUM

S tan's at the Elvisorium, drinking beer and playing Texas hold'em with three of the other Elvises. They don't play for money, they know better than that; they've seen too many despairing punters lose their last dollar at the tables. They play for pancakes – the Baby Stacks Café ones, though you can trade your chits for bacon or peanut butter sandwiches – and there isn't any rule that you have to eat the stuff: too many pancakes and those belts with the silver buckles will fail to make it around the ballooning waists. The core concept is Elvis in his slim-hipped glory days, not Elvis in his blimpy decrepitude. No one wants to remember the tragic decline.

By now Stan knows the civvie names of the UR-ELF Elvis team members. Rob, the tallest, is the founder and CEO; he handles the bookings and the PR, including the website, and keeps an eye on overall performance. Pete, the second-in-command, does the financials. Ted – a little on the plump side for an Elvis – is in charge of running the Elvisorium on a daily basis: the dry-cleaning of the Elvis outfits, the sheets and towels, the basic groceries. UR-ELF is making a profit, says Pete, but only because they keep the overheads low. It's a close-to-the-bone operation: the champagne does not flow, the caviar is not spread. They're always looking at schemes for making a little extra, though not all of these work out. Juggling Elvis was tried but wasn't a success. The same went for Tightrope-Walking Elvis. The fans don't want the Elvises to do things that the historical Elvis would never have done: it would be too much like making fun of the King, and they don't appreciate that.

It's a slow day, so the poker players aren't 'in character,' as Rob calls dressing up. They're wearing shorts, Ts, and flip-flops: the A/C isn't working well, and outside the door it's 104°F. Luckily Vegas is in a desert, so at least it's not humid.

Stan now knows that not all the Elvises are gay. Some are, and there are a couple of bis and one asexual, though who can tell any more where to draw the line?

'Let's say it's a continuum,' said Rob while explaining this to Stan the second day. 'Nobody's either/or, when it comes right down to it. Me, I'm between wives. Boring old vanilla.'

Stan doesn't buy the continuum thing himself. But why should he worry about what other guys do in their spare time? 'The way you were all talking when I got here, you could've fooled me,' he said.

'And we did,' said Pete. 'But it's acting. UR-ELF was founded by actors for when we aren't working.'

'Most of us are just here looking for a part in one of the shows,' said Rob.

'By the way, we do coaching in how to act gay,' said Ted. 'For our new Elvises. Ten tips, that sort of thing. Stan, we might have to give you some help.'

'A straight guy playing a gay guy playing a straight guy, but in a way so that everyone assumes he's gay – that takes skill. Think about the complexity. Though some of the guys overact. It's a fine line,' said Rob.

Stan flashed back to his days with Jocelyn, when he was expected to play out whatever fantasy she'd ordered up that night. 'Okay,' he said. 'I get that about the acting, but why the gay thing? I may be dumb, but Elvis was definitely not gay, so . . .'

'It's the clients,' said Rob. 'And the relatives, the ones who book us for a treat. They prefer the Elvises to be gay.'

'I don't get it.'

'They don't want any uninvited hanky-panky,' said Rob. 'Especially not at the hospitals. With the female patients, the ones in the private rooms. Historically, there have been incidents.'

Stan laughed. 'Not really! Crap! Who'd want to . . .' Who'd want to fuck a hundred-year-old woman with tubes all over her and her insides leaking out? is what he's thinking.

'This is Vegas,' said Rob. 'You'd be surprised.'

⋆   ⋆   ⋆

'Beer?' says Pete, folding his hand and getting up.

Stan nods, broods over his cards. He's within view of another stack of pancakes. He's on a winning streak.

'I hear there's a couple new productions scheduled,' says Ted. 'It's booming in showtime here, so much better than Broadway.'

'Dan just hit it out of the park,' says Rob. 'They're casting for an all-guy *Midsummer Night's Scream,* and he got Tits Tania. That's why he hasn't been around.'

'Let's hope his voice holds up. It's not what you'd call singing,' says Pete with a touch of rancour. 'I wouldn't want to be in that pile of crap myself.'

Stan is way out of his depth – what is Tits Tania? – but once they get into the actor talk, better not to ask.

'At least it wasn't fucking Cobweb,' says Ted. 'With the fairy wings.'

'Or fucking Puck. You can imagine the puns. I hear they're doing an all-guy *Annie* next year,' says Pete. 'I'm going for what's her name, the bitch who runs the evil orphanage. I did it once, in Philly. I could ace it.'

'Five pancakes,' says Rob, laying down his cards. 'You can pay up on Sunday.'

'Go again?' says Ted. 'Win 'em back off you. I'm owed six anyway, from last time.'

'Someone else be dealer,' says Rob.

'Flip for it.'

'With Dan out, we're short an Escort,' says Rob.

'There's a big convention coming up, it's NAB. We're going to have demand.'

'NAB?' says Stan. They're always throwing around these short forms, acronyms for orgs he's never heard of.

'National Association of Broadcasters. TV, radio, all that. They see exhibits and listen to talks in the day, drink horrible coffee, the usual; then they hit the shows at night. Lot of single women, not always young. Stan, up for that?'

'Up for what?' says Stan cautiously.

'Escort Elvis. You've been doing great at the hospitals, nothing but stars and thumbs-up on the website comments, so you should be fine. See a show, eat some food, drink some booze. They might hit on you, offer you extra to go up to their rooms. That's where being gay can come in handy.'

'I can see that,' says Stan. 'Maybe I need some of those gayness lessons.'

'But we want the client to have an overall positive experience. We're all for gender equality. If the ladies want sex-for-cash, we provide it.'

'Wait a minute,' says Stan.

'Not you,' says Rob. 'You'll just give us a call on the cell, over at the UR-ELF Nightline, and we send one of the Elvis bots. Big markup on those! Like a superdildo, only with a body attached. Vibrator built in, optional.'

'Wish I felt like that,' says Pete.

'Then you chat with them, pour them a drink, tell them you wish you were straight. When the

Elvis arrives, you switch him on and he hums a little tune while you run over the instructions with the client: he responds to simple voice commands like *love me tonight, wooden heart,* and *jingle bell rock.* The speed on that last one's edgy, but some of them like it. Then you wait in the lobby. You'll have an earpiece, so you can hear if it's unfolding as per plan.'

Oh great, thinks Stan. Parked in a hotel lobby and eavesdropping while some mildewed hen has an orgasm. He's had enough of insatiable women. He remembers Charmaine, the way she was when they were first married: her quasi-virginal restraint. He didn't appreciate it enough. 'Why wait in the lobby?' he says.

'So you can supervise the re-delivery. Plus, in case there's a malfunction,' says Rob.

'Right,' says Stan. 'How will I know?'

'If you hear too much screaming, time to act. Get up there fast and flip the Off switch.'

'It'll sound different,' says Rob. 'The screaming. More terrified.'

'No one wants to be fucked to death,' says Pete.

WHY SUFFER?

E d has still not returned to the office. All that's happened is that three men with Positron logos on their jacket pockets arrive with a large crate. It's a stand-up desk, they say, and they have orders to install it in the office of the big boss. Once the desk is in they go away, and Charmaine is left to her own devices, which consist of slipping off her shoes and stockings and painting her toenails, behind the desk in case anyone comes in.

Blush Pink is the colour she's allowed. Nothing flaming, nothing flagrant, nothing fuchsia. Aurora bought the Blush Pink for her and presented it in that smug way she has. 'Here you are, this shade is very popular among the twelve-year-olds, I'm told, so I'm sure it will convey the right message.' Aurora gives a lot of thought to those details, which is helpful, but Charmaine can feel herself reaching the moment when she's going to yell. *Darn it, leave me alone! Stop talking at me!* Something like that.

Painting her toenails gives her a lift. That's what most men never understand, how it's a real pick-me-up to be able to change the colour of your toes. Stan got mad at her once when they were living in the car, because she spent some of her PixelDust tip money – he didn't say *spend,* he said *fucking blew* – on a little bottle of polish in a lovely silvery coral shade. They had a tiff about that, because she said it was her money, she'd earned it herself, and it wasn't as if the polish cost a lot, and then he accused her of throwing it up to him that he didn't have a job, and then she said she was not throwing it up, she only wanted her toes to look nice for him, and he said he didn't give a fucking fuck about her fucking toe colour, and then she cried.

She has a little cry now, remembering it. How bad are things when you can get nostalgic about living in your car? But it isn't the car that makes her sad, it's the absence of Stan. And not knowing if he's mad at her. Really mad, not just fucking fuck toe colour mad. They're not the same thing at all.

She tries not to think about Stan not being here any more, because what is is, as Grandma Win used to say, and what can't be cured must be endured, and laugh and the world laughs with you but cry and you cry alone. Maybe it served her right for talking back to Stan, that time in the car.

(*I'll teach you to talk back!* Now who said that? And how had she talked back? Did crying count as talking back? Yes, it did, because after that something bad happened. *Let that be a lesson to you.* But what was the lesson?)

She lets her mind go blank. Then, after a while of staring at the map with red and orange pins all over it like measles, she thinks, Ed will need a lamp for that stand-up desk, which gives her the excuse to go to the Consilience digital catalogue. She browses here and there to find the right section, pausing maybe too long at Ladies' Fashions and Cosmetic Magic, and orders the appropriate lighting device.

Then it's time to go home. So she does go home. Not that it's really a home. More of a mere house, because as Grandma Win said, it's love that makes a house a home.

Sometimes she wishes Grandma Win would bug off out of her head.

Aurora is ensconced on the living room sofa. She's having a cup of tea and a date square. Would Charmaine care to join her? she asks with her wide, tight smile. As if she's the darned hostess, thinks Charmaine, and I'm simply a visitor. But she passes over this, because what the hey, she has to get along with this woman, so she'll suck it up.

'No tea, thank you,' she says. 'But I could really use a drink. I bet there's some olives or something in the fridge too.' There were olives last time she looked, but food has been appearing and disappearing out of that fridge like it has a bad case of gnomes.

'Certainly,' says Aurora as Charmaine sinks into the easy chair, kicking off her shoes. There's a pause while each of them waits to see if the other one's going to get the drink. Darn it, thinks Charmaine, why should I be her maid? If she wants to be the hostess here, let her darn well do it.

After a moment Aurora sets down her cup, pushes up from the sofa, takes the olives out of the fridge and puts them in an olive dish, then rummages among the liquor bottles. There are more of these than there used to be: Jocelyn has a special allowance, she's not limited the way the rest of them are, so it's her that's bringing in the booze. Consilience takes a dim view of drunks because they aren't productive and they develop medical problems, and why should everyone pay because one individual has no self-control? That's been on the TV quite a lot recently. Charmaine wonders if there's boot-legging going on, or maybe people making moonshine out of potato peelings or something. Or more drinking because they're getting bored.

'Campari and soda?' says Aurora.

What's that, thinks Charmaine, some snobby drink unknown to us hicks? 'Whatever,' she says, 'as long as it's got a kick to it.'

The drink is reddish and a little bitter, but after a few gulps of it she feels better.

Aurora waits until Charmaine's drunk half. Then

she announces, 'I'm staying here this weekend. Jocelyn thought it would be best. I can keep an eye on you, just in case anything unexpected happens.'

Oh heck, Charmaine thinks. She's been looking forward to having some Me Time. She'd enjoy a long soak in the tub, in behind the shower curtain where the camera can't see her, and without having to worry about another person who might want to get in there to floss their teeth. 'Oh, I don't want to put you out,' she says. 'I don't think anything unexpected . . . I'm fine, really. I don't need—'

'I'm sure that's true,' says Aurora in her tone that means the opposite. 'But think of it this way. What if he decides to pay you a visit?'

A big What If, thinks Charmaine. She doesn't need to ask who *he* is, but she doubts very much that he'll be visiting, since from what Jocelyn says his dick is in a cast. 'I don't think he will,' she says. 'Not this weekend.'

'You never know,' says Aurora. 'I understand he can be impetuous. Anyway, he'll be happy to hear you've had a chaperone. I also understand he can be quite jealous. And we wouldn't want any undue suspicions to arise, would we?'

It's better than she thought it would be, the weekend with Aurora. You should never pass up the chance to learn something new, and Charmaine learns several things. First of all, she learns that

415

Aurora can make good scrambled eggs. Second, she learns that Ed is planning some sort of a trip, and that Charmaine will be invited on it, but Aurora doesn't know where or when, so right now it's only a heads-up.

And third, she learns that Aurora's face is not her original face. It's always been obvious that she's had work done, Charmaine has known that from the get-go, but what Aurora tells her goes way beyond mere work.

'You may have wondered about my face' is how Aurora opens the face round. This is on the Sunday, after they've watched *Some Like It Hot* while eating popcorn and drinking beer, not that Charmaine likes beer that much but it seemed like the right thing to do. Then they got into the mixed drinks, which by this time are unusual, since the ingredient options are running out.

Now they're feeling like old best girfriends from school, or at least Charmaine is feeling like that. Not that she had any best girlfriends from school, not really close ones. When she was little she wasn't allowed to have them, and then later she didn't want to have them, because they would ask too much about her life. So maybe she's having a belated best girlfriend. Though it might just be the effect of her fourth Campari and soda, or is it a gin and tonic, or maybe something with vodka?

'Your face? What do you mean?' says Charmaine, trying to sound as if she's never noticed anything wrong with it.

'You don't have to pretend,' says Aurora. 'I know what I look like. I know it's too . . . tight. But I used to look very different. And then, for a while, I looked . . . I didn't have any face at all.'

'No face?' says Charmaine. 'Everyone has a face!'

'Mine got scraped off,' says Aurora.

'You're kidding!' says Charmaine, and then she can't help laughing because it's too ridiculous, a scraped-off face, like scraping icing off a cake, and then Aurora laughs too, as much as she can, considering.

'I was in a roller-derby accident,' she says when they're finished laughing. 'It was a charity thing, for the image consultant agency I was working for then. We were raising money for lung cancer. I guess I shouldn't have volunteered, but I really wanted to help out. You know.'

'Oh, yes. I know. But roller skates, that's dangerous,' says Charmaine. She wouldn't have spotted Aurora as being that athletic. Face scraped off! It hurts her to think about it. Aurora is looking blurry, and Charmaine can almost see underneath her skin. Hurt is what's under there. So much hurt.

'Yes. I was young then, I thought I was tough. I shouldn't even say accident, it was a deliberate tripping by Maria in Accounts. She had it in for me because of this man called Chet, not that there was anything. And I landed right on my face, at top speed. I came out looking like hamburger.'

'Oh,' says Charmaine, sobering up a little. 'Oh, terrible.'

'I couldn't even sue,' says Aurora. 'There wasn't even a category.'

'Of course not,' says Charmaine sympathetically. 'Darned insurance companies.'

'So they offered me a full-face transplant,' says Aurora. 'For signing up at Positron.'

'They did?' says Charmaine. 'You can do that with faces?' Pop your face off and pop another one on – you could be a whole different person, on the outside, not just on the inside.

'Yes. They were at the experimental stage and there I was. I was custom-made for them. They wanted to see if they could transplant an entire face. Why suffer? is how they put it.'

'Whose face did you get?' Charmaine asks. It's a tactless question, she shouldn't have asked it. The face of a Procedure is the answer: the face of someone who didn't need their face any more. But they'd have been blissed out or gone to glory while it was peeled off them, they wouldn't have known. And it was all for the best. The better. The good. She upends her drink.

'Those were early days,' Aurora says. 'They're doing things differently now.'

'Differently,' says Charmaine. 'Things. You mean they're killing them differently? Those prisoners? They're not doing the Procedure?' She shouldn't have blurted that out, she knows never to use the k-word. She's had too much to drink. At least she didn't say *murdering*.

'*Killing* is harsh,' says Aurora. 'It was positioned

418

as the alleviation of excessive pain. And happily there are now more ways than one of doing that! Alleviating the excessive pain. Ways that are less harsh.'

'You mean, they don't kill them?' Even to herself, Charmaine sounds like a five-year-old. She's overdoing it on the dumb.

'Hardly at all any more,' says Aurora. 'The thing is, people get lonely; they want someone to love them. That can be arranged for anyone now, even if you look like something the cat coughed up. Why should anyone have to endure that kind of emotional damage? Lord knows I can identify with the whole solution! Considering the way my face . . . this face is, you can imagine I haven't had much of a love life since that happened.'

'Poor you,' says Charmaine. 'Of course, there can be a downside.'

'A downside to what?' says Aurora a little coldly.

'Well, you know. To a love life. All of that,' says Charmaine. She could tell Aurora about a few of her own downsides, but why dwell on the negative?

'Not if the person is devoted,' says Aurora. 'Not if they're fixated on you. Only you. It can be done, they do it by changing the brain, it's like a magic love potion.'

'Oh,' says Charmaine. 'That would be . . .' What's the word? *Amazing? Impossible?* She's never felt she had a lot of choice with love, especially with the hopeless kind. The kind that was mostly sex. You loved someone in that way, and wham! You couldn't help yourself. It was like going down a water slide: you couldn't stop. Or that's how it was with Max. Maybe she'll never be able to feel anything like that again.

'Jocelyn's promised me,' says Aurora. 'If I helped her. She says I can have that done, very soon now, once she's identified the right match. I've been waiting so long! But now I can have a whole new life.' Her eyes tear up.

Charmaine is almost envious. A whole new life. How can she herself get one of those?

ESCORT

'Y ou've snagged your first Elvis Escort gig,' Rob tells Stan at breakfast. Or at Stan's breakfast. It's more like lunch for Rob, but Stan slept in. They're both eating much the same thing, however: undifferentiated foodstuffs. Things that come already sliced, things in foil packages, things in jars. The Elvisorium is not a gourmet establishment.

Stan pauses in mid-crackle. He has to stop gobbling Pringles, they'll make him fat. 'Where?' he says.

'Woman here for that broadcaster convention,' says Rob. 'NAB. She's television, or ex-television from the sound of it. Thought I ought to know who she was. She wants someone to take her to a show. Sounds harmless.'

Stan actually feels nervous. Performance anxiety, he tells himself. What's there to worry about? This isn't his real job, or the rest of his fucking life. 'So, what exactly do I do?' he says.

'What she's ordered up,' says Rob. 'You don't even have to go through the dinner, it's just the show. You won't know about the sex till later

421

in the evening; that can be an impulse buy. But remember to compliment them on their dress. Gaze into their eyes, all of that. At UR-ELF we're noted for our discreet attention to every detail.'

'Okay, got it,' says Stan.

He goes for his usual stroll along the Strip to quiet his nerves, poses for a few photos, collects a few dollars, and one fiver from a big spender from Illinois. When he gets back to the Elvisorium, Rob's still in the kitchen. 'Some guys were here looking for you,' he says. 'They had your picture.'

'What kind of guys?' says Stan.

'Four guys. They were bald. They had sunglasses.'

'What'd you tell them?' says Stan. Four bald guys with sunglasses – that sounds ominous. Jocelyn never mentioned anything like that, and neither did Budge or Veronica. His contact is supposed to be just one person. Has Ed traced the data leak to its source, has he pulled off Jocelyn's fingernails to extract Stan's whereabouts from her? Are these guys Ed's heavies? He sees himself being yanked into a car, then tied to a chair in a vacant garage having the crap smashed out of him until he cries, 'It's in the belt buckle!' Already he's sweating inside his Elvis carapace. Or sweating more than he was.

'I said they had the wrong address,' said Rob. 'I didn't like the feel of them.'

'What kind of picture?' Stan asks. He gets himself a beer, gulps down half of it in one swig. 'Of me.

You think it was taken here?' If so, he's really in trouble.

'Nah, it was old,' says Rob. 'You were standing on a beach with a hot blonde, with penguins on your shirt.'

Stan feels his stomach clench. It's his honeymoon pic, it has to be. The last time he saw a copy of that was at Possibilibots; it was beside Charmaine's head, and he himself had been deleted. Ed and the Project are calling the shots on this, for sure. They've tracked him down.

Fuck it, he thinks. I'm fucked.

He figures it's better to stay in crowds – the bald thugs won't want to call attention to themselves while abducting him – so it's good he has a client for the evening. Her name is Lucinda Quant, which rings a distant bell. Didn't Charmaine used to watch a show this Lucinda did, back when they were sleeping in their car? The first time he heard that name he could imagine the locker-room jokes it must have generated in Lucinda's teenaged years.

He meets her at her hotel, as arranged; it's the Venetian one. The lobby is crammed with NAB convention-goers, still with their badges on. Some of them look as if they ought to be famous, or have been, once; the others, the scruffier-looking ones, are probably from radio.

Lucinda Quant spots him before he spots her. 'Are you my rent-boy Elvis?' she says. He peers down at her tag and growls, 'Why yes, little lady.'

'Not bad,' says Lucinda Quant. She's about fifty, or maybe sixty; Stan can't tell because she's so tanned and wrinkly. She grabs Stan's arm, waves goodbye to a chattering group of her fellow broadcast journalists, and says, 'Let's get out of this freak show.'

Stan hands her into a taxi, goes around to the other side, and slides in beside her. He gives her his best rubbery-lipped smile, which she doesn't return. She's skinny in the arms, teeth-whitened, and covered with silver and turquoise ornaments. Her hair's dyed black, her eyebrows are drawn on with a pencil, and on her head she's wearing two little horns, like baby goat horns, orange in colour.

'Good evening, ma'am,' he says in his Elvis register. 'I sure do admire those horns you got.' It's as good a way as any of starting social chat.

She laughs the hoarse laugh of a long-time smoker. 'Got them here, from a street vendor,' she says. 'Supposed to be the horns of Nymp.'

'Nymp?' says Stan.

'It's a nymphomaniac imp,' says Lucinda Quant. 'Some comic book manga thing. My grandkids know about it, they say it's all the rage.'

'How old are they?' Stan asks politely.

'Eight and ten,' says Lucinda. 'They even know what "nymphomaniac" means. When I was their age I didn't know which end of the lollipop to put in my mouth.'

Is that an innuendo? Stan hopes not. Suck it up, Stan, he tells himself. Be a man. Better still, be

424

some other man. Lucinda reeks of Blue Suede, an Elvis tribute scent Stan has inhaled a ton of lately. A lot of the old babes wear it; it must be sort of like cats rolling around on their dead owner's sweatshirts. It's weird to wear a perfume named after shoes, but what does he know? The aroma – a little like cinnamon, but with an undertone of leather preservative – wafts up from between Lucinda's breasts, the tops of which are on display in the plunge neckline of her scarlet hibiscus-flowered dress.

'So first I thought, those horns are for kids,' says Lucinda, 'but then I thought, why not? Go for it, gal! Live while you can, is what I say. I'm going to tell you right now this isn't my real hair. It's a wig. I'm a cancer survivor, or I am so far, touch wood, and right now I just want to enjoy the hell out of life.'

'That's okay, these aren't my real lips,' says Stan, and Lucinda laughs again. 'You're fabulous,' she says. She slides over and positions one of her bony little butt cheeks up against his thigh. Should he say, in his deep Elvis voice, 'Whoa, darlin', we've got all night'? No; that would hint, unfairly, of delights to come. Instead he says, 'So, since you've shared with me, I feel I should tell you that I'm gay.'

She laughs her smoky laugh. 'No, you're not,' she says. She pats his white-clad knee. 'But good try. We can discuss that later.'

Here they are at the venue, in the nick of time. The casino is a new one, with a Russian Empire theme; it's called The Kremlin. Gold onion domes on the outside, servitors in red boots, a line of fire-eaters dressed as Cossacks waiting to welcome them. One of these helps Lucinda out of the car while raising his flaming torch high in the other hand.

White Russians featured at the bars, and dancers in faux-fur pasties bumping to Slavic rock on several of the gambling tables. Four theatres inside: the shows now pull in more than the gambling, according to Rob, though they make you walk through the gambling on the off chance you'll be seized by the devil of risk.

'This way,' says Lucinda, 'I've been here before.' She steers him toward the theatre where their show will shortly begin.

Stan keeps an eye out for any bald guys with sunglasses, but so far, so good. They make it past the slots and the blackjack and the table dancers without mishap, then into the auditorium. He settles Lucinda into her seat; she puts on her rhinestone-studded reading glasses and peers at the souvenir program.

Stan glances around, locates the exits in case he has to run. There are at least a dozen other Elvises present in the auditorium, each with a crone under his wing. There's also a scattering of Marilyns, in red dresses and silver-blond wigs, paired with elderly dudes. Some of them have their arms around the shoulders of their Marilyns; the Marilyns are throwing back their heads, doing the iconic open-mouthed laugh, flashing their Marilyn teeth. He has to admit it's sexy, that laugh, even though he knows how fake it is.

'Now we'll make some conversation,' says Lucinda Quant. 'How did you get into this business?' Her voice has the neutrality and edge of a professional interviewer, which is what she claims to be.

Watch it, Stan, he tells himself. Remember those four bald guys. Too many questions means danger. 'It's a long story,' he says. 'I just do this when I'm between engagements. I'm an actor, really. In musical comedy.' That's a sure-fire yawner: everyone here is.

Luckily for him, the show begins.

REQUISITION

Early on the Monday morning, Jocelyn comes over to the house. Charmaine's had a shower and is dressed for work, with a white frilly blouse and all, but she isn't feeling up to scratch – it must be a hangover, though she's had so few of those in her life she isn't sure. Aurora is making scrambled eggs and coffee, even though Charmaine has said she doesn't think she could look an egg in the face. She has a dim memory of what they discussed the night before. She wishes she could recall more of it.

'There's an update,' says Jocelyn.

'Coffee?' says Aurora.

'Thanks,' says Jocelyn. She inspects Charmaine. 'What's happened? You look like hell, if you don't mind my saying so.'

'It's the grief,' Aurora says, and she and Charmaine both giggle.

Jocelyn takes this in. 'Okay, good story. Stick to it if he asks,' she says. 'I can see that the two of you had a play date in the liquor cabinet. I'll get rid of the evidence for you, empties are my thing. Now listen up.'

They sit at the kitchen table. Charmaine tries a sip of coffee. She's not ready to tackle the eggs yet.

'Here's his plan,' says Jocelyn. 'Charmaine, he'll tell you he's taking a business trip to Las Vegas. He'll ask you to book tickets for him, and for yourself as well. He'll say he requires your services onsite.'

'What kind of services?' Charmaine asks nervously. 'Is he going to trap me in a hotel room, and then . . .'

'Nothing so simple,' says Jocelyn. 'As you know, he's through with sexbots, for his personal use. He's moving to the next frontier.'

'This is what I was telling you,' says Aurora. 'Last night.'

Charmaine's recollections of last night are a little fuzzy. No, they are very fuzzy. What was it she and Aurora were drinking? Maybe there was a drug in it. There was something about Aurora's face coming off, but that can't be right. 'Frontier?' she says. All she can think of is Western movies.

Jocelyn brings out her PosiPad, turns it on, calls up a video. 'Sorry for the quality,' she says, 'but you can hear quite well.' There's a pixelated Ed standing in front of a large boardroom touchscreen that says Possibilibots in writing that scrawls across the space, explodes into fireworks, then begins again. He's addressing a small gathering of men in suits, visible only as the backs of heads.

'I have it on good authority,' he's saying in his

most persuasive manner, 'that the interface experience, even with our most advanced models, is and can only ever be an unconvincing substitute for the real thing. A resort for the desperate, perhaps' – here there's some laughter from the backs of the heads – 'but surely we can do better than that!'

Murmuring; the haircuts nod.

Ed continues: 'The human body is complex, my friends – more complex than we can hope to duplicate with what is, and can only be, a mechanical contrivance. And the human body is driven by the human brain, which is the most sophisticated, the most intricate construct in the known universe. We've been killing ourselves trying to approximate that body–brain combo! But maybe we got hold of the wrong end of the stick!'

'How do you mean?' asks one of the heads.

'What I mean is, why build a self-standing device when a self-standing device already exists? Why reinvent the wheel? Why not just make those wheels *roll where we want them to?* In a way that is beneficial to all. The greatest possible happiness of the greatest possible number – that's what Possibilibots stands for, am I right?'

'Cut to the chase,' says one of the haircuts. 'You're not on TV, we don't need the sermon.'

'What's wrong with our current position? I thought we were raking it in,' says another.

'We are, we are,' says Ed. 'But we can rake it in even more. Okay, short form: why not take an existing body and brain, and, by a painless intervention, cause that entity – that person – not to put too fine a point on it, that hot babe who won't come across for you – cause her to home in on you and you alone, as if she thinks you're the sexiest hunk she's ever seen?'

'Is this some kind of a perfume?' says another voice. 'With the pheromones, like with moths? I tried that, it's crap. I attracted a raccoon.'

'No shit! A real raccoon? Or just a dame with . . .'

'If it's a new oxytocin–Viagara pill, they don't last. The next morning she'll go back to thinking you're a douche.'

'What happened with the raccoon? That would be something new!' Laughter.

'No, no,' says Ed. 'Let's settle down. It's not a pill, and believe it or not, it isn't science fiction. The technique they're refining at our Las Vegas clinic is based on the work that's been done on the erasure of painful memories, in vets, child-abuse survivors, and so forth. They discovered that not only can they pinpoint various fears and nega-tive associations in the brain and then excise them, but they can also wipe out your previous love object and imprint you with a different one.'

The camera moves to a very pretty woman in a hospital bed. She's asleep. Then her eyes open, move sideways. 'Oh,' she says, smiling with joy. 'You're here! At last! I love you!'

'Wow, that simple,' says a haircut. 'She's not acting?'

'No,' says Ed. 'This is one that didn't work out; we tried it onsite here, but it was too soon, the technique hadn't been perfected. Our Vegas team is up to speed on it now. But it illustrates the principle.' Segue left: The woman is pressing her lips to a blue teddy bear in a passionate kiss.

'That's Veronica!' Charmaine almost shrieks. 'Oh my gosh! She's fallen in love with knitwear!'

'Wait,' says Jocelyn. 'There's more.'

'I don't know what saboteur gave her that bear,' Ed says. 'Trouble is, this thing works on anything with two eyes. The guy who ordered the hit . . . ordered the job . . . ordered the operation was very annoyed when he turned up, but he was too late. She'd already imprinted. Timing is everything.'

'This is dynamite,' says one of the heads. 'You could have a harem, you could have . . .'

'So you designate the target . . .'

'You requisition it . . .'

'Into the van, then the plane,' says Ed, 'off to the Vegas clinic, a quick needle, and then – a whole new life!'

'Fan-fucking-tastic!'

Jocelyn turns off the PosiPad. 'That's it, in a nutshell,' she says.

'You mean, they're snatching them?' says Charmaine. 'Out of their own lives? The women?'

'That's a blunt way of putting it,' says Jocelyn. 'Though not just women, it's a unisex thing. Yes, that would be the idea. But the subject doesn't

432

mind, because their previous love attachments have been nullified.'

'So that's why Ed wants her to go on the business trip to Vegas?' says Aurora.

'He hasn't told me in so many words,' says Jocelyn, 'but it's a fair guess.'

'You mean, he wants to fix it so I don't love Stan any more,' Charmaine says. She hears her own voice: it's so sad. If that happened, Stan would become a stranger to her. Their whole past, their wedding, living in their car, everything they went through together . . . Maybe she'd remember it, but it wouldn't mean anything. It would be like listening to someone else, someone she doesn't even know, someone boring.

'Yes. You wouldn't love Stan any more. You'd love Ed instead,' says Jocelyn. 'You'd dote on him.'

This is like one of those love potions in the old fairy-tale books at Grandma Win's, thinks Charmaine. The kind where you get imprisoned by a toad prince. In those stories you always got the true love back at the end, as long as you had a magic silver dress or something; but in real life – in this real life, the one Ed's planning for her – she'll be under some awful toad prince spell forever. 'That's horrible!' Charmaine says. 'I'll kill myself first!'

'Maybe,' says Jocelyn, 'but you won't kill yourself after. You'll come to when the operation's over, and there will be Ed, holding your hand and gazing into your eyes, and you'll take one look at him and throw your arms around him and say you'll love him forever. Then you'll beg him to make whatever sexual use of you he wants. And you'll mean that, every single word. You'll never get enough of him. That's how this thing is supposed to work.'

'Oh gosh,' says Charmaine. 'But you can't let that happen to me! No matter what I've . . . you can't let it happen to *Stan*!'

'You still care about Stan?' Jocelyn says with interest. 'After everything?'

Charmaine has a flash of Stan, how sweet he was, much of the time; how innocent he looked when he was sleeping, like a boy; how crushed he would be if she turned her back on him as if he'd never existed, and took the arm of Ed, and walked away. He would never, ever get over it.

She can't help it: she begins to cry. Great big tears are rolling out of her eyes, she's gasping for breath. Aurora brings her a tissue but doesn't go so far as to pat her shoulder. 'At least he wants *you*,' she says. 'Not just the robot of you.'

'It's okay,' Jocelyn says. 'Calm down. Ed has specified that I'm going with you. I'm your security, I'm your bodyguard, I'm supposed to keep you safe.' She pauses, to let this sink in. 'And I will keep you safe. I've got your back.'

PART XIII

GREEN MAN

GREEN MAN

The show Lucinda's got tickets for is the Green Man Group. They're a spinoff of the Blue Man Group, who've been going in Vegas for decades. Stan saw a spoof version of them on YouTube when he was still working at Dimple. There are also the Red Man Group and the Orange Man Group and the Pink Man Group, each with a different gimmick. With the Green Man Group, says the program, it's an eco theme.

Sure enough, when the spots and floods go on, there's some fake vegetation with some fake birds in it, and when the first set of Green Men come bouncing out they're not only bald and painted a shiny green but also wearing foliage. Apart from the leaves, it's the same kind of tightly directed comedy, tech, and music show that Stan can remember watching online, or parts of it: tricks with balloons that turn into flowers, munching up kale and spitting green goop out of their mouths, juggling onions, and a lot of drumming, plus a guy with a gong who's used as punctuation. No words – none of the Men ever say anything, since the pretense is that they're mute. Once in a while, there's a bit of message – birdsong, a sunrise on the big onstage screens, a flight of helium balloons with baby trees attached to them – but then the drums kick in again.

All of sudden there's a tulip number, done to 'Tiptoe Through the Tulips.' At first this makes Stan sit up straight: it's the password from his time at Possibilibots, it can't be a fucking coincidence! But as the number unfolds he thinks, Hold on, Stan. Yes, it can be a coincidence, a lot of things are, and considering the barefaced idiocy of what the Green Men are doing up there on the stage, it has to be. If it were a signal, what the fuck would they be expecting him to do in response? Run around screaming? Yell, *Take my belt buckle! Here's the flashdrive?* So, coincidence, for sure.

He leans back in the seat, watches the number. There are tulip-themed pyrotechnics, tulip manip-ulations, tulip transformations: tulips that catch fire, tulips that explode, tulips that grow out of a Green Man's ears. Stan has to admit it's expertly performed, and also funny. It's relaxing to see other guys making fools of themselves. But if they're doing it on purpose, maybe it doesn't count.

Next up, a gong item. The one playing the gong is a clown of sorts. He gets a lot of laughs. But is there only one gong guy? The Green Men are like the Elvises: they're in identical costumes and hard to tell apart. Stan tries to follow the switches, but it's like watching a card sharp: the trick is done, you know it's a trick, but you can't catch them doing it.

The second-last number is an audience participation segment. Three innocents are hauled up on stage, dressed in waterproof outfits, asked to eat peculiar substances, and bombarded with green goo. Then there's a grand finale, with more drums, gongs, and things that light up. Then there's the curtain calls. The bald green guys are sweating.

'So, Rental Elvis, what's your verdict?' says Lucinda as the lights go up.

'Good timing,' says Stan.

'That's it? Good timing?' says Lucinda. 'Men devote their lives to developing those skills and that's all you can say? I bet you're a wow in bed.'

Fuck you, thinks Stan. But I'd rather not. 'Ma'am,' he says, ushering her down the aisle with a swirl of his blue cape. 'After you.' Her orange horns are on crooked; they give her a rakish air, like a demon on holiday.

Lucinda says she's headed for the ladies', and after that she expects Stan to take her to one of the bars in this joint and share a White Russian or two with him, and tell her his life story. The night is young, so after they do that, they can do something else. She fully intends to get her money's worth, she tells him, with a grin, but also in the stern, slightly accusing voice of a high school teacher.

One thing at a time, he thinks. He shepherds

her to the ladies'. As he's waiting for her outside, scanning the thinning crowd for anyone thuggish who looks too interested in him, one of the Marilyns sidles up beside him. 'Stan,' she whispers. 'It's me. Veronica.'

'What took you so fucking long?' he growls. 'There's some Positron guys in sunglasses asking about me at the place where I'm living. You need to move me! Where's Budge? Where's Conor? Am I a small potato? If this crap I'm carrying is so shit-hot, why isn't anyone coming to collect it?'

'Keep your voice down,' she says. 'NAB's always crawling with eavesdroppers. Those broadcasters like to steal scoops and rat on each other to anyone listening. That could be bad for you.'

'I thought Jocelyn wanted to get the news out!' says Stan.

'It's the positioning,' says Veronica. 'She needs to hold back until the exact right moment. Come with me, hurry. We're going backstage.'

'What about my date?' Stan says. Lucinda will raise hell if he vanishes; she's the hell-raising type.

'Don't worry about that. We've got another Elvis, he'll take your place, she won't be able to tell you apart.'

Stan doubts that – Lucinda's not stupid – but he follows Veronica down a side aisle and through the Exit door at the front row of the theatre. There's a corridor, a corner, some stairs. Then the stage door. She knocks on it. It's opened by a bald guy painted green, in a dark green suit and an earpiece. 'That way,' he says. They've thought of everything: themed bouncers.

Veronica hurries along a narrow corridor, Stan trailing. She's got the Marilyn rear action down cold: do they give classes in it? Sprain your ankle, then stuff your feet into the high heels? Veronica, he thinks mournfully. You are so fucking wasted on that bear.

They pause in front of a closed dressing-room door with a green star on it. THE GREEN MAN GROUP.

'Wait in here,' says Veronica. 'If anyone comes, say you're auditioning.'

'Who'm I waiting for?' says Stan.

'The contact,' says Veronica. 'The handover. The one who'll take your info to the press. If we're lucky, that is. You've still got the belt buckle?'

'What's this?' says Stan, indicating his large, ornate midsection adornment. 'Kinda hard to miss.'

'Nobody switched it on you? The buckle?'

'Why would they?' said Stan. 'It's crap silver, it's not real. Anyway, I slept with it under my pillow.'

Veronica shrugs her lovely Marilyn shoulders. 'Hope you're right,' she says. 'It wouldn't be good if they open it up and they're expecting a flashdrive and there's nothing inside. They'll think you flogged it.'

'Who the fuck would I flog it to?' Stan asks. He'd considered such a thing briefly, but he has no leverage. Whoever wanted it and knew where it was would simply take it, then fling him into a ditch.

'Oh, someone would pay,' says Veronica. 'One way or another. Now, in you go. I've gotta run. Good luck!' She purses her Marilyn lips, blows him a Marilyn kiss, closes the door quietly behind herself.

Nobody's in the dressing room. There's a long, lighted mirror, a counter running along underneath it, a bunch of makeup pots, green paint in them. Brushes. A chair to sit in while painting yourself. A couple of Green Man suits on hangers, on the hook in back of the door. Street clothes: denim pants, jacket, black T. Pair of Nikes, large. Whoever's got this dressing room, his feet are bigger than Stan's.

There's only one way out of this room: he doesn't like that part. He bypasses the chair and sits down on the counter, facing away from the mirror. He's careful not to turn his back to the door.

GONG FOR HIRE

There's a knock. What should he do? Nowhere to hide, so he might as well go down trying. 'Come on in,' he says, using his Elvis voice.

The door opens. It's Luncinda Quant. Fuck, how did she track him down? But she doesn't say, 'Where did you get to?' or anything like that. Instead she nips inside, closes the door, strides over to him, and hisses, 'Undo your belt!' She's fumbling at him with her red-tipped fingers.

'Whoa!' he says. 'Wait a minute, lady! If that's what you want, you need to be back at your hotel, and then I can call, we have a service, you'll love . . .' The thought of Lucinda Quant in bed with an Elvis bot makes him shudder. Even in her present diminished form, she'd be odds on to win that one.

'Don't panic, I don't want your body,' she growls with a derisive laugh. 'I want your belt buckle. Right now!'

'Wait,' he says. She can't be the one! She's not at all what he was expecting – not a suave double agent in black, not a tough Surveillance guy working for Jocelyn, not – worst case! – a Positron-sent assassin. How can he know this unlikely biddy is the right handover link? 'Just a minute,' he says. 'Who sent you?'

'Don't be silly. You know who,' she says, tossing her black wig and orange Nymp horns with a hint of the coyness that must have made her a lethal flirt forty years ago. 'This is gonna be my fucking comeback, so don't screw around.'

Wait, wait, he tells himself. You can't just roll over. 'There's a password,' he says as sternly as he can.

'Tiptoe Through the fucking Tulips,' she says. 'Now do I have to pull your pants off or what?'

Stan unsnaps his belt. Lucinda takes it over to the makeup counter, puts on her reading glasses, and holds the buckle under the light. She's got a tiny implement, like a little screwdriver. She inserts it into the top of the buckle, gives a twist, and the thing snaps open. Inside there's a miniature black flashdrive.

She tucks the drive into a small envelope, licks it shut, whips off her hair complete with the horns, and duct-tapes the drive to the top of her fuzzy scalp, which isn't totally bald, but close. Then she pulls the wig back on and adjusts her horns. 'Thanks,' she says. 'I'm off. I sure hope this has a major scandal in it. I don't mind risking what's left of my neck, so long as it's worth it. Watch the news!'

She's gone in a swirl of hibiscus floral print and

Blue Suede perfume. What's next? Stan wonders. Wait until the four guys in sunglasses arrive and start ripping out my molars? *I don't have it!* he'll scream. *It's that wizened-up cancer survivor with horns! She's duct-taped it to her head!* Why can't life hand him something plausible for a change?

The door opens again: four bald guys file in, except they don't have sunglasses, and they're green. They fill the dressing room. 'Stan,' says the first one, advancing in back-pat stance. 'Welcome to Vegas, bro!'

'Conor!' says Stan. 'What the fuck!' They do the pat; something wet comes off on Stan's cheek.

'Right,' says Conor, smiling greenly. 'You remember Rikki and Jerold. It was Jerold let you in backstage.'

Handshakes, grins, whacks on the shoulder. The fourth guy says, 'Stan. Well done.' Could it be Budge? Bald and green? Yes, it could.

'You guys freaked me out,' says Stan. 'Turning up at the Elvis place, with my picture and all.' His honeymoon photo on the beach, the one he'd sent to Conor. That's where they'd got it.

'Sorry about that,' says Con. 'Thought we could cut some corners, make contact earlier, save time. But we missed you.'

'It came out okay in the wash,' says Budge.

'How'd you get out of Possibilibots?' Stan asks him.

'In a box, like you,' says Budge. 'Hard to find

an Elvis outfit my size, but we cut it up the back the way the undertakers do; plus the box was cramped, but apart from that it worked without a hitch. Our mutual lady friend closed my lid at the Possibilibots end.'

'Let's get you out of that dickwit Elvis trash. You look like a twat,' says Conor. 'Who's got the razor?'

Stan, wearing a badly fitting Green Man suit, his head newly shaved, his face a seaweed green, is drinking a coconut water in Conor's dressing room. Conor says the coconut water is a quick energy lift, though Stan really doesn't need any more energy right now: he's buzzing like a bad fuse.

On the small, blurry dressing room screen, the second Green Man show of the night is in progress. They run them through in teams, says Conor, because the act takes so much out of you. Not out of his boys, because they're not really in it, they're just in disguise. They can come and go backstage because everyone in Team One thinks they're in the other team and vice versa. But Conor himself has always craved the spotlight, so he's had himself inserted as a gong player.

'Yeah, I know, it's moronic,' says Conor. 'But you have to admit it's the best cover while we're waiting to pull the job.'

'What job?' says Stan.

'Oh. She didn't tell you? She was extra fucking definite about you. She said you totally had to be in with us; otherwise, it would be a fail. She said you were the lynchpin.'

'Who says? You mean . . .' He stops himself from saying Jocelyn's name. He glances around, then up at the ceiling: is it safe in here?

'I mean her! The Big Wazooka! She said the two of you were fucking joined at the hip.'

The Big Wazooka isn't how Stan would have thought of Jocelyn, but it kind of fits. *Bazooka.* 'So, I'm the lynchpin,' he says. 'Mind if I ask why?'

'Fucked if I know,' says Conor cheerfully. 'Been doing odd jobs for her since before Christ. She's known you were my big brother ever since she saw you at the trailer joint, before you signed in to that body-parts wholesaler corral. But I never ask her why she wants what she wants, that's her business. Deal is I just do the job, no loose ends; then I collect, end of story, have a nice life. But I guess we find out tomorrow, about why you're so fucking central. That's when it's going down.'

Stan tries to look wise. Is it possible to look wise with your face painted green? He doubts it. 'What do I do?' he says. He hopes they aren't going to rob a bank or kill anyone. 'On this job? When it's going down?'

'Figure we'll put you on the gong,' says Conor. 'Not hard to pick up, you just have to know the cues, then hit the gong with the hammer and look like a dumbass. That shouldn't be too hard for you.'

'So I'm onstage?' says Stan. That's not safe,

everyone will be looking at him. But then, so what? He no longer has the thing in the belt buckle; he no longer has even the belt, since Rikki took away his whole Elvis outfit and tossed it into a dumpster.

'Not here,' says Conor. 'Place called Ruby Slippers. It's a retirement home clinic type of thing, lot of rich old farts warehoused or getting themselves cut and sewed. We're the entertainment.'

'That's all?' says Stan. 'All I have to do is hit the gong?' Though he's been to that Ruby Slippers branch as Elvis a lot, romancing old ladies, nobody will recognize him; not in his current disguise as a giant pea.

'Don't be a fucking dummy,' says Conor. 'That's the cover! The real job is a snatch.'

'That place has fucking tight security,' says Stan.

'Hey! This is your brother you're talking to!' says Conor. He rubs two fingers together. 'Those guys get paid off! We just go there, start the green act, knock down the security for the look of it, do the snatch . . .'

Crap, thinks Stan. They're kidnapping someone. That could get them shot, not to mention himself. 'So, I hit the gong . . .'

'You got it,' says Conor. 'And then, whisk-o!'

'Whisk-o?'

'The big snatcheroonie,' says Conor. 'It's genius.'

IN FLIGHT

Ed's up front, in Business. It would look strange for Charmaine to be there too – after all, she's only the assistant, officially. That's Ed's reasoning, says Jocelyn: he doesn't want to call undue attention. Thank goodness for that, thinks Charmaine, because she would find it very, very hard to be nice to him or even civil, now that she knows what he intends to do to her. If she were beside him in Business, most likely he'd be squeezing her arm all the way to Las Vegas, plus dosing her with gin and tonic and trying to get his fingers onto her knee or look down her front, though no hope of that because she's wearing the button-to-the-chin blouse Aurora picked out for her.

And all the time he'd be asking her if she's feeling any less grief because of Stan. Not that he really cares about Stan, or about anything she likes or loves or doesn't like or love, because he has no interest in who she is really. She's mostly just a body to him, and now he wants to turn her into only a body. She might as well not have any head at all.

449

After feeling so sad for weeks, she's really angry underneath. If she had to sit with Ed she'd be sure to snap at him, and then he might figure out that she's learned about his big plan. And then he might panic and do something weird, right on the plane. He might throw her to the floor and start ripping off her buttons, the way Max used to, but with Max she wanted him to do that, whereas with Ed it would be a very different thing, it would be awkward and quite frankly creepy. *Keep your freaking hands off my darn buttons!* That's what she would say.

Well, he couldn't really do that – the floor thing with the buttons – because the flight attendants would stop him. But what if they turned a blind eye, what if they're all his employees, what if everyone on the plane is on his side?

Calm down, Charmaine, she tells herself. That's just foolish. Those kinds of things don't happen in real life. It's okay, it's going to be fine, because Jocelyn is sitting beside her and Aurora is in the row behind them, and there's another Surveillance person on the plane too, Jocelyn has assured her – a man, back near the exit door. And that man plus Jocelyn and Aurora, they'll be more than a match for Ed. She doesn't know what they'll do, but it might involve a judo kick or something. And they have the advantage of knowing about Ed's plan, while he doesn't know a thing about theirs.

Or Jocelyn has the advantage of knowing about Ed's plan. So far she hasn't shared too much of it with Charmaine. She's reading on her PosiPad, making notes. Charmaine has tried for an in-flight movie – how amazing it would be to see a movie that isn't from the fifties, she hasn't been able to watch anything like that for ages, and it would take her mind off things – but her screen isn't working. Neither is the Recline button on her seat, and someone's ripped most of the pages out of the in-flight magazine. In her opinion the airline people do things like that on purpose, to rub it in that you aren't in Business. They most likely have a special team that goes through the planes at night, ripping out the pages and messing up the screens.

Charmaine looks out the window: clouds, nothing but clouds. Flat clouds, not even puffy ones. At first it was so exciting to be on a plane – she's only ever been on one before, with Stan, going on their honeymoon. She reads the remaining piece in the magazine. What a coincidence: 'Honeymoon on the Beach.' Stan got such a sunburn the first day, but at least they did one thing he really wanted, which was having sex underwater, or the lower parts of them were underwater. There were people on the beach too. Could they tell? She hoped they could, she remembers hoping that. Then they had to get their bathing suits on again, and Charmaine couldn't find her bikini bottom because in all the turmoil she'd dropped it, and Stan had to go diving for it, and they laughed and laughed. They were so happy then. It was just like an ad.

Out the window it's still clouds. She gets up, goes to the washroom for something to do. How thoughtless, the last person didn't clean the sink. Really, they don't appreciate their privileges.

It's better to close the lid when you flush: Grandma Win told her that. Otherwise the germs fly around in the air and go up your nose.

Coming back along the aisle, she wonders which one is the security man. Right near the exit, Jocelyn said. She glances around but can't see the heads back there. She reaches her seat, squeezes in past Jocelyn, who smiles at her but doesn't say anything. Charmaine fidgets some more; then she just has to ask.

'What in the heck was he planning to *do*?'

Jocelyn looks over at her. 'Who?' she asks, as if she doesn't know.

'Him. Ed,' Charmaine whispers. 'How was he going to . . .'

'Hungry?' Jocelyn says. 'Because I am. Let's get some peanuts. Want a soda? Coffee?' She looks at her watch. 'We've got time.'

'Just a water,' says Charmaine. 'Please.'

Jocelyn flags the flight attendant, orders some peanuts and a couple of cheese sandwiches, and a bottle of water for Charmaine with a glass of ice cubes, and a coffee for herself. Charmaine is surprised at how hungry she is; she wolfs down the sandwich in no time flat, gulps down a glass of the water.

'He has it all thought out,' says Jocelyn. 'I'm

452

supposed to knock you out on the plane, just before we land. A little something in your drink: Zolpidem, or GBH, or similar.'

'Oh,' says Charmaine. 'Like, those date rape drugs.'

'Right. So you'll go under. Then I'll say you've fainted, and we call a paramedic ambulance to meet the plane and have you carried off on a stretcher. Then you'll be taken to the clinic at Ruby Slippers Vegas, and after the brain intervention you'll wake up, and Ed will be right beside you, holding your hand. And you'll imprint on him and smile at him like he's God, and throw your arms around him, and say you're his, body and soul, and what can you do for him, such as a blowjob right there in the clinic.'

'That so totally sucks,' Charmaine says, wrinkling her nose.

'And then you'll live happily ever after,' Jocelyn continues in her neutral voice. 'Just like in a fairy tale. And Ed will too. That must be what he thinks.'

'How do you mean, he *will*?' says Charmaine. 'The first part of it's not even happening! It's not happening! You won't let it happen. That's what you said.'

'Correct,' says Jocelyn. 'That's what I said. So now you can relax.'

And Charmaine does feel relaxed; her eyelids are drooping. She nods off, but then she's awake again. Awake more or less. 'Maybe I'll have that coffee after all,' she says. 'I need to perk myself up.'

'Too late,' says Jocelyn. 'We're about to land. And look, I think I see the ambulance, right on cue. I sent them an email before we took off. Feeling a little sleepy? Just lie back.'

'The ambulance? What ambulance?' says Charmaine. It's not just sleepiness, there's something wrong. She looks at Jocelyn and there are two Jocelyns, both of them smiling. They pat her arm.

'The ambulance that will take you to Ed's clinic at Ruby Slippers,' she says.

You promised, you promised, Charmaine wants to say. It must have been the water, something Jocelyn put in. *Oh heck! You lying witch!* But she can't get the words out. Her tongue feels thick, her eyes are closing. She feels her whole body leaning sideways.

Bumpity-bump, they must be on the runway. She's so dizzy. Voices, far away: *She's fainted. I don't know what . . . she was fine a minute ago. Here, let me . . .* That's Aurora. She tries to call to her, but there are no words, only a kind of moaning. *Uhuhuhuh . . .*

Don't let her head hit the wall. Jocelyn.

She's in the arms of someone, some man; she's being swung through the air. It feels lovely, like floating. *Easy does it. There.* He sets her down, covers her. Is that Max? Is that Max's voice, so close to her ear? *All tucked in.*

Falling, falling. Gone.

PART XIV

SNATCH

SNATCH

It's better for Stan not to return to the Elvisorium, says Conor, because although the guys in sunglasses who'd come looking for him were only Conor and his three pals, you never knew. Next time they might be more sinister, and better to have left no trails, because after the big snatcheroonie takes place, leaving trails might turn out to be a fucking bad idea. If everything goes as planned there won't be a problem with that because no one will be poking their nose in and asking questions; but if it goes tits up, then there's a risk that all five of them could be toasting on the red-hot barbecue unless they're ready to wipe their whereabouts off the GPS very fucking quick. It's a big fucking risk, what they're about to do.

Conor doesn't seem very worried about the big fucking risk, thinks Stan. If anything, he's excited. Break the window on the mobile home, talk Stan into sneaking inside with him, then, when someone comes, run away very fast, leaving Stan to explain what he's doing with two steaks from the freezer and a lady's underpants. Always Conor's idea of a fun night out.

Conor and the boys have a two-bedroom Emperor Suite at Caesars Palace: whoever's hired Con isn't poor. Con says they can't go out, to a show or a strip joint or the casinos, because he can't run the risk of them fucking up so close to bingo. Budge says that's fine with him, maybe they can watch a game, but there's some grumbling from Rikki and Jerold. Con shuts that down by saying who's running this, and if there's a question about that he'd be happy to settle it. So the five of them end up playing Texas hold'em for grapes and pieces of cheese off the Cheese Assortment plate Con's ordered in and drinking Singapore Slings because Con's never had one and wants to try it, but they can only have three each because they have to be fresh for the next day.

Stan wins a moderate amount of cheese, which he eats; but after three Singapore Slings he's out for the count and nods off on the sofa. Just as well, because there are only four beds, and he has no yen to be in any of them with someone else.

In the morning the five of them sleep in, shower, complain about their hangovers – all except Budge, who'd showed some self-restraint the night before – and order in breakfast. Rikki stands behind the door when the cart arrives, Glock at the ready like something in a cop show, just in case it's a trap. But no, it's only scrambled eggs, ham, toast, and coffee, wheeled in by an agreeable serving wench: they're safe so far.

Then they get suited up and paint their heads green. Con's hired a van; it's in Parking with the Green Man gear already loaded into it. Before they leave, Con goes over Stan's gong cues. Every time he points to his ear – the one with the earpiece – Stan is to hit the gong. He doesn't need to know fucking why, he only has to hit it. That shouldn't be too hard. If Con should suddenly rush off toward, for instance, an ambulance that might, for instance, be pulling up in front of the facility, and if the other fake Green Men should rush off with him, Stan should hit the gong three more times so people think it's all part of the show. Then he should wait for further cues. Then he should go with the flow.

Once they're in the van Stan gets butterflies. What is the flow? Is this going to be another case of Con vanishing over the fence while Stan is left floundering?

'You missed some green at the back,' Jerold says to him. 'I'll paint it in.'

'Thanks,' says Stan. He has a crick in his neck: he's sitting up very straight so the green from his scalp doesn't rub off on the upholstery.

Con has a pass that gets their van in through the Ruby Slippers gate, with its motto: *There's No Place Like Home*.

Inside, the road divides: Main Entrance and Reception to the left, Clinic to the right and around the corner. They park in the Visitors Disabled section at the front and lockstep inside; Con flashes his pass at the receptionist.

'Oh, the special event,' she says. 'You'll be in the Atrium.' She's obviously used to green guys or the equivalent filing in past her desk. Clowns, jugglers, singers with guitars, zombie dancers, pirates, Batmen, whatever. Actors.

In the Atrium there's one special event already at full volume – an Elvis, in the white-and-gold outfit. He's finishing up a gargly rendition of 'Love Me Tender' and gives the Green Men a dirty look as they troop in. The old people in the audience provide a smattering of applause, and the Elvis says, 'Thank you, thank you very much. Would you like another song?'

But Con blows the green New Year's Eve horn he's brought along, which puts a stop to that. 'Can't have that loser cutting in on our act,' he says. 'Let's get that music going!'

The music's on a phone, playing through a small Bluetooth speaker. Con prances around in time to it, shaking a couple of green maracas and grinning like a maniac. Jerold's blowing up green balloons with a hydrogen cylinder, Rikki's handing them to Budge, who doles them out to the audience members. They take hold of the strings, some with confusion, some with distrust, others maybe with pleasure, though it's hard to tell. Several Ruby Slippers Events Assistants in their trademark red shoes help out, wearing green hats in honour of the Men. 'Isn't this nice?' they coo, in case there's any doubt, which there is. But no one has protested yet, so the act must be doing well enough, or at least well enough to convince. Conor points to his ear and Stan whangs the gong.

Con looks at his watch. 'Fuck,' Stan hears him mutter. 'What's keeping them? Squirt some water out of your mouth,' he tells Rikki. 'That's always a howler.'

Now there's the wail of a siren, coming closer. An ambulance drives in through the front gate, heading for the clinic entrance at the side. Con produces a giant rubber tulip from inside his jacket, waves it aloft. It explodes, mildly. That's the signal: Jerold, Rikki, and Budge release a clutch of helium balloons into the air, rush out through the Atrium door, and disappear around the corner.

'Are they coming back?' says a plaintive voice from the audience. Stan nods vigorously and hits the gong again. Maybe they're a success after all.

Now Con is tugging on his sleeve: he's bowing, so Stan does the same. Con links arms with him and lock-steps him out through the door. 'We got him,' he whispers. Who have they got? Stan wonders.

They sashay around the corner. 'Perfect,' says Con. There's the ambulance, back doors open. There's Jocelyn, with another woman. Jocelyn's asshole of a husband is helping Budge with a third man, who appears to have slumped to the ground. It's Ed, the big cheese at Positron, without a doubt: no mistaking that suit-and-haircut combo. Two Ruby Slippers security guards and three other guys in black suits litter the pavement. Fast work, thinks Stan.

'Let's move it, lynchpin,' says Con. 'In here.' He steers Stan to the ambulance.

Inside there's a stretcher, with someone on it, covered to the chin with a red-and-white blanket.

A woman. Charmaine. Is that the robot head? It looks too real. Stan touches her cheek.

'Oh fuck!' he says. 'Is she dead?'

'She's not dead,' says Jocelyn, who has joined him. 'Everything's in order, but we don't have long. The neuro team is standing ready.'

'Let's get the two of them inside the clinic,' says Con. 'Fast.'

FLAMED

Lucinda Quant breaks the story of the big leak on the six o'clock news. She's straightforward, she's believable, and, best of all, she has extensive document trails and video footage. She tells the story about how she came by her treasure trove of dirt, though she doesn't name names – she says 'a brave employee' – and how she smuggled the flashdrive containing the information through the herds of nosy journalists and undercover security agents at the NAB convention by taping it to the top of her fuzzy head under her cancer survivor's wig – here she removes the wig, to demonstrate.

She closes by saying that she is so glad fate has given her this opportunity at what might be the end of her life, because *Live every minute to the full* has always been her motto, and she's humble about the small part she's played in what is after all a much bigger picture, and though she could have been a hit-and-run casualty or found mysteriously dead under a blackjack table or similar, because big money has a lot invested in Positron, she took the risk because the public has a right to know.

The host thanks her very much, and says that America would be a better place if there were more people like her. Big smiles from both of them.

Instantly the social media sites are ablaze with outrage. Prison abuses! Organ harvesting! Sex slaves created by neurosurgery! Plans to suck the blood of babies! Corruption and greed, though these in themselves are no great surprise. But the misappropriation of people's bodies, the violation of public trust, the destruction of human rights – how could such things have been allowed to happen? Where was the oversight? Which politicians bought into this warped scheme in a misguided attempt to create jobs and save money for the taxpayer? Talk shows roister on into the night – they haven't had this much fun in years – and bloggers break out in flames.

Because there's always two sides, at least two sides. Some say those who got their organs harvested and may subsequently have been converted into chicken feed were criminals anyway, and they should have been gassed, and this was a real way for them to pay their debt to society and make reparation for the harm they'd caused, and anyway it wasn't as wasteful as just throwing them out once dead. Others said that was all very well in the early stages of Positron, but it was clear that after Management had gone through their stash of criminals and also realized what the going price was for livers and kidneys, they'd started in on the shoplifters and pot-smokers, and then they'd been snatching people off the street because money talks, and once it had started talking at Positron it wouldn't shut up.

Yet others said that the twin city idea had been a good one at first; who could sneeze at full employment and a home for everyone? There were a few rotten apples, but without them it would've worked. In response, some said that these utopian schemes always went bad and turned into dictatorships, because human nature was what it was. As for the operation that imprinted you on a love object – if not of your own choice, then of somebody's choice – what was the harm in that since both parties ended up satisfied?

Some bloggers objected, others agreed, and in no time at all 'Communist' and 'Fascist' and 'psychopathy' and 'soft on crime' and a new one, 'neuropimp,' were whizzing through the air like buckshot.

Stan's watching one of the talk shows on the flatscreen in the recovery room where Charmaine lies in an anesthetic slumber. There's a small white bandage on her head, no blood. Happily they didn't shave off her hair; that would have been unsightly. She may get a fright when she first sees the new, bald Stan, but that will be fleeting, says Jocelyn, and after that Charmaine will be all his. 'But don't push your luck,' she says. 'Be kind to her. No grudges. Remember, she didn't have

465

any more sex with Max, or Phil, than you had with me – less, in fact – and I intend to tell her all about our little interlude. This new chance you're being handed is your payout for all the help you've given us, so don't muck it up. By the way, get rid of the green makeup; otherwise you'll have to paint yourself up like a zucchini every time you want sex.'

Stan did as suggested, wrecking a couple of hospital towels in the process, because he could see the point of it. Then he settled down to wait for the magic moment when his Sleeping Beauty would awaken and he could say goodbye to frog-hood and become a prince. He's listening to the TV on the earphones, so as not to disturb Charmaine prematurely. Jocelyn has been very firm – he must not leave the bedside, even to pee, or Charmaine may imprint on the wrong love object, such as a wandering nurse – so there's a bedpan handy.

How long is this going to take? He could use a burger.

As if on cue, in comes Aurora, carrying a tray. 'I thought you might like a nibble,' she says.

'Thanks,' says Stan. It's only tea and cookies, but that will hold him till something more carnivore-friendly comes along.

Aurora perches on the foot of Charmaine's bed. 'You're going to be amazed at the results,' she says. 'I certainly am! As soon as Max woke up and gazed into my eyes he swore undying love, and five minutes later he proposed! Isn't that a miracle?' Stan said it certainly was.

'He's so handsome,' Aurora says dreamily. Stan yups politely.

'Of course he's already married,' Aurora says, 'but the divorce is underway; Jocelyn ordered it up in advance, and UR-ELF is taking care of it for them. It's called the Lonely Street Special, they fast-lane it.'

'Congratulations,' says Stan. He means it. The idea of philandering Phil or roaming Max tied by the ankle to Aurora – or to a pit bull or a lamp-post, come to that – does not displease him at all, so long as the fucker is out of commission.

'Jocelyn doesn't care?' he says.

'It was her idea,' says Aurora. 'She says she isn't even being generous. She has something else in the works, and this way, poor Phil will be cured of his sex-addiction problem. Would you like another cookie? Take two!'

'Thanks,' says Stan. She looks so happy she's almost pretty. And for Max, she'll be ravishing. Good luck to them, thinks Stan.

On the screen now is Veronica, more luscious than ever. She's explaining that she's a Positron experiment gone wrong, doomed to be romantically bonded to a blue teddy bear forever. Close-up of the bear, which is looking a little frazzled. The woman anchor interviewing her asks whether there's the possibility of a second operation to

467

reverse her fixation, but Veronica says, 'No, it's too dangerous, but anyway why would I want to do that? I love him!' The anchor looks out at the TV audience and says, 'And that's just one of the stranger-than-fiction angles on this unfolding story! Some of the culpable middle management has been rounded up and warrants are out for more. We'd hoped to be able to talk to the CEO and president of the Positron Project, who hasn't yet been charged with any crimes though an arrest is said to be imminent. However, a news flash has it that he has collapsed from a stroke, and is currently undergoing emergency brain surgery. We'll be back later with more!'

'So where did Ed get to?' Stan asks Aurora. 'Frying in hell?'

'Just down the hall,' she says. 'He's had the operation, but he's still out cold. Now I've got to buzz. Max says he can't get enough of me! See you later!'

Ed's had the operation too? Stan grins. What are they going to love-bond him with? Delicious possibilities float through Stan's head: a plumber's helper, a car vacuum, a blender? No, the blender would be too harsh, even for Ed. Maybe an Elvis sexbot: that would be fucking sweet. It must be Jocelyn who set this up; she has a sick sense of humour, and, for once, Stan appreciates it.

Charmaine stirs, stretches, opens her blue, blue eyes. Stan sticks his head into her sightline, gazes deeply. 'How are you, honey?' he says.

Her eyes fill with tears. 'Oh, Stan!' she says. 'Is that you? Where's your hair?'

'It's me all right,' he murmurs. 'It'll grow back.' Is this working?

She wraps her arms around him. 'Don't ever leave me! I've been having such a bad dream!' She hugs him tight, locks on to his mouth like an octopus. A boiling-hot octopus. Now she's ripping off his shirt, now her hand is reaching down . . .

'Whoa, wait up, honey!' he tells her. 'You've just had an operation!'

'I can't wait,' she whispers into his ear. 'I want you now!'

Fan-fucking-tastic, thinks Stan. At last.

CHARM

Once Charmaine has drifted off to sleep again with what Stan hopes is a satisfied smile on her lips, he gets dressed and goes out into the hall. He's feeling depleted but exhilarated. He's so hungry he could eat a cow. There must be a cafeteria in this joint somewhere, and with any luck they'll serve beer.

He turns a corner, and there are Con, Jerold, and Rikki standing in front of a door. They aren't green any more, and they've changed their suits to black. Each of them has an earpiece, each of them has a slight bulge under the left arm. Each of them has reflector sunglasses, despite the fact that they're inside a building.

'Hi, big bro,' says Conor. 'Everything come out all right?' He flashes a large dirty-minded grin.

'Can't complain,' says Stan. He allows himself a smug little smile. 'Worked like a charm.' In fact, he's walking on air. Charmaine loves him! She loves him again. She loves him more than before. It transcends mere sex, a thing that grimy-minded Con will never be able to understand.

'Way to go,' says Jerold.

'Wicked,' says Rikki. Fist bumps and high-fives all round.

Stan lets himself be congratulated as if it's a football game. Why try to explain?

'Who are you guys supposed to be?' he says. 'In the outfits?'

'Security,' says Con. 'To keep away the reporters, supposing they figure out where our pal is at.'

'The real security's in the men's,' says Jerold. 'Inside the cubicles. Jocelyn gave them some sleepy-time needles, they'll be out for a day.'

'Plausible deniability,' says Con. 'They can't be blamed.'

'So, let me guess,' says Stan. 'It's Ed in the room?'

'Correct,' says Con. 'Rushed him into the clinic. Said he had to have an op. Matter of life and death.' He looks at his watch. 'Where are those two? They better hurry, or he might wake up and get a boner for the night table.'

'Naw,' says Jerold. 'I asked Jos. Whatever it is gotta have eyes. Like, two eyes.'

'I know that, moron,' says Con. 'It was a joke.'

'Here they come now,' says Rikki.

A couple of nurses are hurrying down the hall, wearing the Ruby Slippers Clinics uniform: white dresses, red pinafore, white hat with a border of red flowers, and rubber-soled red shoes with no-nonsense heels. 'Are we in time?' says the first one. It's Jocelyn; she looks really convincing in the outfit, Stan thinks. Like a dominatrix playing nursie. She'd have that thermometer or that

471

cucumber up your ass in about two seconds, and no saying no.

'Stan,' she nods at him. 'Satisfactory, I hope?' Stan nods.

'I guess I have to thank you,' he says. Oddly, he's feeling shy.

'Ever gracious,' Jocelyn says, but she smiles. 'You're welcome.'

The second nurse is Lucinda Quant.

'Help yourself,' Con says to them and opens the door. Lucinda Quant goes in.

'This is better than a freak show,' says Rikki. 'Don't close it all the way.'

'You can close it. Give them some privacy. Channel two on the earpiece,' says Conor.

'I don't have one,' says Stan.

'Okay, leave the door,' says Con.

There's silence. Lucinda must be sitting by the bedside.

'What'll she do with him?' Stan asks Jocelyn. 'Supposing it works? They'll be looking to arrest him, right?'

'She's talking about Dubai,' says Jocelyn. 'Expensive, but we'll pay. No questions asked, lots of orgy-for-two possibilities there, luxury suites with whirlpools; as long as you do whatever indoors. She wants a stellar finale to her life, in case the cancer comes back. And there's no extradition, so Ed will be free to indulge her every last bucket-list whim. She's got quite a few of those, so she's told me. She wants to be covered with chocolate mousse and then licked off, for starters.'

'Where's fucking Budge?' says Jerold. 'With the Buffalo wings? I'm starving.'

'I could eat a hippo,' says Rikki.

'I could eat the chocolate mousse off what's-her-name.'

'I could eat—'

'Shut up,' says Con, 'or I'm eating your face.'

'Why're you letting him off so cheap?' says Stan to Jocelyn. 'After everything he did.' And was planning to do, he adds to himself. Stealing my wife. Messing with her head. Turning her into a sex slave. Turning her into a sex slave for the wrong man. Jocelyn has gone into the details.

'You really think I'd want him giving full testimony in front of Congress?' says Jocelyn. 'Spilling all the beans? I myself am one of those beans, in case you haven't forgotten.'

'Oh, right,' says Stan.

'And more than a few of our respected politicians wouldn't want it either, they were big backers, so it won't be too hard getting him and his new fake docs onto that plane. No clean hands at this party,' says Jocelyn.

'So why not just kill him?' Stan asks. He's surprised by his own ruthlessness. Not that he himself would do that, but Jocelyn is more than capable of it. Or so he believes.

'That wouldn't be fair,' says Jocelyn. 'I'd have to kill all the board members and shareholders too, if it's a question of who's responsible. This is a better way. Cleaner. With benefits to others, such as Lucinda.'

'What happens to Consilience and the Project without him?' says Stan.

'Maybe a modified version. They'll sell off the more legitimate divisions, such as Possibilibots. Maybe condos, for the prison end of it, with a tourist attraction ensuite. Jailhouse Rock, they would call it. They've done prison conversions like that in Australia. My guess is people would pay to role-play in there, don't you think? But it's not my problem, because I'll be living my next life. Anything happening in there yet?' she says to Con.

'I hear some muttering,' says Con. 'Or maybe snoring.'

'Maybe that's how he has sex,' says Jerold, 'with his nose,' and he and Rikki snicker.

'Grow fucking up,' says Con. 'Yeah, yeah, he's coming to.'

Stan applies his ear to the gap between doorframe and door. 'I adore you,' he hears. It's Ed's voice, thick with either anesthetic or lust. 'You're lovely! Take off that pinafore!'

'Hang on, soldier!' Lucinda. 'Wait till I get my bra unhooked!'

'I can't wait,' says Ed. 'I want you now!' A cross between a laugh and a scream, from Lucinda. Then the sound of moans, or are they groans?

'Shut the door,' says Jocelyn. 'Turn off the

474

earpieces. There's some things that're none of our business.'

'You never let us have any fun,' says Con, but he does as she says.

'Lucinda's a client,' says Jocelyn primly. 'We have our standards.'

FLORAL

The wedding is pure enchantment! Or maybe it's weddings, two of them, because although Aurora and Max are getting married for the first time, Charmaine and Stan are renewing their vows, so the wedding is for them too.

A Wedding Elvis performs the ceremonies – it's Rob from UR-ELF, in a white-and-gold jumpsuit with a silver belt and a purple cape with silver stars on it – and a trio of Singing Elvises do the musical interludes, to a backup soundtrack played from a speaker hidden inside one of the floral baskets. Charmaine has chosen the flowers for the chapel area – she opted for the Forget-Me-Not selection, a pale blue medley with sprays of miniature pink roses, and it looks just lovely. The sun shines, but then it always does in Vegas, no matter what is going on in the rest of the world.

As an extra treat, there's a group of five Marilyns, wearing pink taffeta dresses with an off-the-shoulder line, sort of like the big production number in *Gentlemen Prefer Blondes* where she sings the song about diamonds, only without the long train. The Marilyns smile as if they're delighted out of their minds, which is what you want at a wedding, and there aren't any actual relatives to do it, so Charmaine booked this fivesome. They really give value for money, they cheer and laugh and throw rice on all four of them at the end, and one of the Marilyns catches Aurora's bouquet.

Charmaine doesn't have a bouquet as such because she isn't exactly getting married, though it feels like that to her, but she has a spray of pink roses, and that's almost the same. She's wearing a floral print in pink and blue, and Stan has a shirt with penguins on it, she found it online. It's sentimental, but she's a sentimental person.

There's champagne at the outdoor reception, held on a spacious patio with a sun area and a shade area, and a fountain with three mermaids holding mics as if they're a backup group, three surfers playing guitars, and three cupids, each one pouring water out of a fish, with a stone head of Elvis at the top, smiling his Elvis smile. Someone has put a wreath of flowers around his neck. It's totally themed! God is in the details, as Grandma Win used to say.

Charmaine is so happy. The dark part of herself that was with her for so long seems to be completely gone. It's as if someone has taken an eraser and erased the pain of those memories. It's not that she can't remember the things that happened – those things Grandma Win used to tell her not to think about. She can remember them, but only like pictures, or a bad dream. They don't have power over her any more. It must have been something the doctors did when they were fixing the inside of her head so she would love Stan, only Stan, and nobody else. It was the other Charmaine, the Charmaine of darkness, who'd wandered away from him, and that Charmaine is gone forever. It's so amazing what can be done with lasers!

She even watched Max, or Phil, being married to Aurora without a twinge of longing or jealousy. And at the reception, when people were kissing the brides, Max kissed her mildly on the cheek, and though once she would have melted like a microwaved Popsicle at his smallest touch, it didn't bother her at all; it was just more or less like having a fly land on you, she could brush it off and think no more about it. All those things they did, that time when she was so crazy about him – *crazy* is the right word for it – they've faded. It's like she was under some kind of a spell and then, poof, it was gone. She recalls those interludes clearly but distantly, and also fondly, almost as if she's recalling the antics of a child, though not herself as a child. She didn't do any antics then. She was too scared.

There's Max, or Phil, with Aurora now; he's under one of the sun umbrellas, he's got Aurora backed up against the table, his arms are around her, his torso is squashed up against hers, he's kissing her neck. You can tell he can hardly wait to get her into bed and run those skilful hands of his all over her face job. Charmaine searches her heart, and the only thing she can find there in the Max compartment is the best of wishes for Aurora, because it's obvious Max is devoted to her, he follows her around with his eyes all the time, despite what she looks like. Anyway she looks better than she did, because she's glowing with joy, and it's the inner beauty that counts. Most of the time. Some of the time. And Max must be happy too! He must be!

There's Stan over by the cupid fountain with two Marilyns, who are feeding him bites of the wedding cake. The cake is white, with blue-and-pink icing in a design of bluebirds holding ribbons and festoons of roses in their beaks and claws, which is the design Charmaine ordered to go with the total decoration scheme. It's very intricate, but she got it 3-D laser-printed.

The Marilyns are definitely overdoing the act, and in those pink taffeta off-the-shoulder dresses you can peer right down their fronts, which is what Stan is doing, but you can't blame him, because what's a shelf display for except to be looked at?

It's time for an intervention. She strolls over, rather quickly. 'Thank you for taking such good care of my wonderful husband,' she says, linking her arm through Stan's. Then she sees that one of the Marilyns is Veronica, though with a white-blond wig, and everyone knows Veronica can love only her blue bear, poor thing, the same way that Charmaine can love only Stan – that teddy bear story was all over the TV, Veronica's quite the celebrity now – so it's all right.

'Veronica!' she says. 'I didn't know it would be you!'

'How could I miss it?' says Veronica. 'I wanted to see the happy ending. You remember Sandi?'

'Sandi!' Charmaine cries, giving her a hug. The last time she saw Sandi in person she was plasti-cuffed, with shackles around her ankles. 'Oh my gosh! I'm so glad you got out okay! I saw you on TV! It's like a miracle!'

'It was a close one,' says Sandi. 'They'd stuck the hood on and I was just being hauled out the cell door, I figure now that I was on my way to get recycled for spares, though I didn't realize it at the time. Then there was a lot of cellphone babble, it was Jocelyn telling them to hold off on everything till further notice because there'd been an exposé and Ed had gone AWOL with the profits. Those guards dropped me on the floor and ran for it, and by the time I picked myself up and made it to the outside, all the gates were open and it was like, *Out of here!* What a traffic jam! Plus I got a bruised elbow. But hey! Who's complaining? I'm still in one piece, I'm not shishkebob.'

'I keep telling her they wouldn't have cut her up for parts,' says Veronica. 'She's too cute. They would've shipped her out here to the Vegas clinic and done the brain thing on her. She would've ended up with some wrinkly rich dude, acting out his every whim.'

480

'Like the Fuck Tank,' says Sandi, 'only this time with feeling.'

'And with a lot more cash,' says Veronica, and they laugh.

Sandi raises her champagne glass. 'Here's to the old days,' she says. 'May they rot in hell.'

The Marilyns head over to the champagne table for a refill, and Charmaine puts her arms around Stan and squeezes him. 'Oh, Stan,' she says. 'This is so wonderful! Aren't we lucky?' Stan squeezes her back, though in an absent-minded way. He seems dazed, or maybe it's the champagne. He's been drinking it like soda pop, he's had more than enough. But he'll be fine tomorrow, thinks Charmaine. It's worked out for the best, because what's past is prologue and all's well that ends well, like Grandma Win used to say. Not that this is the end. No, it's the beginning, a new beginning. The beginning as it should have been. Not everyone gets a chance at that.

She does have a lingering doubt. Does loving Stan really count if she can't help it? Is it right that the happiness of her married life should be due not to any special efforts on her part but to a brain operation she didn't even agree to have? No, it doesn't seem right. But it *feels* right. That's what she can't get over – how right it feels.

It was Jocelyn who paid for this whole thing, or who arranged for it to be paid. But although

481

Charmaine urged her to come, Jocelyn didn't attend the wedding ceremony proper. 'I don't want to be the wicked witch at the feast' was what she said. Truthfully, Charmaine was relieved by that, because despite everything Jocelyn had done for her and Stan, it must be admitted that some of those things might not be viewed as positives by everyone. Such as Jocelyn humping the jockey shorts off Stan. But Charmaine has no hard feelings about Jocelyn, because she isn't entitled to them. And everything balances out, so it's like having nothing in the bank and no debts owed.

But here she is now, Jocelyn, walking into the outdoor patio area. She's come to the reception, as she hinted she might. She's wearing mauve, which isn't the same as the pink-and-blue colour palette, but doesn't clash with it either. Charmaine is pleased that Jocelyn has given this angle some thought, and has come up with a tasteful solution.

Stan's upsetting brother, Conor, is with her, wearing those reflector sunglasses he thinks make him look so ultra cool, and three of his criminal friends. No, not criminal, Charmaine won't use that word. *Unusual.* That is a better word, because Conor and those men rescued her from Ed, so how could she ever view them as criminals, even if they are criminals in the rest of their time? Though Conor has always been a bad influence on Stan, in her opinion. Or he was when they were younger. Today he's looking more mature, she thinks. Maybe he will meet a wise older woman who will help him become a productive member of society. That is her wish for him, on this wonderful day when everyone should be granted something good.

Charmaine detaches herself from Stan so he and Conor and the unusual friends can do that back-slapping and fist-bumping and name-repeating routine they do. 'Con!' 'Stan!' 'Rikki!' 'Jerold!' 'Budge!' Like they don't know each other's names already. But it's a male-bonding thing, she's seen a TV show about that, it's like saying 'Congratulations' or something. Now they're moving over to where the champagne is, even though Stan should really not have any more of it or he'll be too drunk to do the things she's hoping they'll do, once they get to the hotel room and she's had a lovely shower, with white fluffy towels and almond oil body lotion all over her.

And once Conor and his buddies have dumped some alcohol into themselves, Conor will think about kissing the bride, and kissing Charmaine as well; he'll want to plant some aggressive smooches on her, to annoy Stan. She ought to warn Aurora about Conor – the way Max is, now that he's truly in love, he might resent any other man laying a finger on Aurora, and then there could be a fight, which Max would lose, because four against one, or maybe five, counting Stan, and Max would get a nosebleed at the very least and ruin the cake or the floral arrangements, and that would spoil this beautiful, perfect day – but as she looks around the reception space, she sees that Max and Aurora have already disappeared. Hot to trot, though it won't be trotting, it will be galloping, she thinks, without a shadow of regret. Or is that a tiny shadow? It can't be, since every shadow of regret, and every shadow, period, has been lasered out of her. All of her shadows.

She decides to glide as far away as she can, over behind the fountain where Conor can't see her, because out of sight, out of mind. Jocelyn comes with her.

'So, joy and fresh days of love,' she says.

'I guess,' says Charmaine. Jocelyn says weird things sometimes. 'For me and Stan, that's really true.'

'Good,' says Jocelyn. 'I have a wedding gift for you. But I'll give it to you a year from now. It isn't ready yet.'

'Oh, I love surprises!' says Charmaine. Is that true? Not always. Sometimes she hates them. She hates the kinds of surprises that pounce on you out of the dark. But surely Jocelyn's surprise won't be that kind.

'I can't thank you enough,' she says, 'for everything you've done for us. For me and Stan.'

Jocelyn smiles. Is that a real smile, warm and friendly, or is it a slightly scary smile? Charmaine has trouble figuring out Jocelyn's different smiles. 'Thank me later,' Jocelyn says. 'Once you know what it is.'

Then, after the handshakes and goodbyes, and after Conor has kissed Charmaine after all, but only on the cheek, Jocelyn and Conor and those other men get into a sleek black car with tinted windows and drive away.

Charmaine stands beside Stan with her arm linked through his and waves at them until the car is out of sight. 'Do you think they're an item?' she asks. 'Conor and Jocelyn?' She'd kind of like it if they were, because then Jocelyn wouldn't be prowling around uncoupled, so she'd be less likely to make a grab for Stan. Though Charmaine is grateful to Jocelyn, she still doesn't trust her, after those lies she told and the tricky numbers she pulled.

'I'd put money on it,' says Stan. 'Con always liked the hard-nosed ones. He says it's more of a challenge, plus they know what they want, plus they've got more RPMs.'

RPMs is a car engine term, Charmaine knows that. But it isn't very polite. 'That isn't very polite,' she says. 'Women aren't cars.'

'It's Con's way of talking,' says Stan. 'Not polite. Whatever, they're in business together.'

'What kind of business?' says Charmaine. It would have to be something they're both good at, such as bluffing. Maybe they're working for the casinos. If the two of them are an item, she wonders how long that's been going on.

'I'd say their business is none of our business,' says Stan.

PART XV

THERE

THERE

S tan has a new job. He's an Empathy Module adjustor for the newly opened Possibilibots Vegas production facility. He's in charge of perfecting the Elvis grin, which has never been quite accurate. Too tight and it's a snarl, too loose and it's a drool; they've had complaints both ways. But Stan is making progress: he's going to ace this! After that's done, he's already booked for the Marilyns, where some tweaks to the pout are required.

It's the weekend, so he's home, his own home, trimming the cactus hedge, his own cactus hedge. And with his own trimmers; he keeps them in razor-sharp condition. On the lawn – his lawn, or rather their lawn, which is covered with AstroTurf because of the Vegas watering restrictions – little Winnie, already three months old, gurgles on a blanket covered with cute little ducklings. Stan wondered about naming her Winifred – her nickname would sound too much like a kids'-story bear, and she'd be called Poo at school and teased for being named after a turd, but Charmaine said it was a tribute to her

Grandmother Win, because what would have happened if it hadn't been for her, and anyway it was only little boys who had such potty brains. So they could jump that bridge when they came to it, when they could always opt for Winnie's second name, which is Stanlita. Charmaine insisted on that; she said it was like a memorial to their undying love. Stan said there wasn't any such name as Stanlita, and Charmaine said there was, and he looked it up online, and fuck if she wasn't right.

Under the shade of a sun umbrella, Charmaine sits in a lawn chair, knitting a tiny hat for what she hopes will soon be the next baby, and keeping an eye on Winnie. She hovers over the kid: there have been some unexplained baby disappearances in the news lately, and Charmaine is worried that the babies are being stolen for their valuable, age-cancelling blood. Stan tells her it's not likely to happen in their part of town, but Charmaine says you never know, and a stitch in time saves nine.

She's keeping an eye on Stan too, because she has this notion that he might ramble off and get involved in adventures, with or without predatory women. She never used to be so possessive of him, but ever since that thing they did to her head she's been like this. A micro-manager of Stan. At first it was flattering, but some days he feels a little too examined.

Nor can he dump the fact that Charmaine was

once willing to kill him, no matter how much she'd boo-hooed about it. The story – the story Jocelyn subsequently fed him – is that Charmaine always knew that scene was fake, which is what they both pretend to believe. But he doesn't buy it; she'd been serious.

Not that he can use it against her. And he can't use her fling with Max either, because thanks to Jocelyn, Charmaine has the counter-weapon, namely his fling with Jocelyn. He could say he was coerced into it, but that won't wash: Charmaine would only say the same thing about herself. *I couldn't help it,* and so on. Plus, Charmaine knows about his pursuit of the imaginary Jasmine, which is more than humiliating for him: to be a rascal is one thing, it's almost respectable, but to be an idiot is pathetic. They're evenly balanced on the teeter-totter of cheating, so by mutual consent they never mention it.

On the other hand, his sex life has never been so good. Partly it's whatever adjustment they made inside Charmaine's brain, but also it has to be his repertoire of verbal turn-ons. They're straight from the videos of Charmaine and Max that Jocelyn made him watch, and though it was hell at the time he's grateful to her now, because all he needs to do is haul out one of those riffs – *Turn over, kneel down, tell me how shameless you are* – and Charmaine is toffee in his hands. She'll do it all, she'll say it all; she's everything he once longed for in the imaginary Jasmine, and more. True, the routine has become slightly predictable, but it would be surly to complain. Like complaining that the food's too delicious. What kind of a complaint is that?

GIFT

Charmaine is basking like a seal. Or like a whale. Or like a hippo. Like something that basks, anyway. Even her knitting is going better than it used to, now that she knows what it's for. She knitted a bear for Winnie, though a green one, not blue, and she embroidered the eyes to avoid a choking hazard. And this hat will be darling once she's finished.

What a beautiful day! But all the days are beautiful. Thank heavens she had that adjustment to her brain, because she couldn't ask for more out of life, she appreciates things so much more than she used to, even when something goes wrong, such as the drain water spitting up into the dryer like it did yesterday, with a full load in there too. That would once have taken her mood way down. But after the plumber came and fixed it, she put that load through again with an extra dose of lavender-scented fabric softener, and it was just like new.

And that's good, because her white cotton top with the peasant frill was in that load, and it's what she wants to wear to the Positron Survivors'

Reunion. She'll see Sandi and Veronica there, and catch up on their news. They're both doing well, according to their online pages: Sandi's in hair-weaving, she has a real knack for it, and Veronica's with a speaker's agency and goes around talking about how to work with your sexual orientation if it doesn't happen to fit in with society's norms. Just last week she spoke to a gathering of shoe fetishists, and instead of giving her a bouquet or a plaque or whatever they gave her the cutest pair of blue shoes, with peek-a-boo toes and ginormous high heels. Charmaine can't wear shoes like that any more, they give her pain in the Achilles tendon. Maybe she's getting middle-aged.

Max and Aurora might be there as well. She hasn't kept up with them. There's still a little needle of hurt buried somewhere in the cushions of warm wishes she takes care to send their way whenever she thinks about them. Or thinks about Max. She still does think about Max, from time to time. In that way. Which is odd, because those feelings about Max were supposed to have been wiped.

What she tries not to think about is the work she used to do, back in her other life at Positron Prison, before her shadows got erased. If you do bad things for reasons you've been told are good, does it make you a bad person? Thinking too much about this could really spoil everything, which would be selfish. So she tries to put that side of things right out of her mind.

★   ★   ★

Stan turns the hedge trimmer off. He raises the visor he has to wear because of the flying cactus prickles, takes off his leather gloves, wipes his forehead. 'Stan, honey, want a beer?' Charmaine calls. She's not drinking herself, it wouldn't be good for Winnie.

'In a minute,' he says. 'Just got a foot more to do.' Charmaine thinks maybe they should take the cactus hedge out and put in a fence of woven sticks, but Stan didn't go for that idea. He says why fix it if it's not broke? Actually he said, *Not fucking broke* and told her to quit nagging him about it. She wasn't nagging, but she let it rest. Let him keep on believing anything he wants to believe, because when he's grumpy he won't have sex, and the sex is amazing, way better than before; how can it not be, now that her brain's been reborn?

Stan can still get a little impatient with her in daily life. Even though everything's so wonderful. It's the pressures of his work. Charmaine will get some work too, in a while, maybe part-time because it's good to receive some validation from the real world.

A dark hybrid car's pulling up in front of the house. Jocelyn gets out of it. She seems to be alone.

Stan lowers his visor, switches on his trimmer, turns his back. So that's all right, thinks Charmaine: it means he's not interested in Jocelyn, despite the way she's flashing her legs.

'Jocelyn!' says Charmaine as Jocelyn walks across the AstroTurf toward her. 'What a surprise! It's so good to see you!' She sets down her knitting, makes flailing motions in the lawn chair.

Jocelyn's wearing a fashionable dark grey linen sheath, white Cuban-heeled sandals, a floppy-brimmed sunhat. 'Don't get up,' she says. 'Cute baby.' You can see she isn't much interested; if she was, she would've picked Winnie up and gone *Ooochie-kootchie* or some normal thing like that. But then Winnie might spit up on Jocelyn's expensive outfit, and that would not improve their relationship. Not that they have one: Charmaine hasn't seen Jocelyn since the wedding. She and Conor are in Washington, doing something top, top secret. Or that's the version Stan got from Conor.

'Can I get you a cold drink?' Charmaine says dutifully.

'I can't stay a minute,' Jocelyn says. 'I just came by to deliver your wedding gift.'

'Oh,' says Charmaine hopefully. 'How great!' But what is it? Jocelyn isn't carrying a package. Maybe it's a cheque, and that would be nice too but not so tasteful. A personally chosen item is better, in Charmaine's opinion. Though not always.

'It's not an object,' Jocelyn says. Charmaine has a memory flash of Jocelyn's head when it was in a box. She used to think that head could read her thoughts, and here was Jocelyn doing that very same thing, only not in a box. 'It's a piece of information, about you.'

'About me?' Charmaine says, dismayed. Is this another trick, is it some blackmail thing like those videos of her and Max? But those were supposed to have been destroyed.

'You can choose,' says Jocelyn. 'To hear it or not. If you hear it, you'll be more free but less secure. If you don't hear it, you'll be more secure, but less free.' She crosses her arms, waits.

Charmaine has to think. How could she be more free? She's already free enough. And she's already secure, as long as Stan has his job and she has Stan. But she knows herself well enough to realize that if Jocelyn goes away without telling her, she'll always be curious about what it was.

'Okay, tell me,' she says.

'Simply this,' says Jocelyn. 'You never had that operation. That brain adjustment.'

'That can't be true,' says Charmaine flatly. 'It can't be true! There's been such a difference!'

'The human mind is infinitely suggestible,' says Jocelyn.

'But. But now I love Stan so much,' says Charmaine. 'I *have* to love him, because of that thing they did! It's like an ant, or something. It's like a baby duck! That's what they said!'

'Maybe you loved Stan anyway,' says Jocelyn. 'Maybe you just needed some help with it.'

'This isn't fair,' says Charmaine. 'Everything was all settled!'

'Nothing is ever settled,' says Jocelyn. 'Every day is different. Isn't it better to do something because you've decided to? Rather than because you have to?'

'No, it isn't,' says Charmaine. 'Love isn't like that. With love, you can't stop yourself.' She wants the helplessness, she wants . . .

'You prefer compulsion? Gun to the head, so to speak?' says Jocelyn, smiling. 'You want your decisions taken away from you so you won't be responsible for your own actions? That can be seductive, as you know.'

'No, not exactly, but . . .' It will take Charmaine a while to think this through. There's an open door, and standing just on the other side of it is Max. Not Max as such, because his brain really has been altered, he's bonded to Aurora now and he'll be devoted to her forever, not that Charmaine begrudges Aurora that, because she's suffered so much in her previous life, and doesn't she deserve a little out-of-your-mind ecstasy, like . . .

Never mind like what. Better not to dwell on that in too much detail. The past is the past.

So not Max, but a shadow of Max. A Max-like person. Someone who isn't Stan, waiting for her in the future. That would be so destructive! Why is she even considering it? Maybe she ought to see a therapist or something. 'Of course not!' she says. 'But I need . . .'

'Take it or leave it,' says Jocelyn. 'I'm only the messenger. As they say in court, you're free to go. The world is all before you, where to choose.'

'How do you mean?' says Charmaine.